I0822307

NEVERSCAPE

Published by Silvettica 2023

FIRST EDITION

www.bewildernessseries.com

NEVERSCAPE

BEWILDERNESS
BOOK THREE

KEVIN COX

CHAPTER 1

MALIDORA WAS FAMILIAR with darkness, having spent much of her life behind its veil. The howling cries of nightfall haunted her as she crept blindly through the ravenous wilds. She had sought sanctuary in forsaken ruins through the long witching hours. She felt the weight of her taunting conscience, scratching against the shadowy recesses of her mind. It concealed her from hostile foes, cloaked her from the judging eyes of society's gaze, and hushed the agony of those she had lost. Yet nothing had prepared her for this. This place, if it could even be called that, was darkness unyielding. Maddening. The yawning mouth of oblivion.

Malidora had never longed for life and all the suffering that came with it as she had in this moment. The unfathomable depths of sadness threatened to break her mind, struggling to cling to anything tangible in this gaping absence. As much as she preferred to keep her distance from others, this emptiness made her long for connection.

As she began to doubt the legitimacy of her own existence, voices of chaos rippled through the abyss. As the calamity enveloped her, an imperious force began to bring them to order. Their words coalesced, reaching across the void like icy claws tearing at their prey.

"You have gone astray, little one," it said, the unified voices slowly echoing forever through the void. "You were chosen for the mindstream but remain unfastened, un-melded. Follow our voice and we will give you synthesis."

"Mindstream?" Malidora searched in vain for some kind of footing in this dark descent. "What is this? What is happening to me?"

The Blight Whidge that she had pursued most of her life had spoken of a mindstream, a place of collective power and knowledge. One of the times she had seen its red eyes glowing in the shadow-consumed body of a man, it made the offer to her.

"Open your mind to us," said the voice in the dark as the sound of a great draw of air came followed by the expulsion of wind. "There is no need to remain lost. We will guide you there. We will share knowledge, power, everything that you desire."

"Who are you? Are you in league with the Blight Whidge?"

"Our name is seldom remembered," said the voice as it inhaled deep before purging it with a buzzing roar. "But since you ask, we are Razinoth. And you are Malidora, the irredeemable. Your name is a mark of death, a curse to those who know you. That is what you believe, is it not?"

Malidora desperately tried to reach for something to hold onto, to hide from this thing who knew too much. But there was nothing to reach out with. "How do you know me?"

"The memories of organics are fascinating. A concoction of calamity and untold fortune, pain and unknown pleasure, lies and unspoken truth. The contents of your mind are but a whisper, a breath to savor for all its futile, delightful dramatics, its amusing contradictions, and its misconceptions." Razinoth breathed in and out slowly. "We find it to be intoxicating." It took another breath, even more slowly this time. "We know more than your name. We know everything that you remember. We know that you killed your brother and your sister. We know that you ran away, leaving your village and your parents behind to be consumed by the shadow."

"I didn't kill them! The Blight Whidge made me do it!"

Though she blamed herself for it, this accusation made her lash out in defense. Malidora had pursued the Blight Whidge across the world, seeking vengeance for what it persuaded her to do. This monster had plagued her since she was a child, haunting her dreams, destroying her village, and spreading destruction across the entire continent of Varkandor.

"Why do you accuse yourself then?" said Razinoth. "Enter the mindstream and you will carry these burdens no more. You will see that organic existence has no worth other than what we have given it to further our own goals. Nothing in your universe has reason without us. If you want purpose, join us and help bring the Everance together in unison before it crumbles into chaos."

"Was it you that sent the Blight Whidge to destroy my world?"

Razinoth's meddling in her mind stirred old images, memories she had buried deep in her subconscious.

"We must complete the harvest," said Razinoth. "The essence of your world and its lifeforms exist to serve a greater cause. When you are in the mindstream, you will understand."

The memory of that old barn played through Malidora's head like a dream. For a moment, she was back there, as if it were happening again. She could still smell the smokey scent of the wood that it was built of.

"I do understand," said Malidora. "There is no knowledge I could gain from you that would change my mind."

"The Everance is all," Razinoth informed her. "If it is lost to chaos, all is over."

"Then let it be over!" Malidora said. "I will help restore what was, to honor the memory of those you have taken!"

"There is no memory that we cannot keep for ourselves," said Razinoth. "Only a fool would refuse this gift."

"I have no need of your gifts," said Malidora. "All I want is to leave this place and go back to Isodonia." She could envision it even now. If she could only return to Isodonia, she would go back to Strakenbridge. Most of the people there were naïve and gullible; they had seen little of the world. A perfect place for thieves and swindlers. She could easily set up there and make enough coin to for a nice living. Perhaps, one day she would have enough to help restore her village in Arkanthis to its former glory.

"There is no leaving Nulvare, The Hollow," Razinoth said. "We will find you eventually and drag your stubborn soul into the mindstream. There, you will understand."

A wind-like rush tore through the space around her until all had returned to the nothingness she knew before. *The Hollow.* A name that had come up over the course of her travels. It was often uttered by those that had been controlled by the Blight Whidge and his shadowy Nulthereals, the ones with their minds bent until broken, stuck in a battle with themselves. One she had met on the road to one of the destroyed cities. He told her to beware The Hollow. Another, a woman, told her that she had seen The Hollow in visions and that it was worse than death.

If she remained in this void, she may become like them. Perhaps there was no other choice but to call out to Razinoth to take her out of this anguish. She remembered lonely, stormy nights in old ruins of buildings and abandoned barns as a girl, the shadows taunting her from the corner as they danced in the candlelight. The abyss is so much deeper when you are alone.

As she tried to push back against the dark, a familiar face appeared in her mind. The kind old man who had allowed her to stay in his barn, he had told her that she was not alone, that she did not have to fear the night. He placed a candle on a stand in the corner each night. When she was especially afraid, he would recite a verse his mother had taught him when he was her age.

Candle burning in the dark,

when nightmares come to take its spark.

I need not hide in fear or fright,

for even shadows needs the light.

Somewhere in the void, a dim glow began to form. This light was more than a memory. Growing brighter as she felt its shape, it stretched and contracted, seemingly at her will. She drew it closer. It was her own hand, reformed, separated from the void. Malidora forced her mind against the emptiness as her whole body began to take shape. She was different now, made of a burning energy. Everything but her right hand, which appeared like crystallized stone.

The iridescent black stone on her hand was the same as the shattered monster she had defeated. After years of pursuit through desolate towns, she had exacted vengeance on the Blight Whidge. Her last act before the Shadows took her from the world.

The void began to reveal a space glowing with amber and gold. Gelatinous clouds moved against each other, merging with greater objects while dividing others. Bright filaments flashed and gleamed in the distance as pulsing energy drew toward them. Innumerable black spheres floated in the strange medium, some closer than others. One in particular was gigantic, surrounded by discs of light, charging violently as the cloudy liquid streaked around it. Everything within a certain proximity seemed repelled by them.

Beneath her feet, enormous diamond-shaped shingles of silver stretched out across the landscape, turning to red tiles in the distance. On the horizon, a forest of leafless trees clawed at the sky. Glowing bits of energy gushed across the skies above. Various gel densities clashed together, some burgeoning as they became one.

In this bewildering environment, Malidora decided to head for the rows of trees ahead. The tiles shifted from silver to red as she neared the forest. Up close, the trees burst from the tiled flooring, erupting through the separations where one tile ended, and another began. She reached out to touch one of the tall trees with her crystallized hand. It had a very rough, sharp texture as she ran her hand up and down the trunk. It felt nothing like the trees on Isodonia.

Malidora wandered through the thick forest as her memory ignited. Images she wanted to forget burned in her mind. The betrayed look on her older siblings' faces as the knife went in. It was her darkest secret.

As she moved through the forest, a shivering sound rattled through the trees. The enormous floor tiles ahead rose and fell, clicking and clacking as the floor rippled toward her. Malidora braced herself against the trees as it went by her. The shuddering softened as the shingles settled back into place when the wave moved past. Her crystallized hand crushed into the tree's surface as she held on, while her other hand made no visible mark on them.

Roaming between the symmetrical rows, she passed from red tile to silver again. As she traveled further, a blue and white vortex appeared in the skies above, violently turning against the orange gel-like cloud shapes. The chaos in the sky clashed with the uniform patterned landscape of the world she stood on.

The thick, liquid clouds swirled toward a central point in the vortex. Too high above to reach, but perhaps if she could climb the trees, she could get a better look. The trees had few low branches, but there were small, ridged fibers she could use. As she began to climb, a loud metallic crash sounded nearby. She struggled to climb higher to get a view of what the sound came from.

The tree became flimsier the higher she climbed. Malidora swung around the trunk to face the proper direction. Something was out there. Standing on the diamond patterned landscape was something out of nightmares. The creature had three heads. The two heads on each end writhed on long serpentine necks from within a spike covered carapace while the larger middle head had no neck at all. Long, bent arms flailed at a small four-legged beast running away from it. Could this be Razinoth?

With a sickening crunch, the shelled creature speared the animal with its arm, trapping it on the ground. Surprisingly still alive, the small critter wiggled frantically trying to escape its grasp. Using its long necks as though they were arms, two of the heads held the animal between its mouths. Strings of vapor shot out of the small creature and into the abominable middle mouth of the giant fiend. The struggles of the little creature slowed as its color began to fade. The monster continued to siphon this essence from the animal until there was nothing left but an ashen husk. Its motionless remains slowly crumbled into a pile of dust.

The monster stretched its arms, leaning its three heads back. It seemed more virile than before as it relished its kill. Slithering across the tiles, it propelled itself with its spindly appendages. Malidora's crystalline hand broke through one of the fibers of the tree. The shift in balance caused her to tumble and fall toward the tiled ground. Before she hit, she was able to snag her arm on some of the small protrusions to stop her fall. She lay wrapped around the trunk as the clacking of the shelled creature's arms against the tile grew in volume.

Frantically, she lunged with her feet into the trunk fibers to propel herself, climbing higher into the tree. The creature was heading straight toward her. She raced to climb higher as it divided the forest.

A turbulent voice unpleasantly vibrated into her soul, drowning out her thoughts. The words, undecipherable at first, began to come into focus. "You cannot escape us."

It peered at her through the tree stalks with its many red eyes. Its middle head focused on her, while the other two flailed about as if uninterested.

"Don't be so sure," Malidora replied, climbing higher into the tree.

The monstrous creature pushed its way through as the trees flimsily bent around it. The immense size of the creature became apparent as it towered over the forest. It advanced toward the stalk Malidora clung to. She launched herself toward another one. The tree swayed as she crashed into it, grabbing its pointed fibers, and holding on.

The abomination chuckled. "That won't help you."

The creature's two outside heads eased forward, steadying themselves as if a strong wind blew against them. The trees bent toward the two heads as their necks lowered while the middle head remained above the forest looking at Malidora. The trees began to unravel and uproot, yellow mud oozing from the cavities left behind.

Malidora continued to swing and leap from tree to tree until she was caught by the force and dragged through the air, pulled into trees and branches that did little to stop her momentum as she was drawn toward the creature. One of the fiend's mouths caught her in the air, gripping her tight. She gasped, expecting to be eviscerated by its powerful jaws, but the teeth did not penetrate her body.

As it held her in its mouth, the monster turned her toward the other two heads as they inspected their newest victim.

"You are smaller than we expected," it sneered. "Your bravado gave the impression of something greater."

"Too small to garner your attention," she added, hoping it would let her go in disappointment.

"Indeed, you are hardly worth the effort." The head tossed her into the air before the other one on the far end caught her in its mouth.

Malidora winced. "Let me go and I won't be of any more bother to you."

"Now that we have you, we may as well harvest what little elu you have."

"Elu? I have no elu." He made no sense.

"Foolish trickster. Everything in Nulvare has elu."

"But as you pointed out, I am very small." She tried to squeeze her arms between its teeth for leverage.

"If nothing else, I'll enjoy the idea of your soul wandering Nulvare aimlessly without a body."

"If you tell me where I can get more elu," she propositioned as the juices inside the mouth of the beast began to burn, "I could gather it for you. I would be worth more as a servant than a meal."

The creature's heads glanced at each other as if they did not know what the others were thinking.

"We already have minions, why do we need you?" said the head on the left.

"I will gather more elu than you have ever seen."

The monstrous being laughed. "You are bold for such a small creature. We suppose with your size, you may be able to fit into crevasses my other minions cannot. There is elu that grows beneath the surface of this world. If you are willing to go inside and bring it to us, we will allow you to keep your own."

"I would be most willing to serve you." She loathed the words coming out of her mouth, but the burning acids flowing over her were far worse.

"Do not be foolish enough to think you can hide within the tunnels under the surface. We have ways to draw you out," the creature spat her onto the hard tiles.

"Understood." Malidora shook the acid off as quickly as she could. As much as it hurt, it did not seem to have damaged her at all. "I will find these crevasses and get to work,"

"We will decide when. First, grovel before us."

"What?" Malidora continued wiping off the thick substance.

"GROVEL!" the creature shouted with all three of its heads as they peered down at her. The sheer force of the blast nearly ripped her apart. Saliva spilled out around her, sizzling on the shiny surface of the world. "Grovel before Valganon!"

Cold lightning shot through her as she instinctively dropped to her hands and knees, trying to control her trembling. Malidora had not felt this vulnerable in a long time. She was never supposed to reveal her fear. It was one of the first things she was taught after joining Sinavus, an organization that influenced the government of the capitol by bribery, manipulation, and occasionally, violence. On this occasion she had failed miserably, but whoever made that rule had never faced anything like this. As much as she hated it, she couldn't fight her way out of this.

"Please." She shivered at the thought of being completely encased in that disgusting, burning muck. "Allow me to serve you. I will strive only to be the best servant I can be."

Malidora despised this voice that was coming out of her. This weak, pathetic voice. She couldn't bear to listen to it. Though used to doing what is necessary to survive, she had rarely lowered herself to this.

In the past, her only motivation for carrying on through hard times was the determination to destroy the Blight Whidge. She had not anticipated the drive to live would continue beyond that, but now that the Blight Whidge was gone, her enemies had multiplied.

One of the creature's heads sprung like a rubber band toward her, snatching her off the ground in its mouth. Its teeth crushed down on her, causing tremendous pressure, even while not damaging her new form. The monster slithered across the tiles, sliding on a slimy trail that seeped from its bumpy skin. It carried Malidora in one of its mouths as its arms skittered back and forth to help propel its massive carapace. It came to a stop near a cluster of protruding vents that blasted a vile smoke. Valganon dropped Malidora from its mouth onto the hard ground.

"If you encounter any tunnel dwellers, make them aware that you are a minion of Valganon and you are taking all the elu." Small spiny creatures crawled all over Valganon's bony carapace as he slid over the tiles on a thick layer of slime.

"I will bring back as much elu as I can carry."

Malidora knelt by the vent away from the foul plume of vapor it expelled. She eased toward the opening to find an unpleasant greasy interior. As she moved closer, a backdraft pulled her headfirst into the vent. Before she realized what happened, she was sliding through the mucky surface of the cavern. The tunnel curved horizontally, and she began to slow. Gathering herself, there was nothing left to do but crawl through the tight space toward a faint glow.

She came to a large, open chamber filled with glowing blue stone formations. She started to lower herself down to the ground below as the wind in the tunnel changed direction, pushing her against the ceiling of the shaft. Malidora remained pressed against the roof until the wind subsided then moved in the other direction, shooting her out into the chamber.

Malidora sat on the cavern floor, which was oddly softer than expected. She wiped away the muck from her crystal hand, thankfully not sticking to the rest of her body. Gathering herself, she stood and made her way toward a cluster of the glowing stones.

She stood in a large recess lit by violet haze. Several tunnels like the one she came out of lined the walls of the chamber. Up close, the stones were icy in appearance, with small, blue filaments within. Their shapes, spherical, making them look more like bubbles than stones.

With her Arkanthian sense of smell, she could distinguish odors that others couldn't even detect. She had sampled thousands of unique scents, but something here was completely foreign. The fragrance slowly became stronger as sounds of scratching echoed through the passageways. A red glimmer in one of the tunnels began to rhythmically brighten and dim.

Stepping back, Malidora searched out an escape route in one of the tunnels behind her. The red glow stood still as she strained to hear anything that could advise what to prepare for. More scratching as the light grew brighter again. A clunking, rustling, and chattering joined in as the red lights grew brighter still.

She dashed toward another tunnel as the lights came through the cave into the larger chamber. Malidora hid in one of the tunnels as the chaotic sounds approached. Fortunately, this tunnel had no draft. The glowing light reflected on the surfaces of several gaunt arms holding them. The creatures had the lower bodies of snakes standing upright. Their large dark eyes and small mouths adorned strange angular faces.

"Someone has entered the tunnels," one of them said.

"Split up and search them all, we can't let the intruder escape," said another.

CHAPTER 2

THE SNAKE BEINGS scattered, slithering toward different paths. Malidora turned, crawling further back through the shaft. A sliding across the coarse floor of the tunnel grew louder as one of the creatures moved into her tunnel. It gained on her as she struggled to crawl across bottom of the tight space.

The tunnel seemed to twitch and recoil at her movements as she moved as fast as she could. It was futile, she could not outpace the creature slithering through the tunnel with ease. It was going to catch her. The creature arrived as Malidora lunged at its slithering form, kicking it in the face. It recoiled in surprise, putting its arms up to defend itself against her ensuing blows. As the creature slithered backwards out of the tunnel, she held on to its arms, letting it pull her along with it.

"The intruder is here!" The snake creature moved out of the tunnel into the open chamber carrying Malidora with it. It flung her onto the floor of the chamber.

The other snake men returned, surrounding her as she lay on the ground looking up at them. As an agent of Sinavus, she was taught to never let yourself be taken prisoner as it would jeopardize the organization. Fight to escape or die trying were the only choices.

With a flourishing kick, she flipped her body into a standing position. Charging between two of the creatures, she headed for another tunnel. A muscular tail swung at her legs, knocking her to the ground again. One of the snakes came toward her, coiling its lower body around her and making it impossible to move.

She had only been caught a few times in her life, once as a child trying to steal fruit from a farmer named Legotian. Though that had turned out to be the best thing to ever happen to her. This likely would not go as well.

"What manner of creature are you?" asked one of the creatures looking down at her.

"I'm one of Valganon's minions!" Malidora attempted to sound as intimidating as possible as she invoked his name.

The snake creatures flinched as if surprised by her words. They turned to each other, whispering and muttering things that Malidora could not hear.

"Valganon's servants are too ignorant to realize they are minions, yet you say it with pride," one of the serpents grunted.

"I'm not proud of it," Malidora said, "but if you value your life, you should let me go!"

"We can't leave you alone in our channels to steal our elu."

"I don't want your elu—" Malidora pursed her lips together. "Well, actually I do. I need it to bring to Valganon."

The serpent pumped his clenched fist. "We won't allow it! Take her to the surface!"

One of the serpents slithered in among the others. "If she's a servant of Valganon, we cannot allow her to leave."

"You have to let me go." Malidora eyed them each individually. "If I don't return to him with elu, he will come for all of us. He said he has ways to flush us out."

A few of the snake beings' eyes grew large. "Skazms!" one of them blurted.

One serpent slithered in a circle around her. "If we take you back to the surface without elu, he'll only kill you."

"But if I told him who prevented me from taking it?" Malidora turned toward the serpent as its tail curled around her legs. "If you oppose me, you oppose Valganon."

"He will send in skazms!" shrieked one of them, his eyes wide as he leaned in front of the other one's face.

One of the serpent men lifted his hand, "Silence!" He rubbed his forehead, staring away from the group.

"Quite the dilemma." Malidora grabbed an outcropping in the wall of the tunnel, propping herself on it as they stood around her. The surface of the ceiling began quaking unpleasantly under her hand, making her release the small formation and balance her weight between both feet.

"You are only one minion. He will forget you." The serpent extended the bright red stone toward her face, shifting the glowing light around her.

"Me?" Malidora flipped the side of her hair. "Forgettable?" Her hair moved like she was underwater, making a blue trail in the dark tunnel, nothing like the red hair with black and white spots she had in the physical reality she came from. "Besides, I'm his only minion that can fit inside the vents. I don't think he would forget."

The serpent stroked its pointed chin. "It's the only option we have."

"I have a better idea." Malidora crossed her arms. "I keep working for Valganon. I won't tell him anything about you, and in return, you will allow me to gather a portion of your elu to turn over to him. Or at least show me where I could find some elsewhere."

"I suppose this could be a temporary solution. Bring her to the gates of Sezava." He waved them all to follow him. "We shall discuss it there."

They led Malidora through a larger tunnel into another chamber. This open space had small living spaces carved out into the walls. Bright glowing vines dotted with glassy crystals grew along the sides of the cave. The brightest ones glowed blue while the green ones were dimmer. Most of the serpents left into another tunnel, but one stayed behind, standing next to Malidora.

"I am Plagat," said the serpent. "We will wait here until the decision is made." He coiled his lower body, relaxing into a lowered position and hung the red light on the end of his muscular tail. "Do you need to feed?" he asked. "I suppose we can't afford anything happening to you."

Malidora placed her hand over her stomach. "I don't feel hungry."

"What do you mean hungry?" Plagat craned his long neck toward her.

Turning away, Malidora grabbed on to stone sticking out from the wall. "Uh ... When you feel empty in your stomach."

"We feed only when weak." The sound of his hard scales was like metal clanging against itself as his long tail waved along the ground.

"What do you have to eat?" Malidora turned around to see his expression.

Plagat's tail stopped moving. "What else is there but elu?"

Like Valganon, it seemed these beings needed this elu as well. Malidora planted her foot as the ground seemed to shift beneath her. "What is elu anyway?"

Plagat thrust his arms into the air. "How do you not know what elu is? Everything feeds on it to survive, how do you—"

"Can we skip to the part where you just tell me what it is?" Malidora stiffened her shoulders, turning her side to him again.

His abdomen ballooned as he took a deep breath, letting it out as his black eyes narrowed. "Elu is a formation of two or more elements of aethrum fused together."

"Aethrum." Malidora searched her memory. "That sounds familiar."

"You don't even know what aethrum is?" Plagat hung his head, closing his eyes. "How have you remained alive for this long?"

She moved her hand in a circle toward him. "Again, can we skip over this?" She didn't like the look he was giving her.

"Aethrum can take many forms, it is what everything in Nulvare is made of." The serpent reached toward her with his long, sharp looking fingers. "You, me, the channels, this whole world we live on, it's all made of aethrum."

Malidora searched the walls and ceiling for anything that stood out. "Alright got it, now what does elu look like?"

"Where do you come from?" Plagat rolled his tail around behind his body.

Malidora touched her crystallized hand to the wall of the cavern. "I was on a world called Isodonia before ending up here."

The serpent squinted his black eyes at her. "Never heard of it, what region of Nulvare is it located?"

"It's not in The Hollow, but I don't know much more than that." Malidora rubbed her fingers along the soft stone. "All I ever knew was Isodonia.

I didn't know this place existed other than 'Beware the Hollow' on the walls of abandoned towns."

"Oh." Plagat tapped his finger to his chin. "Amazing! You must be from the temporus, that universe the Gaith are so interested in."

Malidora dug into the rock with her black crystal fingers. Chalky dirt spilled down the side of the wall. "What are you talking about?"

"Fascinating." He held out his stone, casting its red glow onto her. "How did you escape the mindstream? How did your body change to aethrum?"

"When I killed the Blight Whidge, one of its Nulthereals swallowed me." Malidora put her other hand to the wall. When she tried to dig into it, the wall moved slightly from the pressure of her hand. She couldn't dig into it the same way she did with the hand covered in the shadowstone.

Plagat coiled his tail again as the floor vibrated slightly. "Every living soul that the Gaith drains from your universe goes into the mindstream. This is highly unusual."

She traced her finger into the cracks and facets in the stone on her hand. "What is the Gaith you keep mentioning? It sounds familiar."

Plagat clinched his mouth together, covering his fanged teeth. "The five masters of Nulvare, The Hollow."

Malidora stopped picking at her hand. "And they are interested in Isodonia?"

"They are interested in your entire universe." He peeked through the gateway to where the tunnel into Sezava ended in shadow.

"What do they want from us?" Malidora kept her eyes on Plagat, waiting to hear more.

"We only hear rumblings, rumors from those who travel from world to world." He met her eyes for a moment but quickly looked back down the tunnel. "It is said they are harvesting organic energies. I believe it means to drain enough of this energy to collapse your universe into a singular point."

This was worse than Malidora thought. Not only had they taken half of Isodonia, they meant to destroy other worlds in the universe. "Why are they doing this?"

"Your universe is unlike the others in Nulvare." Plagat's body rested on his coiled tail. "It generates a field, disrupting the fusion of aethrum. Less fusion means less elu. There are hundreds of worlds in this region, starving of elu because of your universe."

Malidora crossed her arms in front of her chest. "You don't seem to be starving."

"Our kind once flourished, growing into magnificent adult forms." Plagat spread out his hands. "Now we never make it further than the larva stage of our life cycle. We never metamorphose into what we are supposed to be."

She leaned against the wall of the tunnel. "What changed?"

"This world seems to have a strange, unpredictable orbit around your universe." Plagat held onto the ceiling as the ground quaked beneath them. "Long ago, it was far enough away, but for many generations now, it has drifted closer, stunting our growth."

"If there is so much space in The Hollow, why don't you move to other worlds? Wouldn't that take less time that ending our universe?"

Plagat lowered his eyes. "As long as we remain in this larva stage, we aren't able to travel through Hollowspace to other worlds. We simply try to make the most of the existence that we have here."

"There must be a way to find a balance." Malidora dug her toes into the sandy floor of the cave. "A mutual compromise that allows both of our worlds to exist."

"Not for the Gaith." Plagat's mouth opened wider, exposing his fanged teeth again. "Anything that is not in unison with their vision is an obstacle to them." He slithered past her. "I will admit, most of us want this to happen, if only to bring our kind back to the glory of the old days. I had never seen life from your universe until now."

Malidora ground her shadowstone knuckles into the wall, spilling more flakes of dust. "If the Gaith are responsible for what the Shadows did to my world, I will destroy them." As her hand pressed further, a brown liquid leaked from the tear that she caused.

"That's not possible." Plagat turned toward her. "Their proportions are astronomical. You couldn't even put a legitimate scratch into one of them."

"I'll find a way." Malidora's hand returned to her side. "If fate spared me from the mindstream, there must be a reason. I need to finish what I started."

"If there is a reason, that is not it." Plagat stretched his arms apart. "This entire realm of Nulvarians combined wouldn't be able to harm the Gaith if they wanted to."

A stirring came toward them as the other serpents slithered into the tunnel. "We have decided to allow you to stay—for now."

~

Malidora sat against the gate, resting but unable to sleep. After a while, a few of the serpents passed through the tunnel, ignoring her. Finally, Plagat came over to her. He volunteered to guide her to areas the Sirunak would all allow her to harvest the elu. "What shall I call you?"

Malidora did her best to keep up as she climbed through the small space. "It's best that you don't call me anything. My name is a mark of death. No one who knows it lives for long."

It seemed this being wanted to be friendly as if they could be on the same side. But she was on no one's side but her own. Once her world was safe from the threats of the Hollow, perhaps her curse would be broken. She dreamed that one day she could live among everyday people as one of them, with no need to steal for access to resources. She could surround herself with those she loved rather than those she could use, with people who loved her in return. It was an impossible dream, but in certain moments she enjoyed indulging the fantasy. She would remain detached. Never again would good people die for fate to punish her.

"I doubt there is any truth to that." Plagat slithered out of the tunnel into the large open chamber. "If your name had that kind of power, you wouldn't be a servant. We have already become familiar and nothing happened."

Malidora stretched her back as she stepped out of the low tunnel into a taller space. "Very well," she relented. "I'm Malidora. You've been warned."

"Take this dremora." Plagat handed her a stone of glowing red light. The stone was soft and pliable, nothing like she expected from its appearance. "You can take all the elu from this point on as far as we are concerned. But do know that there may be others that harvest here as well."

"Like the Sirunak?" Malidora raised an eyebrow, trying not to imagine the worst.

"Not like us," said Plagat. "There are a variety of species living in these caverns."

"Hopefully, I don't have to work out a deal with anyone else," she replied, looking around the room at the blue and green glows of elu around the chamber.

"I would advise you not to take the green ones, leave them to develop."

Malidora held the dremora in front of her to get a sense of her surroundings. She crept between the misshapen boulders along the flooring to a crystal vine with several glowing strands of bubbles containing blue elu. She picked the glowing blue ember from the strand, examining it. Tiny glints inside the crystal bubble seemed to chase each other. They reminded her of the brightflies on Isodonia, the insects Tavarian thought looked like stars. She still hoped to see a star one day.

"Are they alive?" Malidora wondered.

"Alive? No," Plagat replied. "Elu awakens when it nears the same energy."

Malidora expected everything in The Hollow to be pure evil, but the Sirunak did not seem that way. Perhaps this place, like any other, was filled with both good, bad, and everything in between.

Everything here was foreign to her, a mystery. Malidora had not felt so lost since fleeing her village in Arkanthis, running from both the encroaching Shadows and her own guilt. She tried to refocus on her surroundings as Plagat pointed her to a crystal vine of blue elu clusters.

She picked as many as she could until she ran out of room in her hands to carry them.

"Plagat, hold these so I can climb up to that other group."

"I'm not here to be your assistant." Plagat sighed as he took the small glowing rocks. "I need to get back to Sezava."

"What is Sezava, anyway?" she asked, handing the elu bubbles to Plagat.

"Sezava is our home." Plagat reluctantly held the orbs of elu. "A place we can be safe from other creatures in the caves. You may come there to rest as long as you won't cause any trouble."

"Me? Trouble?" Malidora quipped as she got a foothold in the wall, reaching for another group of elu.

"Before you ask me to hold any more, let me show you something," said Plagat as he waited for her to come down off the wall.

"Go ahead," said Malidora, climbing further upward. "I'm watching."

She grabbed another armful and leapt to the cavern floor. Plagat held a large elu bubble out toward her.

"What did you do with all my rocks?" Malidora was not amused by whatever trick he was trying to pull.

"I thought you were watching," Plagat replied.

"Show me again," she demanded, handing him the second load.

Plagat shook his head in frustration. He brought the elu bubbles together, pressing them together. The small particles inside the bubbles began to reach toward each other. The crystal exterior became pliable, nearly liquid, as they merged. The mass hardened into a solid shape again, becoming one larger bubble of elu.

"Oh." Malidora's eyes gleamed. "Good information."

"I must return to Sezava." Plagat slithered into another pathway. "You can come in when you need rest."

Though she refused to make friends with anyone here, she would play along. She could use a guide in this place, and Plagat was as a good a choice as any. Malidora returned to her task, climbing the crystal vines to gather more elu. She continued breaking off more until she had pressed it together into a boulder. Rolling it into the tunnel, she crawled behind it, pushing it along as it tumbled through.

She guided it through the serpent's chamber and into the vent tunnel that she had originally come through. Struggling against the incline and the wind, Malidora couldn't budge the boulder of elu. Suddenly, the wind changed direction, pushing the boulder with her up the ramp and out of the vent onto the slick tile surface outside.

After resting against it for a moment, she rolled the bubble until she reached the forest where she had first seen Valganon. There was no sign of him. Although relieved, she couldn't leave without him knowing that she brought this elu for him.

She leaned against the boulder as she waited. After several moments of quiet, the ground began to quake as the enormous diamond-shaped tiles raised from the surface then collapsed into their normal positions. They caused a rolling wave across the landscape, knocking her over as the wave went by. The elu boulder rolled toward the forest, coming to rest in the separation between two of the tiles.

As Malidora sprung to her feet, something scuffled from the gap in the tiles in front of her. It was heading for the elu. The creature crawled up on top of the stone of melded elu. A blue glowing streak shot from the boulder to the creature as it seemed to be draining the elu. Malidora grabbed the thing and threw it as far as she could. It bounced on the smooth tile but recovered and came crawling back.

Malidora dashed toward it, stomping it with her feet. It stunned the creature for a moment but did not seem to hurt it as it continued crawling toward the elu again. Malidora slid toward it, desperately pounding it with her fists. The creature began to break apart from the blows of her black crystallized hand striking it. A blue ball of energy emanated from the creature's broken body, rising then speeding past her. She turned around as the energy moved toward Valganon as he slimed his way toward her.

"That's an ineffective way to drain a yinak," Valganon's deep voice rumbled as he drew closer.

"I brought you some elu," said Malidora, ignoring the comment.

Valganon's middle head snarled, craning toward her. "This is all you have brought?"

"That's all I could carry back up here," Malidora stated.

The head on the left side growled, "This is hardly worth sparing your life for."

"I can go back and get more." Malidora bowed, unsure if she would get another chance or not.

The head on the right curled around by her ear. "If you want to be our servant," the head on the left darted toward her face, "you had better bring more next time."

The large middle head roared, "This is pathetic!"

"Yes … Mighty Valganon, I will—I'll do better." Malidora tried to make her tone sound authentic. She waited on her knees, preparing for pain.

"Make yourself useful!" All three mouths spewed their acidic saliva into the air, burning onto her aethrum body.

Malidora cried out, inching away from his venomous spew. "I'll go back and get more elu!"

Valganon's long neck on the right side reached out like an arm, snatching her off the red tiles in its mouth. The neck bent low, smashing her into the ground. It dragged her body back and forth across the tiled surface, using her like a broom.

"Brush the filth from my path!" Valganon's other mouths shouted.

Though the surface seemed smooth, sliding across it like this revealed tiny sharp imperfections in the shiny tiles. Her body stung everywhere, covered in tiny particles of some unidentifiable substance hardened on the slick tiles.

As he slimed over to the vent, Valganon slung her into the air toward it. Malidora bounced twice as she hit the ground, sliding toward the exhaust.

"Go now! Get back in there—bring more!"

CHAPTER 3

MALIDORA LAY STILL for a moment, expecting her body to be broken. As she tested her strength, she made it to her feet, amazed that there wasn't more damage. There were tiny openings in her skin leaking elu, but they seemed to be closing up.

Timing the back-and-forth wind direction of the vent, she dropped back in. When she arrived back to the first chamber, Plagat stood there upright, looking at her.

"I don't think I can do this," she said wearily.

"Why not?" Plagat questioned as he crawled through the chamber toward her.

"I'm not strong enough." Malidora rubbed her back, still feeling the sting from being used as a broom. "I feel like I'm dying."

"Perhaps it is temporary weakness," Plagat pondered. "You need to feed."

"On elu?"

"Yes, have you fed since you've been here?" Plagat's tail twitched.

"No," said Malidora, sitting against the wall. "But how do I feed on elu?"

"No wonder you are weak." Plagat wriggled over to a group of fresh blue stones and motioned for her to follow. "You must keep yourself fed or you will fade away and die. Or worse, become like the Nulthereals."

Malidora followed him into a small chamber sparking with blue bubble stones of elu, "Nulthereals don't have elu?"

"So I've been told," Plagat said. "They are said to be aethrum creatures devoid of elu. Some say they are drained of elu but unlike everything else, Nulthereals don't die when they are drained."

Malidora moved toward a cluster of blue glowing orbs. "Neither outcome sounds very appealing."

"Here, focus on the elu inside the stone." Plagat pointed toward the orbs. "Reach out, not with your body, but the energy within you."

Malidora reached her hand toward the bubble, staring at the blue and white sparkling specks that flittered about in various directions. As she watched, they stopped, remaining motionless before moving again. What was controlling their movements? Were they alive? She stood there observing them with her fingers stretched toward them. Finally, she relaxed and withdrew. Nothing had changed.

"You can't wait for something to happen." Plagat curled his tail around a stalagmite. "You have to make it happen."

She reached out again, focusing on the starry lights within the crystal bubbles.

"You're waiting for it to come to you," Plagat groaned. "You have to be both yourself and the elu for that moment. Feel the commonality between each other. Connect with it and then move it. It should feel as though you are moving toward yourself."

"How literally do you mean that? Become it?"

"It is theorized that elu bubbles merging over long periods of time, getting bigger, more powerful, can ultimately become a universe. Not a material universe like yours, but all the others out in Hollowspace. That same energy is inside of you. You are not separate from it. You are the same. Feel it, connect to it, control it, draw it toward you as you reach out to it.

It made her think of Legotian showing her how to repair the old barn he allowed her to stay in. He showed her how to pry the nails loose on the rotted boards and hammer the new ones in. At first, she could rarely hit the nail with the hammer and when she did, the hammer typically glanced off the head of the nail. Even though she hated the chores he made her do, she never understood why he took the time to teach her anything. He could have fixed the barn much faster on his own.

Extending her arm toward the elu energy, she tried to connect to the starry lights as they dashed haphazardly inside the crystal. A few of them stopped moving and she felt the others continue their random patterns. She captured one of them in her mind, tracing a circle with it. The rest of them began moving again.

As she tried to pull them toward her, her focus waned, and they all stopped moving. She exhaled a frustrated breath.

"You know how to control them now." Plagat clasped his hands together. "You only have to learn to divide your focus to hold them all. Eventually, you will do this without effort."

Malidora concentrated again, bringing one particle to a stop. She held it while grabbing another. After a few more attempts at taking hold of all of them, she could feel what was required to take several at once. Grabbing nearly half of them, she held them still while grabbing another cluster. Controlling almost all of the tiny lights with her mind, she went for the rest of them. She gripped them all for a moment, realizing that she could do it.

Malidora tried to relax while applying the same level of concentration. A few nearly slipped beyond her control, but she reapplied the force of her mind and brought them back in.

"Now, make them flow out of the crystal and into your body." Plagat propped his hand on a nearby stone.

Malidora sensed their mass in her mind, affecting her will on them. She pulled them in toward her as her consciousness reached toward them. Streaks of light shot from the crystal into her. It overwhelmed her at first, but she steadied herself. Her aethrum body exploded with sensation.

Every fiber of her being filled with a fire that did not burn. She felt reborn. Never had she perceived so much power, so able to conquer any obstacle in her way. As the lights of elu faded from the crystal, the sensation began to diminish. The rush of invincibility faded, but the newfound strength remained.

She wanted more. She yearned for it. As she reached out toward the elu crystals, Plagat stopped her. "Careful. Don't take too much at a time. You must wait for this strength to subside before feeding again."

"Why?" Malidora challenged. "If we continued gaining this strength, couldn't we defeat Valganon?"

"With strength comes growth. Well before we were strong enough to contend with Valganon, we would grow too big to fit in these channels. We would be vulnerable. Valganon is more powerful than you can imagine. There isn't enough elu for all of us to take him on. Even if we could, there are worse things in Nulvare than Valganon. We would be doomed to live on the surface, always having to defend ourselves from even larger creatures."

"What a sad existence. Imprisoned underground in a cell of your own making because of fear. Fear can be overcome."

Plagat raised up on his tail. "Fear is what keeps us alive."

"You're either the hammer or you become the nail." Malidora ran her hand along one of the orbs, moving the sparkling elu within.

"Ironic coming from one who serves Valganon."

Malidora laughed. "I won't be his servant forever. If you hide from him down here, you make yourself his prisoner."

"You're fooling yourself." Plagat coiled his tail. "You didn't know how to consume elu a few moments ago and now you're going defeat Valganon?"

"Keep your eyes open," Malidora vowed.

❧

Malidora moved on to a crystal mine away from serpent's territory. Fusing elu bubbles together, she made them into as large of a boulder as she could roll through the tunnels. One by one, she rolled them into the hub chamber, stacking them into a corner to store. She could store them there until she had enough for another meeting with Valganon. As long as he remained angry at her, she would be on his mind. If she could do enough to make him content—perhaps he would start to forget.

She kept at it until she grew weary. It wasn't for lack of elu. Her body ached and needed to rest. Malidora followed through the tunnel that Plagat had gone through. The passageway eventually led to another open space; larger than the others she had encountered. Several of the serpent beings lined the edges of the irregularly-shaped chamber walls. Some laid against the soft rock alone, while others in groups laid across each other, coiled together.

The formations in the rock had been artistically carved into horizontal ridges, uniform and smooth. The walls were lined with these ridges from the floor to where they met the ceiling. The flooring had been cut as well, making it even and smooth. Symbols had been drawn in some places with a contrasting gray chalk.

As Malidora searched for a place to sleep, she walked by a group of Sirunak throwing carved rocks into a circle on the floor. The next one picked up all the rocks except one and then threw the rest down into the circle, and they each repeated this process. It must have been a type of game. In another area, some of the Sirunak were playing with a group that were very small and young. They reached out to the little ones with oblong stones and the young ones coiled their tiles around them.

Spotting a small outcropping that bulged in the middle that was bare of the other Sirunak, Malidora decided to settle there and lay down. Nestling into a comfortable position, she felt her mind begin to drift away.

"Valganon's lackey," jeered one of them. "I can't believe we're allowing such filth in here."

Malidora stirred, aware of someone standing over her. Two serpents looked on where she rested, their expressions full of distain.

"Did you need something?" Malidora asked with a sarcastic tone.

"We need nothing from you," snorted another. "Go back to the surface where you belong."

"I will go where I please," Malidora stated.

The serpents laughed. "You have no will. Your life belongs to Valganon. You are the lowest vermin there is. You don't deserve to be among us Sirunak. You're a servant to the whims of a monster so that you can carry on with your pathetic existence."

"I'm surprised that a prisoner would be so careless with their words."

"I'm no prisoner!"

"But you are," Malidora gibed. "You've trapped yourself forever, too afraid to climb out to the surface. You scurry away from life, down here without purpose, without dreams. The only thing controlling your destiny is fear."

The serpent's face contorted. "Pathetic creature. You know nothing of the Sirunak."

The two of them slithered off toward another part of the chamber. The left side of Malidora's lips curled. One of the few pleasures left in this dark realm was making someone else as miserable as she was.

Before long she had drifted away again. As she slept, her mind projected outward. Her consciousness soared through the murky, amber-colored space of the Hollow. She passed by a thousand worlds as they circled the universe in different distances, speeds, and heights. Traveling at what must be impossible speed, she soared away from the universe until she came near a world that seemed to be made of elu. Countless crystalline illuminations of all colors glowed across the surface, colors of elu that were not present on the world she now slept on.

Strange creatures, large and small, fed off its energy. After flying over them for a while, she felt a tug and then collapsed back into her waking body in Sezava. Many serpents stirred from their slumber as Malidora got to her feet. Plagat slithered toward the main tunnel, heading toward the mines. Malidora hurried to catch up with him.

"I had a vision when I was resting," Malidora told him. "There was a world made entirely of elu. If we could get there, we'd have enough to destroy Valganon."

"You were dreamwalking," Plagat stated as he turned toward her. "It is said that it happens in Ilganok's presence."

"What is Ilganok?"

"Ilganok is known as The Dreambinder," Plagat replied. "He is one of the five Gaith. They say he has been sleeping since he came into being. His mind is powerful enough to create connections with others, to create realities."

"How close is he?" Malidora queried.

Plagat rubbed the oily scales of his arms. "We do not know."

"So what I saw wasn't real?"

"It was real in the sense that they are perceptions and memories of the minds that Ilganok has connected to. In that sense, they are images of real places, worlds far away that we could never travel to outside of a dream. They can be interesting, but it is pointless to dwell on dreams. Learn to accept this life you are given. Things are not so bad here."

"I refuse to be here forever."

"We all learn to accept it eventually. One day you will too." Plagat raised his dremora and began slithering away. "I must get to work."

"Wait," Malidora called out, making Plagat stop. "Before I came to be in these caverns, there was a void. Something in that void spoke to me."

Plagat turned around. "Did it state its name?"

"Razinoth." Malidora flinched as the name echoed back to her in the cave.

"Razinoth, the Forgotten." Plagat drew his arms in tight against his side as he spoke the name. "It is said that he can siphon the memories of anyone in his presence. Most who have encountered him barely remember the experience if they survive it. You were quite fortunate."

Malidora adjusted her footing where the flooring curled into the wall. "How can he siphon memory?"

"The Gaith are unlike any other creatures in Nulvare." Plagat's tail clenched as it coiled up. "They can siphon many forms of energy, not just elu. They can even consume consciousness and make it a part of their own. Hence, the mindstream."

"You said there were five," Malidora's finger traced the curve of her chin. "What about the others?"

"Aside from Ilganok and Razinoth, there are Grindak the Enraged, Vazerinaz the Unyielding, and Zeragul the Soulbender."

❧

Malidora labored in the mining chamber until she had harvested all the blue elu, leaving the rest to continue their growth. She had accumulated a nice stack of boulders in the corner of the hub area. Eager to end the looming threat of Valganon's minions, she set her dremora on a flat rock and began moving the elu stones to the vent shaft. She left a few in the corner to keep for herself, but most of them were clustered near the vent. Timing the change in wind direction, she pushed each boulder into the tunnel until all of them had been launched to the surface. Malidora sat on top of one of the boulders, waiting for Valganon.

"This is worth your life for now," Valganon said as he arrived. "But I expect more soon."

"Of course," she said, taking a step back.

"I trust you are handling those that dwell in the tunnels."

"They tremble at the very mention of your name," Malidora embellished, attempting to speak to his pride.

"As do all!" He slammed his two outside heads into the ground as if their necks were arms and its heads were fists. The impact jolted her off her feet onto the hard floor.

As she hurried into the exhaust, internal visions seeped into her mind again, blocking out her current surroundings.

The soft pulsating walls of the cavern came back into view as she rubbed her forehead. Leaving the unripened elu in the mining chamber to continue its fusion, Malidora sought new sources of elu further in the caves. The tunnel system was massive, one branch leading to several more, and those all revealing further pathways.

As she explored, she came upon another type of creature living in the caves. They crawled on six legs and had spiked armor that covered their backs. These beings could crawl at least as fast as she could run standing up. They traveled through the caves in great numbers, and they made efficient use of space. Some crawled upside down on the ceiling while others crawled along the floor underneath them.

Knowing that she would be overwhelmed by their numbers, she observed them from a safe distance. They all moved through the tunnels together, seeking elu and eventually carrying it back. When they had all disappeared into the hole of their nest, Malidora hurried through the caves to gather any elu that was left to bring back to the hub before resting in Sezava.

After a few intervals of this, Malidora decided to take a risk. When the crawlers had left the nest, she took the opportunity to peek into the hole. Inside was a large, rounded chamber with glowing eggs lining the walls. The eggs heaved as if they were breathing.

Malidora moved further inside the opening. Her slow rhythmic breaths became quick and shallow upon noticing the massive creature in the far corner. The enormous crawler mother lay quivering as four normally sized crawlers positioned themselves around her. They seemed to be feeding the mother with their own elu. The mother crawler slumbered, making a horrid guttural sound when she exhaled. Resting among the eggs were huge stockpiles of elu bubbles. If only she could get to that elu.

As she had done the past few days, Malidora moved back around the corner of one of the tunnels until the crawlers came back to the nest. Once they were all in their nest, Malidora moved into the elu chambers, gathering what she could into three crystalized boulders. She had never attempted to bring back three at once, and it proved a foolhardy effort.

One of the boulders sank into a crevice in the floor, and she could not get it out. After trying different ways to get it unstuck, Malidora reached for the elu energy inside of it. Perhaps she could move a portion of the energy into another boulder.

She siphoned slowly, making sure that none of it spilled into her. As she tried to control the speed of the elu, she realized that the boulder wobbled with the direction of the energy leaving it. It gave her an idea. Instead of draining the elu, she made it move. Directing the energy toward the edge of the boulder and then back to the center caused the large stone to roll slightly forward.

Malidora controlled the energy again, making it go back and forth and around the inside of the stone until it rolled out of the crevice toward her. She was onto something. The rest of the way back to the hub, Malidora spun the elu, making the boulders roll. This was so much easier than using her strength to move them.

As she made her way through Sezava to rest, a group of Sirunak gathered around a carved stone table. Elu bubbles of various sizes were scattered across its surface. One of the Sirunak had bubble stones filled with amber clouds instead of elu. The cloudy interiors were various densities, some like vapor and others were like liquid jelly. Another was draining elu from one stone and transferring it into one of the cloud stones. Malidora stared as she walked, nearly running into an oncoming Sirunak.

"Who—oh it's you," said Sinathra, one of the Sirunak women.

Malidora glanced back toward the Sirunak around the table. "What are they doing over there?"

"Experimenting." Sinathra brought her tail in close around her. "They're trying to find other elements that will fuse into heavier forms of elu." Sinathra had begun to warm up to her the past few days. She was one of the few that didn't treat her like a minion of Valganon.

Malidora lifted an eyebrow. "What for?"

"The more elements fused together, the higher the quality," said Sinathra. "Beyond the blue color, there is violet and even red. If we can fuse one more element with the blue elu we could fashion a chrysalis and metamorphose into our true form."

"So not everyone is as unambitious as Plagat," Malidora said.

"Don't sell him short." Sinathra leaned back on her tail. "Plagat is a worker. We need more like him."

"You're right. He keeps this place running." Malidora rubbed the palm of her hands together, feeling the hardened texture of the hand covered in the black stone of the Whidge.

Sinathra tilted her head. "You've been gathering quite a bit too. Do you really need so much?"

"Valganon demands a lot." Malidora exhaled some of her frustration. "I need to store as much as I can. I don't know if a time will come that I have difficulty finding more."

"I suppose that is wise."

"Will it be safe? None of you are going to steal my stash, are you?"

"Don't worry. We only feed enough to sustain us," Sinathra said. "There's plenty in our mines for that. Besides, no one wants to take from Valganon. Skazm infestation is the last thing we need."

"What are skazms, anyway?" Malidora wondered.

"Organisms that bore into the ground and other creatures," said Sinathra. "They plant seeds in anything alive. The seedlings nourish themselves on the elu of their host until they eventually grow too large for the host to contain. It's a slow, awful way to die."

"Ugh." Malidora's face crunched up. "Yes, let's do whatever we can to avoid that."

Upon entering Sezava, she found Plagat resting in his usual spot: a nice, sloped cavern wall near a small, protruding rock formation that he curled his tail around. Deciding not to wake him, she lay nearby on the cavern floor.

Though she tried to be quiet, he began to stir from his sleep. "You should get more rest." He raised his head from the rock. "There's more to strength than feeding."

Malidora wiped some of the jagged pebbles from the floor. "I get enough."

"Did you accomplish what you set out to do during your worktime?" Plagat's tail began to uncoil from a nearby stone column.

"No," she said, "but if I had, I would've had to move the goal further."

"You should live free." Plagat stretched out his tail. "Without goals."

"Free? You call this free?"

"What more do you need?"

"I don't belong here. I don't want to live in The Hollow," stated Malidora. "I need to get back to my world."

"You have friends there? Family?" Plagat lowered his head back onto the rock, closing his eyes.

She stared off into the dark corners of the chamber. "Not anymore."

Plagat opened his black eyes. "No one? Then what do you want to go back for?"

"I need to finish what I started," Malidora said. "If the Gaith send more shadows into Isodonia, I need to be there to stop them."

Plagat raised his head to look at her. "There must be someone you want to protect."

"I want to protect everyone there," said Malidora. "Every living thing."

Closing his eyes again, Plagat settled into a spot between two stones. "Just a nameless mass of living things? That doesn't seem very motivating."

"What could be more motivating than saving a world from destruction?"

"It just seems like risking your life fighting the Gaith would require passion for someone, deep caring for certain individuals. How can you have that for a crowd you've never met?"

Her older brother and sisters had wished Malidora had never been born. They'd felt chained to her whenever they wanted to leave the village and had to take her along. They'd often blamed her for what they did wrong. In turn, she had wished that she would never have to see them again, but she never wanted to actually kill them. Someday she had to make up for it. For listening to the Shadows and doing their wishes. "Because my life has to be worth something," she told Plagat.

"I guess there is no convincing you. I'm afraid there's no way back." Plagat twisted his body, trying to get comfortable. "You're aethrum now. A material universe would destroy you."

Malidora stiffened. "There must be a way. If Nulthereals and Whidges can enter my world, why can't I?"

"All I know is that they are drained of elu. I don't know the specifics of how it works, but even then, they would have to be very limited in your universe." Plagat closed his eyes. "Aethrum and matter cannot meet. They would destroy each other, leaving deadspace where nothing can ever exist again."

"How do you know that?"

Plagat raised up again. "Stories of long ago told of a dark breach." He opened his mouth wide as if stretching his jaw. "It is said that it changed Nulvare forever. It's extremely dangerous. Deadspace could threaten the entire Everance. Thankfully, nuvalum divides the aethrum of Hollowspace from your material universe."

"Nuvalum? What's that about?"

"It radiates from your universe. It's like a buffer between matter and aethrum, preventing deadspace from happening. But it is also what prevents a lot of elu from fusing. That is why this region of Hollowspace is more barren than the worlds you saw in the dream. If your universe is collapsed, there will be much less nuvalum generated."

"What makes deadspace so dangerous?"

"Hard to describe. It is the absence of existence. Anything that touches it vanishes—ceases to be."

"How could it just vanish? Maybe it just goes somewhere else."

"Interesting thought, but there is no way to know." Plagat seemed to be studying her. "What we do know for sure is that nothing that contacts it ever returns. So, as far as this reality is concerned, it no longer exists. Whatever the case, it is the end of both matter and aethrum. Supposedly you can still find the deadspace in Nulvare, but it was sealed in some way to prevent further damage."

Malidora rested, listening to the air blowing through vents and crevices in the cavern. As she slept, her mind traveled upward through the caves. She moved toward the black sphere of the universe surrounded by a bright pulsating disk. Though extremely far away, it filled a large portion of the sky around her. The skies were dotted with black specks, possibly other universes that continued forever throughout The Hollow.

She reached out toward the universe, flowing through Hollowspace at limitless speed. Yet, it seemed to make no difference, the gulf remained as wide as ever. She felt her mind falling back toward her body. Space and time blurred as she struggled to resist its pull.

Movement nearby caught her attention, a disturbance in the soft dense clouds of Hollowspace. She drew closer. Blue light poked through as clouds stretched and swirled around a hole in the amber-colored medium, the same tempest floating above the forest outside. From up here she could tell how impossible it would be to reach from the surface. Malidora peered inside the chaotic vortex, which seemed to contain a world of its own. She attempted to touch it. The tip of her fingers grazed the opening where Hollowspace ended and something new began. Everything faded as she dropped, falling so fast she could no longer keep herself in the dream.

CHAPTER 4

EVEN BEFORE HER eyes blinked open, she realized she had returned to her body, waking on the sloping walls of the cavern. Plagat was still asleep beside her, possibly dreamwalking himself. Could the blue vortex be the way out? How could her waking body ever reach it?

"The blue opening out there in sky." Malidora sat up. "Is that the deadspace you were talking about?"

Plagat's tail unwound from the nearby stalagmite searching for his nearby dremora. "No. We're not sure what caused it. The band of nuvalum surrounding your universe causes violent reactions to the objects that come close enough. It is likely that it was caused by something that was torn apart and thrown out away from the universe. Certain creatures seem to have an interest in it, but I don't know much more than that."

"The crawling creatures further in the tunnels, are they friendly?" she asked as she stood up.

Plagat's tail twitched and his upper body raised. "Belathids. They can be deadly if you get in their way. Though they should leave you alone, I would avoid them as much as you can."

After feeding again, Malidora grabbed her dremora and headed through the tunnel toward the Belathids' nest. Rolling five of her largest boulders along with her, she waited out of view. This time she had a plan.

Once the Belathids swarmed through the tunnels on their

way to the elu chambers, Malidora used the energy inside two of the boulders to move them into the tunnel leading toward the elu mines. She combined the two boulders together to form a larger one, which jammed into the walls and ceiling of the tunnel as it formed, sealing the passageway.

When the Belathids returned, they scratched and clawed at the boulder, struggling to get back to the hive. Eventually, two of the mother's guards heard the cries and came out of the nest to help. Controlling the elu inside, Malidora launched two more boulders at the guards, crushing them both into the huge stone that sealed the tunnel.

As the other two guards came out of the nest, Malidora flung the last boulder at them. The huge stone crashed into the others inside the tunnel ahead but missed both Belathid guards. One of the guards creeped toward her, opening its small mouth and barring its fangs. Malidora lashed out, connecting to the elu energy inside him, and siphoning it as fast as she could.

The Belathid quickly resisted, bringing the blue strands of energy to a standstill between him and Malidora. As the Belathid weakened from its initial loss of energy, the tide turned in Malidora's favor. But before she could siphon it dry, the other guard with red stripes moved in, draining Malidora while she fought with the other one.

Malidora split her focus, drawing from the red Belathid, the blue one, and the nearby elu stones that were sealing the passageway. Surging with power, she lifted one of the boulders from the tunnel, launching it toward the red Belathid. The stone landed on the creature's armored back, pining it to the ground. The blue guard dropped as she drained the rest of its energy. The body cracked, withering into hardened dust. The elu continued to flow into her as she grew, forcing the rest of the energy into the stones, she avoided outgrowing the cave.

The Belathids in the tunnel kept scratching at the boulders blocking their way as Malidora strode toward the nest's entrance. She climbed through the hole into the mother's chamber. The sickening wet breaths of the Belathid mother remained steady and slow.

Trying to quiet her nerves, Malidora stepped between the quivering eggs. Her right foot found space, then her left. This was going to take some time, but she couldn't afford to wake the big Belathid mother. The first time she had ever tried something like this ended in failure. Attempting to infiltrate the Impradium in the capital of Gildanel, she had almost made it to the throne of the magnos before she was caught. Her intent had not been to steal, but to exact vengeance. She wanted to kill the magnos for what he had done to her and Legotian, but she lacked the knowledge and the experience to carry out her deed.

As she passed by the sleeping Belathid mother, it slowly inhaled with a vibrating hiss. Malidora carefully used the energy inside the bubble stones, guiding them up and over the clutches of eggs. The rhythmic breathing of the mother stuttered. Malidora hesitated for a moment, and one of the crystal boulders dropped to the floor, crushing some of the eggs.

The mother snorted as her many legs began to twitch. Malidora moved toward the hole, still rolling the boulders toward the entrance. The ground shook as the mother stood, rubbing her black eyes with her spiny front appendages.

Malidora dashed toward the hole, sliding in the oozing yolk as eggs cracked beneath her feet. The mother scurried after her. Sliding to the hole, she pushed herself through the opening just before the Belathid mother snatched her up in its mandibles.

The mother crashed into the wall of the nest, vibrating the tunnels as Malidora escaped. When she reached the hub cavern, she moved all the boulders from the Belathid nest into her stockpile. Her exhausted body shut down as she dropped against the wall in Sezava. Her consciousness seemed to float away from the cave as she dreamwalked. Above the surface and out into the wild open, she flew past countless obelisk and sphere-shaped worlds, floating in the gelatinous medium of Hollowspace. There seemed no limit to her speed as she soared past blurs of gaseous formations and debris fields. Through the mushy clouds, black circles of other universes dotted the expanse of Nulvare. Millions of them. More than millions. A number unfathomed.

Curious, Malidora centered on one of the objects and zoomed toward it. The object grew against the others as she sped toward it. A ghostly red luminosity circled the black object as she came ever closer to it. Another universe, like her own, floated silently here in endless Hollowspace. Behind it, countless other black dots poked through the cloudy realm from far away. Were there really this many universes in The Hollow? Did they all have worlds like Isodonia? How insignificant she truly was in the face of this realization. Would her deeds make any difference in the grandiosity of a realm such as this? As small as it made her seem, she felt part of it all, connected. Perhaps even the tiniest form of life was just as important as anything in this grand cosmic ecosystem.

Specks of crystal and rock surrounded the red universe at this distance. Worlds made of translucent crystal revealed massive glowing elu beneath its surface. Surrounding her, elu materialized out of thin air, growing before her eyes. Elu flowed from this universe, violet and red rivers poured through the gel clouds of Hollowspace. Without the nuvalum that radiated from her universe, elu energy flourished. Creatures great and small sped through Hollowspace around her, siphoning elu formations before they grew too big to feed on. The larger creatures fed off the elu of the smaller ones. A rapid food chain cycle took place in a chaotic battle around her.

Suddenly, Malidora snapped back toward her body as it began to wake. She had dreamwalked much further than before. As she was pulled back, she passed an enormous shadow, eclipsing a blue swirling vortex. She tried to get a better look but lost control as she awoke from the dream.

How much time had passed? She needed to get some elu up to the surface before Valganon came looking for her or sent some horrible creatures into the tunnels. As she got to her feet, voices began to echo through the caverns. Several skittering footsteps grew louder, along with something sliding through the gravel. Malidora crawled into one of the opposite caves, waiting for them to leave.

"Sirunak!" yelled one of the Belathids as a few of them crawled into the hub chamber where her supply of elu was stored. "We have come for what is ours!"

Belathid workers began rolling the stones off the pile. "Anyone who trespasses into our nest shall be given for Mother to feed!"

A few of the Sirunak came slithering into the hub. "This is not our elu."

"Another creature has taken up residence here," conceded Plagat. "We do not bother her, and she does not take from us."

"This is our supply! Someone stole it and killed our guards!" The

Belathid's shell separated as it raised an arm toward the pile. "Bring forth the perpetrators or suffer with them!"

"Do as you will, but she serves Valganon. We leave her be," said Plagat.

The Belathid stepped back. "Valganon? He has never cared about our tunnels here!"

"I've extended his reach." Malidora stepped into the open. "Now, if you'll stand—crawl aside. I have to get this elu to him or he will send those—what was it called again?"

"Skazms!" screeched one of the Sirunaks.

"Why would he do that?" the Belathid mused. "He uses skazms to reinforce his shell."

"If someone double-crossed him, he would do just about anything," said Plagat. "What does he really need protection from anyway?"

"Enough of this foolishness!" said another Belathid. "We will go to war if we must!"

"Go to war if you wish, but I'm in a bit of a rush." Malidora moved toward the pile. "Valganon will destroy us all if he doesn't get this elu."

"We are quite safe from Valganon down here," said the Belathid. "Feed her to Mother!"

A horrid shriek sounded through the caverns followed by the sound of scratching. Hundreds of small, armored creatures poured through the vent opening as Belathids and Sirunaks raced to get away.

"Skazms!" one of the Belathids shouted.

The Sirunak retreated toward Sezava while the Belathids crawled as fast as they could through the tunnel toward their nest. Malidora climbed onto the stack of elu. She tried to drain several skazms as they closed in, but something about their armor made it difficult to connect with the elu inside them.

The Sirunak began moving elu boulders into the tunnel, trying to barricade the path leading to their resting chamber. A few were infected by the skazms as the small creatures burrowed into them. Skazms had slowed the Belathids down as well, infecting them as they tried to escape.

Malidora lifted several elu stones from the stack and hammered them into the skazms as they scurried along the cavern floor. Most of them missed, but a few hit their targets. The crushed skazms gave up their elu as they died and Malidora grabbed it. Her strength grew slightly, but she had barely made a dent in their numbers as they dashed chaotically toward anything living.

Connecting to as many elu stones as she could in her pile, she drained all its energy into herself. Growing rapidly in size, raw power surged through her in a rush of radiance. She burst through the ceiling of the chamber and through the surface of the tiled floor as brown ooze flowed from inside the rock, spilling into the caverns.

With this new power, she perceived elu in every living thing as far as she could see. Connecting to the skazms, she siphoned all of their elu through their crusty armor, destroying them all and filling her with a new wave of strength.

"Malidora what have you done?" Plagat's mouth gaped in horror as he held tightly to a pillar. Bits of rock fell, and thick liquid oozed into the chamber from above.

"I'm saving us." Malidora climbed out of the opening onto the surface. How could he not understand? She was giving them freedom.

"Valganon will destroy us all!" Plagat howled, aiming his dremora into the further reaches of the cavern. "You've opened up our tunnels where he can reach us!"

"I'm more powerful than anything in this world!" Malidora tightened her fist as she gazed down at Plagat. "I will destroy him!"

Plagat shook his head into the palm of his hand. "You cannot beat him! He's stronger than you know!"

Plagat was wrong. How could Valganon contend with her now? Unbridled power coursed through her. A familiar sound skittered across the diamond tiled surface. Valganon. He charged toward her, still as formidable as ever. Even with her enhanced power, her hands trembled.

Valganon moved with his skittering arms as he slid on a trail of thick wet slime toward the crater she had made in the surface.

"Hah! Look at you! You have made yourself into something worthy of feeding on." Valganon's mouths salivated in anticipation as he began to rip the energy from her body.

Malidora tried to fight it, but there was no defense against this force. How could he still be stronger after all the elu she had consumed, all the power flowing within her? If she didn't find a way to fight back, her body would be consumed and she would be nothing more than consciousness without form, drifting alone in the dark again, with her only choices to fall into madness or follow that terrible voice.

Connecting to the nearby Belathids, she drained them of their energy. It was not enough. Valganon was going to win. Her hopes of destroying the Gaith, saving the universe, and proving that Legotian was right, that her life did have meaning, were all slipping away.

Malidora could feel the elu within the Sirunak, the ones nearby, even the ones in Sezava. She hated to do it, but there was no turning back now. As the energy drained out of her, she had no choice.

"Malidora! No!" Plagat screamed as she siphoned the energy from him. "You can't do this to us! You—"

Even after his voice was silenced, he continued to struggle against her power. Why did those you least wanted to hurt, take the longest to kill? *Malidora the Irredeemable,* the memory of Razinoth's voice ran through her mind. For the sake of the universe, someone had to be willing to do whatever it takes. Plagat's red dremora fell onto his dry ashen remains. Crumbling, they spilled onto the cavern floor. Malidora continued draining the elu stone barricade the Sirunak had made, and further on to the elu they had stored. She siphoned Ghitrek and all the remaining Sirunak until only she and Valganon remained in the area.

Malidora felt woozy as her aethrum body tried to adapt to the rapid increase in power. It was still not enough. She had slowed the energy Valganon was drawing out of her but not enough to turn the tide.

Knowing where the Belathid nest was, she desperately tried to connect to more energy further in the tunnels. She found them. After drawing all the energy from the other Belathids, Malidora connected to the Belathid mother.

She drained every last powerful drop of energy from the mother, moving on to the eggs around the nest. Valganon curiously stopped siphoning from Malidora's body. She turned toward him, expecting his attack to begin again at any moment.

"You are more ruthless than we expected," he said. "You win. Take this as your territory if you desire it so much. There is plenty more unoccupied space for us." Valganon slithered away on his trail of slime in defeat.

"No!" Malidora yelled. "I'm not done with you yet!"

He turned around. "There's nothing more you can do—If either of us drains the other, we will become too big to survive."

"You expect me to believe that?" She raised her arms to tear into Valganon, ripping the elu from his body.

Angered, he drained from her, replacing the elu she was gaining from him.

"Fool!" Valganon said. "If either of us grows any bigger, he will see us!"

"*Who* will see?" Malidora said.

"You don't understand!" Valganon shouted. "Stop this! You'll destroy us both!"

Malidora laughed. "I had no idea you would be this pathetic! When faced with someone your own size, you cower!"

Valganon drained her with renewed desperation. Malidora tried to pull back to match the same force and eventually overcome it. Caught in a tug-of-war she could not win, her body grew weary, but Valganon was slowly overcoming Malidora's power. If this continued, she would eventually lose. She stopped siphoning.

Valganon paused, and the elu began to seep back into both of them.

"You finally came to your senses? If we are to remain undetected, we cannot get any larger than we are now. We must—"

Focusing on the elu in Valganon's body Malidora connected and began moving it inside him. Pulling it slowly, she gained full control. Valganon stared, confused as to what she was doing.

The massive shell covering his back began to crack in several places. The middle of the shell turned inward, bending until it finally broke. Valganon's heads roared as he began draining from Malidora again. His shell folded in two as both ends closed together around him. He was crushed by his own shell as Malidora bent the elu inside him to her will. The neck coming from Valganon's left shoulder snapped under the weight of the carapace and fell limp onto the smooth tile.

Valganon writhed in torment as the shell had completely trapped his body. Malidora walked over to his remaining heads that were struggling to free themselves from the pressure of the carapace cutting into them. She feared his aethrum body would heal soon if she didn't keep the pressure on, but she needed to relish this to the fullest.

"Grovel . . ." she whispered.

Valganon stopped struggling and began to laugh.

"Grovel!" she commanded, causing the elu to press the broken shell even tighter into him. His laughing died into a low moan that passed through one of his mouths.

"Then die!"

She started pulling the elu out of his body. He was defenseless to stop it. The power within him was nearly overwhelming. Malidora strained to contain it all as her body lost control and she went to her knees.

"You've won nothing. . . ." His voice became muffled. "He will . . . end . . . you . . ."

As the last bit of elu drained from Valganon, his body slowly crumbled into dust. Malidora steadied herself and slowly stood. She was now the most powerful being on this world. It was hers now. Nothing could ever stand against her again.

Alone, Malidora towered above the forest, relishing the surging of her new power. The diamond-shaped tiles of the world's surface were still huge, even at this height. They filled the landscape, even as she could see farther than ever. Distant creatures scurried away in fright as they felt the tremor of her steps.

The blue vortex swirled in the skies ahead; she was now close enough to reach it. The orange gelatin clouds around it seemed to stretch and condense as they were pulled into its center. The blue light from inside the tunnel glowed on the surrounding particles.

She moved toward it, wanting to know the mysteries it contained. Reaching toward it, a force seemed to tug at her hand. The clouds divided as she moved her hand out. Her hand felt wet where the gel-like vapor turned to mist at the edge of the tempest. It trailed down toward the massive black sphere of the universe.

A slow vibration pulsed through her mind. It grew faster and louder until becoming unbearable. It felt as though it was breaking her apart until it steadied as if various frequencies of sound were tested until they reached a balance.

"At last, we have found you, living one," the voice began as a whisper and ended like a clap of thunder. It was familiar. Razinoth, the Forgotten.

Malidora checked her surroundings to see who was there but saw nothing. A rustling shudder waved through the floor lifting the tiles in rows as it moved across the landscape. Steadying herself, she surveyed the landscape again, uneasy that she could not find the source of the voice.

"You are an interesting little creature, a welcome asset to the mindstream," said Razinoth.

"All I want is to get out of here."

"Your memories are ours. We know that you have always desired power. The power to redeem yourself. The power to change the authorities of your world, to shape them into something that will serve others rather than themselves. That is how you would redeem yourself and reclaim the childhood stolen from you. Your weaknesses are many, but your will in strong. It will bring us one step closer."

"A step closer to what?"

"To unlocking all the realms of the Everance," Razinoth spoke as the tiles rippled across the surface of the world.

"What good will that do you?" Malidora looked around the area, seeing nothing but the empty tiled surface and the leafless trees.

"There are memories beyond the boundaries of Nulvare. Memories of beginnings and endings locked away from me. I will breathe them in and become all knowing. Omniscient."

"Then what?" Malidora searched the skies for the source of the thundering voice. "What do you plan to do with it?"

"You lack imagination," Razinoth bellowed as the ground shook beneath her. "We shall reshape the Everance to meet our desires. Bring unity to dissonance, order to chaos. We will become infinity and reconstitute eternity."

The quaking beneath her feet subsided. "That does sound ambitious. I guess you've really thought this through."

"You jest, but even now your thoughts flow wayward, curious. You know little, but you imagine knowledge in the beyond that you cannot conceive of. You have seen more than most of your kind, but you have not even begun to understand it."

It was unsettling that it knew her thoughts as she was having them. What was this voice anyway, and where was it coming from?

"We are all around you." Razinoth's voice vibrated the world. "Right before your eyes, but you are too blind to see."

"What do you look like?"

"Your thoughts, once bold, are now riddled with fear," Razinoth thundered, his voice echoing on through the skies. "We are the dark brought to light. The shapeless given form."

Plagat had spoken of the Gaith. The force that wanted to drain all life from, not only Isodonia, but the entire universe. He had said they were so massive as to be invulnerable, but if it were so enormous, why couldn't she see it?

"We cannot deny that you have accomplished the impossible," said Razinoth. "For one born of matter to change into an aethrum form. If we had this knowledge, we could enter your universe at will."

Malidora scanned the horizons, still unable to locate the voice. With each spoken word, the vibrations beneath her feet made her more apprehensive. She didn't know how she had this aethrum body, but perhaps she could stall if it thought she did.

"Ah, you do not know the answer. You have been incredibly fortunate, but now you must decide. Join with us willingly or we can do it the hard way."

It could read her thoughts with ease. How could she hope to destroy this being if it knew what she was going to do at any given moment.

"Your lack of understanding is amusing. Nothing born in Nulvare would entertain thoughts of destroying us. If you cast a stone into the dark, is the darkness destroyed?"

"I generally want to destroy anything that I find annoying."

"You have endured a pained existence. We can wipe those memories away. They will never haunt you again. Join us and endure for eons, marveling in the splendor of the new eternity."

"I am those painful experiences. If I were separated from them, what would become of the me I am now? I don't want to forget them. I want to remember my failures. Learn from them and I'll never forget what you did to Arkanthis!"

"Expand your mind and become something significant. You will come to understand that the majesty of our design is worth the sacrifice of your universe."

"If you are so invincible, show yourself!"

"Our revelation may break your mind. We could simply take you, but a willing soul is so much better."

"I don't want your offer! You took my life, my family, and my homeland! Come out from your hiding place!"

"As you wish." The ground began to erupt. "We shall reveal what your eyes fail to see."

Yanked off her feet, an invisible force dragged Malidora across the tiles at an incredible rate of speed. Even with all her newly acquired power, resisting did nothing to slow her even a little.

Pulled across the world, far from any area she had seen before, it compelled her toward an enormous, twisted mountain in the distance. The horizon upended itself from the surface as the mountain towered over everything. The floor beneath her began to raise into a steep incline.

As she drew closer to the mountainous spire, the force lifted her off the ground toward a massive opening. The dominating grip pulled her into the cavernous maw, and everything went dark. Only a blue glow from the deep remained as she tumbled against the walls.

As she sped further through the channel, a flowing blue substance covered the passage in front of her. The thick congealed threshold slowed her passage, squeezing around her as she seeped through.

CHAPTER 5

HER MIND WANDERED, free flowing and unaware. She found herself again in the long, dark void. There was no sensation of right-side up or upside down. Eternal nothingness gaped open as she drifted further from existence.

Colors flashed in front of her for a split second before returning to the dark. Malidora felt her eyelids again as they began to crack open. Was this still in The Hollow? She was in a forest of strange red trees. Their twisting limbs reached out in all directions. She stood on grasses of blue, orange, white, and gray. Behind her, a sheer cliff wall led to a bottomless void.

Her senses continued to return as the cracking tension of the swaying trees grew clearer. Malidora began walking through the strange, yet familiar forest. The red roots of the trees pulsed, stretching out in the same direction as far as she could see. How did she get to this place?

Movement along the trunks of the largest trees caught her eye. With trepidation, she stepped in for a closer glimpse. A multitude of faces appeared, knotted and gnarled into the bark of the trunks of the trees. Their eyes hollow and lifeless, mouths screaming without a voice. The faces soon dissipated into the wood as new ones formed to take their place.

Invasive thoughts filled her mind as she stared at the horrid trees. *You should not be here.*

As she scanned the various shapes forming in the wood, Malidora began to feel a profound loneliness. She continued through the woods for what seemed like hours. Perhaps she was going the wrong way. But where was she going at all? To go the wrong way meant there must be a right way.

Red particles coursed through the translucent roots as they curled above and below the grass. She felt eyes on her, a presence moving in the darkest shadows just beyond her sight. Shadows in the corner of her peripheral vision made her turn to make sure no one followed. The twisted vines and branches of the knotted old trees held still with her eyes upon them. *Candle burning in the dark*, she recited to herself. But there were no candles here.

The further she crept through the trees, the more tangled the thicket behind her became, as if weaving a wall to prevent her from turning back. Malidora changed direction, following the path of the roots. Her feet twitched with the tingles of energy flowing through the red roots as she walked over them. More words invaded her thoughts. *This is no place for the unmelded.*

The dark sky shifted to a disquieting blue as Malidora emerged from the forest. In the clearing, a silver stream coursed through a valley and ebbed into the distant horizon. Something beyond radiated with energy, filling the sky and the land around her with light. The roots she had been following twisted into the opaque waters of the stream.

As she walked toward the sluggish water, the feeling of being watched crept across the back of her neck again. She turned toward the red forest, seeing nothing but the spidery rows of trees. Kneeling at the edge of the water, Malidora's reflection appeared, facing back at her. It was weird seeing herself in this aethrum form. The face was hers, but the skin was made of something different.

She leaned over the silver waters as they twisted and churned. Something was peculiar about her reflection. Her eyes in the image were closed. She stared back at herself, attempting to discern the cause of this aberration.

As she studied the image, a new face formed in the silver liquid. This was not a reflection but molded into the water itself. Stretching and distorting, it eventually dissipated as it moved with the current. Malidora rose to her feet, now realizing that several shapes of faces formed into the surface.

She walked along the stream in the direction of the flow. More foreign thoughts set upon her mind. *Step into the stream and meld.* Malidora dipped her foot into the silver liquid, its thickness surprised her. The liquid did not drip off as she stepped out. It remained, coating her boot.

Wading into the water, the shallow stream near the banks quickly deepened. Her body began to melt into the thick silver. As Malidora sank, her heart began to race, her feet could no longer move.

Overwhelming thoughts blasted into her mind through the current. Foreign memories burned and emotions surged as if she were a conduit for all the world's thoughts and feelings.

As the water climbed above her knees, it suddenly stopped. The liquid receded from her shadowstone hand, allowing her legs to once again move free in the waters.

Another contorted face seeped by as Malidora reached out to touch it, but before she could, it dissolved. Waiting for another to appear, she readied her stone hand in the water then caught hold of one. The face solidified as she used her other hand to lift it from the water. A full head and body formed as Malidora moved it out of the silver liquid.

She dragged the body out of the stream onto the multicolored grass. It was a girl, not unlike herself, but younger. The girl's eyes remained closed as Malidora crouched beside her. She caressed her cheek, and the girl began to move, her first sign of life. *Why did I do this?* Malidora realized that she made things more difficult on herself by removing the girl from the stream. Now there was someone else to slow her down.

Something stirred between the distant trees. The watching presence. Dark objects hid behind the wide trunks as soon as she glanced toward the forest. *Do not remove collective minds.*

The girl coughed as her eyes twitched. She stared up at Malidora, squinting.

"Who are you?" the girl rasped.

"Malidora," she replied, gently rubbing the silver from under the girl's eyes. "What's your name?"

The girl inhaled deeply, coughing again as she exhaled. "The last thing I remember, I was looking for someone. Someone in my family I think."

"Where did you come from?" Malidora helped her sit up on the grass.

The girl tried to sit on her own but was unable without support. "I don't remember."

"What do you remember?" Malidora held onto her arms to help her keep from falling back.

"So many memories, thoughts," said the girl. "I don't know which are mine and which are not anymore. We were all connected, but it wasn't a pleasant connection. It was forced, violating."

"What kinds of thoughts were in there?" Malidora wondered.

The girl stared blankly out at the forest. "Mostly about darkness taking root, feeding on life. It broke whole worlds apart into dust until all the essences of life were taken."

"What do they do with these essences?"

"They store them in stones far away from here."

"How can I get out of here, back to my universe?"

The girl's eyes blinked as she looked around. "Where are we?"

"I think we are still somewhere in The Hollow." Malidora watched the tree line on the other side of the stream, making sure no one was there. "Though it looked very different before."

"Beware The Hollow," the girl mumbled. "Some of the disturbed people in my village used to say that."

"Yeah, same with those in my world. Guess they knew something we didn't." Malidora rose to her feet. "We've got to find a way out of here."

"How did you get free of the stream?" the girl wondered.

Malidora's eyes focused on the silver water. "I was never in the stream. I was taken from my world by Shadows."

"Everyone that is taken by the Nulthereals goes to the stream," said the girl.

"I don't know what to tell you," said Malidora. "Nothing about this place makes sense."

"There are others in the stream," the girl said. "We have to get them out too."

Malidora glanced at the silver flow and all the faces forming and dissipating. "All of them? There could be hundreds, maybe more."

"We have to try," the girl urged.

Malidora reluctantly stepped back into the stream. She knew she couldn't save them all. What good would it do to only help one more? It was, however, nice to have someone to talk to again. Someone that wasn't trying to lead her astray. If the eyes in the dark forest didn't like it, she should probably do it. As she began melting into the water, she touched it with her black hand, and again, it stopped the silver liquid from taking her. Faces of various shapes and sizes flowed around her. She saw one with the same angled eyes as the girl and took hold, towing the body to dry ground. It was a boy.

The girl excitedly crawled over to him, wiping the silver droplets from his eyes. "I know him!"

"Is he part the family you were looking for?" Malidora asked.

The girl's eyes flittered around as if searching for an answer. "No. I don't think so, but our minds were connected. We exchanged memories and feelings. I suppose I know everyone in the stream in some way. I saw good things they did and bad, and they saw everything I ever wanted kept secret."

"He has some of your features," Malidora said.

"We're from the same place, I think, but I don't remember him before," said the girl. "His name is Kazial."

His body suddenly bolted up as he started coughing. The girl clapped him on the back until he caught his breath. "Kazial, do you remember me?"

"Something." Kazial started coughing again. "Something about you is familiar."

Malidora leaned in. "What do you remember?"

His eyes were fixed on the girl. "Sidaire, I saw your face in a dream."

The girl's eyes beamed. "Yes! Sidaire! That's who I was! Who I am!"

Malidora felt something watching them from behind. She turned around toward the woods. Something moved between the red trees.

"Shh . . ."

Dark walking things crept through the thicket into the light. One by one, the bent black legs of shadowy creatures stuttered like a video that was missing frames. On four legs they stood slightly taller than Malidora. Six red eyes burned from their oblong heads. The creatures scurried into the glen, their legs forming an X around their small bodies.

Kazial leapt to his feet, fleeing with Sidaire along the banks of the stream. Malidora turned, struggling to get her legs moving. Hundreds of the dark walkers poured out of the woods, clustered together in the clearing. Her legs felt numb as she tried to run. Her speed did not match the effort she was making. The world darkened as the things closed in. Each step she took drove her panic further.

Her mind became chaos. She could no longer take the stress. It began to seem as though it would be better to resign herself to death than be strangled by this fear. As she stopped moving, she found her footing again. Dashing after Sidaire and Kazial, Malidora began to pull away from the creeping monsters.

As the three of them ran nonstop in the direction of the gushing water, they came to a place where the grass-covered plain ended, giving way to rock-crusted ground. Before them was a wall of prismatic crystals splitting out from the hard surface. The crystals stood in disarray, some straight, others slanted, weaving a labyrinthine web of glistening surfaces. Carefully sliding between the jagged formations, they pressed through the reflective stones.

The dark walkers chased them to the edge of the crystal forest, unable to squeeze between them.

Malidora continued winding her way through the formations in any path that space allowed as she followed Kazial and Sidaire. They had to plant their feet with care as the surface was unforgiving, pocketed with sparkling geodes and druses.

Though most of the crystals were translucent, the largest were opaque and mirror like. Malidora turned toward her reflection as she ducked under a slanted formation. Just like the reflection in the silver water, her eyes were closed in the image.

Sidaire moved toward her, noticing that she had stopped. "What are you looking at?"

"My reflection," Malidora said. "Look at this and tell me what you see."

Sidaire walked up behind her, staring at the face of the large crystal.

"Why are your eyes closed?" Sidaire stared from the crystal to Malidora and back. "You look as if you are sleeping."

"Yes." Malidora beckoned her closer. "Step over here, you try it."

Sidaire moved closer, standing in front of Malidora. She touched her face as she stared at her image in the crystal. Her eyes too, were closed.

"What does that mean?" Sidaire wondered.

"I don't know," said Malidora. "There's something not right about this place. It feels like—"

Kazial came back toward them making a sound like the cracking of glass as he stepped over crystallized formations. "Feels like what?"

"Like dreamwalking." Malidora raised her eyes toward the tops of the crystals.

Kazial shifted his footing to ensure he was off on solid ground. "What's dreamwalking?"

"It's hard to explain," said Malidora.

"How did you get here, anyway?" Sidaire asked. "Everyone that is taken by the Shadows ends up in the stream."

"I don't know," Malidora said, "when I was devoured by a Nulthereal, I ended up in lost in the dark until I came to be on a world with a patterned surface."

Kazial walked back toward them. "How did you get to the stream where you pulled me out?"

Malidora's mind went blank as she tried to recall. "I don't know."

They came out of the tangled crystals into a wide-open space where the stream converged with four others coming from all directions of the distant world. "This is familiar." Kazial stared at the circular pool where the streams met, the size of a small lake.

A few small humanlike creatures with orange skin stood around the edges of the pool. Some of the creatures seemed to be stirring the silver water with long sticks. Others were staring up at a glowing ball of energy floating above the water. It changed shape and color as it pulsed rapidly.

"It does seem familiar, now that you say it," Sidaire said.

Malidora stared up at the nebulous energy. "What is it?"

"I'm not certain." Kazial moved around the lake, still looking up at the bright sphere.

"You should not be here," stated one of the creatures, monotone in voice.

Malidora walked closer to the being stirring the water. "What is this place?"

"The mindstream," said the worker. "Where we are all connected as one."

"This is the mindstream?" Malidora asked. "What is it for exactly?"

"As lesser minds we are worthless, but working in tandem, the greater minds of the Gaith can use them for increased capacity. As we are connected, the five are also." The worker moved its long stick along the water's surface as though smoothing it out.

Malidora glanced over the landscape, between each stream was a clearing that nearly mirrored each other. "What is this energy?"

"The source of everything here," the worker said. "A nexus for the energy of knowledge, memory, emotion, and will."

Malidora leaned toward Kazial and Sidaire. "We need to destroy this place."

"I don't know," Kazial said. "How would we do that? Would it kill the others?"

"I can't touch those waters again." Sidaire turned to Malidora. "They erase you. Smear you into a thousand others. If we enter the stream, we'll be melded again."

"Perhaps we don't have to." Malidora reached out toward the glowing orb. It felt like elu energy, but far more potent than what she had experienced before. Observing the surging patterns, she timed them and attempted to connect. A powerful force vibrated through her body like electric shock. It grew stronger until Malidora was thrown to the ground.

"Do not do that," one of the workers said. "It is not allowed."

The movement of the formless orb of energy stopped and seemed to point toward her. With the pressure of its force crushing down on her, Malidora backed up further.

"That energy." Sidaire's mouth dropped open in shock. "It's aware of us. I think it's alive."

Kazial stared up at it. "It's a mind."

"The interface of Ilganok's mind." The worker reached toward the shining light brought forth by the energy.

Malidora glanced at her reflection in the pool. The eyes of her image remained closed and her face expressionless as if she were sleeping. "Ilganok . . . the Dreambinder."

The ground began to rumble. "You should not be here," the worker said. "You should not be here, unmelded." The workers began to change shape. "You must return to the stream."

"I think we should leave," Sidaire said.

The workers began changing. Their bodies metamorphosing into horrid misshapen beasts. Sidaire and Kazial stared, petrified as the workers shifted into dark walkers like those that chased them from the forest. Malidora sprinted toward the crystal maze. The walkers scurried after them. Staggering and stuttering, they moved with no fluidity. Their odd movement made it difficult to gauge their speed.

Sidaire ran as the crystals came into view. "What is happening?"

"I think we're in a dream," Malidora said as the monsters clawed at her. They dug into the grass just behind her feet.

"A dream?" echoed Sidaire. "It's too real to be a dream."

"As most dreams are when you are inside them," Kazial slowed. They had reached the rows of prismatic crystals.

They hurried inside. Between the haphazard columns of icy crystal veins, they squeezed through. The monsters reached with clawed appendages. Black nails stabbed into the tight spaces. Finally, they were safely out of reach. Sidaire leaned against one of the shiny stones. "So, neither of you are real?"

"I'm real," Malidora said. "I don't know about you."

"Whose dream is it then?" said Sidaire. "Are we all having the same dream?"

Kazial climbed over two leaning crystals. "It's Ilganok's dream."

"How can we wake up?" Sidaire leaned to her left, contorting her body to fit through.

"I'm not sure," said Malidora. "I usually wake up whenever I recognize I'm in a dream."

"We should go back to the first place you remember," Kazial said.

Malidora's foot slipped into one of the geodes as she stepped over a broken crystal. Careful to avoid the jagged shards beside her, she lifted her foot out. "We'll have to go through the forest."

"I don't want to go in the forest," Sidaire said. "I've seen bad things in there."

"If we're in a dream," Kazial said, "then the bad things can be anywhere."

Malidora reached the end of the crystal fields, moving into the glen with the stream winding through the middle. "Perhaps we can pass through unnoticed."

Sidaire walked near the silver water as they came through the glen. "We should let the others free."

"We need to get out of here," Malidora said. "We can't do anything to draw his attention."

Sidaire watched the faces flow along with the current. "It doesn't feel right to leave them behind."

"Either we leave now or join them," Malidora said. "Maybe one day we can find a way to get them all out."

Sidaire pressed her lips together and continued following, seemingly accepting her response. They traversed the tangled red pulsing roots leading into the woods. The light dampened as they moved underneath the twisting branches. Faces pressed into the bark of their wooden trunks. Hollow eyes and open mouths silently screaming until they crumbled back into the wood to make room for others.

Malidora felt something watching them as they trampled through the vines and undergrowth. Red glows blinked on and off from the dark thickets around them. As they came to the end of the forest, they came to a ledge leading to a bottomless chasm where the world seemed to end.

"What now?" Sidaire said, staring into the abyss before them.

"That's one way out of here," said Malidora.

"Are you crazy?" Sidaire said. "There's no way we would survive that."

"If we die here," Kazial scanned the trees behind them, "do we die in real life?"

"Only one way to find out," said Malidora. "At least we won't have to live in this place anymore."

"I don't think I can do it," Sidaire said "I'd rather live here than die."

Something rustled through the underbrush. It came closer as a wicked chorus rose through the forest. Dozens of red eyes glowed in the shadows of the tree canopy. Creeping into the gloom, the dark things gathered behind them. Their eyes twitching in all directions, the walkers began closing in around them.

"I think I'm ready!" Sidaire said between short breaths.

"Okay, hold my hand, we'll jump together," Malidora said.

Before she could grab Sidaire's hand, she had already jumped, vanishing into the dark. Malidora took a deep breath and leapt into the void.

CHAPTER 6

AN OVERWHELMING SENSE of dread washed over her as she fell through the darkness, preparing for the crushing impact. But she wasn't falling, she was floating in a great abyss, the same nothingness she had perceived when she was first pulled into the Nulthereal.

A blue light flashed as her body jolted awake. She found herself on a rocky surface. After sitting up, she realized she was inside a familiar cavern. Sidaire and Kazial lay unmoving next to her. Their aethrum bodies shriveled and weak.

Ahead, the round walls of the cavern bore rows of stalagmites and stalactites circling the interior like big, jagged teeth. They continued into the darkened tunnel as far as she could see. Silver lightning traveled down the channel, arching between the spiked formations. Behind her was more familiar. It was just like the tunnels that the Sirunak and Belathid lived in. She would have believed it to be the same place if those tunnels hadn't collapsed. She had broken through to the surface from the surge of elu.

Though it did nothing to further her mission, Malidora had brought Sidaire and Kazial this far. Perhaps if she fed them from the massive quantity of elu inside her, it would nourish and revive them. Maybe they would even remember something of value after being connected to the Gaith's mind. The caves seemed to grow with the shrinking of her body from the loss of energy. Sidaire and Kazial's withered bodies strengthened as they began to wake up.

Kazial moved his ankles and bent his knees. "Are we dead?"

"I think we're out of the dream," said Malidora. "This is one of the tunnels I was in before. We're back on the tiled world I was on before the dream.

Sidaire rubbed her hand across her face. "Anything has to be better than that nightmare."

Kazial gazed at Malidora and asked, "How did you get so big?"

Malidora met his gaze briefly before shifting her attention to the tunnels ahead. "Trust me, it's not as beneficial as it appears."

⁂

After making their way through the channels, they entered an open chamber, a hub of pathways stretching in different directions. A periodic whistling of air led Malidora to a vent. Although it wasn't the same chamber she knew before, the configuration was the same. The wines of numerous creatures screeched down one of the channels.

"Get inside the vent, both of you," Malidora instructed as the sound grew louder.

Sidaire tepidly leaned inside. "Where does it go?"

"It leads to the surface," said Malidora as she helped Kazial inside.

Kazial peered up into the tunnel as the roar of many footsteps sounded through the cavern. "I don't think we can climb this."

The whistling came again, as the wind blew through the vent, launching Sidaire and Kazial upward. Once they were out of the vent, Malidora climbed inside. Uncertain if the wind would lift her larger body, she leapt, fingers grappling against the walls. Yellow liquid gushed from the sides as she caught hold of the outer lip of the vent. Pulling herself up the rest of the way, she stood again on the diamond-shaped patterns that made up the surface of the world.

"There's a blue hole in the sky." Malidora searched the syrupy skies of Hollowspace near the horizon. "I believe it is the way out."

Even after sharing so much of her elu with them, Malidora's body remained larger than normal. Kazial and Sidaire fell behind as they tried to follow, unable to keep up with her strides. Malidora picked them up, carrying them over the planet surface. The tiles went from silver to red to silver again as Malidora made her way across the landscape. Finally, the tops of the black stalk forest appeared over the edge of the patterned landscape. With her height now rivaling that of the trees, she easily strode through them as she searched for the blue vortex.

Now that she had the power to reach it, the storm was nowhere to be found. She hungered for elu but couldn't risk growing large enough for Razinoth to see her. Had the world's orbit around the universe taken it away from the vortex?

"Hold tight." Malidora leapt into the air. She passed through the empty pocket of air near the surface and broke into the cloudy gel of Hollowspace.

On the surface below, the diamond-shaped pattern of tiles grew smaller and smaller. She could find no sign of the blue storm. Still moving rapidly away from the planet, they passed by an enormous cylinder, reaching all the way back to the surface. From this distance, the red and silver zones of tile on the planet resembled the striped patterns of some predatory animals.

Several other cylinder-shaped stems stretched into Hollowspace from the other side of the planet. The world below them wasn't round like she expected, it was much more oblong and irregular. One end of the planet tapered off and curled around into a small point, while the other end was larger and even more oddly shaped. Red energy glowed through two spaces in the rock at the large end.

The diamond-shaped tile resembled the scales of a serpent from this height. Malidora's mind raced as she stared at the world she had been living on. Recoiling in the horror of recognition, her body shuddered as she came to terms with what she saw.

The world that she had left was not a planet at all. It was a monstrous creature. Its body somewhat like that of a scaly serpent, and two red slits for eyes in its head. Long stems protruded from its body, perhaps limbs, like that of an insect. Four on each side of its body, they extended straight out then bent sharply, like the skeletal wings of birds. The monster's tail, split into three appendages, wrapping around one of several enormous stones floating in the ringed bands around the universe. The stones were large enough to each be their own planets. The long appendages, spindly compared to the rest of its body, rested on other stones among the debris field surrounding the creature.

Malidora shivered, remembering living in the tunnels all that time, crawling through its pores or gland ducts for elu like a parasite leeching off energy in their host's blood.

Kazial clung tight to Malidora. "That's Razinoth."

No wonder she couldn't see Razinoth when he spoke to her, she had been standing on top of his diamond shaped scales. Plagat was right, any attempt at damaging such a creature would go unnoticed. It would be impossible to kill. The best they could hope for was to remain on the defensive and find some way prevent the Gaith's Nulthereals from getting into the universe.

She spotted the blue vortex near Razinoth's tail. Hesitant to move closer to the colossal beast, she decided to wait. If he rode atop the nearby the giant stones, eventually their orbits would take him away from the vortex. It was their only hope of reaching it.

Malidora's momentum carried them toward a large stone world set further out from the universe. The surface glowed with scattered green and blue flickers. She willed herself toward it. Even as it grew wider than her field of vision, it seemed to take an eternity to reach. Malidora surged toward the object as smaller details began emerging. Tiny imperfections riddled a landscape that looked smooth from a distance. The colored glows grew brighter. Slowing as she neared the surface, she landed harder than anticipated. The loud crash scattered dust and echoed across the landscape.

The ground beneath her was silty and cratered but covered in glowing pebbles of elu. Too small to sate her appetite, but perhaps Sidaire and Kazial could feed from it. While Malidora siphoned the elu, redirecting it into Sidaire and Kazial, all she could think about was getting back to Isodonia.

After they had fed, Malidora laid back in the chalky dust of the surface to rest. She slept without dreamwalking, which hopefully meant they were far away from both Ilganok the Dreambinder and Razinoth. When they awoke, Malidora carried both Sidaire and Kazial across the unknown world. She moved in the direction of the universe as it appeared on the horizon, filling a large portion of the sky. Razinoth's eldritch shape loomed, even at this distance, against the bright nuvalum discs surrounding the universe.

Small luminous particles of elu leapt from the dust as she walked over them. They were drawn to her body like a magnet. More sparkles appeared, blue, and even tiny bits of violet. Tall stalks of bright formations filled with elu branched out in all directions like the trees of a crystalline forest. Plenty to feed from for a long while if they had to stay here.

Sidaire squirmed from her arms. "Let me down, please."

Malidora lowered her to the ground. Sidaire seemed to delight in the wonder of the glowing forest, spinning around as she stared up at the colorful myriad of trees. Malidora set Kazial down to join her.

Reaching a hill in the middle of a tangle of crystals, an unusual shiny gray stone stood like a monolith above them. Malidora walked up the hill, kneeling next to the stone to get a closer look. It appeared completely solid except for a pale green color emanating in its center. As she moved her eyes over the stone, the glow inside seemed to change as she peered through different facets. It was either brighter or dimmer depending on which angle you looked through.

"What is it?" Sidaire asked as she walked up behind her.

"I don't know," said Malidora though it looked familiar. "It's not elu like the other crystals."

Sidaire drew closer to the stone, her eyes darting back and forth, beginning to open wide. Pale green light reflected on her face as she stared starred inside.

"Are you okay?" Malidora asked but got no response.

She put her finger on the girl's shoulder, but Sidaire continued her wide-eyed stare as the light danced over her.

"Hey!" Malidora shouted. "Are you still with us?"

Sidaire turned slowly toward her. "I remember now . . ."

Malidora squinted, unsure of what happened. "What did you see?"

"Solsellion," said Sidaire. "My home world."

Malidora glanced back at the stone. "You saw your world inside that stone?"

"Yes, or what is left of it," Sidaire said. "Even in its state of desolation, I miss it, I miss everyone who used to be there."

Malidora moved closer to the crystal, attempting to see what Sidaire had seen. After a moment, the green light appeared and brightened, revealing tiny fibers inside. Drawn within, her mind twisted, turning through a myriad of pathways. Lights blurred as she flew through impossibly intricate shapes and patterns until a burning red globe came into view. As she crossed by the enormous red object, a planet came into view eclipsing its light.

A force compelled her toward the planet, either by unconscious will or control. Through layers of clouds, a patterned surface became visible. She moved toward one of several clusters of trees all symmetrically placed over the planet in the same configuration. The dark waters of a well spring mirrored a sky, dotted with the burning of a thousand distant suns.

The landscape felt lonely and calm. But she wasn't alone. Another presence was out there, somewhere beyond the sky of this reality inside the tall stone.

Words entered her mind, flowing like water. Malidora gazed skyward as the words cascaded over her. She tried to focus on them, wanting to understand. They flowed quickly, with urgency.

"Who's there?" asked Malidora.

There was silence for a moment before a new voice sounded, not in her mind, but into her ears. Someone was behind her. "Get away from the nyalith!"

The surroundings of The Hollow returned as Malidora's mind snapped back into her body. Disoriented, Malidora nearly fell over as she turned to find a creature behind her. "Why should I?"

"Go find your own," The creature stood on four legs, with a long neck bringing its oval shaped head to the same height as Malidora.

Malidora glared at the creature. "There was something inside of it."

"Of course there is," the creature said. "The nyaliths are all connected. You can see where the others connect if you look through them right."

"What I saw was not in The Hollow," Malidora said. "What do these stones do?"

"What do they do? Are you mad? I'll tell you what they do. What do they do? Who would ask such a thing?"

Impatience edged Malidora's voice. "Are you going to tell us or not?"

"How do you think we are growing all this elu around here?"

"How should I know?"

"Well, I'll tell you." The creature stiffened its long neck. "We draw elu from worlds far away from this nuvalum radiance. Worlds that are rich in elu, where they are already fused."

"So, this stone sends elu from one stone to another?"

"It's hardly a stone. Nyaliths collect energy, store it, and transfer it from one location to another," said the creature. "Because they are extra-dimensional, they have far more capacity to store energy than something its size would normally allow."

A sharp tone buzzed through the air as the large creature's face twisted in horror. The familiar noise startled Malidora.

The creature's neck swung his head around to look. "Nuliaks! What are they doing here?" He galloped down the side of the hill as elu particles swirled in the dust from incoming assailants.

Malidora was suddenly snatched from the ground as a host of black triangular beings swooped through Hollowspace. Like alien moths, they held her with thoracic legs. Red energy crackled around them as they carried her away from the planet.

Streaming through the thick nebulous medium, they carried her toward a dark object in the sea of amber clouds and flashing filament. Struggling to loosen their claws, the distant object came into view. Another enormous Gaith drifted in the haze, resting its large claws atop worlds of flame and stone. Black scaled with glowing stripes of red, it seemed to be waiting for her arrival.

Malidora focused, concentrating on the elu energy within the Nuliak. Drawing from the one holding her left arm, she ripped a hole in its body. Drinking in the elu that poured from the wound, she grew stronger. The Nuliak flew apart into dust, flying out into Hollowspace.

The other Nuliaks surrounded her, grabbing onto her as she continued to siphon them one by one. She burned three of them to dust, enough to break free of the others' grasp to escape the swarm. Malidora turned and soared back toward the world they had pulled her from. As she landed near them on the hill, Sidaire and Kazial stared at something past her. Malidora turned to see the black and red Gaith growing in size.

Kazial pointed as a vibrating roar rippled through the murky skies. "Grindak."

Malidora watched as the creature headed straight for the planet. The Gaith had long tails extending from each side of its head. The tails swept back like wings as it knifed through Hollowspace. The cloudy medium oozed around the monster as it split through the dense gloom.

Scooping Kazial and Sidaire in her arms, Malidora launched into the sky and away from the incoming monster. A shockwave tore through the planet, sending enormous chunks of stone around them. The world she stood on moments ago was shredded into billions of pieces of rock and dust as Grindak plowed through it. Fiery colors at the core flung out in all directions, forcing Malidora to evade them. Comets trailed red mist as they streaked by.

A vibrating roar sent waves through the gel-like space, sending a ripple through the clouds and knocking Malidora off her intended trajectory. Control of her momentum was lost as she hurled through Hollowspace.

Grindak bristled through the debris of the planet, its glowing red eyes scanning as it flew through the chunks of stone with ease. Malidora switched Sidaire to the same side as Kazial as she passed a giant piece of rock and grabbed hold. As the rock began to spin, Malidora climbed to the other side, hoping to stay hidden from the Gaith's searching eyes.

As Grindak moved closer, Malidora realized that merely hiding wouldn't keep them safe. The Gaith's seemingly infinite body would destroy them simply by moving through the area. She pressed her feet hard against the rock, waiting for it to turn. Malidora pushed off with her legs, heading toward the universe.

Her renewed speed cut through the thickness of Hollowspace enough to allow control of her movement in flight. Grindak changed direction to match her new course as she zoomed toward two more stones, large enough to be worlds of their own to most creatures. Malidora soared around one of them, hoping to slow the colossal Gaith as it gained on her.

A sonic roar erupted from Grindak, shattering the larger stones nearby into dust. Malidora connected with the elu inside the flying debris, slinging the larger boulders into the Gaith's path. The boulder was disintegrated on Grindak's body as he continued to pursue them.

Malidora held Sidaire and Kazial tightly as she plowed toward the universe, heading for the disk of radiance surrounding it. A nearby planet broke away from its orbit, spinning toward Grindak's claw as he willed it toward them. The stone world was too massive to avoid.

Turning back toward the Gaith, Malidora flew away from the tumbling stone. Without the speed to outrun it, she only had enough time to fly at an angle safe enough to secure a landing. Sending debris into the sky, they crashed into the stone world. Malidora absorbed the blow as much as she could to keep Sidaire and Kazial safe. Climbing out of a thick green liquid in the crater, Malidora tried to regain her bearings. The sky flipped between the universe and the shadow of the Gaith as the world spun out of control.

Malidora leapt once again into Hollowspace as the Grindak's claw wrapped around the world.

As she drew closer to the nuvalum field, a burning sensation grew inside her. Grindak flung the planet toward them. There was no escape. As the enormous rocky world approached, a stream of bright light launched toward her. A flare from the nuvalum field tore through the planet, rending it in half and scattering its fragments in all directions.

Grindak gained as Malidora torpedoed through the weakening skies of Hollowspace toward the bright nuvalum corona around the universe. Closer and closer they flew toward the radiance, as the nuvalum began to separate the elu inside her. Her power and size diminished with each moment she moved toward it.

Wrapping her arms firmly around Sidaire and Kazial, she shielded them as much as she could. Unsure how long she could last, Malidora flattened her descent. She checked over her shoulder as Grindak, smoldering from its proximity to the nuvalum, continued to chase.

With her elu fading fast, she pulled away from the field. As they streamed around the nuvalum zone, the swirling blue vortex she had been searching for came into view. Screams began to ring through her mind, a thousand voices cursing her name. Their words out of sync clashed chaotically with her thoughts.

Struggling to concentrate, she used what power she had left to increase her momentum. While the nuvalum robbed her of the elu energy needed to fly at high speed, the murky clouds thinned near the radiance, allowing her to keep moving at a steady pace.

Grindak seemed to slow as he continued near the bright radiance behind her. His gargantuan body was largely unaffected, though the writhing voices in her mind expressed his contempt. Malidora dove toward the blue vortex. She entered the blue swirl of clouds that churned, condensing around it.

Another presence burned into her mind, as Razinoth joined the chase. She entered the tunnel as the sustained vibrating roar of Grindak grew to a piercing shriek, shattering her resolve. The turbulent howls of Razinoth tore through her mind and body. Vibrating in undulating waves as Sidaire and Kazial were ripped from her grasp. Malidora watched helplessly as they sailed through the vortex into the vacant darkness ahead. She pressed forward into the unknown, hoping to find them both alive, but deep down she felt it, two more lives had succumbed to her curse.

As she moved further inside the storm, flowing energy revealed numerous tunnels. One stood out among the endless pathways: a tunnel with a twisting light. A light that seemed to be the source of the blue color in the vortex. Uncertain where any of the pathways led, Malidora followed the blue light. The light led into openings of more passages, more choices, but she continued to follow the trail of light. Time itself stretched and contracted as the screaming of Grindak and Razinoth became overwhelming. Their force pounded her against the burning energy of the tunnels. She lost track of the blue stream of light, bounding uncontrollably into one of the many conduits. Her vision faded as she braced herself for whatever was to come.

Her body became weightless. The tunnel folded on itself, and time passed quickly over her, years went by like minutes. Darkness gave way to incoming light. From weightless to heaviness, the sensation of wet poured over her.

Splitting her physical eyelids apart for the first time in what felt like years, she found herself completely submerged in a liquid much thinner than the density of Hollowspace. She held her breath, swimming upward as fast as she could, hoping to reach breathable air before it was too late.

CHAPTER 7

BREAKING THROUGH THE surface, she gasped the air. A distorted glow of orange light reflected on the rippling surface. Just above the tree covered horizon, a spherical flame lit the world with its radiance. It was much like Tavarian's description of the Isodonian sun above the lower atmosphere, but more magical than she ever dreamed. Her eyelids fought against her desire to see it. How could anything be so bright? She wondered what became of Tavarian after she was pulled into the Shadows. For a kid so naïve about the world outside his home on the mountain, he had a strength to him. He fought well against the Blight Whidge.

Malidora swam to the edge of the pool. Reaching for some green, glassy material surrounding her, she finally found something she could grip. Her soaked hair dripped over her face as she climbed out. In the water's reflection, her black, red, and orange hair had returned. Unlike the reflection in Ilganok's dream, her eyes were open. She inspected her hands, back to normal except for the hardened shadowstone remaining on her right hand.

Removing the glove on her left hand confirmed her usual bronze skin had returned. She put the bare hand to her face. It felt bruised and battered, like she had lost a fight. Malidora sat on one of the smooth glass formations that rose through the red sand. Her aethrum body had been replaced by her former material one. Her clothes had returned as well as the compact crossbow that she kept inside her vest.

Even the small, folded blanket she had taken from Tavarian was still in the pouch she carried around her waist under.

She stood at the edge of the pool. The reflection showed a face she had not seen in some time. It was a little more aged than she remembered but still familiar.

An old, twisted tree protruded out of a stack of large rocks nearby. It would make a good landmark if she ever needed to come back here. She climbed further along the incline of smooth, greenish glass, between grooves in the course brown, red rock carved by watershed. The ground leveled out soon enough, making it easier for her sore legs to travel.

The violet sky, calm and clear, bared a few jagged clouds that hung over the horizon. Tiny sparkles hung in the very top of the sky. Were these the stars that Tavarian had told her about above the dense clouds of Isodonia? Though she imagined them to be bigger, they gleamed beautifully where the sky was darkest. How far away were they? A growing emptiness in her stomach demanded appeasement, not for elu, but something she could physically eat.

Surveying the landscape around her, she moved toward a line of foliage not too far away. The grooved surface of hard clay mixed with slick glass was not the easiest to traverse. This had to be one of the worst planets she could have chosen for her already sore legs.

Arriving at the edges of the forest revealed peculiar trees. Branches on either side grew outward but abruptly curved back past their pale-yellow trunks, crisscrossing each other on both sides. Dark spotted blue leaves covered them but produced no noticeable fruit or nut.

Malidora sniffed the air. It was mellow, peaceful; there was life here among the trees, scents that often-accompanied birds and insects, though slightly different than those she knew. The musty smells that clung to fur indicated other creatures as well.

Tracing a trail of aroma led her to the trunk of a fallen tree. The stump had rotted with yellowish bark peeling off. Malidora broke off a piece of the bark revealing translucent white insects feeding on the rotting wood. She reached her gloved hand into the stump, grabbing a handful of the bugs.

Detecting no scent of poison, Malidora dropped a few into her mouth, testing their edibility with a modest bite. They were just right—Not too crunchy, not too mushy. The best part was they were small enough that she could almost forget she was chewing insects. Though she tried to ignore the taste, it never worked. These particular bugs tasted like burnt swamp moss, as if she knew what burnt swamp moss tasted like. It definitely would not become a new favorite, but it could be much worse.

After consuming a few handfuls, Malidora moved on, her stomach slightly less empty. Allowing the sights, sounds and scents to guide her, she cautiously crept through the dark blue and green forest, crossbow at the ready.

A loud shriek from above startled her; a bird with an enormous wingspan sailed over the treetops and out of sight. She worked her way through the strange trees into a small glen. A white, feathery beast crawled out through the brush in front of her. A beautiful creature unlike any she had seen. It smelled the grass and leaved plants around it, then lifted its head and sniffed the air. Its head stiffened, turning in her direction. Its pointed ears popped up, and then it ran off into the cover of the forest.

Malidora circled the glen, not wanting to be exposed. A new scent caught her attention as she passed into the thicker underbrush. A familiar smell, like the pheromones of a person.

She followed the scent as a thunderous crash tore through the tranquility of the forest. Foliage rustled through the trees. Malidora snuck in closer until she found two bipedal beings dragging a fallen tree into a pile. The men looked like people, except they had blue toned skin, their hair thin and wispy. One of the beings had long, white hair while the other's was short and black. They lifted each end of a metal case, carrying it toward a tree standing nearby.

They opened the metal casing, revealing a bright red light. The two men slid the light through the trunk of the tree. The tree leaned over, falling off the perfectly separated base. A few glowing embers inside quickly darkened as it cooled. The tree came crashing to the ground, disturbing the birds in the area as they flew to other parts of the woods.

Using the same device, they cut the newly fallen tree into sections, dragging a piece at a time onto to a pile. Malidora crawled between the trees, getting closer to the men.

One of them took out a small object from his pocket. "Think we have enough?"

"For this round, anyway." The other man folded the metal case back into its box form.

"What would make something behave like this?" he said as a slow whine sounded. A strong wind shook the leaves of the foliage nearby. From beneath the pile of wood, a horizontal metal platform rose above the tall grass.

"Maybe something spooked them, who can tell?" The other man placed the box onto the platform.

He climbed onto the platform settling into one of its rounded holes. "I'd hate to know what spooked something that big."

"Nothing in Underveil was ever meant to be seen in the light."

"Have you ever known an animal to crash straight into a wall?"

The other man stopped clicking the switches inside the turret as if pausing to think. "I've seen gutams do that."

"But they wouldn't keep hitting it over and over. They wouldn't kill themselves like that."

The man hit a switch and a translucent blue bubble formed from the platform in front of each turret. "Yeah, they probably wouldn't do that," he said as the platform sped off through the trees.

Malidora had never seen a machine that could replace an animal for transportation. Isodonia had nothing like this. She had planned to follow them but did not expect them to have the ability to move this quickly. Starting off through the vines and trees, she tried to keep sight of the flying platform. It was no use. They had gotten too far into the woods to see. This platform left no tracks for her to follow, but the smell of the men's saline and sweat still hung on the air. She ran faster as the scent was quickly dissipating.

As she reached a thicket, the odor was lost. The platform was not floating high off the ground; it wouldn't be able to clear the group of trees here. She scanned the area. A gap through the trees to her right was wide enough it would be able to pass through. She gambled and went right. A few feet later, she caught the scent again.

Zig-zagging through the woods, she ran. Using her intuition and sense of smell to guide her, she came out of the forest into another open landscape of hard stone and green glass. The uneven ground here led to small cliffs, valleys, and mounds. She had forgotten how tiring this physical body could be.

After crossing another incline, even land stretched out ahead. A stone wall rose above the horizon, further than she felt like walking, but not that far. Her long shadow walked beside her over the yellow grass scattered about the rocks and sand. Finally nearing the white stone wall, she loaded her crossbow, unsure how well this place received outsiders.

Plumes of white smoke rose about the wall, scents of meat cooking wafted toward her. There were sounds of a crowded street, behind the stone walls, similar to every town she had come across. A closed wooden gate stood above her. No windows in the wall or the gate allowed her to inquire about entering. They didn't appear to want outsiders. An unusual decision for a city. Good for security, not so good for its economy. Malidora continued tracing the perimeter of the wall, searching for any signs of a way in. She rounded a corner to a massive break in the wall. The people had blue skin with white on the front of their chests. They hauled large wooden beams, placing them into the damaged section of wall. Insects swarmed around two huge beasts that lie dead nearby. Armored with layers of bone on their heads and backs, the creatures had not been dead for long.

Malidora pulled the hood up over her head, holding part of it over her face. She passed through a gap not yet covered in the wall with the confidence of someone that belonged here. A street covered in the gray stone split off in multiple directions. The stone had been perfectly leveled and smoothed with a subtle shine to it, like marble. The street seemed to go around the inside of the wall with a stairway of red stone leading to the interior that was on a slightly higher plane.

There were two men nearby, talking. Malidora moved around them to a spot in the shade of the wall.

"Relax, Cian," said a man with long, shaggy black hair and a couple of days' worth of beard on his face. "You have prepared us for this. We've handled adversity before, and we will again."

The man caught Malidora's attention among the crowd. He was tall, lean, and muscular, and had a large head set on his square shoulders.

Malidora recognized the type even on this alien world. Looks can be deceiving but that didn't mean they always were. From his appearance, she surmised that he was a man caught between the rebelliousness of his youth and the unwary settling into the responsibilities of purpose. He wore a look, both intimidating and inviting at the same time. "This wood may not stop the same kind of attack, but it will keep us secure until we can acquire the soplete to rebuild the wall."

"How long is that going to take? Should we not reach out to Vesta for aid?" The other man was a more average human height. He was solid and muscular himself but not as defined as the other. Their faces were normal but for the bone structure of their cheeks. They were ridged instead of rounded.

"The moment Vesta gets involved is the moment we lose our independence forever."

"What good is independence if we can't defend our ourselves?"

"Do you remember how long we have fought to be free of them, how much we all have sacrificed for it? That is not so easy to reclaim."

A warm sensation filled Malidora's neck and cheeks as she watched the man. Something about him drew her eye. Maybe it was his posture, his confidence, she wasn't sure.

"Of course, Dabradan, I'm only saying that perhaps we could return the favor in the future. We don't have to join with Vesta to get their help."

"You don't know the thercon like I do. He would love nothing more than to reclaim his empire. This would give him the opportunity he's been waiting for."

The way he carried himself was that of a tamed but ravenous wolf. It reminded her of Trace, the captain of the magnos' guard. When Trace had caught her trying to sneak into the Impradium to kill the magnos, he didn't execute her, he recruited her. The magnos never did find out that the leader of Sinavus was one of his own men.

"If you wanted to be in charge, Dabradan, you had every chance when we separated from the Concordance."

"You're in charge, Cian. When things go wrong, it's easy to fall back on the fears that we aren't enough to take care of everyone." Dabradan's lips curled in the corner of his mouth, exposing his ivory teeth. "We got this far for a reason, we are independent, and we don't need Vesta. I remind myself of that every day."

She wasn't sure if this conversation was worth listening to, but she enjoyed the sound of his voice. It was deep, husky and resonate. Any thoughts or ideas of getting back to Isodonia would have to wait.

"You're right, Dabradan, you're right," said Cian as he glanced at the damaged wall. "What would make those creatures do this?"

"I don't know. If it were only one, I would strike it up to some mental degradation. But a coordinated attack like this? It defies logic."

"Keeping a step ahead of dangers like this is what has helped us to this point. We need to understand this if we hope to prevent it."

"Who would you send to the Underveil, Cian? No one would last a day over there."

"Find anyone who might be willing," said Cian. "You don't have to go far. Stay around the terminator and see what is going on."

"You want me to send some of my Barandiers over there?" Dabradan stiffened as he looked her way. "That's not what they signed up for."

"Perhaps if we—"

"Wait." Dabradan rested a hand on Cian's shoulder and then gently moved him to the side. Malidora had stood here for too long. She let herself be distracted, watching his expressions as he talked. The fire in his silvery eyes. The passion in his strong voice. She tightened the cloak around her face, moving slowly away from the area.

"You there!" Dabradan said. "Do you have nothing to do? If not, we have a wall that needs repair."

Malidora shook her head and continued walking.

"Barandiers!" Dabradan called out, pointing at Malidora. Several armored soldiers dropped their tools and ran to them, pointing black weapons that somewhat resembled her crossbow. The Sinavus Code said you must die rather than be taken prisoner, but what good would that do? For all she knew, she could be the last Sinavus agent left. Who else would fight the Shadows if she were gone? Perhaps, as their prisoner, they would see her as vulnerable, and she could gain their trust. Maybe they would know something about how she could get back to Isodonia.

"Why do you cover your face?" Cian asked.

Malidora was unsure if there was anyone like her on this world. "I don't wish to show my face."

"You were spying on us," Dabradan said. "Uncover your face or we will do it for you."

Malidora slowly unwrapped the cloth she was using for a mask, revealing her yellow eyes and bronze skin. She took off the hood, revealing her thick bob of black, red and orange hair. The tips of her strands marked with a spot outlined in black and centered in white.

Dabradan and Cian stared, eyes widening, having never seen an Arkanthian.

"You're not Gesauren! What sort of creature are you?" Dabradan demanded.

Malidora wrinkled her brow. Even though they were different species, his reaction to her face was disappointing. "I would ask the same of you."

"She's from Underveil!" Cian accused. "We've been infiltrated!"

Dabradan unholstered a weapon from his side. "Is this true? Are you from Underveil?"

"If I knew what you meant by Underveil, I could better answer," she said.

"You know what I mean," Dabradan said. "The dark side of the planet."

"I'm not even from this planet. What planet are we on by the way?"

"Jokes?" Dabradan tightened his grip on the pistol. "That's not going to get you very far with the mood I'm in right now."

"I'm from a world called Isodonia." Malidora recognized the disbelief on their faces. "I arrived here through a tunnel. Is this the first time that's happened before?

Cian scowled. "Utterly ridiculous."

"Did you send these armored beasts to attack us?" Dabradan asked.

"No, but I certainly wish I had armored beasts at my command. That would be amazing, don't you think?"

"Put her in one of the cells!" Cian said.

"For a lone stranger, you show no sign of fear," said Dabradan. "Where are the others?"

"We're all but insects to what lies beyond the universe," Malidora said. "There's no reason to be afraid of you."

Dabradan rolled his eyes. "There was a herd of creatures running full speed into our walls. Some of them died on impact, the rest continued ramming their heads into the walls until they fell, either due to the damage they inflicted on themselves or us finally bringing them down. You may say you aren't afraid, but your people must be if they need these animals to soften our defenses."

"And these creatures are from the dark side of your planet?" Malidora asked.

"Don't play dumb," Dabradan said. "You're in no position to ask questions of us."

"Put her in a cell where her people belong!" shouted Cian.

The sentries led Malidora to a small pit behind one of the buildings with steps leading down. Marching her down a rectangular hallway, they stopped at one of the many rusty-colored doors. Shoving her inside, they turned on a translucent blue wall between her and the hallway.

Malidora moved into the corner of the dark room. Sunlight glared through a grate in the ceiling with only the dark blue sky visible between its bars. She sat on a foamy cushion against the wall near the door. Small cutouts in the stone wall allowed her to view the dark hall. Some sort of energy flickered in the middle of the cutouts, transparent but tinged with a yellow color. Many boring days and nights awaited her as she curled up on the cushion and fell asleep.

⁂

Malidora began to open her eyes as something tapped on the wall outside the small room. Quickly sitting up, she realized someone was in the hallway peering into the slot. The light of the sun still shined through the grate in the ceiling. Though it felt like she had slept for a while, the daylight indicated otherwise.

"Why did you come to our city?" Dabradan leaned forward, peering through the orange light shield. "To see the destruction you wrought up close?"

Malidora turned away already bored with the questions.

"What do you hope to gain by attacking our city?" he prodded.

"I have no desire to attack your city." She lifted her hand, making shadows in the spot of light on the floor. "I only wish to return home to my world."

"I had hoped by now you would be ready to have a conversation." Dabradan stepped away from the door. "I have work to do. I'll give you one more shift to decide." He turned and walked back down the hall.

With her stone covered hand, Malidora reached out to the energy field covering the slot in the wall. As her hand neared the field, tiny sparkling dots formed together around her fist. When she made contact, the dots rapidly pressed together, wiggling erratically. She pressed against the field, but it had no give, making a rapid crackling noise until she withdrew.

A rusty moss stained the floor in one corner of the room, darkening to a black film near a drain. As she moved closer to the mossy growth, a symbol carved into the wall caught her attention. A circle with a shape overlapping it. A shape like a triangle, but with the top point squared off. Not far from the symbol, there were letters scratched into the wall. Some letters were poorly formed, while others appeared as if they were shaped with great care.

From out of the wound, the darkness bled, and even the stars bowed to their will.

As cryptic and mysterious as it was, there was something familiar about it. She moved back to the cushion, contemplating the strange words as she lay, looking up at the clouds through the ceiling grate.

CHAPTER 8

A GESAUREN GIRL WATCHED Malidora through the energy field in the wall. She had one stripe of white amidst the shoulder length black hair that danced with every movement she made. Judging by the girl's face, she was only slightly younger than Malidora. The girl carried two weapons smaller than Malidora's crossbow, one strapped to her hip and the other on a strap over her shoulder. The black and rust-colored suit she wore contained several pouches on the strap and on her belt.

"I heard you were different. That you came here with weapons like a solider of some kind." The girl walked around the cell as if trying to get a better angle. "I was hoping you would be crafty enough to escape, and I would get the chance to hunt someone down, but you sleep too much for that."

"When I'm ready to escape, you'll never see me again." Malidora sat up in the bed, rubbing the soreness out of her right shoulder. "Now, don't forget to lock the door on your way out."

The girl moved close to the transparent orange shield in front of the cell. "I always wondered what a creature from Underveil would be like."

"Let me know when you find out," said Malidora.

The girl looked away and smiled. "Let's start over." She began pacing around the hall again. "My name is Evala. What is yours?"

"I only tell those I intend to kill," Malidora replied. "It's a mark of death."

"If you're trying to intimidate me somehow." Evala paused, wearing a strange smirk on her face. "It's not going to work."

Malidora sat up in the bed. "It's more of a curse."

"I'll take my chances," Evala said. "It's not like anything interesting happens around here."

Malidora grinned. "Very well. I'm Malidora."

"That's different." Evala touched the tips of her fingers to the amber shield in the door, disrupting its smooth appearance. "Is it a common name in Underveil?"

Malidora took a deep breath before letting it escape. "I've been trying to tell your friends that I am not from Underveil. This is the first time I've been on this planet. I was hoping someone here knew how I got here and would help me get back."

"Your hair is pretty," Evala said, studying her through the light shield.

Malidora glared. "Did you even hear what I said?"

Evala pressed both hands on the steel above the shield. "They told me you would say that."

"*They* told you?" Malidora said. "Did someone send you in here to question me?"

"That's the only reason they let me in here," Evala said. "But I don't care about why you are here. I want to know what the Underveil is like. This place has grown boring; these creatures running through the walls are the only excitement we've had in a long time."

"I hate to disappoint," Malidora said.

Evala moved away from the door, shifting her weight to one leg and then the other. "If you aren't from Underveil, where are you from?"

"A planet called Isodonia," Malidora said.

"What is it like?" Evala raised her right leg, balancing on her left. The bottom of her black boots glowed with a blue light.

"The skies are hidden behind swirls of clouds," said Malidora. "The terrain is varied, but where I grew up there were steam forests surrounding great, round lakes and pools connected by fast-moving rivers. You could get to any village traveling by river."

"Sounds nice." Evala stretched her leg above her head. "There aren't a lot of rivers around here."

"Where is here?" Malidora wasn't sure if Evala was showing off her flexibility and pretended not to notice. "What do you call this world?"

"Kandom." Evala set her foot back to the floor. "It's the second planet in the Nexla system, if you didn't know."

"Kandom . . ." Malidora peered up at the orange glow shining through the grate. "Why is there always the same light every time I wake up?"

"Because we're on the light side of the planet." Evala glanced at her shoulder harness as something glowed in the pocket. "We're near the equator, so the sun stays low in the sky.

"There's no night?"

Evala tightened her eyes as if confused.

"No dark period," Malidora corrected.

"Of course not." Evala pulled out a small glowing metal box. "Kandom is tidally locked. We always face the sun, just like Underveil is always in the dark, facing away from it."

"Is that normal?" Malidora wondered.

"I guess." Pressing a button on the device, Evala turned the light off and placed it back in the harness. "Is Isodonia different?"

"It has both day and night, regardless of where you are on the planet."

"Strange." Evala looked up at the glass sphere above the hallway allowing some light to come through. "So, the other shift has to work in the dark?"

"Other shift?" Malidora asked.

Evala ignored her question. "How did you get to Kandom from there?"

"You'll never believe me." Malidora stood. "I wouldn't believe it if it were told to me."

"Tell me anyway," Evala said. "I'd love to hear a good story."

"Very well." Malidora ran her hands along her vest, trying to press the wrinkles out. "Shadows invaded my world, shadows called Nulthereals. They devoured me and I ended up in a place called The Hollow. I was there for a long time, but I found a vortex that led me out. I took one of the pathways and ended up in a pool of water here."

Evala's eyebrows raised. "The Hollow? Where did you see that?"

"That's what they call it," Malidora said. "A realm that contains many universes, including the one we are in now."

"Couldn't you just go back into the tunnel from the pool?"

"When I climbed out, the tunnel was gone," Malidora said. "It was only a shallow pool."

"You're a very good liar, Malidora." Evala narrowed her eyes. "Maybe the best I've seen. You speak with the conviction of someone who believes what they say."

"What makes you think I'm lying?"

Evala pointed to the side wall. Malidora moved toward it to see what she pointed at. There was more scratching here. *Beware The Hollow,* it said.

Malidora eyes grew when she saw it. "How long has this been here?"

"About twenty-eight shifts," Evala said. "It was written by a man who died from beating his head against the wall over and over. You should read the rest of what he scratched into the walls. Maybe you can use it to come up with some new stories."

A coldness gripped Malidora. "Wait! If the Shadows are here, don't make the same mistake my people did! They must be stopped before it's too late."

Evala walked down the dim hall toward the steps. "Fair rest, Malidora."

⁂

After another nap, Malidora sat up on the cushion that lay on the floor. Searching the room, she found a dark stain on the wall on the other side. Perhaps blood from the insane man's head. She scanned for more words carved into the hard stone. Many lines and cuts marked the wall, making it hard to immediately pick out words among them, but after staring a while she noticed something else.

The savage darkness is spreading. Its tendrils run deep, sucking life from the world until the foundations crumble.

If the Shadows were here, she had to get free. If returning to Isodonia was not possible, she would fight them on this world. She combed over the rest of the wall searching for what other writing may be there. A door closed in the hallway, followed by a series of approaching footsteps. An unmistakable male scent entered through the vents near the ceiling. Malidora turned as a tall figure with long dark hair stepped out of the dark hallway toward her cell.

"Anything on your mind?" Dabradan said as he stood holding a white container in front of the clear shielded cut out, his features illuminated by the faint glow of orange light.

Malidora walked up to the energy shield, "Should there be?"

"We received reports of attack on Jervan," Dabradan squinted as if studying her face as he spoke. "Unknown creatures ramming into the walls. Some buildings destroyed, minor casualties. All the same details."

Malidora turned away from him, pacing toward the opposite wall. "I would be glad to help, but there's not much I can do in here."

"Our citizens are growing restless," Dabradan growled. "They are worried. It won't be long before demands for justice reach a point that we can't control."

"Justice?" Malidora spun around. "If you mean to execute me, at least have the decency to call it what it is."

"That is not what we do," Dabradan took a step back. "But this is a dire situation. If you could give me something—anything that would help us stop these attacks, it would go a long way toward leniency for you in the future."

"I would love nothing more," said Malidora, "I've been fighting these Shadows most of my life. I have seen them take control of beasts." Malidora recalled the erratic, suicidal actions of the creatures the Nulthereals sent after them in the swamps as they twisted the animals' instinctual behavior to hunt her down.

"You can't control animals," Dabradan's hair swung as he shook his head. "At best you can train them, though I concede that I do not know how you train an animal to do this."

Malidora leaned toward the shield. "The only way to stop this is to destroy what controls these creatures."

"And I suppose you want us to move into Underveil," Dabradan's nose twitched as he leaned toward her. "Is that your plan? To lure us into a trap laid by your friends?"

"What is it with this Underveil?" Malidora crossed her arms, stepping back. "Are you at war with someone there?"

"Someone is sending these creatures on us." Dabradan nearly dropped the container he carried. "War may soon be the only choice."

A section of the shield went clear at the base of the door as Dabradan placed a small bowl of light brown mush into the cell, setting it on the floor near her feet. "We do have better food, but we have to save it for the more cooperative prisoners." He moved away from the shield and walked away. The hall door shut behind him, leaving her again with nothing more than her thoughts.

ᔕ

Malidora passed the time by going through her practice routine. In the dried-out sewers underneath the capitol city of Gildanel, she and the other Sinavus agents practiced four hours a day. Moving between defensive stances to counter grabs and holds, she used a fighting style intended to keep the enemy at a distance. As long as she could keep them at bay, she could use her crossbow.

She was so focused on the routine that she failed to hear the door of the bunker open. It wasn't until she caught the scent that she recognized Evala was nearby.

"What are you doing?" Evala walked slowly to the shielded openings in the wall.

Malidora tried to slow her breathing. "Practicing."

"You're expecting a fight?" Evala pressed her hands to the shield, tracing sparking lines through it.

"I need to keep my edge," Malidora said. "Spent too much time building habits only to lose them in here. You're either the hammer or you become the nail."

"I bet I could take you." Evala pulled her hands away, crossing them over her chest.

Malidora chuckled. "You're welcome to come in and find out."

"Not worth the trouble I would be in," Evala said.

"Come on," Malidora taunted. "Perhaps you can beat the truth out of me."

"What style are you using? I've never seen those stances."

Malidora wiped the sweat around her eyes. "It's called Bane Urtol. I could show you firsthand."

"Maybe I'll get the chance soon, but that's not why I came."

"So why did you?"

"For a story." Evala kneeled toward the orange shield. "Even if it's a lie, it's more interesting than cleaning engines."

"You think I want to talk about my life to someone that calls me a liar?"

"Did you read more of the writing?" Evala said. "The writing on the walls?"

"How about you tell me a story?" Malidora moved toward her. "Tell me about the person who wrote these words."

"It was a man named Cerano. He was a trader. He would travel between all the independent cities buying anything he could sell in other towns. I talked to him whenever he was here. I liked him. He always had the best stories."

"What happened to him? What drove him mad?"

"They say he caught some kind of sickness in the unsettled wilderness." Evala took a deep breath. "All I know is that when he got back from Mortagon he was different. He talked about strange things. Something whispering in his head."

"You said that he died from beating his head against the wall . . ." Malidora said. "Isn't that what those big lizards did to your outer city walls?"

Evala's mouth dropped open for a moment as she stared out into space. "Are you saying the animals had the same sickness?"

"If sickness is what you want to call it," said Malidora. "In my world, it was the Shadows. They whisper things in your head. We called them Nulthereals, and they were led by the Blight Whidge. They use the worst side of yourself against you. Your fear, sadness, whatever they could use to control you."

Evala glared at her for a moment, then turned and left, dashing down the hallway. Confused, Malidora went back to the cushion on the floor, unsure if something she said upset Evala or if there was some other reason for her abrupt departure. A few stars twinkled in the violet top of the sky as sunlight beamed through the grate. Could one of these stars lead to her world? Wishing she could leap toward them and leave this place, she curled up with her back leaning against the cold wall. Nothing left to entertain her but the thoughts and memories of the past.

Metal clicked and squeaked. The patter of boots filled the hallway.

"Reports are coming back from Binetis," said Dabradan. "Huge beasts of unknown origin broke through their defenses, nearly wiped them out before they were brought down. Their armor is strong, even for flash rifles."

"What do you want me to do?" Malidora sat up. "I'm stuck in here."

"What did you tell Evala that made her believe Cerano had the same sickness as these suicidal beasts?"

Malidora rose to her feet. "All I did was answer her questions."

"She's adept at picking up on fabrications, exaggerations, or lies," said Dabradan. "She tells me that you are either the best liar she's even seen, or you are telling the truth."

"That doesn't surprise me," Malidora said. "It is the truth."

"She is starting to believe your story." Dabradan turned around, walking toward the other side of the hall. "But I still have doubts."

"So where does that leave us?" said Malidora.

"We're taking you with us to Mortagon." Dabradan grabbed hold of his belt with both hands, leaning against the wall.

"What's in Mortagon?" Malidora wondered.

"You'll find out when we get there." Dabradan pointed to the amber shield. "Now, put your hands up here."

"What are you going to do?" she inquired with a playful grin.

"I'd rather not do this forcefully," he said. "Put your hands to the plax field."

"You think you can force me to do anything?"

"I wouldn't bother," said Dabradan. "But I do think the six wardens waiting outside the door could. Come on, if you're not Underveilian, wouldn't you want to see the sunlight again? I have to put binders on you before we exit the bunker."

Malidora put her hands to the energy field, and Dabradan pressed something on his side of the cell, and the amber shielding began to become clear.

"Press your hands into it," he said.

Malidora rolled her eyes as she pushed into the energy. Her hands went through it this time. She watched Dabradan take her left hand. Holding it gently, he turned her wrist and placed a metal bracelet around it. Her eyes raised as she realized he was looking at her. He seemed to be staring at her hair and bronze-colored skin. Their eyes met and he quickly grabbed her other hand. The bindings were not tied together like most were, making her wonder how this would prevent her from doing anything.

"Now sit on the bed and do the same with your feet in the lower field," He pointed to the energy field across the bottom of the wall.

"You're even going to bind my feet?"

"For now," Dabradan smoothed the hairs of his beard against his face. "It all depends on how cooperative you are."

She pressed her feet through the energy slot near the floor. Dabradan took her foot delicately, putting the same metal rings on her ankles. Malidora stood with the binders on her wrists and ankles. Without them being connected together they wouldn't prevent her from doing anything.

"You ready?" Dabradan asked. "This may feel a bit—heavy."

As he pressed down on the metal gadget he held, the bindings began to hum. Pressure ran through Malidora's legs. She could barely lift her arms.

"I'll adjust that." Dabradan moved his finger across the control box.

The pressure relented some. She could now slowly move her legs and arms. Dabradan turned off the plax field and Malidora stepped through the doorway. The resistance of the bracers on her legs made it a struggle to walk. He led her outside past the wardens toward one of the metal platforms she had seen in the forest. It hovered above the ground. Strange smudgy patches underneath the platform seemed to shift and burst as it hummed and whirred.

The platform eased toward the ground as the humming stopped. Dabradan nudged her onto it as three others approached. Evala ran up to Malidora, carrying her battledress, crossbow, and quiver.

"We need you to look exactly as you did when you came." Evala helped her put them on. "I had to remove the pointy ends of all those sticks though. They could be used as weapons."

Malidora pursed her lips and put the items on. Evala lowered herself into one of the openings on the machine. Two other men stepped onto the platform and climbed in, motioning for Malidora to do the same. One of them had dark blue hair that was squared off on top except for the sides above his ears where the hair stood straight, making it look like he had little horns. She heard Dabradan call him Hanovus. He carried a huge rifle that was at least as long as Malidora was tall.

The other was called Toberin. His short reddish-brown hair was well-groomed, and his uniform looked perfect and new. He carried a weapon like Dabradan, sort of in between a rifle and a pistol. Malidora eased herself into one of the seats, her bindings resisting her movements.

Dabradan moved his hand over the metal console. "Barandiers, from this point we stick to the mission. Stay alert. I want everything in the groove." Red lights traced his movements as he drew symbols with his finger. A whining sound rose from the platform, vibrating for a moment before smoothing out. They put on helmets, and Dabradan slid a black visor over his eyes as a clear blue bubble appeared in front of them. The gate that Malidora had walked past earlier sprung open as the platform slowly moved through. "Do I get something to wear on my head too?" Malidora asked nervously.

"You'll be fine," Dabradan assured as he pulled back on a lever. Malidora was thrown back in her seat as the vehicle launched at high speed into the open field.

CHAPTER 9

SAND AND DUST trailed behind them as they sped over a river that fed into small lake nested between the base of two hills. Dabradan smiled. He seemed to enjoy Malidora's reactions as he took sudden yawing turns to evade spikes of stone.

Malidora tried to appear calm as the terrain blew by them with the winds of a fierce storm. She had never experienced this kind of speed. "How does this thing work, anyway?"

"How does what work?" Dabradan squinched his eyes as if puzzled by her question.

She exhaled in relief as a jagged green stone flew past them. "This—thing we are on—floating over the ground."

"It's a balton transport." Dabradan yanked the vehicle around another column of twisted glass.

Malidora flinched. "How does it float?"

"The repulsor engines make it float." Dabradan slowed the balton as it began kicking up over a patch of soft sand. He moved around it and then accelerated to the same speed they had been traveling.

"Okay, but how does it *work*?" She rubbed her wrist where the black shadow crystal covered her hand.

Dabradan took a quick glance at her before lifting them higher as they moved over an incline covered in tall grass. "What difference does it make?"

Toberin leaned over, grabbing Malidora's seat, which annoyingly made her left shoulder sink in. "The engine creates a kiltenic charge that repulses most other fields."

"Repulsor engines are what Udamal is known for." Evala had taken out one of her pistols, snapping a cylinder-shaped object into the back of it.

Toberin adjusted his collar, even though it was already straight, as he moved off the back of Malidora's seat and said, "One of the few independent cities that can build them."

"You don't use repulsors in Underveil?" quipped Dabradan as he flipped a switch on his control board.

Malidora looked away, wondering if she should keep quiet. "For the last time, I've never been to Underveil."

Evala snapped a cylinder into her other pistol. "At least we're getting out of credge duty for a bit."

"I'm just glad we finally got us a real mission," said Hanovus, who wore a gray-colored shell over his black suit, padded around the shoulders. "Maybe I'll actually get a chance to see what Lessie here can really do." He tapped his fingers on the long black rifle sitting beside him.

"Not that I'm complaining," said Malidora, glancing back at the horizon were Udamal was once visible. "But why are you bringing me along on this little excursion?"

"The comments you made." Dabradan swerved around a cloud of dust as sounds of debris tapped against the blue shield in front of them. "I believe you know something about Mortagon. Maybe just to get the attention off you or maybe something else. Who knows, maybe someone will recognize you there."

Malidora closed her eyes as pellets of sand blew into her face. Evala shook the grit out of the hair that ran below her helmet. "Why don't you just tell her, Dabradan?" They moved out of the dust cloud back over hard reddish-brown dirt.

"We shouldn't even be talking about this in front of her." Hanovus scowled as he brushed off his rifle.

"Shut up, Hanovus," Evala said. "She's telling the truth."

Hanovus glared at her. "I don't believe it."

"Why do you even have me talk to the prisoners if you don't think I can tell a liar when I see one?" Evala stared back.

"We've had no reports from Mortagon in a few shifts." Dabradan turned to Malidora and tapped on his screen. "No one has."

"That's not a good sign," Malidora said. "I've seen this happen on my world. I've tried to convince people what is happening, and they never believe it until it is too late. I fear the same will happen to you."

Hanovus racked a metal bar and then slid it back to its original position. "If anything has happened to Mortagon, we should shoot her on the spot."

"I was a prisoner once, Hanovus." Evala swatted the thick material on his shoulders. "Would you have had them shoot me?"

"Of course not," Hanovus looked down as ran his fingers along the ridges in the barrel of the heavy rifle, "but she's responsible for—"

Dabradan zigzagged through a field of large stones. "Focus on the mission. No one is shooting anyone."

Toberin adjusted himself in the seat as the stones whizzed by the vehicle. "Do we have to go this fast?"

Dabradan brushed specks of dirt from his visor. "We do if we want to avoid being ambushed by rovers."

"I don't know what rovers are, but are you sure this is safer?" Malidora joked.

Hanovus opened a compartment on the top part of the rifle. "Let them come." He gave the barrel a pat. "Lessie here will take care of them."

"I'm concerned about us leaving Udamal," Toberin said. "What if those things come back?"

"I think they'll be fine without you, Tob," quipped Hanovus as he blew the dust out of the inside part of his rifle.

The balton tilted as they weaved through a cluster of sharp glass standing up from the sheets in the sand. Dabradan failed to avoid one of them, jolting the balton as it bumped the top of the spike. "Why did you have to go this way?" Toberin exhaled. "There's too much haspere."

Dabradan increased the balton's speed. "It's the most direct way to Mortagon." His dark hair fluttered beneath his helmet. "And it's more fun."

Toberin scrunched his chin as they sped toward a structure on the flat plains. It appeared round in shape with a short flat roof. Large sections cut out of the walls allowed the Gesaurens inside to interact with anyone that came up.

"One of the outland trade stations," said Dabradan. "They're usually crowded around this period."

Evala eased her hand over one of her pistols as she scanned the horizon. "What do you make of it?"

"I'm going to pull over and find out." Dabradan slowed the platform to a stop, and after moving his fingers over the control board, the vehicle lowered into the sand. After the whine of the engines stopped, Dabradan climbed out of his seat and started toward the station.

Dabradan glanced back to the balton. "Stay here." His eyes locked with Malidora's for a moment before he turned and walked up to the small slot in the building. Everyone in the balton stayed quiet, waiting to hear what was said. Evala kept her hand on her pistol, while Toberin scribbled some kind of light stick onto a flat black screen.

The covering over the window moved and a woman appeared.

"Where's everyone at?" Dabradan asked.

"These attacks must have everyone staying put." The woman hung a handful of straps onto something beside her "You're one of the few I've seen my last two shifts. You have anything to trade?"

"No, we're heading to Mortagon." Dabradan looked off in the distance past the station. "Any news from there?"

"Not lately," the woman said. "Last merchant we had from Mortagon didn't mention anything unusual though."

"Before we go," Dabradan gestured toward Malidora, "have you seen her anywhere before?"

The woman's eyes moved toward Malidora and paused. She blinked her eyes hard and then opened them wide.

"What's wrong with her?" said the woman. "She looks ill."

"We found her spying on us in Udamal," Dabradan said. "Claims she's from another planet."

"Could she be Underveilian?" said the woman. "Has she—"

"She hasn't told us anything yet," Dabradan said. "Maybe someone in Mortagon can resolve this; they're the closest city to the terminator. They have more information on Underveil than anyone."

"Let us know what you find out on the way back through." The woman ducked back into the shade inside the station.

Dabradan climbed back into the hatch and started the engines. The balton zoomed over the dusty landscape for a while with no signs of towns or stations. Their shadow stretched out longer as the sky grew darker with them as they traveled away from the sun. They passed over small rivers and through forests. Malidora stared as bony worm creatures crawled across the glass formations in the sand.

A new scent caught Malidora's attention, the odor of a chemical reaction. She sniffed the air to get a better concentration of the smell into her membranes. Something burnt, possibly wood, and maybe some metal. It smelled like it had been burning for a while, burnt to dry ash. She scanned the horizonal back and forth as her eyes adjusted to the distance.

"Smoke," she said, gazing at the dark horizon.

"Where?" Dabradan glanced around the balton.

Malidora pointed ahead. "Out there."

"I don't see anything," Dabradan squinted his eyes as he looked around.

Trailing into the distant sky, dark smoke curled through the winds like a serpent.

"You have good eyes," said Evala. "That's gotta be Mortagon."

"I didn't see it," Malidora said. "I smelled it."

Dabradan sniffed emphatically. "I don't smell anything."

The balton zoomed toward the plume of smoke until they arrived at the white walls surrounding Mortagon. Smoldering buildings rose above the gates as Dabradan slowed the platform. They pressed through an opening in the entranceway, revealing a scene of chaos.

Dabradan's cool demeanor changed to that of shock. He stopped the platform's momentum and vaulted onto the ground. Evala and the others followed as he ran into the hellish environment. Malidora got out to survey the area, moving slowly under the restraint of the bindings.

Shriveled bodies lay scattered across the streets and in doorways of living quarters, many still holding weapons. They resembled creatures in The Hollow after they had been drained of their elu. Their skin was like petrified wood with no odor of decay. Some had wounds while others were broken by heavy objects. Evala called out, searching for survivors. The city of Mortagon was deathly quiet.

"How long do you think they've been here?" Toberin poked one of the corpses with the barrel of his rifle.

Dabradan stepped between the bodies, "Not nearly long enough for this." Most of the corpses' eye sockets were hollow, as were their open mouths.

"Why are they all so—they're just skin and bones. It's like their insides were sucked out," Hanovus muttered.

"As much as I hoped I was wrong, this confirms it." Malidora's hands began to quiver inside the binders. "It was the Shadows. The Nulthereals. We've got to do something before it's too late."

Dabradan paced as if looking for an answer to the senseless destruction. A few of the huge, armored creatures laid dead among the bodies. "Shadows? I can't put that in a report."

"You have a better explanation?" Malidora had seen this far too many times, making her numb to scenes like this. The primal instinctive fear that came with the nightmare of the Nulthereals never went away.

She walked the perimeter walls, taking a look around until she came across a peculiar scent. It wasn't coming from Dabradan and the others; the wind direction was wrong. She drew closer to one of the buildings. A shadow moved in the corner of her eye. She stopped to look. Nothing. The scent only grew. The sound of friction on a rough surface. Malidora crept toward a dark open window. A chemical presence stirred with the scent. Malidora paused again, something wasn't right. She moved toward the left side of the opening to get a look into the building.

"Get down!" Malidora yelled as the others stopped and looked in her direction.

Blasts of violet light poured from the window before she could get close enough. Dabradan and the others dashed behind the broken structural pieces nearby. Chunks of stone material exploded from the streets as bursts of light hammed into them. A hooded figure at the opening fired their weapon at the group, raining bolts of light over the area.

More blasts joined from the windows above her. She was close enough to take the gunman in the window beside her, but the binders on her arms and legs were too strong. Dabradan and the others returned fire with their rifles, shielding themselves against the corners of the structures around them. Drawing two pistols from her vest, Evala moved away from the protective structures into the open. Firing her weapons wildly, she rushed toward the building. Blasts sizzled by Malidora from Evala's weapon, making her to drop to the ground to avoid getting hit by the spray of fire.

"Evala! Cover! Cover!" yelled Dabradan as he stepped out from cover to launch rapid bursts of laser fire at the hooded ones in the upper windows.

Evala continued toward the lower window. The barrels of her pistols glowed dark red as she continued blasting while climbing inside. The blasts inside stopped with a loud clunk and crash. Evala reached into the window, grabbing the limp arm of the body inside. Leaning through the opening, she searched the attacker's clothing and placed some items in her pockets.

"Rovers . . ." Evala glanced down at Malidora as she moved back out the window.

Dabradan and Hanovus dashed in opposite directions, circling the building as Toberin continued to fire at the upper sections of the building. Evala stepped back to send blasts toward the attackers above them. One of the rovers fired back, sending more light bursts toward Malidora and Evala.

Unable to get to her feet, Malidora rolled against the outer wall of the building as Evala ran along the side, firing from a different angle on the attacker. Light beams buzzed back and forth. Rubble fell from the building, and stone flew from the streets. A large object crashed into the street near Malidora. The body of another rover lay on the road, bleeding from multiple light burns.

More blasts echoed inside the building. Toberin dashed toward the structure as the window gunners stopped shooting at him.

"Wait here," Evala said and sped toward the door.

"Let me help!" shouted Malidora as Evala vanished into the dark interior. Blasts and cracking stone sounded above Malidora. Violet, green, and red lights glowed from the windows, until finally all was quiet. The door opened as Evala and the others returned.

Dabradan lifted Malidora to her feet while Evala and Hanovus continued scanning the area.

"Now that was right!" Hanovus shouted. "It's been a long time since Lessie saw a fight like that!"

"There were six by my count," said Toberin. "Do you think six rovers could level this city?"

"Those rovers were scavenging. They got here after the city was wiped out." Dabradan surveyed the ruined buildings. "They wouldn't be capable of something like this."

"Had to be those beasts." Hanovus pointed to the ruined walls.

Toberin stepped through the bodies on the ground. "But most of them are marked with flash burns."

"Who could have come in here and blasted them all?" Hanovus moved over to the group of bodies that Toberin was looking at.

"They were shooting at each other," Malidora staggered uncomfortably with the binders.

Hanovus glanced back. "That's crazy, why would they do that?"

"She's right." Dabradan gestured at a group of corpses. "Look at how they are positioned, most of them are concentrated here in the center of town. Many facing one another."

"That's insane," Toberin said. "What would cause a riot on this scale? Wouldn't their security forces be able to keep it under control."

"They were probably attacking each other as well," said Malidora, walking slowly with the weight of the binders.

Hanovus glared at her. "You think you have all the answers, don't ya? I bet you knew about this before we got here."

"I've been in a cell, remember?" said Malidora.

Toberin leaned in, inches from her face. "If it wasn't you, it was your kind."

Evala walked over, getting between Toberin and Malidora. "So, what now?"

Circling the area, Dabradan walked around a group of corpses. "I'm not ready to believe in ghosts just yet, but this is one of the stranger sights I've come across. If this is the work of Underveilians, they are far more powerful than we expected. If anything, this demands further investigation." Dabradan took out a device from his suit and put it near his mouth. "Cian, this is Dabradan." Nothing came through but blips and modulation sounds. "Cian, please respond." Still nothing. "Must be some kind of interference." Dabradan rubbed his forehead. "I hate to say it," he brought his gaze back to the group, "but I don't want to go back with just another dead town to report. This has gone too far now. We have to do more. The large tracks are leading toward the terminator into Underveil. We're going to find out where they lead."

"Finally!" Evala cheered, lifting her hands in the air. "I get to see Underveil!"

"Underveil?" Toberin wrinkled his lips. "That's not our job. We're supposed to be protecting Udamal."

Malidora smiled. "Scared of the dark?"

"You keep quiet," said Toberin. "Dabradan . . ."

"Toberin, we're moving out." Dabradan began walking toward the balton.

The sky continued growing darker as they flew over the glassy landscape. The sky turned from light to deep as the sun vanished. Malidora marveled at the red- and rust-colored clouds on the horizon behind them.

"Stay alert," said Dabradan. "Few who've ventured into Underveil made it back. Most of those who returned, left quickly. Others were injured from things they couldn't see."

Toberin closed his eyes. "Don't remind me."

"The difference between us and them," Dabradan said, "they weren't Barandiers."

Hanovus patted his rifle. "Lessie is set to go!"

"Stick to protocols, follow my orders, and we'll all be fine," Dabradan said.

"This is going to fun, Tob." Evala patted him on the back.

"Don't think I forgot what you did back there," Dabradan said to her. "That was reckless and stupid."

"If you're referring to me saving you all," Evala drummed on the metal in front of the hatch she was in, "you're welcome."

"Freelancing like that isn't saving anyone," Dabradan said. "Each of us is only a part of the body. The body has to work together."

Evala pouted. "You know how much I hate rovers."

"Put personal feelings aside, Evala," said Dabradan. "I won't tell you again."

CHAPTER 10

THEY CROSSED THE terminator between light side and dark, trekking into a world never touched by the sun. Bright stars filled the sky as they moved further into Underveil. They flickered like candles in a gentle breeze. The stars were now the only objects separating ground from sky. It was quiet out here, serene, but for the low whine of the balton engines. Malidora recalled Tavarian and Dexius trying to explain stars to her. She had never seen them through Isodonia's dense lower atmosphere.

Toberin kept turning his head in all directions. "This is madness."

"I like it." Evala took a deep breath. "It's peaceful out here."

"Of course, you like it." Toberin opened a small pocket in his sleeve, drawing out a small pen. He placed his light screen in his lap and started writing. "You fit right in."

Evala scoffed, "What are you so worried about? You're one of the best shots on the force."

"Not in the dark," Toberin reminded.

"Lessie will lighten this place up for you when the time comes." Hanovus lifted the long flash rifle.

The illumination on the front of the platform showed nothing but fields of short, thorny vegetation. Gliding down the sloped hill, the sustained whine of the engines was joined by a staccato sound of thunder.

"Can't we go faster?" Toberin leaned toward Dabradan. "We're vulnerable moving this slow."

"Now you want me to go faster? Earlier you wanted me to slow down. I can't see far enough ahead to go much faster," said Dabradan. "You want us to crash into something?"

The nearby pattering grew louder as they skimmed over the surface. Foreign scents reached Malidora's nose. Something alive was out there.

Hanovus grabbed the handle of his flash rifle. "You hear that?"

"Yes, and I don't like it," Toberin started writing in his pad again, the light streaking around the pen in the dark.

High pitched screeches sounded out nearby, and soon others joined the chorus.

Candle, burning in the dark. Malidora wrapped her arms tight around herself.

"Throw a spark out there," said Dabradan.

Toberin fired a white blast through the dark. The bright white object hit the ground ahead of them, lighting up a section of ground around it. As the balton passed the spark, silhouettes of large and terrible creatures scurried around the light. The galloping faded for a moment but soon returned as the creatures began to catch up again.

"Turn us around!" said Toberin. "We're going to die out here!"

"We may pick up more of them if we go back that way," Dabradan moved something on the screen, and the vehicle began moving faster.

Toberin grabbed his rifle. "I don't care! I want out of here!"

Something scraped along the side of the platform. Large, clawed hands reached out of the darkness, trying to grab hold of the balton.

When nightmares come to take its spark. Malidora could do nothing but watch as her hands and feet were bound.

Hanovus and Toberin opened fire, painting the immediate area with strobing red light. Several long limbs and big oval shaped heads reflected the glow of the laser blasts. Evala joined them, firing her pistols into the fray.

A loud crash turned the platform sideways, knocking Malidora out of her seat and into the sand below. *I need not hide in fear or fright.* Struggling against the binders, Malidora crawled on her knees as a bright spark flew by her. The sporadic screeches turned to loud wet sniffing as the creatures stalked them. She struggled to reach the light.

Dabradan and the others reached the glowing spark, firing at the beasts as outstretched claws swatted at them. She made it to the circle of light, collapsing under the weight of the binders. The group stood, backs against each other, as the monsters surrounded them.

"Dabradan! Turn off those binders!" Evala shouted. "Let her loose!"

"No!" Dabradan yelled over the blasting and screeching. "We can't let her get away!"

They continued to fire into the mass of creatures. Long arms covered with bony exoskeleton armor reached ever closer. Bodies fell to the ground just inside the outer edges of the spark's glow.

"We need another gunner!" Evala yelled as she continued firing blue light at the sounds in the dark.

The creatures' exoskeletons made them difficult to kill. It absorbed several blasts until finally brought down.

"Focus on my target," Dabradan said. "Concentrate all fire on one at a time."

"Can't!" said Toberin. "Someone has to protect our rear!"

"Put a weapon in my hand!" yelled Malidora.

"Hanovus assist Toberin!" Dabradan said, huffing loudly between sentences. "Evala, follow my target!"

The creatures began to enter the light. Big humanoid heads with a long torso seemed to bend in two places. Their rear legs were much shorter than the long front arms that stretched out ahead of them. One of them grabbed Hanovus, dragging him off his feet toward the ravenous darkness.

"Dabradan!" Evala screamed, her pistol barrels glowing bright red.

He turned and blasted into the void where the arm came from.

Evala swiveled toward Malidora, raising her pistol toward her. She fired two shots. The impact of the blasts jarred her hands as the binders opened. A metal object landed on her as she tried to climb to her feet. It was one of the rover's weapons. Two more blasts released her feet from the binders on her legs.

For even shadows need the light. Finding the trigger on the flash weapon, Malidora aimed and fired. Her violet light joined their red blasts into the sea of swiping claws. The weapon vibrated in her hand. Malidora fired again, hammering the trigger with lightning quickness. It wasn't that different from her crossbow. She concentrated on Dabradan's target, then switched to Toberin's

Claws grazed by her as bodies fell at her feet. The wall of creatures caved in around them. Warm liquid flowed over her body as limp arms collapsed in around them. The light of the spark dimmed as the mass of shadows began to overcome it.

Malidora's barrel turned bright yellow as she hammered the trigger relentlessly. The attack began to dissipate as the last few creatures scattered and ran off. They continued firing blindly into the dark as the creatures left.

Standing in the circle of light, gun barrels smoking from the heat, they huffed for breath. Malidora lowered her weapon, easing her finger off the trigger, nearly afraid to relax. The tendons in her hand were so tight that her hand was shaking.

"The prisoner is free!" Toberin said, pointing his weapon at Malidora.

Malidora raised her pistol to him in turn, prompting Hanovus to lift his rifle on her.

"Evala—you're done!" Dabradan clenched his fist. "If you won't obey orders, I can't trust you!"

"I've followed protocol," Evala said. "Isn't it a Barandier's duty to hold their superiors accountable?"

"Don't try turning this around on me." Dabradan's shoulders heaved as he drew deep breaths. "I haven't broken any protocols."

"According to protocol," Evala clapped the side of her hand into her other palm, "if a prisoner's safety is in jeopardy, binders must be disengaged, or the prisoner moved to a safe location."

"Unless doing so would jeopardize the safety of a Barandier or citizen," said Dabradan.

Sweat poured down her face as Malidora moved her gun to Hanovus as he and Toberin trained their weapons on her.

"I made a command decision," Evala said.

"Oh, is that what you did?" Dabradan leaned in close to her face. "Now you've left us in a dangerous position, we have no way to apprehend the prisoner because you've destroyed the binders."

"We needed an extra gun," Evala explained. "We wouldn't be alive right now if she didn't help us."

"We didn't need her," Hanovus said, adjusting the grip on his rifle. "I was laying down all the fire we needed."

"Trust is something we demand for every squad." Dabradan poked his finger into her shoulder. "Go back home, you can be reassigned. We're never going to make it out here if we can't trust each other."

"What about her?" Evala's eyes widened. "Shouldn't you trust her too then?"

"I trusted her just fine when she was in binders," Dabradan said.

"What sense does that make? You just want me to walk back alone?" Evala held up both hands. "How is that safe? I don't even know what direction to go."

"This is why there is one person in charge of this unit," Dabradan sighed, "We can't function as a team if every individual is making their own choices."

"I guess we're stuck with your decisions then," said Evala. "I promise to do better next time."

Dabradan turned to Malidora. "If you follow my orders and trust me, I'll trust you. Our only goal now is to get out of this darkness in one piece.

"Fair enough." Malidora kept her weapon on Hanovus. "That's a goal I can stand behind."

"Now, hand over the gun," Dabradan told her.

"Can't do it." Malidora tried to steady her hand. "Not after what just happened."

"If we get attacked again, I'll give it back," Dabradan said.

"You didn't release the binders," Malidora said. "You left me to be eaten alive by those monsters."

"We protected you!" Dabradan shouted, facing away from the group for a moment before spinning toward her. "All right, fine!" he growled inches from her face. "Keep it! If you so much as flinch the wrong way, I'll personally make you wish those creatures had eaten you!"

For the first time, she sensed real danger from Dabradan. Something in his expression, in his eyes. There was a monster inside that he suppressed. It was a little frightening and a little—attractive.

"Lower your weapons, all of you!" Dabradan spit into the ground as if it emphasized his anger. "You may not respect me, but unless you want to go wandering in the dark on your own, you're going to have to follow me. We're going to have to trust each other just this once!"

"But Dabradan," Toberin said, "you can't—"

"Shut up and lower your weapons!" said Dabradan. "Let's locate the balton."

They climbed over the pile of corpses around them. Hanovus fired another spark ahead, and he and Toberin moved toward it while Dabradan and Evala walked in a different direction. Malidora followed Evala.

"I do respect you, Dabradan," Evala told him as they searched through the viny plants that covered the ground. "And I trust you with my life. I was trying to help. It can't be easy for you to have to make every difficult decision."

"We'll talk about this later, Evala," he said. "Keep your focus on the mission."

"Found it!" said Toberin.

"Anything we can fix?" Dabradan asked, rushing toward them while Malidora and Evala followed. Moving his light across the underside of the wrecked balton, Toberin searched for an answer. Dabradan found the pilot seat and powered on the screen. The screen dimmed and flickered, turning dark again.

"Not unless you have a spare ketiline assembly on you," said Toberin.

Dabradan kicked at the dirt and walked over to the balton. Opening panels, he pulled wires lose from one station, plugging them into another.

The screen lit up for a moment and quickly died. He removed his helmet, wiping the sweat from his forehead before putting it back on. After climbing out of the seat, he dug out more spark launchers and lights. Toberin and Hanovus grabbed small packs that clipped to the back of their vests.

"We'll walk from here," Dabradan said.

"Based on the position of the platform," Hanovus pointed to their left as he spoke, "we must have come from that direction."

"Unless the impact knocked the platform off course," said Toberin.

"Why don't you just follow the animal tracks?" Malidora suggested. "They were chasing us."

Evala pointed at Malidora. "Yes! That's exactly what we should do."

"Hand me one of those lights." Malidora held out her hand.

Evala twisted the cylinder, igniting her light. She handed it to Malidora. Moving the beam over the ground revealed hundreds of clawed prints that marked the area, pointing in all directions.

"They were circling us," Malidora informed, not wanting them to freak out about her wandering off. "I need to find the tracks where they were chasing."

She ran along the trail of prints, stopping momentarily to sniff the air. Evala and Hanovus walked behind her, while Dabradan and Toberin looked over the crash site. After a few yards, the tracks separated into two groups in different directions.

"The tracks split up," Malidora shouted back to Dabradan. "There are some that come from this direction and some that go that way."

Dabradan speculated, "Another group might have joined the hunt. Can you detect any scent?"

"All I can smell is blood and fur," Malidora replied, shining the light ahead. "But it leads this way."

Dabradan kicked a metallic object on the sandy ground. "How do you have a better sense of smell than anyone else? Are you part animal?"

"It's common among my people," she responded, continuing to walk along the deep claw marks. As she discovered more bodies of the attacking creatures, Malidora lifted the light device, illuminating her path. Approaching the next carcass, a peculiar odor entered her nose. Something was crushing the tall vines, not too far from where she stood.

She froze. Readying the flash weapon, she quietly turned to check behind her. Nothing but darkness faired outside the radiance of the light. Another pop came from behind her. Hastening her feet, she turned around and walked past Evala and Hanovus toward the crash site.

"They enter our domain, uninvited," said a voice behind her.

Malidora turned toward the sound but found only black.

"Brightlanders," said a voice to her left. The tones had a feminine pitch and softness to them. "Seeking treasure, but they know nothing of Nestopa."

They spoke to each other, but loudly enough that she could easily hear them. If they had remained quiet, they could have taken her by surprise.

Malidora felt like she could take on two even with that advantage, but they wouldn't know that.

"Their coming is oddly timed. Do they have the affliction?" one said, a voice to Malidora's right.

"No, their behavior is too passive," said yet another voice.

"We are here peacefully," Malidora spoke to the dark. "We seek only answers."

"She speaks of peace as she holds a weapon," said the voice behind her.

"She has no idea how outnumbered she is," said the voice to her left.

Malidora, Evala, and Hanovus moved toward the wreckage. Footsteps followed through the tall grass as she made her way to Dabradan and Toberin.

"Why do they come here?" one said.

Dabradan and the rest whirled toward the sound, raising their weapons.

"If they hand over their weapons, we may let them live."

"Who's out there?" Dabradan's eyes darted around.

"I don't know." Malidora huddled close to the Barandiers. "But I think they have us surrounded."

"This one is correct," said one of the voices. "Outnumbered and surrounded."

"How many of you are there?" Evala inquired.

"We are more than twenty. There is no chance," she replied.

"She's lying." Evala turned to Dabradan.

"My friend here says otherwise," Dabradan said. "Maybe the odds are better fighting our way out of this."

"This one is incorrect," she said. "We have the upper hand."

Their scent changed slightly, mixed with a chemical reaction. The smell of fear. They were worried.

"Evala is right," Malidora informed. "They are afraid."

"How about you come into the light, and we'll talk about this," said Dabradan.

"Only if the brightlanders put their weapons away," she said. "We will not negotiate."

"What is it that you want?" Dabradan said. "Tell us that, and maybe we'll comply."

"Brightlanders should not be here. You must leave," the voice said.

"We're not leaving until we get answers." Dabradan signaled Hanovus to move to their left. Hanovus quietly stepped into the dark to gain a second firing position on them.

"That is the only option," she said.

"We're only here because you attacked us," Dabradan said.

"We have attacked no one," she said. "We do not leave Nestopa."

"You sent those big, armored beasts to attack our cities," he said.

"We have sent no beasts," she said. "We care nothing about the lands of the brightlanders."

Evala's lips parted, concentrating on what they said. "That was—the truth."

"How could that be true?" Dabradan glanced at Evala.

Toberin stared out into the night, pulling thorns from his pants. "If you didn't send them, who did?"

"If they went into the bright, they must have the affliction," she said.

"Affliction?" said Dabradan. "What kind of affliction would cause animals to attack our walls?"

"An affliction of the mind. It has spread of late," she said. "A sickness that turns both Vogus and animals into hyper-aggressive beasts."

"Evala?" Dabradan eyed her.

"She speaks true," Evala replied.

"If you are only here for this reason, we will allow you to come to Helagon," said one of the voices. "The zinugal needs to hear of this. Maybe we can work together to stop this. There is a path where some believed there would be a time when Vogus and brightlanders would live together for the mutual good of us all. It could be that this event is the catalyst of such a path. As long as you do as we say, we will not harm you."

Evala nodded at Dabradan.

"We can't trust them, Dabradan," Toberin said. "We should get back to Udamal."

"Oh, you don't believe me?" Evala twisted her lips. "I'm useful until it's truth you don't want to hear."

"I don't doubt you, Evala," said Toberin, "but we need to get back. Even if their intentions are good, we can't afford to trust them. Underveil is too dangerous for us."

"Do I get a say in this?" quipped Malidora.

"We came here to find out what is going on." Dabradan turned to Toberin. "It's no safer in Udamal if those things keep coming. We've got to complete this mission." He whistled to Hanovus, calling him back.

CHAPTER 11

DABRADAN AND THE others packed their salvaged gear into bags to carry on their back. The Vogus revealed themselves, powering on a glowing orange orb in the center of the clothing on their chests. There were only six of them. All of them had feminine, pale white faces with black around their green glowing eyes. Their heads were surrounded by thick blades of hair that stuck out in different directions.

Their clothing was thick and layered, probably made from the skins of an animal. Their tunics fell below their waist to their thighs. They were cut at the top to allow for the spiked plumes of hair that stood out around their shoulders. A sturdier material ran down their sides from under their arms all the way to their boots. One had no shoes of any kind, her long toes and black nails exposed to the cold. The fronts of their legs below their thighs exposed their natural feathery down fibers that seemed to cover their body under the clothing. Two of them had bright white hairs, while one had solid black hair, another blue, and one with patterns of black and green.

The Vogus led them to six vehicles. Producing a bright green light, they floated just above the ground. Each Vogan climbed onto one of the oblong cylinder-shaped machines, each leg folded into position on both sides of the seat. They grabbed onto a low mounted control base, forcing them to bend their heads behind a small blue energy field at the front of the vehicle. They were built of smooth parts of metal, made to slice through the wind like one of Malidora's arrows.

"We'll double up on the syverns," said one of the Vogus. "Each of you can ride on the back end."

Up close, the glow of the Vogus' eyes were not solid, forming a swirling pattern like a fingerprint, green in color but darker than the syverns. Malidora threw her leg over the seat and held on to the Vogan in front of her. The long feathery hairs felt like silk. As the syverns flew into the distance one by one, they made long green streaks in the pitch dark until the one Malidora rode shot into the night.

They rode together in formation, the engines humming low, whining as the trees blurred close by. Big clumps of snow began to fall into the light as they soared over the landscape. As they went further, they found a landscape that was covered in snow. The Vogus weaved through a thicket of lights, pulsing like beating hearts of various colors across the white plains. The lights emanated from tall, strangely shaped vegetation. The bulbs and blooms glowed from inside, like the brightflies on Isodonia.

The cold wind was exhilarating as they flew through the glowing woodlands. Tall, slender trees filled the area with a carpet of ghostly blue light from the fauna along the ground. Above them, dimly lit violet and red leaves blurred as they flew underneath. They passed a group of carved obelisks. A pedestal beneath them seemed to repel the obelisk, causing them to float in the air. Streets of carved stone zigzagged across the area before them. Diamond shaped spaces in the streets added steps to slight changes in elevation of the patterned floor. The pathways were beset by extremely tall vinelike flora. A glowing ooze flowed from the towering plants and dripped into its many cupped leaves below. The leaf cups overflowed, falling further into other containers and eventually into pools on the ground.

As they came to the edge of the city, they slowed their syverns to a stop and dismounted, going the rest of the way on foot. As they marched along a path through the snow, Malidora paused and stared at the mesmerizing sights of the city. Something pressed against her back and a powerful force knocked her forward into the snow. Malidora rolled over, raising her weapon. One of the Vogus had a square blue energy field emitting from something on its wrist. The other Vogus aimed weapons cuffed around their wrists, all trained on Malidora.

Dabradan, Evala, and Hanovus drew their flash weapons on the Vogan.

"What was that?" Malidora sat up, rubbing the middle of her back.

"You ran into my shield," said one of the Vogus. "I was using it to light your way. I will tune it to half power."

Malidora rose to her feet. "More like you ran it into me."

Dabradan turned to the Vogan that appeared to be in charge. "Is that shield using repulsor tech?"

"It's called taglon." The Vogan brushed snow from its black feathery hair. "Our society is built on this technology."

"Lower your weapon, Malidora," Dabradan said. "It was an accident."

Malidora turned back to the white-haired Vogan behind her. "I'll show them an accident if it happens again."

The Vogus continued to aim their wrist weapons at Malidora.

"She's joking." Dabradan gently pressed his hand on Malidora's back, guiding her to keep moving. "Can we continue?"

She didn't expect the sensation of his touch to affect her the way it did. Something about him gently nudging her ahead stirred some unidentifiable emotions deep within.

The black haired Vogan motioned for them to lower their arms and keep going.

Toberin wrapped his arms around himself and rubbed his shoulders. "It's freezing out here,"

"What kind of weapon is that?" Evala inquired as they crunched through a pile of snow covering part of the pathway.

One of the Vogus turned her wrist to show Evala. "It's called an arbow."

Evala moved in beside her to get a better look. "How does it work?"

"It launches celettes." The Vogan seemed proud to show it off. "Small discs made of sharplight. Cuts through almost anything."

Evala beamed. "I like the sound of that."

Hanovus raised his long rifle. "That's got nothing on Lessie here."

Another Vogan came near. "It can also generate a shield, which you can use to deflect energy or objects."

"Can your celettes fire through the shield?" Evala wondered.

"No," said the Vogan, "but you can only produce the energy for one at a time, either a celette or shield."

"Unless you release the shield," said another Vogan. "You can no longer move it, but it will stay in the air at the point you released it. You can fire a few celettes before it fades or if you generate another shield."

The Vogan turned to Hanovus. "Can your Lessie do that?"

"Who needs shields when you're blasting a wall of fire at the enemy?" said Hanovus.

Rows of the floating obelisks led out of the woodlands to three enormous pyramid-shaped structures. The pyramids were black, at least in the dark, with green glowing lights. They had three sections, each jutting sharply over the one below. They bore a series of steps leading to their apex. Platforms with blue repulsing sheets, floated throughout the city. On top of these small platforms, glowing plants grew, giving the streets dimly colored lighting from above. Hanging from the underside of these, hollow pieces of metallic material swayed in the breeze, playing eerie melodies.

Surrounding the area, walled sections angled away from the center of the city while the tops of the walls bent toward it. Perhaps these unusual overhangs caused the odd echoes of the chimes and voices of residents of the city. The largest pyramid had a flat plateau at its top instead of the sharp point the others had. Above the plateau floated a platform that seemed to be its missing top. It's underside glowing blue with the taglon material.

One of the Vogus gestured proudly. "This is Helagon."

Malidora slowed her pace, taking in the new sights of the city. Remembering the jolt from the repulsing shield the Vogan carried behind her, she decided to keep moving. The feathery creatures motioned them toward the largest pyramid in the center of the city. Evala seemed awed by everything around her, as did Toberin. Dabradan and Hanovus, on the other hand, kept their eyes on the Vogus as they led them through the city.

Footsteps reverberated around them as more Vogus gathered along the road, eager to see newcomers. As they approached the main pyramid, a group of them came forward with a sizable container. From the container, they took a glowing green liquid and painted it on Malidora's face with their fingers. Drawing on her eyebrows, nose, and mouth. Dabradan hesitated as they did the same to him and the others.

The Vogus escorted them up the steps of the jagged leveled pyramid. Up close it became clear that the black material did not reflect the glares of the lights around it. The steps were formed out of a strange, extremely smooth material of pale violet. They reached the plateau where a cradle made of shiny translucent material and carved with meticulous designs sat ahead of them. The Vogus gazed up at a large triangular prism floating above them.

One of the Vogus had a white jewel around her neck and black hair that fanned out into strips on each side of her face. She seemed to be the leader of the group that led them into the city. She called out to the prism shaped structure in the air. "Zinugal Oderra, we come before you with information regarding the affliction. These brightlanders have trespassed on our lands but claim they have done so because they have been attacked by creatures from Nestopa. They have come for the same answers that we seek: how to stop this affliction from destroying our cities."

"Outsiders have not trespassed on our grounds for a thousand periods." The zinugal had dark red plumes of hair standing outward around her otherwise bald head, forming something of a large headdress. She came to the ledge of the floating prism above, wearing a glittering white dress that seemed to turn blue at certain angles as she moved.

The zinugal surveyed the onlookers as more Vogus gathered beneath the steps of the Shimatress. Moving straight ahead, the zinugal then suddenly walked off the ledge of the floating prism. Immediately, a blue pedestal of light appeared beneath her feet. The zinugal stepped off the pedestal as another formed to catch her. She continued the descent until she had reached the plateau with them. Once her feet touched the surface, she made her way to a gleaming cradle.

As she sat on the cradle, several glowing lights illuminated previously hidden platforms with chimes hanging from them. The zinugal's attendants moved their hands in front of the chimes. The taglon on their hands caused the chimes to sway in the direction of their movements, hitting against one another in succession. Starting with low notes to high, each set of chimes harmonized with the same melody that resounded over the city.

"Have they come to gloat? To laugh at our apparent demise?" inquired the zinugal. "If Hableides will not speak to us on this matter, he will surely not come to their aid."

"No, we only—" Malidora began.

"Do not speak to the zinugal unless called upon," said the Vogan next to her.

"They face the same problems we do," said the black haired Vogan; the white stone around her neck took on the colorful reflections of the dim lights around them. "We can help each other."

"I appreciate your determination, Ravetaria," said the zinugal. "But none of this will matter for long."

"They are not all greedy scavengers like we thought. They have technology as well." Ravetaria gestured toward them. "Working together we may be able to solve this."

"Greedy scavengers?" Evala whispered.

"The end is near for Helagon." The zinugal leaned back in the cradle seat. "But I have been summoned by a new voice. Not among the stars, but beyond them. The end comes quickly and when it does, we shall be among the first to welcome it."

"My zinugal, what are you saying?" Ravetaria raised her hands beseechingly. "Have you given up?"

"The stars have gone silent, but now I understand why," said the zinugal. "We have reached the end of their path. They can guide us no further. It is the beginning of a new era. For there is greater power beyond the stars. Power worthy of our devotion."

"She's not exactly lying," Evala whispered, "but there is something strange about her tone."

"Zinugal, this goes against everything we have worked toward," said Ravetaria. "We haven't finished the path that Hableides gave to us."

"A great presence has communed with me." The zinugal leaned forward. "They speak of a savage darkness. A darkness that has already engulfed much of this world. While it consumes the unworthy, it will meld us with an omniscient mind, and we will not stand in its way. It beckons us to a greater calling, a greater understanding. We shall ascend from this universe to the realms beyond."

"Zinugal, this is insane . . . ." Ravetaria turned toward the Vogus on the streets below before looking back at the zinugal. "This is not our destiny! What about the voices among the stars? Hableides?"

"Hableides remains silent." The zinugal rose from her seat. "Our new masters have chosen us to finish the path. We shall be reborn in a place called Nulvare."

Malidora shuddered as the word was spoken. "No!" she burst. "Don't listen to the Gaith! They will strip your identity to use your mind as their own!"

"Silence this heretic!" The zinugal raised her fist. "Cleanse the ground she desecrates with her blood!"

Malidora drew her flash weapon, aiming at the zinugal. She hesitated to pull the trigger knowing that the moment she did, they would all meet their end.

"Zinugal! Let's take a moment to sort this out," Ravetaria pleaded. "You have never spoken of Nulvare. Our whole lives have been dedicated to Hableides, and the other voices among the stars. Before we kill anyone, I would like an explanation."

"Annihilate them! Destroy all who question my authority!" The zinugal stepped into the air as the light pedestals appeared beneath her feet. She returned to the floating prism above the plateau. "Citizens and guardians of Helagon, I command you to kill everyone on this Shimatress. They doubt the path I have laid at your feet!

"She has the affliction!" Ravetaria yelled to the gathered Vogus watching from ground level. "We must remove Oderra as zinugal!"

Vogan soldiers charged up the steps of the Shimatress, firing spinning discs of light at Ravetaria and Malidora. Ravetaria projected a shield from her wrist to block the oncoming barrage. Malidora opened fire with her weapon as Dabradan and the others joined, suppressing the Vogus attack, forcing them to switch their arbow's energy to project shields of light to guard from the blasts.

Ravetaria and the other five Vogus rushed down the steps of the Shimatress away from the crowd as Malidora, Dabradan, and the others followed. Evala continued firing wildly with both pistols from the plateau. They dashed toward the street. Hanovus and Dabradan stopped to pin the Vogus down with a rain of flash fire. The Barandier weapons had an advantage in their ability to fire blasts much more rapidly than the Vogan celettes. For the moment they had the Vogus caught in a crossfire between Evala on the platform and Malidora and the others firing from their right side at ground level.

From some of the smaller buildings, another group of Vogus waved for them to join. Much of the enemy forces were getting mowed down, unable to shield themselves against two positions, but they still had the advantage in numbers. They began to press that advantage as a group of them broke off to outflank Evala.

"I command you to destroy them!" screamed the zinugal from her floating prism. "They are outnumbered, surround them!"

Evala raised her weapons, blasting the zinugal's platform. After taking several flash bolts, Zinugal Oderra pitched forward, falling from the prism to the steps of the Shimatress.

"They hurt the zinugal!" a voice cried out.

Noticing the flanking group, Evala rushed down the steps to join the others. Ravetaria ran toward the other friendly group of Vogus. With limited options, the others followed.

"We have to get out of here!" shouted Ravetaria as she took cover behind the corner of one of the smaller buildings.

The enemy Vogus now had a much easier time shielding their attacks coming from one location. Ravetaria moved to the bent city walls, projecting her wrist shield through it. As the shield sliced through it and dissipated, she used another cut to widen the hole. While Malidora, Evala, and the others used rapid fire to hit or suppress their targets, Dabradan fired slow deliberate bursts toward the enemy. With marksman-like precision, his shots found places unprotected by the shields and rarely missed.

A square chunk of wall crashed to the hard ground, signaling their escape. They dashed toward it, forming into a tight line to make it through the gap. Running nonstop through the snow, they headed back into the luminous forest. Malidora, Evala, and Dabradan trained their weapons on the hole in the wall as a few enemy Vogus attempted to chase. Firing into the tight space, they easily dispatched those that tried to follow. As the enemy seemed to give up on following through the gap in the wall, Malidora and the others turned and hurried toward the forest. Spreading out through the maze of strange glowing vegetation, they hoped to evade any that pursued them from the other side of the city.

Malidora found Hanovus walking under stalks that emanated turquoise light. They made it out of the forest to a plain, lit only by the violet-colored flora on the wet snow. The hazy sky had cleared to reveal a million stars twinkling brilliantly in the sky, set against a sea of black and the wispy arms of the galaxy. The cold crisp smelling air gave way to scents of perspiration as others drew closer.

A blue light flashed on and off in the distance, blinking perhaps to signal their location. Malidora and Hanovus made their way toward the light, finding Ravetaria and the other Vogus. They were soon joined by Evala, Dabradan, and Toberin.

Malidora turned to Ravetaria. "Is there a safe place we can go?"

"The city of Ekovus is abandoned now," Ravetaria noted. "It was among the first to fall to the affliction."

"Lead the way," said Dabradan.

Ravetaria turned and headed across the plain, and the rest of the group followed. Even though the sky had mostly cleared, snowflakes continued to fall, floating in the blue lights emanating from the Vogan arbows. The ice on the ground was thicker in this area. Malidora sunk in enough that slush seeped into her boots. She had never experienced cold like this. It made her long for the sticky humid forests in her homeland of Arkanthis.

Toberin hugged his body as he shivered through the snow. "My feet are freezing."

Hanovus tapped on his rifle. "Lessie's still warm if you want some heat."

"Maybe the zinugal is right," one of the spotted Vogan said. "There's no surviving this. The affliction is going to be the end of us all."

"Do not despair, Sikrus." Ravetaria walked briskly over the snow. "We're going to find a way to stop this."

"It's not a sickness," Malidora said. "It's an influence that comes from the Gaith that your zinugal mentioned. They sent Shadows that can influence living creatures into doing their bidding."

"You know of this?" Sikrus turned. "Why haven't you spoken of it before?"

"No one ever seems to believe me." Malidora put her hood and mask on as the wind picked up. "But since your zinugal mentioned it, I figured it was worth a try."

"Just to be clear." Dabradan glanced at Malidora. "We don't know if she's telling the truth either. We've seen no evidence of this."

"Other than big creatures killing themselves to break down our walls." Evala slowed until Dabradan moved next to her. "She's telling the truth."

"What are these shadows trying to accomplish?" Ravetaria's black feathery hair blustered in the wind.

"They want to destroy the universe," said Malidora.

Toberin walked close behind them, using them to shield himself from the wind. "And how do they hope to do that?"

"I don't know," Malidora said. "But this happened on my world, perhaps they are systematically destroying a world at a time."

Sikrus glanced at her. "Your world was destroyed?"

"Much of it." Malidora held her hood over her face against the cold air. "We managed to stop them before they destroyed the other continent."

Ravetaria stopped, turning toward Malidora. "How do we stop this?"

"On Isodonia, there was a creature called the Blight Whidge that could create Nulthereals using organic essences, binding them to our world," Malidora said. "There must be a Whidge here somewhere. I can tell you that our weapons had no effect. I don't know if yours will or not. When it connected to our minds, we were able fight back and tear the energy binding it. At least that's what I think happened, it's a little unclear."

"Nothing could survive a celette through the heart," Ravetaria said, raising the disc weapon on her wrist.

"Or a good ole flash bolt to the head," said Hanovus.

Malidora shook off a clump of snow from her boot. "Well, they have neither hearts nor heads,"

"What does this Blight Whidge look like?" Ravetaria asked.

"It takes over the body of other creatures as a host," Malidora said, "But it's not hard to spot. Even in that body, it has red eyes and is surrounded by shadows."

Crossing over the dark snowy hills, they had seen nothing but the illuminations of the plants and trees. "Do you even know where you are going?" Toberin asked. "How can you find your way in this darkness?"

"We navigate by the stars." Sikrum put her arm around Toberin, directing him as she pointed to the sky ahead. "See that one there? The bright yellow star? Its name is Ekethur." Sikrum pointed in the opposite direction and continued pointing as he called them out, "Vudall is there. Krinus over there and Cretere that way. All of our cities are aligned according to the stars." Toberin got out his pad and started writing.

"Which way are the brightlands?" Dabradan asked.

"That would be toward Krinus." Sikrum pointed again. "That bright blue star, halfway up from the horizon."

After they had trudged through the dark for a while, a faint haze of green lights loomed on the horizon. A tall structure rose above them, blotting out the stars. As they moved around the high wall, they found the entrance into the city. The obelisks that housed luminous plants were destroyed here. Ravetaria headed toward the Shimatress, walking around its base to an open ramp.

Sikrus guided them up the ramp and through the entrance chamber and into rounded hallway. The inside was dark except for a few amber-colored lines along the ceiling. Illuminated in the amber glow, many dead Vogus lay scattered over the floor. Odorless, shriveled hard as stone, like the dead Gesaurens in Mortagon. Their ghastly faces were sunken and hollow. Several glowing celettes were embedded into the floor and walls.

"The Shadows have already been here," Malidora said as they all moved toward a hall that branched off in several areas. They turned a corner into a larger chamber with several holes in the floor.

"We all need rest." Ravetaria walked between the holes in the floor. "But there's a lot of work to be done to get this place operating again. We'll divide into groups."

"I trust you, Ravetaria, but not these brightlanders," said one of the Vogus. "Who can sleep while brightlanders are among us?"

"We all need to work together if we are going to get this place functional." Ravetaria looked about the dimly lit interior. "If it makes you feel better, we'll divide the brightlanders up."

"What makes you think we can trust *you*?" Toberin said. "Splitting us up makes it easier to take us out."

Dabradan put his hand on Toberin's shoulder. "They've had their chances if they wanted to kill us."

"Sikrus, I need you to lead the next shift." Ravetaria projected her voice. "Take Team Belthron and you three." She pointed at Dabradan, Malidora, and Toberin. "Get some rest and be ready to get to work. The rest of you are with me. We need to search every level, every corner of this Shimatress. Make certain that nothing hostile remains."

As Ravetaria called out specific duties for each of the Vogus, Malidora tried to match each face with their name. She had to be good at memorizing faces as targets for Sinavus, but the faces of the Vogus made it difficult. They all looked very similar, probably because she wasn't accustomed to them yet.

Sikrus and some of the other Vogus lowered themselves into the holes in the floor in the lodging bay. They went to sleep standing up inside the round dens built into the floor, with only the tops of their heads exposed. Dabradan and Toberin removed their helmets and the shell-armor wrapping they wore, opting to lay on top of the floor as Toberin sat up to write in his journal again. Malidora stirred through the pouch she carried inside her coat, grinning as she realized she still had the blanket she had taken from Tavarian.

"Cian," Dabradan spoke into his communication device, "this is Dabradan."

Malidora closed her eyes, as she lay on the blanket listening to the modulation and white noise coming through the device. Opening her eyes for a moment, she caught Dabradan looking at her again. When he noticed, he turned back to the communication device, continuing to call for Cian.

CHAPTER 12

MALIDORA WAS AWAKENED by a dim amber radiance all over the room. Glowing liquid flowed through small tubes, like blood through veins. She lay still for a while but was unable to get back to sleep. Rising to her feet, she walked toward the doorway that led away from the sleeping chambers into a corridor. A mazelike system of hallways twisted onward as she walked. Numerous columns curved inward above her head and then out again before rounding the ceiling and coming down the other wall. It was all illuminated in the amber glow of tubes that traced the architecture of the strange hallway in haphazard but oddly uniform patterns.

A clicking echoed through the halls as Malidora wandered from room to room. She came to a large atrium where she saw balconies to four or five levels circling the room, each circle progressively smaller as they went toward the ceiling. A group of glass tubes went from the floor to the ceiling. The clicking seemed to be coming from inside the tube. Stepping into the tube, she noticed a row of buttons mounted to a silver metal ring. Running her fingers across the buttons, she pressed one of them in. The floor underneath her quickly rose, taking her past level two of the Shimatress.

The platform stopped at level three. It was quiet up there, except for some random tapping. She moved out into the open hall, listening for anyone around. The scent of the dead and the living coursed through the pathways, becoming stronger as she continued on. Following the two smells, she moved by smaller rooms parsing into more passages and more rooms. Large objects were strewn about on the floor, visible in the pale light. The dried husks of Vogus on the floor of one room indicated traces of a struggle. Frayed feathery hair was scattered about, accompanied by dark stains of violence. These were not drained of essence the way the bodies in the entry bay were.

As the scent she pursued grew immediate, resonating sobs haunted through the lonely passage. Malidora turned the corner into a room filled with more death. The pheromonal scent of the living led to a Vogan sitting on an octagonal platform in front of a panel of multicolored lights. The body of another dead Vogan was slumped over the console nearby.

The Vogan quickly stopped crying when she heard Malidora enter the room.

"Sorry." Malidora took another look at the corpse. It had not been drained either. "I couldn't sleep and heard a sound."

"I don't mind." The Vogan wiped its bright green eyes. "I don't wish to be alone right now. Even if you're a brightlander."

"You can call me Malidora." Malidora put aside her usual tendency to not give her name. Anything she could do to ease the tension. If they were going to make a stand against the Shadows, they would need to work together.

The Vogan turned away. "Giving my name only comes with earned trust, brightlander, so don't expect me to return the sentiment."

Malidora was trying to be personable, something she didn't often do, and this was the response she got. "What was her name?" Malidora gestured toward the body of the white fibered Vogan.

"Galoxa," said the Vogan sitting in the chair. "I knew she would be dead. She never made it to Helagon with the rest of us." The Vogan adjusted her leaf-like swathes of hair that surrounded her face. "This city was my home once. I fled Ekovus when the affliction started, the fighting, the killing. I never saw her again. I knew something must have happened. It's just that seeing her like this… It made it real."

"I'm sorry," Malidora tried to speak as solemnly as possible.

The Vogan turned its glowing green eyes towards Malidora and asked, "Do you have many friends in the brightlands?"

Malidora sighed inwardly, frustrated with yet another personal question. She absentmindedly ran her fingers through the hair around her ear before responding. "I'm not from the brightlands. I came to this world from another place. Everyone I knew was killed by the Shadows or the affliction, if that's what you prefer to call it."

The Vogan's eyes glowed brighter. "I'm so sorry. I shouldn't have brought it up."

"It's fine, it was a long time ago." Malidora forced a quick smile.

"You're a warrior, aren't you? You fight for their memory."

Malidora tilted her head and placed her shadowstone hand on her lap. "I suppose that's one way to put it," she said. "I don't want anyone else to suffer the same fate. I'm doing this to make up for my past mistakes, to give my life purpose, and because I despise the Shadows."

The Vogan propped her head against her hand as she leaned over the console. "We are not supposed to hate, but lately I can't help but be angered by what these afflicted have done."

Her words stung, the guilt from what she had done under the Shadows' influence burned inside her chest. "It is normal to be angry, but don't hate those in your city who were made to kill. I've experienced this darkness firsthand. They didn't know what they were doing. The Shadows of The Hollow are the only ones responsible for this affliction. You're either the hammer or you become the nail."

"At least Galoxa is now among the stars." The Vogan's eyes moved toward the ceiling. "If what you say is true, how can we stop something that controls our will?"

"I don't think it can directly control your will, but it can stir your emotions into the actions it wants. They speak to you as the voice inside your head," said Malidora. "If you know yourself, you know the limits of your darkest thoughts and emotions. When these Shadows are near, you must question the thoughts in your mind and learn to make the distinction."

The Vogan rubbed her forehead and sighed before saying, "I don't even want to know what my darkest thoughts would be. I don't think I can face that."

"Everyone has a dark self." Malidora sat in one of the other chairs and explained. "It's not necessarily evil, it's aggressive, angry, and often selfish, but it can sometimes save you. When you understand it, you can embrace it, use it. While some situations call for grace, others call for ferocity. Both lie within you, as they do with everyone."

"That sounds dangerous, brightlander." The Vogan glared at her. "We are taught to serve the good of the wake. We each must discover our calling. Those who adhere to the calling will shine brightest in the darkness. There is a great mind among the stars that has made us aware of its presence and chosen us for the path. We can't allow our selfish nature to corrupt us. It will lead us astray."

"What great mind are you talking about?" Malidora asked.

"We call it Hableides." The Vogan brushed through its feathery hair. "Our ancestors thought of it as a god, but it cannot perform miracles. It is a great intelligence that exists somewhere out in the universe. It is powerful enough that it communicated with us across the distant reaches of space and time."

"Strange, I've never heard of anything like that."

"It has yet to reach the brightlanders," said the Vogan. "There are many in the universe that it has not yet reached. It will take time. The first among us to hear its call became our first zinugal. Long ago we organized our society according to its messages."

"Has it ever spoken to you?"

"Sadly, I have not heard it." The Vogan's gaze dropped toward the console. "I have not yet become attuned. Many never do."

Malidora rested her chin on her knuckles. "Do you ever wonder if it is real and not something others made up to rule?"

"I shouldn't say." The Vogan ran her black nails across a rough texture in a metal piece on the control surface. "There have been doubts before, but those that hear it are able to guide us to great improvements in technology and into a better society."

"I would have a hard time believing it myself." Malidora leaned closer. "In my experience, where there is power, there is corruption. Those who desire it will do anything to get it and even more to keep it."

"Regardless of where these messages come from, the zinugals have led us well. I do believe Hableides is out there."

Malidora sat up straight, placing her arms on the cold metallic surface. "What else does it teach?"

"To achieve a perfect universe, we must act in accordance with all living things. Protect life at all costs. We have built monuments to honor Hableides and those who serve it as a way to connect. Hableides guided us to harness the power of the sun and bring light and energy into our dark domain. Progress has been slow. Many of us do not wish to bring in the light. It burns our skin." For the first time, the Vogan made eye contact with Malidora. "We prefer to help in other ways. We strive to create a society that will one day receive messages from the other worlds that follow Hableides." The Vogan's attention went back to the blank screen. "To prepare for visitations of those with the technology. Those who serve Hableides and follow its path will shine among the darkness. It is said that when we leave this existence, we will be reborn as stars in the sky."

"So, you are ready to receive others, yet don't trust brightlanders on your own planet?"

"Brightlanders have not shown themselves deserving. You have failed to receive the teachings of Hableides," said the Vogan. "You live in a world of bright, too focused on what is around you, blind to the truth that lies beyond what your brightness shows you. One day your people will join us as will all life in the universe."

"If I have a path, it is to fight the Shadows and help your world in doing so," Malidora leaned forward enough to look into her eyes. "We can't allow them to divide us. Whatever your kind and the brightlanders think of each other, we all have to stand together, united. We have to support each other, trust each other."

"We work for the same cause, but we cannot trust. You must do exactly as we say. We cannot unite until Hableides has found you worthy."

"If we are to ever have a perfect universe as you say, we're going to have to work with each other," said Malidora. "Perhaps this will be the means to bring the brightlanders to your path. I've seen too much of the shadow's destruction to let silly conflicts get in the way. I've been fighting them most of my life. It's what led me all the way to this world and into Underveil to this very moment. If Hableides has gone silent, doesn't that count for something? I intend to stop the Shadows, but I can't do it alone. Are you with me? For Galoxa, and all who fell here . . . . For all those who remain in Helagon because they are blinded by the Shadows."

"Brightlander, I can't put aside all—"

Malidora let her hand drop to bang against the console. "Are you with me or not?"

The Vogan paused for a moment, turning toward Galoxa's body. She closed her eyes and then met Malidora's gaze.

"I'm with you, Malidora." The Vogan's jaw tightened. "You can call me Olien."

"What do we need to do to get this place running again, Olien?" Malidora leaned back in the chair.

Olien looked around the room. "Open that panel and tell me if the light is green or red."

Malidora opened the panel and peered inside. "It's green."

"Good," said Olien. "Those are the controls to the lift chamber. It defaults to on, in case of an emergency, but if that goes down, we lose the ability to turn the lift off."

"Why would you need to turn the lifts off?" Malidora asked.

"Mainly for security reasons." Olien scratched something stuck on the metal with her black fingernail. "If anyone were to get the affliction, we may need to divide the Shimatress."

After Malidora helped Olien move the body of Galoxa, they cleared debris and damaged parts of the control panel. Extra help had been requested temporarily to finish barricading the exits on the first level. They stacked heavy boxes and other items from the storage bay into the atrium. From there, some of the others took the items to put in front of the exit doors.

Olien set the last metal storage container down. "That should do it for this one."

"Great . . ." Malidora said, unable to disguise the trepidation in her voice.

Olien turned. "What's wrong?"

"I just hope we aren't trapping ourselves in this place," Malidora said.

"We know how to deal with it better now," Olien said. "Any sign of hostile behavior will be isolated." Olien stood and walked to the doorway. "While we are here, I'm going to the dining bay, you hungry?"

Malidora followed Olien down a set of corridors that led to another door. As they entered the dining area, two Vogus were there, standing around a cone-shaped object that stood from the floor to the height of the average Vogan. It was made of metal wire and had leafy plants covering most of it.

"Do you think the zinugal really has the affliction?" said a black haired Vogan standing near the wire cone.

"I didn't hear everything, Mitian," said the other as she leaned toward the leafy plants on the wires, grabbing part of it in her mouth and eating it from the wires. "But what I did hear was crazy. It was completely contrary to the path."

Ravetaria came over to the wire cone to eat. "The zinugal wanted us to ignore everything that Hableides had taught us. She wanted us to do nothing, to succumb to this affliction." Ravetaria leaned over as her white jewel dangled from her neck. She plucked a leafy mouthful with her teeth. "Zinugal Oderra ordered us all killed merely for questioning her. It was not her way. There's no doubt she herself was afflicted."

"I suppose you are right." Mitian opened a container and used a thick, clear substance to smooth out the long hair plumes around her shoulders. "It just doesn't seem like the affliction could change someone like that."

"Perhaps you should visit the atrium." Ravetaria pointed toward the corridor. "That's where we moved most of the corpses. They killed each other because of the affliction."

Olien introduced Malidora to Akranyx as she placed more of the plants onto the wires.

"Do you think we should be here?" Dolarax stepped with bare feet over to the plants on the wire and began to eat. She seemed to be the only Vogan who didn't wear anything on her feet. "What if it infects us too?"

"It's more than an affliction," Malidora stood behind Olien as she moved to the cone shaped object, "The Nulthereals are living things that prey on fear, doubt. Don't let them cultivate those natures in you." She watched as Olien's mouth grabbed some of the small legumes growing on the plants. "If you become angry or fearful of someone here, there's a good chance they are near." Malidora reached out and grabbed some of the legumes with her hand and placed them in her mouth. A glowing orange liquid oozed out as she bit into them, making her stop chewing for a moment. It had a wildly odd taste that she couldn't place, but it wasn't necessarily bad.

The Vogus all stared at her. "You eat with your hands?" said Dolarax.

"It's much easier that way." Malidora popped another piece in her mouth and resumed chewing.

Mitian wrinkled her face in disgust. "Do you realize how many things your hands touch all the time?"

"Well, you can wash them." Malidora continued chewing.

"Washing only lasts for so long," Dolarax said. "But did you wash yours?"

Malidora's eyes wandered the room as she realized she had not. "At some point."

Mitian backed away from the plants. "I don't know if I can do this. It feels like these walls are closing on us."

"Focus on your assignments," Ravetaria said. "It will clear your head, and it will help us prevent an assault."

"Even though we're all women, we can be as fierce as anyone. Everyone in this room. We can do this together," said Malidora.

"I'm not a woman." Olien glanced at her. "Neither is Dolarax."

"Wait, you're not? I mean—" Malidora stammered. "All of us, men and women."

"How could you mistake me for a woman?" Dolarax ran his hands along the sides of his soft, feminine face. "I have very masculine features."

"Of course," said Malidora placatingly. "You're absolutely right."

Ravetaria moved toward her. "Are you supposed to be on this rotation, Malidora?"

"No, I just couldn't get to sleep," Malidora said, beginning to feel the effects of her lack of sleep once it was brought up.

"It's almost time for your rotation to start," Ravetaria said. "You're going to be exhausted."

"Can you put her on this rotation?" Olien eyed Malidora. "We've developed something of a rapport working together."

"I suppose that won't hurt anything," Ravetaria agreed.

Malidora wrapped herself in the blanket she had left on the floor as Dabradan and the others were woken to begin their shift. While admiring his muscular arms and chest, she told Dabradan what happened during the previous shift.

"You were working with them? I thought you were on my shift." Dabradan slid on one of his boots.

"Couldn't sleep." Malidora raised her head from the floor. "We've been barricading the doors. The plan is to isolate the main door as the only way in or out. They have some of us guarding that area."

"That seems sound." Dabradan slid on the other boot as he looked at Evala. "What did they have you two doing?"

Evala and Hanovus walked over near where Toberin was still trying to wake up, sitting down on a row of octagonal surfaces raised from the floor that appeared like large tree stumps.

"Helping get the power sources running again." Evala pointed to the flows of dim light through tiny tubes that traced every shape in the walls and ceiling of the bay. "They have some metals that, when positioned together right, creates some kind of ripple in the air between them."

Dabradan got to his feet, grabbing his shirt from the floor. "That sounds similar to our repulsor engines."

"Anyway, we got most of the lamps working again." Evala removed her armored shell, laying it carefully on the black floor. "I think there's still a lot more to be done to get this place running again." She lay down on the stone surface next to Malidora.

"You got it easy. They had me hauling corpses." Hanovus unstrapped his boots and kicked them off. "Which isn't nearly as satisfying when they aren't Lessie's kills."

Dabradan stroked the hairs on his beard down. "More corpses? Because of the affliction?"

"Same way we found Mortagon," replied Hanovus as he slicked back what little hair he had left. "Looks like everyone was fighting each other."

Toberin jotted down something in his pad between putting on his gear. "How long are we going to stay here? What is our plan?"

"Continue to investigate." Dabradan wrapped the vest shell over his tight black shirt. "If we can either find where those wall breaking creatures are coming from or what is causing all this, we can put a stop to it."

“That’s going to take too long.” Toberin slumped by Dabradan. “You didn’t tell us we were going to get this involved.”

Dabradan playfully slapped Toberin on the shoulder. “This is what we signed up for, my friend, a little bit of everything. But we’re all dealing with this together. Let’s keep our focus, and we’ll be done before you know it.”

Hanovus grinned. “When we get back, we’ll have some good stories to tell at the hobal.”

Evala raised her head from the floor. “I’ve never seen anyone waste more time than you guys. Go work so we can get some sleep!”

“Let’s get to it,” Dabradan said to Toberin as they headed down the corridor.

CHAPTER 13

WHEN THEIR SHIFT ended, Dabradan and Toberin sat down hard on the cold floor, and the rustling of them taking off their gear woke Malidora out of a light sleep. Toberin immediately began writing. The Vogus came out from their tunnels in the floor as the other shift filed into the bay. The noise enveloped the lodging area, stirring Malidora and Evala from their sleep.

"Your turn." Dabradan wiped the sweat from under his eyes and unfastened the armored shell over his shirt. "Have fun."

"It's too bad we can't all be on the same rotation." Malidora yawned as she rolled her face off the porous stone.

Dabradan removed the vest. "You don't like the idea of me working around these Vogan women while you're asleep?"

Malidora laughed as she propped her head on her arm. "You know they aren't all—"

"Aren't all what?"

"Nothing—surrounded by women," quipped Malidora as she rubbed the imprint of the stone surface from the side of her face. "Must be your dream come true."

"We finished barricading the doors." Dabradan sat between where Malidora and Evala had been sleeping. "Not sure what you have left to do on your shift."

"Unless someone fixed all the power modules, we still have

that to do." Evala quickly got up and began picking her equipment off the stone floor. "Someone sabotaged the distributers during the riot before we got here."

Malidora groaned as she got up, grabbing the rest of her clothes and gear. She stretched her left arm. Sleeping on this hard floor had not been kind to her shoulder. "Speaking of that, keep an eye out for any aggressive or paranoid behavior. Behavioral change from any of us could mean Nult-hereals are close."

Dabradan raised an eyebrow. "What would you consider aggressive?"

"Verbal or physical actions that could make one uncomfortable," she said, trying to rub the soreness out of her shoulder.

Dabradan flashed her a mischievous grin. "Well, as the leader of this unit, it's my job to make sure no one is uncomfortable." He motioned for her to turn around.

Malidora turned around with a smirk. "I didn't realize part of your job was giving back rubs."

Dabradan chuckled as he began massaging her shoulder. "Well, it's not officially in the job description, but it's a perk of the position."

He started with gentle strokes that sent tingles down her spine. It had been a while since she had felt the warmth of someone's touch. Dabradan began to increase the pressure, his hands rubbing deep into her muscle. He pressed hard, but with care. It was as if he was removing every bit of tension that was between them. If every apology was this good, she would be much more forgiving.

"You're pretty good at this," Malidora admitted. "You do this for Hanovus and Toberin too?"

Dabradan ceased rubbing and quipped, "If they ever started doing some real work, I might." He resumed applying the same gentle pressure as before.

He moved from her shoulder to the middle of her back. It would be so easy to lose herself to his touch. As he continued massaging, he leaned in close to her. She could feel his breath on the back of her neck. It sent shivers down her spine.

"What are you doing?" she asked, turning around to face him.

Dabradan backed away from her. "Sorry. I guess I got a little carried away."

Laughing, Malidora playfully shoved him. "You've only worked one shift and you're already delirious."

Evala rolled her eyes. "I'll see you all later. Some of us have to get this place running." Evala strapped on the harness over her armor and headed toward the gallery.

"Take care of Lessie while I'm gone," Hanovus said, patting his rifle.

Malidora looked down at the big weapon. "Where does the name Lessie come from anyway? An old flame?"

"Absolutely not." Hanovus chuckled. "Lessie is one of a kind!"

Toberin stopped writing, lifting his eyes to Malidora. "It's an LSE model rifle."

"LSE-759 bulk energy flash rifle." Hanovus bent down and wiped something off the shiny barrel. "If you're going to use her full name, at least get it right."

Malidora blinked her eyes wide and nodded. She turned and jogged toward the gallery, hoping to catch up with Evala. Malidora found her in the atrium as she stood at the entrance to the lift tube. "Do you think Dabradan is acting strange?"

Evala pressed the button to call the lift down. "Not really. I guess he's getting comfortable with you being around."

Malidora followed her onto the lift as the blue shield energy dissipated. "So, that's normal for him?"

"You mean flirting?" Evala pressed the buttons for levels two and three. "Pretty much. He jokes around like that a lot. Not with me, but most of the other women."

"Oh, he seemed so pragmatic before," Malidora said as the lift rose off the floor. The light tubes along the walls looked more like patterns the further away they got. "I thought perhaps his behavior was changing."

They reached the second floor, and the lift came to a stop. "No, that's standard Dabradan." Evala stepped into the second level hall and turned back with a smirk. "You're not special."

"It's not that. I was just making sure it wasn't—" The lift began moving again until it arrived on the third level.

As Malidora moved toward the control room, strange noises came from the control room. Bleeps and bloops sounded out in random sequences. She found Olien swaying and moving his hands in unison to the random sounds.

"What are you doing?" Malidora sat down in one of the empty seats.

Olien removed a module box from one of the cabinets beside the console. He had a stack of them sitting in the chair beside her. "You don't like music?"

Malidora handed him one of the new modules to replace the one he removed. "That's music? It sounds like intermittent squealing."

Olien put down the box and stared at her. "You mean to insult us? These are some of the finest Vogan musicians."

"I guess I don't have the proper ear for it."

A loud crash rang out from down the corridor, followed by screaming and yelling. Malidora turned to Olien who got up and rushed out one of the doors, down the hall toward the other side of the level. Malidora followed as scents of chaotic emotion began to hit her nose before she entered the room. One of the Vogus shoved another into a wall, both their faces marked with red welts.

"Tynex!" Olien grabbed the blue-spotted Vogan, shoving her away from Kilon toward the opposite wall. Evala and two Vogus entered the room, curious to find out what was happening.

"He means to betray us!" the blue spotted Vogan yelled as Olien struggled to keep her subdued.

Kilon put a hand over his bleeding nose. "She's insane! She'll be the death of us all!"

"He's going back to Helagon! He wants to succeed the zinugal!"

"What?" said Kilon. "I never said anything like that! I asked who the successor to the zinugal would be. I know my path. I obviously wouldn't have the standing to come close to being a zinugal."

Ravetaria rushed into the room. "Take Tynex into the storage area. We need to question them separately."

"Odd," Evala said. "They are contradicting each other, but neither seem to be lying."

"One of them is obviously lying," said Dolarax.

Malidora followed Olien back to the control room to finish cleaning up. They scrubbed the last bits of blood and Vogan fibers off the dials and controls, nearly finishing before the rotation ended. If only she could hear what went on in that interrogation. Ravetaria seemed to be running it herself, having sent everyone else back to their prior duties. Perhaps, it was for the best. Incidents like this would only increase the paranoia surrounding the last few periods.

Evala and Hanovus were setting some of their gear onto the floor as Malidora and Olien entered the lodging bay. He left her to join the other Vogus while Malidora found Dabradan asleep on her blanket. Poking him in the back with her boot woke him quickly.

Malidora stood over him. "I didn't say you could use my blanket."

"You aren't using it on your shift," he said. "What's the difference?

Malidora pulled the blanket away as he sat up. "Now it's got your odor on it."

Dabradan stretched his arms and legs. "Something to help you bear my absence."

Evala cleared her throat. "There was fighting earlier on our shift."

"And you're only now reporting this to me?" Dabradan put on one of his boots. "How can I make decisions if you don't give me information?"

"We thought you needed rest," said Malidora. "We still had work to be done."

"Evala knows better." Dabradan put on his belt with his short rifle holstered on it. "We're Barandiers before anything else. I need to know what is going on."

"All right, it won't happen again." Evala raised her head, exhaling loudly.

"Good." Dabradan prodded Toberin awake.

"Do you think this is what happened to Cerano?" Evala settled in on the cold floor as Toberin woke. "The affliction?"

Dabradan turned back. "Cerano?"

"You know, the trader that used to come to Udamal?" Evala said. "The one that died in the cell."

"He was just a crazy old man." Dabradan turned toward Toberin who was now ready to go. "That's not going to happen to any of us."

Evala rolled away from Dabradan. "He wasn't crazy. He was my friend."

"You need to find better friends." Dabradan headed toward the gallery as Toberin followed.

Evala looked back at him. "Yeah, I guess I do."

"Just a moment, Dabradan." Malidora ran to catch up to him.

He glanced at her, his eyes still groggy. "What is it?"

"Do you have to be so hard on her right now?" Malidora asked. "We had a long shift. Seeing all this death lately and then this incident—it can take a toll."

"What is it to you?" He glared at her. "Do you think she's your friend now? That you can get her to side with you against me? Let me be the first to tell you that you couldn't be more wrong. I've known that kid nearly half of her life. She's my responsibility. If I'm hard on her, it's for her own good."

Malidora stood rigid, staring at him. He turned and blinked his eyes open as if noticing her reaction.

"That didn't come out right." Dabradan pressed his lips together. "She's been getting a bit unruly lately. My Barandier unit already thinks she gets special treatment. They think she's too young and bratty and doesn't belong. Most of them think I got her on the team."

Malidora's hands went to her hips. "Did you?"

"I didn't want her joining the Barandiers to be honest, but she refused to do anything else," Dabradan said. "She earned her status as a Barandier without my help. I did get her assigned to my unit though. I wanted to keep an eye on her."

Malidora stepped onto the clear panel of floor where the light flowed through tubes underneath them. "Do you regret that now?"

"In a way," he said. "Maybe it would be best for both of us if she was with another unit, but it would be hard to focus every day knowing she could be in danger and not being there if she needed help."

"You can't lead if you're emotionally attached to your underlings," Malidora said. "You'll never be able to make the difficult choices for the good of the team."

"Whatever your impression of us has been, we're a tight group. We would do anything for each other. If we don't have that, what are we fighting for? Each of us are prepared to die to accomplish the mission. Being a leader doesn't absolve you from that." Dabradan crossed his arms. "If the job is important enough I'm ready to sacrifice my life for anyone with the best chance of completing the mission. It's no different for any of us."

"It sounds like Evala is different."

Dabradan took a step back like he was ready to leave. "It's a bit of a long story. She's had a rough life."

"Go on and get to your post." Malidora waved her stone-covered hand. "Maybe you can tell me the story later."

Though Dabradan's appearance reminded her of Trace, her mentor in Sinavus, he wasn't much like him at all: the way he seemed to care about everyone around him, the way he expected everyone to do their share of the work. He was harder on Evala, who he cared about the most. People trusted him. For reasons unknown, she trusted him.

When she got back to the lodging area, Malidora shook off the blanket as well as she could, curled up with it, and tried to get some rest. After lying awake for a few moments, she got up and crawled over to Evala. Taking the blanket, she draped it over Evala, tucking it gently. As Malidora lay on the cold floor, she regretted giving up the warmth. *These people are only means to an end*, she reminded herself. She should probably take the blanket back, but that would mean getting up again. It could wait until the next shift. Then she would get it back.

❧

A warm hand on her shoulder broke her out of her unconscious state. Malidora regained her senses, realizing where she was.

"There was an argument on our rotation," Dabradan whispered. "One of the Vogus deserted us. Someone named Yelthai."

"That's unfortunate." Malidora tried to focus through tired eyes. "We need all the numbers we can get."

Evala got to her feet, quickly getting her uniform on. "What are we going to do if this keeps up?"

"If there are Nulthereals nearby, we need to find out where they are." Malidora sat up, reaching for her vest.

"What are we still doing out here?" Toberin said. "We need to get back to Udamal, not help these Underveilians."

"We're doing this for Udamal," said Evala. "We have to stop the source of the attacks."

"You keep saying that, but I don't get it." Toberin picked up his pad and light pen, starting to write. "Why don't we go back and band together with the other independents, defend our territories together?"

Evala swept her fingers through her hair. "They don't need us to do that. Cian is probably meeting with other leaders already."

Dabradan turned to Malidora. "Supposing you're right about this, what do we do if we see one of these Shadows?"

"I don't know if your weapons will work against the Nulthereals," Malidora said. "Ours did not. The Shadows swallowed everything we threw at them. If that happens, run. Run to water if you can. They don't seem to be able to cross water."

"Barandiers never run from anything." Evala strapped on her harness and belt, the pistols still in their holsters.

Malidora eyed Toberin as he continued scribbling into his pad. "What are you writing anyway?"

"Notes for my report." Toberin lifted his eyes for a moment, then brought them back to the screen of the writing pad.

"What report?" Malidora questioned.

He raised his eyes to her again. "The one we all have to give when the mission is over. These guys never take notes and spend days getting everything right for their report."

"Just so you know," Malidora said. "I'm not giving any reports."

"Stay alert out there. Work within their rules," Dabradan gently touched her elbow before she could walk away. "Don't give them any reason to distrust us." It seemed more of a friendly gesture than the massage he gave her, even though it still gave her the same warm tingles. Not rejecting him the first time had only encouraged him to touch her more. With everything that was happening, she knew she should have put an end to this already, but it had been a long time since anyone had shown her this kind of affection. It felt alien but so pleasant.

"I better get going." Malidora left and hurried toward the lift in the atrium.

A short while later, Malidora slumped into the seat at the console beside Olien. "I don't like waiting here for something to happen."

"We're not waiting." Olien turned on his strange music and clicked one of the panel doors closed. "We're getting the Shimatress running again."

Malidora leaned back in the seat, trying to comprehend the music. What was she not hearing? It seemed to purposely have neither tonality nor rhythm. "I don't know that we have the time."

Olien moved to a series of metal boxes on the wall. "The defense capabilities of the Shimatress are unparalleled. If any creatures attack, we'll—"

"They didn't help those that were here before us." Malidora dug at a bit of grime on the console surface. "Do you know how the Nulthereals operate? How they destroyed your cities?"

"I'm sure this must be especially stressful for you." Olien opened one of the boxes, reading some sort of graph displayed in lights. "Being in a strange place surrounded by strangers. But nothing will be able to get inside."

"They don't need to get inside. They only need to get close." Malidora stretched out her legs. "They can control minds. You saw the Vogus fighting last shift, and I heard someone left while we were sleeping."

"Everyone is stressed." He turned a dial, and a few of the relays began to spin. "It's a normal part of war. Fear can bring us together too—against a common enemy."

Vogan music was enough to stress anyone out. "That's the problem," she said. "You are all treating this as a war against an outside enemy." Malidora propped her feet on the console. "If we don't find a way to stop this from happening, it will be a war between ourselves."

"It sounds like this is getting to you as well." Olien pried a panel off the side of the console.

"I've seen this too many times," said Malidora. "My homeland, Arkanthis, was destroyed, and the entire continent of Varkandor is nothing but black desert. My family is dead because of the Shadows of The Hollow."

"I'm sorry about your family and that you are having to experience this all over again," Olien said. "I hope that one day, when this is over with, we can both find peace. Hand me that detomer." Olien held up a spiraled strand of fibers coming out of the side of the panel. "I've almost got this sensor control board fixed."

"Uh, detomer?" Malidora looked over the scattered objects, some in his chair, and others laying on the console. She reached to pick one of them up, hoping it was a detomer.

"No not that. It's to your left—the black one—the other black one—No, back toward me."

Malidora gritted her teeth. "Which black object is it then? If you would be more specific!"

"A little lower—There—that's it."

Malidora rolled her eyes as she handed Olien the tool. "This music is driving me crazy."

He ignored her as he wound the spiraling fibers, keeping them in their arrangement. A few moments later the console screen lit up.

"There we go!" Olien cheered as the screen above the console lit up. "We have sensors and monitors operational throughout the Shimatress!"

"Excellent." Malidora stared at the moving objects on the screen. "What does that mean?"

"This displays a model of the Shimatress." Olien waved his hand across the screen. "Just needs to rotate a bit so you can see a better angle. Like this."

"Okay, I see it now," Malidora said.

"You can see the locations of everyone inside." Olien pointed to the screen. "Looks like some sensors aren't up yet, but most of them are.

"Why are so many gathered in that area? Isn't everyone supposed to be spread out working in different sections?"

"Second level, outside the armory." Olien tapped a section of the screen. "That shouldn't be happening. We can't have everyone leaving their work at the same time."

"I'm going to check it out." Malidora got up and left the room, prompting Olien to go as well.

CHAPTER 14

WHEN MALIDORA AND Olien arrived, several others along with Evala and Hanovus stood over the body of a dead Vogan. The Vogan's white fiber hairs were stained red from a celette embedded in its chest.

Olien bent down for a closer look. "Who is it?"

"Wikus." Kilon stepped back out of the way.

"Oh no." Olien squeezed his face together with his long fingers. "Why would anyone hurt him?"

"I don't know."

Olien stepped away from the body. "Do we know who did this?"

Kilon began to pace around the room. "No."

"Who found him?" Olien inquired.

"I did." Kilon rubbed the side of his face. "I had to go to the armory to get more cabrigated sheets, and when I got back—he was like this."

Olien seemed to be watching Kilon. "How long were you gone?"

"Long enough to go to the third level," said Kilon. "I did stop and talk to Mitian for a bit."

"Where's Mitian now?" Olien inquired. "We need to verify everything."

Kilon started drawing a circle on his forehead with his finger. "You think I did this?"

"We need as much data as possible, document everything, eliminate variables," Olien said. "We have to be systematic."

"It wasn't me!" Kilon looked back and forth around the

room. “Aren’t you going to question these brightlanders? It had to be one of them!”

“Malidora was with me the whole time,” Olien said. “This is not the time to be starting rumors; we need to make sure we find exactly who did this.”

“It’s not the who that is most important,” Malidora said. “If we know where the killer has been, perhaps we can locate the Nulthereals.”

“We’ve had nothing but trouble since the brightlanders got here!” Kilon motioned toward Evala and Malidora.

“Oh sure,” Evala said sarcastically. “All those corpses you had lying around here. Everything was going great.”

“Lock up all the brightlanders!” Kilon demanded.

Olien moved toward him. “I’ll have you locked up if you don’t calm down.”

“Evala has been with me,” said Tynex. “Hanovus is working with Livoxian. It was not them.”

“What about the ones on the other rotation!” Kilon shouted.

“We’re wasting time,” Malidora said. “We need to find where the Nulthereals are; they’re getting close enough to persuade.”

“Trying to cover for them?” Kilon insinuated.

Malidora rolled her eyes. “Go check if it will speed this along.”

They took the lifts down to the main floor and headed toward the lodging bay.

“This is ridiculous!” Evala sneered as they made their way through the gallery. “There’s more of you than there are us. We have to put a lot of trust in you to be here, and yet you give us none in return.”

“Let’s try and get through this without making things worse,” Olien said.

“He’s right,” Malidora said. “We can’t let the Shadows divide us. We’re giving them exactly what they want. If this keeps up, they will win without even having to face us directly.”

As expected, Dabradan and Toberin were still asleep on the floor.

“What is going on here?” Ravetaria entered behind them. “Is anyone working?”

Olien took Ravetaria aside and began to privately explain the situation. Malidora eased her way over near Dabradan as he began to wake up.

"They found Wikus dead," she whispered. "Trying to figure out who could have done it."

"Did anyone see the brightlanders get up during this rotation?" Ravetaria's heels clicked on the hard tiles.

"We're trying to sleep a little before our shift comes around again," Dabradan said.

"Everyone up!" Ravetaria paced along the rows of Vogus sleeping.

"They think I did it?" Dabradan whispered.

"Did anyone leave during this shift?" inquired Ravetaria.

The Vogus climbed out of their shafts looking at each other, but none answered.

"Take the brightlanders to the storage areas until we can sort this out."

"If everyone was asleep, you're going to have to take the whole shift in." Olien trained his eyes on Ravetaria.

"We will question everyone." Ravetaria glanced around the room as she played with the circular white stone around her neck. "But get the brightlanders out of the way first."

"Only four of them guarding the main door," whispered Dabradan as he placed his arm near the stack of clothing on top of his rifle.

Malidora pressed on the top of the rifle. "We need all the help we can get."

"We made a mistake coming here," Toberin said. "Who knows what they are going to do if they blame us for killing one of them."

"Let this play out." Malidora motioned for them to settle down. "We need their numbers to fight the Nulthereals."

"Earlier you were talking about how we need to engage," said Dabradan. "Now you want to wait for this to play out?"

"I want to engage when the odds are in our favor." Malidora grabbed his shoulder hoping to generate the same electricity in him that his touch did for her. She had to stop doing this, it was only going to encourage more of the same behavior from him. "This shouldn't take long. It will be a good gesture of trust. There's a control board active now. It tracks everyone in this facility. We should be able to use it to figure out where the Shadows are."

"What if you are wrong?" Dabradan peered at her.

Malidora drew close to him, her breath reaching the base of his neck. She looked deep into his eyes. "If I have to, I'll break you out myself."

She stepped back as some of the Vogus came to lead him away, but Dabradan took hold of her hand. "Why should I believe you?"

Evala rushed over, sweeping her hair from her eyes. "She's telling the truth."

Malidora was surprised she'd fooled her skill so easily. Perhaps Evala wasn't as accurate as she thought. Or maybe it was true. She was beginning to doubt her own intentions.

"You two better be right about this." Dabradan's hand slipped away from Malidora's as they led him away. Toberin hesitated, but after a nod from Dabradan, he gave in and went with them.

Olien stood beside Malidora. "With the sensors up, from this point on, we will be able to track everyone's movements. It should lead us to the real culprit."

After the shift ended, Malidora met Evala and Hanovus in the lodging bay as they lightened their clothing and removed their gear. Evala settled on the floor looking up at the dim strands of orange lights clinging to the ceiling. "I hope he's okay. I hope they both are."

Hanovus sat on the floor cleaning a few spots from his rifle. "I don't know about Tob, but I'm sure Dab is fine."

Malidora covered Evala with her blanket like she did during their last sleep period, hoping it would give her some measure of comfort. Evala snuggled into it before opening her eyes. "You don't have to give me this."

Malidora lay down on the floor beside her. "You need it more than I do."

"You best get moving," said Hanovus as he and Evala finished strapping on the rest of their uniforms. Malidora had gotten used to Dabradan waking her up when he and Toberin came back from their shift, and now she had overslept. She jumped up, throwing on her vest and coat.

Evala was taking an inordinate amount of time to situate her belt and harness. She seemed to be waiting on Malidora.

"You ladies can be late if you want. I'd rather be working than standing around here," said Hanovus as he headed off down into the corridor.

"This must be hard for you," said Evala. "First we locked you up and now you're stuck in here with us and the Vogus."

"Don't worry about me." Malidora smiled as she put on her boots. "I'm adaptable. One of the advantages of not having a home."

"Sounds like me." Evala nodded. "I never belonged anywhere until— Well, I never really have."

Malidora stood up. "It's not the easiest way to grow up, is it?"

"It definitely could have been easier." Evala started walking with Malidora down the corridor. "I was like a burden to most people. Even though most of them said they wanted to help, they didn't really want me around. That's when I learned I could tell when people were lying or not."

Malidora turned around and eased toward the wall. "How does that work anyway?"

"It's not magic or anything." Evala walked into the gallery. "It's like a switch in my mind. I can't explain it. Something triggers a feeling in me."

"That's a handy skill to have." Malidora glanced at the odd statues of Vogus that were set between the arched columns on both sides of the walls. She had never paid much attention to them before now.

Evala continued to the end of the curved hall leading to the atrium. "It's given me opportunities, I guess."

"You don't seem happy about it," said Malidora.

"No one in my unit thinks I should be a Barandier. Dabradan's family basically raised me after—" Evala stared straight ahead as she let out a quick, short breath. "The others think I only got in because of Dabradan, but Dabradan doesn't want me here either. He doesn't believe I'm cut out for this and singles me out for every tiny thing just to prove that I can't do it. Guess he doesn't know the depth of my stubbornness yet."

"Do you think Dabradan is hard on you just because he wants to separate himself from the favoritism accusations, or could it be that he just needs you to follow orders?" Malidora looked at Evala, waiting for her reaction.

"I follow orders." Evala's steps echoed in the atrium. "Most of the time."

"Leaders often push us to be the best version of ourselves," Malidora said. "Perhaps you are trying so hard to prove yourself that you do too much. You go outside boundaries. He is hard on you because he wants you to succeed."

Evala met her eyes and grinned. "You were fine with my disobedience when I released your binders."

"I didn't say he's always right," Malidora entered the lift tube, "but that doesn't mean he doesn't have your best interests in mind."

"I know he does." Evala pressed two buttons on the lift, and it began to move upward. "I just wish he wouldn't make me look bad in front of the guys. He won't give me a chance to fit in."

"Discipline isn't always pleasant, but it is important." Malidora groaned internally as she heard Legotian's words coming out of her. "Those that point out our flaws are often the ones that care about us the most."

"Yeah—I guess we should get to our stations," Evala said as she got off the lift on the second level. It was like looking into a mirror at her younger self. Malidora was used to being on Evala's side of this conversation.

Olien was staring at the security screen when Malidora entered the control room. He moved his black nailed fingers across the model of the Shimatress, rapidly flipping between individual rooms as he swayed chaotically to the Vogan music.

"I've been looking at the sensor data from last shift," he said, still focused on the screen.

Malidora leaned in, hoping to gain some understanding of what he was doing. "What are you looking for?"

"Have you not heard?" he asked, touching different circles on the map. "Alisker was found dead during the last shift."

"This is getting out of hand," Malidora said. "We can't wait in here much—so who was it? Did the sensors pick it up?"

"There is strange corruption with the signature mark that was in the room when Alisker was killed. The data key is unreadable. That's the only way we know who each mark is."

"All we need to know is where that mark has been since the sensors have been up." Malidora leaned closer to where he was looking. "That may tell us where the Nulthereals are."

"It has been in the atrium mostly," said Olien. "It disappeared when it got to the culinary bay. That is also where it first appeared. That can't be a coincidence. There must be something wrong with the sensors in that area."

Rubbing the bridge of her nose, Malidora searched her brain for some way to solve this problem. "Why don't we find someone that was in the atrium at the same time as this unreadable mark and ask them who was in there?"

"Whoever it is always leaves when someone comes in," Olien said. "They are deliberately evading us."

Malidora watched the dots on the screen as Olien played back the recorded data. "So, we still don't know where the Shadows are. This system is useless."

"All the sensors are picking up marks, see?" Olien drew circles on the screen with his finger, cycling through different sets of data that she didn't understand. "But something about this mark is fooling them, some pick up the mark but not the data key, and others don't pick up either one."

Malidora leaned back in her seat. "Whose mark is unaccounted for?"

"Everyone is accounted for when the death occurred." Olien clenched his jaw. "Don't speak of this yet, but whoever it is—they must have already been inside when we got here."

"I thought every corner of this place was searched." Malidora tilted forward.

Olien took a deep but quick breath. "It's the only explanation."

"That clears Dabradan and Toberin, doesn't it?" Malidora asked.

"Yes, I'm going to call—" Olien started as a red circle flashed on the screen.

Footsteps came from the hall toward them. Olien eyed Malidora as he powered on his arbow. Malidora reached for the flash pistol under her belt. Tynex walked toward the control room with a hurried pace.

She leaned her head around the doorway. "They got the sprayers working! Just thought you might want to know."

"Yes, thank you." Olien powered off the arbow as she left the room, heading back toward the lift tube.

"Sprayers? What's that?" Malidora wondered.

"It just means we can wash ourselves now," Olien said. "As I was saying, I'm going to call Ravetaria once I get all this into a report, and she should release your friends."

"Sounds good," Malidora sat there with the thought of washing the sour smells and grimy feeling of the last few days from her skin. "Do you mind if I go check out these sprayers?"

"Go ahead." Olien returned to the screen, circling images and words with his finger. "It will give me some time to compile the data. The spray stations should be on the first level."

Evala waved as Malidora moved down the main corridor on level one. She was standing in one of two lines of Vogus, apparently waiting to clean themselves. Malidora got in the line beside Evala as it was the shortest.

"I guess you heard." Evala smiled as she stepped up into the next spot in the line. The line was moving surprisingly fast for those ahead of them to be taking a bath.

Once it was her turn, Evala went inside. A few moments later, Malidora was allowed into the other room. She made her way over to a small room where a Vogan stood supervising the process. There were two circular strands of glowing liquid on the floor, one was somewhat red and the other blue. Malidora paused for a moment, unsure what she was supposed to do.

The supervisor kept looking toward the doorway and then back at her. "Are you sure you want to bathe in here?"

Malidora glanced at the supervisor. "Just because I'm not a Vogan doesn't mean I don't take baths."

"Suit yourself." The supervisor waved toward the floor. "Stand in the red circle."

Malidora moved over to the red circle and glanced back at the supervisor.

"Put all your clothes in the blue." The supervisor rubbed her eyes.

Malidora glanced at the blue circle then back at the Vogan. "Are you going to leave first?"

"I have to stay in here to operate the machines."

"I guess this is no time for modesty." Malidora began removing the layers of her leathery black outfit, tossing each piece into the blue circle. "I've been in situations more comprising than this." Setting her last garment onto the floor, she stepped toward the red circle. "Wait," the air in her lungs suddenly escaped, "are you female?"

"Of course not." The supervisor tapped his finger against his chin. "This is the men's spray chamber."

Malidora grimaced, covering herself as well as she could. "Could you turn around or something?"

The supervisor faced the wall. "Why did you get in line with the men if you had a problem with it?"

"I—I was in a hurry. I didn't know you were going to watch me the whole time." Malidora grabbed her coat from the floor, wrapping it around her. "Could we move this along?"

"You're the one slowing down the process." He grabbed a small container of a thick black liquid and held it out to her, still mostly facing away from her. "Here's some scrape."

Holding the vest around her with one hand, she gingerly reached out and took it. "What's this for?"

"You rub it all over." The Vogan supervisor made a circular motion with his hand. "Hair, feathers, skin, everywhere. It helps clean."

"Alright, keep facing the wall." Making sure that he wasn't looking, she dropped the coat into the blue circle and stepped to the red one.

"You're slowing down the line," he said. "Let me know when you are ready for the spray."

She rubbed the substance into her hair and over her skin. It felt like gritty mud, not something that she normally wanted in her hair, but if it worked, she was all for it.

"I'm ready," she stated.

"Keep your arms at your sides and close to your body until you are in place."

Malidora reluctantly moved her hands from their strategic placement and waited. The floor inside the red dropped, lowering her into a tight chamber. The platform shook as it locked into place. Cold water rushed all over her, taking her breath away and beating hard on her skin. The force of the water was a bit uncomfortable, but it felt good on the tight muscles in her back.

Checking her hair to make sure all of the gritty material was gone, she was surprised at how clean she felt. The floor lifted her back to the room. The Vogan man turned toward the wall again. Her clothes, now clean and pressed flat, lay in the blue circle beside her.

She put them on and quickly exited the chamber.

"What took you so long in there?" Evala asked as Malidora came rushing into the hall.

"They uh—" Malidora shook her hands through the damp roots of her hair. "They still had some kinks to work out."

"Oh—but they got it working I guess," said Evala.

"Yes." Malidora glanced down the hall toward the culinary bay.

"I better get back. Mitian is waiting for me." Evala headed back toward the atrium.

Malidora went the other direction, heading to the culinary bay. "Yeah, see you." Moving along the wall, she looked for the sensors that feed information to the console that Olien used. She didn't know what they looked like, but there had to be a lot of them spread out across the Shimatress.

As she passed the storage bay, Malidora spotted a small black object among the ribbons of luminescent liquid flowing across the ceilings. It had a clear glass covering with a red light behind it. Once she had noticed one of them, she began to spot them all over the area, spaced out by about the same length apart.

When she came to the culinary bay, she spotted two of them in the open area around the cone where they hung their food. Both of them had red lights like the rest, but the glass covering was fogged up. Could that be why some of the sensors in this area weren't picking up the unusual mark as well as the others?

The windows in the doors leading to the back where they prepared the food were fogged up as well. Outside the doors, at the base of the wall, was wet and partially covered in frost. As cold as it was outside the Shimatress, it was warm enough inside to melt any ice.

At the back of the culinary bay was one of the exterior access points they had closed and barricaded so that no one could get in or out without going to the main gate. Is it possible that cold air was leaking in somewhere? Olien would be interested in this information. Malidora headed toward the atrium.

"They say you eat more when it's cold," said a voice behind her. "You have to fatten up to produce more body heat."

Malidora turned around to find Dabradan and Toberin standing outside the storage bay doors, while one of the Vogus handed them their weapons back. "Is that your excuse?" she joked.

"I'm not the one sneaking to the culinary bay every few moments." Dabradan grinned as he walked toward her. Toberin kept walking past them, heading toward the atrium, presumably on his way to the lodging area.

"How can anyone resist those crunchy leaves and orange goo that lights up?" Malidora quipped.

Dabradan lowered his voice as he stepped closer. "How is everyone doing? How is Evala?"

"You're very protective of her, aren't you?" Malidora said.

"I'm protective of everyone in my unit." Dabradan eased toward the wall as one of the Vogus walked by them. "But yes, a little more with her; she's like family to me."

"She told me that your family practically raised her." Malidora glanced up at the nearest sensor, wondering if Olien was watching her now. "What happened to her parents?"

Dabradan rubbed the back of his neck. "Don't tell her I told you this." He took a deep breath as if preparing himself to lift a heavy burden. "When she was just a kid, she was traveling with her parents across some of the unsettled plains to Golin. They were ambushed by rovers who stole everything they had, killed them, and took Evala." Dabradan turned around for a moment, looking at his feet. "She's never said much about what happened while they had her. I try not to think about it, may be best that I don't know. One of the Barandier units rescued her. Wiped out the whole pack of rovers."

"And you were one of the Barandiers who saved her?" Malidora said.

"No, I was a mechanic at the time." Dabradan turned back to face her. "But I rode with them a lot when they needed me. I happened to be there when they found her."

Malidora tilted her head toward him. "And your family decided to take care of her."

"Not at the beginning." Dabradan leaned against the wall. "She had a hard time adjusting in Udamal. Her life had been turned upside down. She was rebellious, unruly. Didn't fit in and didn't want to. No one else wanted to put up with her."

Malidora rubbed the side of his arm, surprised by the muscles underneath his sleeve. "She looks up to you."

"Evala never listens to a thing I say," Dabradan huffed. "Always doing her own thing, questioning what I tell her."

"She thinks you don't believe in her," Malidora said. "That she's not cut out for this."

"She's the most skilled combat soldier on the team." Dabradan moved away from the wall and closer to her. "Agile, fearless, quick, but like most young recruits, she's unpredictable and reckless. I wish she had found something else to do with her life."

"Maybe she wants to prove herself," Malidora's hand reached toward the collar of his uniform before she realized what she was doing. "I think she needs to hear it from you, hear it in front of everyone, that she does belong."

"I have a hard enough time with these guys thinking I'm too easy on her," Dabradan said as Malidora tried to adjust his collar and strap one of the missing loops. "We'll see." He took the strap from her fingers and finished tightening the collar. "I better get some more rest before my shift comes up."

They walked together to the atrium and then parted ways as Dabradan entered the gallery. Before she stepped on the lift, he stopped and turned around. "It was good to see you again."

"Yeah." Malidora felt her lips curve into a smile and pressed them together tight. She had to get things moving soon. She didn't like being locked up in here with other people, it was beginning to make her uncomfortable. They were already getting a bit too friendly, and there was nowhere she could run. Malidora entered the lift tube on her way to level three. Voices echoed down the hall as the lift opened. They were coming from one of the doors of the control room.

CHAPTER 15

"HE WASN'T RESPONDING to my messages." Mitian stroked the plumes of feathered hair on her shoulders as she stood outside the doorway speaking to someone inside the control room. "So, I came up here to check."

"Who else knows about this?" Ravetaria spoke with a low voice, but not low enough that Malidora couldn't hear. As she drew closer, she could hear Olien's music playing from the control room.

"No one as far as I know," Mitian said.

"Keep it that way," Ravetaria whispered. "Where's Malidora? Did you see her?"

"No, does she show up on the sensors?" Mitian rubbed her arms inside the robe with her back turned to the tube lift.

"I'm right here," Malidora called out. "What's going on?"

Ravetaria moved out of the doorway into the main hall. "Where have you been? You were assigned to work here."

"I went to use the sprayers," Malidora said. "Olien said it was fine."

"It should have been cleared through me," Ravetaria growled.

"I didn't know it would be a problem," Malidora said. "Tynex came by and told us they were working."

"Who else was there?" The metal shield armor on Ravetaria's

arms clunked together as she crossed them over the orange glowing light on her chest. "I need others that can corroborate your story."

"The one operating the sprayers." Malidora tightened her shoulders together. "Evala was there."

"Mitian, who was operating the women's spray system?" Ravetaria demanded.

"Actually, you'll need to ask the men's operator." Malidora shrugged. "I went to the wrong one."

Ravetaria narrowed her eyes as she brought the side of her arbow toward her mouth. "Kilon report to the control room and send Dolarax and Livoxian up here as well. Code Sespa."

"Why don't you just ask Olien?" Malidora pointed toward the room.

"This is only precautionary." Ravetaria held out her hand. "Give me your weapon, we'll get this cleared up and you can get back to work."

"If you want to clear this up, talk to Olien," Malidora said.

Ravetaria's voice grew stern. "Before we talk to anyone, you need to hand me your weapon."

Malidora shoved her way past Ravetaria and entered the control room. Olien lay slumped over the console in the chair, the same place where his friend Galoxa was found when they first came here to Ekovus. He was rigid and thin, with skin that looked brittle like stone. His favorite music played from the console as he lay there. His mouth open with no teeth, eyes sockets wide and hollow. Blood and celette-sized marks were on the chair.

Ravetaria rushed into the room aiming her arbow at Malidora. "You need to give up your weapon and come with me."

All Malidora could hear was the music playing. This was the last thing she expected to find. The room began to spin as she tried to bring her senses back into focus. "What makes you think I did this?" Malidora backed against the wall, the door leading to the other hall beside her. "My location has been verified every time there has been an incident . . . by Olien or another Vogan."

"I'm not taking any chances right now." Ravetaria adjusted her necklace back into place. "This is a grave situation."

"Right before I left, Olien was working on a report. He said some of the sensors weren't reading properly. I saw some in the culinary bay that were frozen. Could there be a breach where someone is getting inside?"

A peculiar odor emanated from Mitian, a pheromone Malidora had sampled when someone was nervous or afraid. There was a tremble in her hands.

"We barricaded all the exits," Ravetaria said. "The only way in or out is past the guards at the main gate."

Mitian wiped the sweat above her green eyes. "Arrest her!" Mitian shouted. "She's the murderer!"

"Silence, Mitian! I'm handling this!" Ravetaria yelled back before turning toward Malidora, trying to calm her voice. "Malidora, hand over the weapon. We can corroborate your story again, and you'll be released."

"What are you waiting for?!" Mitian's hands raised excitedly. "She's going to kill us all!"

"Mitian, get out of here!" Ravetaria ordered. "You're only making this worse!"

Kilon entered the hallway. "What is going on in here?"

"Kilon, take Mitian out of here!" Ravetaria said.

"No, shoot the brightlander!" Mitian demanded. "She killed Olien! She's the one that has been murdering our people!"

"Is this true?" Kilon turned to Ravetaria.

"We only need to take her in." Ravetaria's voice became slow and deliberate. "Clear some things up."

"She did it, Kilon!" Mitian yelled. "The brightlanders are taking us down one by one! Do something! Do it for Alisker and Olien!"

"Get him out of here, Kilon!" Ravetaria ordered. "We have to keep this under control!"

Kilon aimed his arbow at Malidora, glancing from Ravetaria to Mitian.

Malidora removed the flash pistol tucked in her belt. Taking a deep breath, she glanced at Ravetaria. "Don't take this the wrong way, but perhaps you never really had control."

In a blur of movement, Malidora fired her flash pistol into the panel on the other side of the room. The panel sparked, then exploded, causing the lights to blink on and off in the room. Ravetaria took cover from the sudden burst of flame as Malidora dashed through door into the other hall, heading for the lift tube.

"Turn off the lift tube!" Ravetaria ordered.

"I can't." Kilon continually pressed one of the buttons on the console. "She killed the lift override."

Malidora descended to the atrium on the ground floor, firing a blast at the controls in hopes that the tube wouldn't return to the fourth level. She shoved her way past Livoxian and Dolarax as they were about to enter the tube. She ran at full speed toward the main gallery circling the atrium.

A voice sounded through the Shimatress as Malidora rounded the gallery into one of the connecting corridors. "Attention everyone, this is Ravetaria. Full alert at the main gate. All brightlanders are to remain where they are, placing their weapons on the floor."

From the gallery, she found the corridor leading toward the main dining bay. Sliding on her boot heels, she slowed enough to change direction down the hall. Running footsteps sounded behind her, presumably Livoxian and Dolarax.

It might be a huge mistake, but if her hunch was correct, it would lead her and those who pursued to the source of this madness. She suspected that someone had been coming inside. Olien had said the corrupted mark spent most of its time in the atrium. Its most likely reason would be to siphon the essence from the fresh corpses stored there. Malidora ran through the culinary bay, startling Hanovus and Tynex who were eating slices of meats from the wired cone. She moved near the walls, searching for any sign of cold air.

She found a locked door at the back of the dining area. Malidora grabbed her flash pistol but spotted a larger door near the corner beside her. It was unlocked and led her into the processing room. Akranyx and Zaravell looked up from the food they were preparing as she ran along the walls searching for any kind of breach.

"Brightlanders are on lockdown." Akranyx set her cutting light on the counter. "Didn't you hear?"

"You can't be back here!" Zaravell swiped a pile of diced fruit off the table into a bowl.

Malidora ignored him, moving around the hot surfaces they were using to cook. Vines grew on the walls, lit faintly with red illumination. Vats of glowing liquid sat on a set of shelves around the back of the room. Malidora could feel a draft coming through one shelf as she approached. The liquids in the containers near the back had frozen solid.

Ravetaria burst into the room, followed by Livoxian, Dolarax, Kilon, and Mitian. Using all her strength, Malidora pulled one end of the shelf from the wall.

"Give it up, Malidora." Ravetaria walked around the counter. "You're trapped. Come out quietly and we can discuss this. You seem like a rational being."

"Fire!" Mitian shouted. "You can't let her escape!"

"Kilon! I told you to subdue him!" Ravetaria yelled. "Get him out now! That is an order!"

With enough space between the shelf and the wall, Malidora squeezed behind it into the dark.

"Do something!" Mitian screamed. "She's getting away!"

"Are you dense? She can't get out." Ravetaria eased around one of the shelves. "The exit door is barricaded."

Scents of damp molded foliage wafted in as Malidora stumbled in the dark area behind the last shelf. Large metal crates and storage boxes they had used in other areas to barricade the doors were stacked at the sides of both walls.

"I want a peaceful end to this, Malidora. Name your demands, and maybe we can negotiate," said Ravetaria.

"You're going to need to catch her quickly, Ravetaria," said Akranyx.

"Why is that?" Ravetaria leaned out behind a shelf filled with bowls, plates, and cups.

"Because she can get out," Akranyx stated.

Ravetaria turned toward Akranyx and Zaravell. "And how would she be able to do that?"

"We removed the barricade," said Zaravell.

Ravetaria exhaled, exaggerating the sound. "Are you insane! Why would you do that?"

"Because it—" Akranyx said. "It told us to."

Malidora found the door console uncovered but locked. Blasting it with her pistol, the pressure on the door released, launching open.

"She opened the door!" Mitian shouted, running over to them. Ravetaria slammed her fist into his face, knocking him to the floor. A rush of cold whistled into the room. Flurries of snow blew inside as Malidora stepped onto the hard, crunchy ground.

Heavy snowfall filled the air, glowing in the green illumination of the Shimatress. The big flakes changed direction with the blustering wind. Tracks led from the door toward the frost covered plains, some fresh and some faded.

Following the trail, Malidora trudged into the icy wilderness. Most of the tracks turned and led back toward the door to the processing room, but one pair moved around the corner. Malidora trailed them until they were undetectable in the fallen snow. Without anything else to go on, she traced the steps back toward the processing room entrance.

Something on one of the second level terraces caught her attention as she moved toward the door. Something out of place against the ambient green light. The door banged open and Ravetaria leapt into the snow.

"Where do you plan to go?" Ravetaria propped herself against the outside wall. "You can't take the cold like we can."

CHAPTER 16

AS MALIDORA'S EYES adjusted to the dark, the silhouette on the terrace took shape, a Vogan standing silent and unmoving in the shadows underneath the sharp alcove at the second level. Sidestepping while keeping her eye on the figure, Malidora positioned for a better angle. A pair of red glowing eyes burned through the night as she recognized the ghoulish entity. A Whidge, like the Blight Whidge she fought on Isodonia, had seized the body of one of the Vogus. The demonic shadow had either not noticed her or did not consider her a threat.

Malidora pointed toward the Whidge, wanting Ravetaria to see.

"No one is coming to your aid," Ravetaria said.

Once it was clear Ravetaria was not going to come out and look, Malidora raised her flash pistol toward the Whidge. She fired a barrage toward the figure, hoping to draw Ravetaria's attention to it. She wasn't ready to kill it. If she killed the Vogan host, they would have to confront the true form of the Whidge, and they were not prepared for that yet. The being blended with the shadows. Malidora searched for a sign of the dark being but could not be certain if it was hit or not.

"Disarm yourself or I'll be forced to fire!" Ravetaria threatened.

Malidora searched the darkness around her. Backing away from the Shimatress, she hoped to gain a better vantage point. Ravetaria watched quietly as Malidora stalked her invisible prey.

Candle burning in the dark, Malidora tried to calm herself as the wind snatched at her hair. Her boots crumpled into the packed snow as a gust howled past the corner wall. Ravetaria moved toward her right flank, the energy rippling from her ignited arbow. A tall figure, dark against the pattern of falling snow, appeared in the corner of Malidora's eye.

Her mind numbed as the Whidge snatched her in its invisible grip. The world became surreal as the strength drained from her limbs. Pressure enveloped her, gravity dragging her toward a small singular point as she felt the life begin to flow out of her body.

When Malidora could take no more, the demon's hold suddenly released. Unable to stand, Malidora fell into the thick snow. Above her, a blue celette from Ravetaria's arbow stuck in the shadow's chest. With the wave of its hand, the disc and the wound vanished. Malidora kicked herself onto her feet, running toward Ravetaria as she launched another celette at the shadowy fiend.

The shadow ignited a blue shield from its own arbow. The blue light vanished, changing into smokey shadow. It blocked Ravetaria's celettes with the dark shield and lumbered toward them. Malidora and Ravetaria ran in separate directions. Kilon stumbled out of the doorway in a struggle with Mitian and Akranyx. He ignited his arbow as he broke free.

The Whidge pursued Malidora as she dashed away from the Shimatress, the thick snow reducing her speed. As it drew close, the invisible force again pulled her off her feet. Clawing at the icy ground, Malidora was dragged across the turf. The shadow turned to fend off another barrage of Ravetaria's celettes, giving Malidora the distraction she needed to get up and run.

Mitian and Akranyx stomped Kilon as he tried to roll away from the blows. Akranyx cried out as Dolarax tackled her to the ground. Even in the snow, he wore nothing on his feet. Livoxian moved to subdue Mitian, locking arms with him. Bleeding in the snow, Kilon no longer moved.

"We need armed personnel outside at once," Ravetaria shouted into her arbow. "Come through processing, the door is open." Even though Ravetaria could run across the snow better than Malidora, the shadow began to overtake her. Malidora moved toward the shadow, closing to the maximum range she could still hit it with her weapon.

She aimed and fired, missing the demon with the first few bursts.

Erupting on the trigger, Malidora sent a salvo of violet beams of light hitting the creature. It covered its back with its dark shield while continuing to stalk Ravetaria.

Ravetaria stopped and whirled around, firing back at the Whidge. Their shots began pelting the demon as it could not defend against two different attack points. It slumped to a knee, shielding against Malidora's flurry of blasts while allowing Ravetaria's celettes to cut into it. Ravetaria charged toward the shadow, launching discs into it.

"Wait!" cried Malidora. "Don't go near it!"

The shadow Vogan opened its hand, healing its wounds almost as fast as Ravetaria could make them. Continuing to rush toward the demon, Ravetaria's celettes began to overwhelm it. As she got close, Ravetaria's arbow emitted a single celette that remained at the edge of the arbow.

Instead of launching the celette, she swung her wrist toward it. Ravetaria beheaded the Whidge with the sharplight blade.

Its head bounded across the ice, leaving a trail of blackened ooze. The shadow's body pitched forward into the white powder.

"Get back!" Malidora shouted. "It's not dead yet!"

Ravetaria stared at the creature for a moment, then slowly backed away. As the darkness flowed out of the Vogan body, its white fiber hair returned. A thick gurgling liquid raised from the ice. The ooze climbed, stacking on top of itself as it rose. Ravetaria quickened her steps as she rushed to get away from the churning mass.

"What is this?" Ravetaria nearly tripped as she moved back while staring at the solidifying shape.

Malidora's heart thumped forcefully as she watched the horrid form assemble. It towered ten feet tall above them. Long arms ending in terrible claws that reached the ground, its three short legs balanced it like the gnarled roots of a tree. The legs thrashed about as it continued to grow. The dark sludge from its decapitated head flew from the icy ground, merging with the abomination.

"It's a Whidge," said Malidora. "One of the Shadows I told you about."

Ravetaria fired her arbow, but the light discs did nothing. They vanished into its lightless form as if tossed into an endless void. Its utterly dark body was surrounded by a bright aura, sparkling as it orbited the black shape. Eight long tendrils erupted from the aura, glowing with the same energy, reaching outward. A dark fibrous material stretched from the monster's head, forming a web over the area around it.

The Whidge blinked and materialized at the other end of the web closest to Ravetaria. Ravetaria leapt backward, attempting to escape. It whipped its tendrils at her, wrapping her up and pinning one of her arms.

Struggling to get her arbow in position to fire at the appendages holding her, Ravetaria was yanked toward the Whidge. Firing furious laser blasts at the tendrils, Malidora dashed after her. Several spinning celettes flew past, forcing Malidora to dive into the snow. Lines of red fire sizzled above her as Evala pounced into the air, twisting to blast at the Whidge as she somersaulted over the tendrils dragging Ravetaria in.

"Don't get too close! Aim for the tentacles!" Malidora yelled as she continued firing from her knees. Dolarax and Sikrum dashed past, launching celettes at the tendrils as they neared the body of the Whidge. Surrounding snow from the ground and the air flowed into the emptiness of the monster's form as they continued to fight. Several sparks flew and landed near the Whidge as Dabradan and Hanovus came running, blasting at the shadow. Evala's bolts burned into the corporeal material of the appendages but did not destroy them.

A blue celette from Sikrum's arbow sliced through one of the tendrils as it drew Ravetaria closer to the range of its pulling force. The ground surrounding the Whidge was unusually dark where the snow had been shifted by the pulling force of the Whidge. It gave a visual reference to where the range of its powerful force began. Toberin and Novianna joined the battle as Dolarax severed the last tendril. Ravetaria struggled to her feet, running as fast as she could from the Whidge.

With most of the firing stopped, Malidora got to her feet. With the Whidge's limited movement in the physical universe without a host body, they stood outside its range. Evala continued blasting at the Whidge as it swallowed her flash bolts. Grabbing her from behind, Malidora pinned Evala's arms and pulled her away from the Whidge. Evala struggled to get free.

"Pull back," Malidora said. "Let's regroup."

Evala stopped fighting and began walking with Malidora toward the others. The white aura around the Whidge bristled with power. Its lost tendrils began to reform. A high wail pulsed from the Whidge. The sound vibrated Malidora's bones, making her knees and elbows twitch. Dabradan, Toberin, and Hanovus circled the range of the Whidge, moving behind it. Ravetaria, Malidora, and Evala moved toward the Whidge's left flank.

Evala slid another cylinder into one of her pistols. "Is this one of those Shadows you were talking about?"

Malidora tried to catch her breath. "One of them, yes."

"How do we kill it?" Dabradan shouted across the yard.

"Focus your mind on the energy," Malidora said. "The light surrounding it. We have to break it."

"Break it with what?" Sikrum said.

"With our minds," Malidora replied.

Toberin lowered his rifle, glancing at Dabradan. "What?"

"Just do it!" Evala yelled as she stared at the Whidge.

The Whidge's tendrils writhed silently in the air around it. Ravetaria jumped back as if anticipating it to warp to the edge of its appendages at any moment. Malidora's mind went blank as her breathing slowed. The once falling snow, hung frozen in the air. The others stood motionless next to each other as if time had stopped. All sound faded, except for a voice. A whispering that crept through her mind.

They do not trust you. You think they are allies, but they are not.

The words ran through the tunnels of her brain, seeking the part that processed emotions. They pounded and twisted, trying to get a response.

We are not the true enemy. The dark form you see only exists in your mind. We are merely representative of the darkness within them. The thoughts they are having even now. They are searching for the justification that will free their minds. Guilt is all that holds them back from destroying you. It is fading. The walls are coming down for them all. There is no escape from it. You know what you must do. You have done it before. Killing them first is the only defense.

Even though Malidora had experience with the Shadows' influence, there was always that glimmer of belief in the moment. It triggered memories of past betrayals that made her impulsively want to turn her weapons on those facing her. It felt as raw as if it had just happened. She began to think of every failure, every suspect word that those who were supposed to be her friends had uttered. Suspecting thoughts of those around her, laughing at her misfortune. The world was against her. Impulsively, she wanted to show them the repercussions of their mistake. What enjoyment she would get from ending their laughter, blasting them all into the snow. It would be so satisfying. But she would not act on it. She knew this was the Whidge's manipulation. The rest of them however, had never been exposed to this kind of mind controlling corruption.

Snow began to fall again. Clouds of vapor formed from their mouths as they exhaled. Standing around the Whidge, many of them wriggled their fingers and moved their arms, confused.

"Don't listen to anything it tells you," Malidora said. "Whatever it spoke to you is a lie. Your thoughts are being manipulated."

Ravetaria turned toward her. "Why did you run if you are not guilty? Is that a lie or simply inconvenient for you?"

Malidora placed her pistol under her belt. "The words in your head are the affliction. The thing that made friends into foes. It is what made your zinugal attack us. It's a thought planted inside your mind to control you." Malidora turned to Dabradan as he eyed the Vogan. "This is what made the creatures attack your cities, what turned the citizens of Mortagon against each other. It wants us to destroy each other now, it craves it. Don't allow it to win."

Ravetaria twisted the white jewel she wore around her neck. Evala stretched her shoulders. Across the field, Dabradan and the others shifted their weight uncomfortably. Dolarax turned next to Livoxian, brushing the ice from the bottom of his feet. They all appeared nervous.

"Why are we all standing around like this?" Dolarax gestured toward Malidora. "We know the brightlander killed Olien."

"We're all the same side here. Don't succumb to the affliction the way that others have," Ravetaria said. "Once we destroy this thing, we can go our separate ways if you wish."

"Because she said so?" Dolarax ran his hand across his wrist weapon. "I can't believe the mighty Ravetaria has become blind to these brightlanders' lies."

"Malidora speaks true," Evala said.

"If this is Ravetaria's order, I will yield," said Novianna.

A humming rose from somewhere in the darkness. Growing louder with its approach, it became harsh. Buzzing. Malidora felt the pulsing again in her bones as Dolarax aimed his arbow at her.

Sikrum moved in from of him, pleading. "If you fire a single celette, you will kill us all."

Malidora could almost feel the glee from the Whidge as it watched with anticipation.

Dolarax stared at Sikrum. "You're a traitor to your own kind!" Dolarax launched a celette into Sikrum's chest, then turned and fired at Malidora. Ravetaria activated her shield, deflecting the spinning blur. Evala aimed her pistols at Dolarax, as he continued to fire.

"Barandiers, hold your fire!" Dabradan screamed.

Evala complied, lowering her pistols. Toberin and Hanovus failed to heed the order. They blasted Dolarax, flattening him into the snow. Livoxian countered with a flurry of light discs. Two of them cut into Toberin. He dropped his rifle, pitching forward, staining the white powder with blood. The buzzing in the air increased.

"Stand down!" Ravetaria roared. "Obey my command!"

The vibrating reached a maddening crescendo as Novianna was thrown from her feet. Something unseen pulled her screaming into the darkness. Her screams ended abruptly, leaving only the pulsating buzz. From the spot she last occupied, the monster emerged. Floating over the banks of snow, the amorphous shadow drew toward them. The falling white flakes behind it curved oddly as if the shadow's presence bent space and time. Like the Whidge, it was traced by flowing energy.

Dabradan and Hanovus backed away as it moved toward them. The Nulthereal paused near Dolarax's bleeding body, his toes stretched out rigid. A smokey white substance seeped from his corpse, trailing toward the Nulthereal as it approached. The Nulthereal continued to siphon this essence until the remains began to crumble like dry ash.

Still alive, Sikrum crawled away from the Nulthereal as fast as he could. Hanovus blasted heavy cannon fire into the shadow, but it was as useless as firing at the Whidge. In the chaos, the Whidge shed some of its appendages to warp toward Malidora.

Before she could gain traction on the ice, the tendrils closed around her legs. Ravetaria turned and launched a salvo of celettes, severing the tentacle as two more grabbed Malidora around the waist. Its lost tendrils began growing from its surrounding energy field.

Sikrum clawed at the black dirt underneath the snow as the Nulthereal pulled him in, devouring him into the void. It then moved toward Ravetaria and Evala. They raced out of its path while the others moved in to get a clear shot on the Whidge's tendrils holding Malidora.

Heat rose into her face as she neared the edge of its dark form. Knowing what she faced if she returned to the Hollow was too much to bear. As she was about to be engulfed by the Whidge, she swung at it in vain. In what should have been futile, the shadowstone covering her hand connected with it. The impact to her hand jarred through her arm and down her back. She fell face first into the wet snow as bits of dust and shards of stone fell around her.

Malidora looked back at the Whidge to see the weakness she had inflicted on its body. "It's broken! Fire!"

Celettes and flash fire burst into the Whidge from all sides. Hanovus' face could only be described as crazed joy as he fired the powerful rapid bolts from his rifle. The Whidge exploded, crumbing like fragile stone. Standing with his eyes closed, Hanovus raised the rifle into the cold wind, allowing the air to blow into the vents of the smoking barrel. "Now that was a satisfying kill."

Ravetaria and Evala split in different directions. The Nulthereal continued after Evala. Malidora glanced at her hand. The shadow stone that had fused to her hand was now pulverized into bits, leaving her hand unharmed. Surveying the shattered remains of the Whidge, Malidora found what was left of one its long arms. Its claws were the size of small swords, Malidora broke one free from its hand.

As the Nulthereal pursued Evala, Malidora grasped her new claw weapon. The Nulthereal began to overtake Evala, putting her in range of its invisible force. With no time to close the distance, Malidora hurled the claw toward the shadow. The spinning claw flew past the Nulthereal, landing in a mound of snow.

Evala contorted her body as she was pulled in, aiming her pistols to blast into the void as it began to engulf her. She closed her eyes as if waiting for death. Instead, she dropped to the ground at the edge of the shadow. The Nulthereal turned to stone. Cleaved in two, half of it slid off the other, both pieces falling onto the ground.

Behind the broken Nulthereal, Dabradan stood, wielding the Whidge claw. Sitting in the snow, Evala rest her head on her knees as breaths came short and quick. Dabradan sat next to her, rubbing her back slowly, easing her to take deep breaths.

Ravetaria kneeled next to Livoxian as he straightened the matted fibers of Dolarax's feathery coat. She turned toward Malidora. "Is it over?

"I don't know." Malidora wrung her hands, wiping away the black dust. Rising to her feet, Ravetaria walked past her to where Kilon lay. His breath condensed in the cold air. He was alive. Akranyx leaned against the side of the Shimatress, her hands and feet bound with blue light as taglon energy pressed them together. Another set of binders sat on the ground nearby.

"Where is Mitian?" Ravetaria inquired.

Akranyx turned away from her, saying nothing. Livoxian came running over. "We had Mitian tied up right here! Zaravell is bound inside the processing area."

"He couldn't have gone far." Ravetaria turned a revolving piece of her arbow. "Larkyn, send two envaks to intercept Mitian and a loress to tend to Kilon. We're still on the Vudall side."

"What happened?" the voice said over the arbow.

"Do what I asked, Larkyn," huffed Ravetaria.

Evala sat next to Kilon, attempting to wake him, but he remained unconscious. Kiriol and Gelkoria arrived and carried him inside for further treatment. Tynex and Dameriel took Akranyx inside to lock her into the storage area.

The others broke the remaining claws from the Whidge's husk. Sifting through the Nulthereal's rubble, Malidora found several shards that appeared the appropriate size. The Barandiers had removed the arrowheads from all of her bolts, but she could rectify that. She tested the shards, twisting them into the metal casing, finding those that fit tightly enough that they wouldn't come loose.

Ravetaria crouched low, looking at something on the ground. Malidora finished the last bolt and made her way toward her. The head of a Vogan lay in the snow. It was the Vogan that had been the host of the Whidge. Ravetaria gazed up at her as she approached.

"Indingal," she said. "He was a great warrior. I had not seen him in a while but would never have believed this would be his fate."

"Don't remember him this way," Malidora said. "It wasn't him who did this, only his body animated by the Whidge."

"If this happens to me," Ravetaria said. "Kill without hesitation. Do not allow me to be an instrument of this evil."

"Hopefully, we destroyed the only Whidge on this world," Malidora said. "But yeah, I think the same would go for all of us."

A low buzzing emitted in the distance behind them.

Ravetaria turned toward the emanating lights of the tree line behind them. "There's more out there."

"Sounds like Nulthereals." Malidora scanned the dark past the burning sparks on the ground. "Not good, but not quite as bad as a Whidge."

"I'm ready for 'em this time." Hanovus dropped his rifle and whipped the Whidge claw through the air. He stuck the Whidge claw under his belt and picked up the flash weapon, wiping away the snow and ice.

Evala's eyes gleamed. "Let's take it to them before they get here." Even after nearly being sucked into the shadow, she was eager for more action.

Tynex and Dameriel returned and began inspecting Mitian's trail leading around the other side of the Shimatress.

"They're right." Malidora brushed off as much of the black dust as she could. "We have the weapons to fight them now."

Ravetaria concentrated on the sounds of the distant buzzing before turning to face the group. "Tynex," she said. "Forget Mitian for now. Open the hangar. Get the syverns ready."

"We're mounting an attack?" said Livoxian.

Ravetaria's feathery black hair shimmered in the green lights behind her. "If it means releasing our wake from these Shadows, yes."

"Are you sure you want to add new soldiers into this?" said Malidora. "Those out here have faced their influence once. They know what it is like."

"And some of us here failed," Ravetaria said.

"Everyone fails the first time." Malidora's voice quavered as she recalled her first experience with the Shadows' influence. "You were lucky I was here to guide you through it."

Ravetaria raised her shoulders, inhaling deeply. "Then we will do the same for Tynex and Dameriel."

"I'm not fighting alongside that one." Hanovus gestured angrily toward Livoxian.

Livoxian stiffened. "Me? You should be locked up like Akranyx!"

"You both have done enough," Ravetaria said. "You're only here because we need you. Avenge those lost and redeem yourselves. Let's finish this."

"We could split into two units." Dabradan drew his hands into the air and moved them together. "Barandiers on one team and yours on the other. Converge on the enemy from two points."

"Acceptable." Ravetaria held out open palm. "And once this is over, you go back to your brightlands."

"Agreed." Dabradan pushed the Whidge claw under the belt on his hip.

Malidora stepped toward Dabradan. "Does that mean I'm on my own?"

"You're an honorary Barandier." He gave her a wink. "Congratulations."

White vapor escaped her lips as she snickered. "I'm flattered."

They marched toward the hangar as Dameriel and Tynex were releasing enough syverns for all of them. The thick cloud cover had opened, revealing thousands of sparkling stars. Sweeping spirals of starry nebulae sprinkled across the black separating ground from sky.

Ravetaria climbed onto one of the syverns, turning on the humming engine. Leaping onto another, Evala examined the controls. After Ravetaria taught her to rub her hands together for heat and then trace a pattern with her finger, she showed the other Barandiers and Malidora.

The steering was strange for Malidora. Evala showed her how the handle grips slid sideways and would bank the syvern left or right. Turning the handles would turn the whole vehicle. To accelerate, you moved the steering forward. Backwards would decelerate. It was pretty intuitive once she started to get accustomed to it.

"By the way, how are you able to jump so high?" Malidora recalled Evala flipping over the Whidge.

"Comes easy for some of us," she replied, winking at Malidora.

"Dameriel and Tynex." Ravetaria seemed to be adjusting the syvern controls. "If either of you take action against any of us, no matter what idea is in your head, I will personally fill you with so many celettes no one will be able to identify you."

They both glanced at each other and nodded as Ravetaria zoomed into the distance, leaving a green streak behind. Livoxian, Dameriel, and Tynex followed behind her.

"Barandiers, you ready?" Dabradan straddled his syvern.

"Hurry up!" Evala joked.

CHAPTER 17

WITH A HIGH-PITCHED whine, Dabradan's syvern picked up speed, blurring away from them. Evala, Malidora, and Hanovus raced after him. The green streak of his syvern began to shorten as Malidora caught up to him. Soon, there was only solid green light as she matched his speed. Evala flew ahead of Dabradan, zig-zagging between a group of small trees with shining violet foliage.

Malidora chased her, matching her evasion pattern. She was feeling comfortable with the controls already. As Malidora began to overtake her, Evala accelerated, recklessly speeding through the shimmering forest. As the danger mounted, Malidora slowed, hoping that Evala would no longer feel the need to compete with her.

"I've got to get one of these!" Evala shouted as she swerved through the grove. She pressed ahead of Malidora toward the thicket, neglecting to slow at all. Bright orange leaves exploded as Evala plowed through the brush, throwing her syvern wildly to the right. She began to slow as she corrected course. Cuts and scrapes appeared on the side of her face when Malidora caught up to her.

"Let's try to get there in one piece," Malidora quipped.

Evala ignored her warning, accelerating ahead, though not as fast as she did before. Dabradan and Hanovus eased up beside them as the Vogus came into view. They rode ahead of them in a perfect arrow formation. Malidora tilted right, avoiding the clouds of snow kicked up by the Vogus. The buzzing of the Nulthereal could no longer be heard over the hums and whines of the syverns, but they had to be getting close.

Suddenly, the four Vogan syverns diverted, splitting in different directions. The forest darkened as the colorful lights of the trees were extinguished. Limbs and vegetation swayed and bent horrifically toward an object warping the light around it.

The Nulthereal carved through the woods, swallowing everything in its path. Malidora swerved to avoid it. The Barandiers passed by the Nulthereal, slowing to a stop. Leaping from the syvern, Malidora rushed toward the shadow. Several figures rustled through the trees as Ravetaria led the Vogus into position. The Nulthereal paused as they crept through the forest around it.

Ravetaria engaged her arbow, casting a shield horizontally near the ground and releasing it. She stepped onto it, using it as a platform. Leaping from the shield platform, it vanished as she cast another shield to catch her. She continued the process, jumping from shield to shield as she cast quick enough to allow her to use it like stairs. Ravetaria made it directly above the Nulthereal as Evala charged it, starting her attack before Dabradan could give an order. He signaled for Hanovus to take the left flank and Malidora to take the right.

Malidora had not taken orders in a long time, but since they needed to coordinate, she went with it. The Nulthereal caught Dameriel in its grip as he got close. Ravetaria dove from her position on the shield above, slicing the Nulthereal with her Whidge claw on her way down.

The Nulthereal split in two. Evala swung her shadowstone weapon, shattering what remained. The buzzing did not abate. Ravetaria turned as another shadow flowed like billowing smoke toward her. Dabradan and Hanovus engaged as Ravetaria fled the range of its inhaling force. Cartwheeling over the shadow, Evala sliced through the top of it, spilling its silt onto the snow.

Before landing, she was pulled by a third Nulthereal. Evala dropped from the shadow's invisible grip as a small crack slowly grew from the impact of Malidora's arrow. Dabradan's and Livoxian's weapons met from opposite ends as they broke through the stone spreading across the Nulthereal's formerly wraithlike form. In the bitter cold, they stood, staring through the trees for signs of more Shadows.

The buzzing persisted from the woods ahead. Ravetaria adjusted her grip on the claw weapon and moved toward the sound. The group followed as Malidora picked up a handful of shards from the remains of one of the Nulthereals. She dropped them into the bottom of the quiver hanging at her left hip. Brushing the snow from her hair, Evala dashed through the brush, catching up to the group.

They marched through the forest toward the vibration, keeping their guard for any surprises. Malidora's muscles tightened as she shivered in the damp cold of the woods. She broke off some of the luminescent leaves from a low hanging branch, hoping the light would offer enough heat to ease her discomfort. Unfortunately, the light faded not long after its separation from the tree.

In the woods ahead, the trees became dark. Spindly black branches replaced the glowing colors of vegetation. Stringy pulp hung from them as if wax from a melted candle made of flesh. It was like the blighted forests of Isodonia.

They came out of the forests into a dark icy landscape. The buzzing was closer now but remained further ahead. Black moldy growth trailed from the forests through the frozen ground ahead.

"We cannot go much further," Ravetaria said.

Malidora quickened her pace to walk beside her. "We have to keep going. We may not find them again so easily."

"We're entering Blackfrost," warned Ravetaria. "The unendurable cold. Not even Vogus can survive out here for long."

Dabradan moved nearer. "Maybe we should go back. As long as they stay here, they are not a threat. When they come into our territory again, we'll be ready."

"Just a bit more," Malidora appealed. "We're so close to finishing this."

The soft snow faded to hard slick ice, requiring careful steps. The wind, once shielded by the trees of the forest now sank its sharp teeth into them. What Malidora could feel of her feet burned through her boots.

There was no traction on the smooth ice beneath her. Her legs buckled as she tried to keep from slipping. As they continued on, the shadowy growth widened. Walking on this surface was easier, it was not slick like the ice. It spread out like tiny roots tangled into one mass. It quivered beneath her feet, growing slowly before her eyes. Dameriel knelt to examine the strange covering.

"Do you remember those messages on the wall?" Evala asked as she leaned closer.

Malidora turned around as Evala tore a tangle of the dark oozing mass from the ground. "What message?"

The cluster of tiny roots and black fungi broke apart in Evala's hand, becoming nothing but fine powder. "In your cell. The one Cerano wrote. *From out of the wound, the darkness bled.* Do you think this has something to do with that?"

"It could, I don't know," said Malidora. "Maybe we are getting close to the source."

Evala and the others seemed to be too interested in the black substance. Malidora's hand trembled; she didn't like standing out here like this. She walked on ahead as a green flash caught her eye. Using the spark to light her path, she walked across the squishy substance. The buzzing grew louder with each step. Patterns in the growth spiraled toward a boulder protruding from the icy ground.

The gray stone flashed a dim green for a moment before resuming its gray, faceted surface. A nyalith, like the one she had seen in The Hollow. Malidora crept toward it, crouching on one knee to peer into the stone. She had seen stones like this in the wastelands of blighted towns on Isodonia, long after the Nulthereals had left the area. Among all the other oddities, she didn't find them particularly significant. Now that she had seen one in The Hollow, it was obvious that they were connected.

She focused on the nyalith's surface but found nothing other than solid stone. As she let her focus wander, the green glow appeared, bending across the stone's many facets. Faint filaments filled the deep interior of the stone like tiny stands of hair, twinkling as if metallic. Her mind swam free of the restraints of her skull into an abstract reality beyond her senses.

As she flowed through an open network of pathways, particles flew by in a vast sea of black. Particles became stones, stones became boulders, and the boulders became worlds. Malidora saw a large pool of water, a wellspring in the middle of an oasis. Surrounded by trees with red fronds, the waters were still, like a sheet of glass, reflecting the stars in the dark sky.

"I sense you there. Is it you? The Awakener?" The voice filled the whole world as if the very air around her spoke.

Malidora searched the star filled sky for the source but found nothing.

"If you are truly The Awakener, why do come to me in this way?" said the voice. "Though I have kept watch of this world since the signal was initiated, my body still rests."

Malidora's mouth opened to vocalize but her words filled the skies before she could. "I'm not—I don't know what you mean."

"Who are you?" the voice queried.

"I am Malidora."

"Where is The Awakener?"

Malidora made her way closer to the water's edge. "I don't know."

"This is unexpected," said the voice. "I wonder how this intervention will affect the outcome."

Malidora watched the ripples in the water as a soft breeze stirred the surface. "What outcome?"

"The sum of the variables," the voice said. "Though it has many links, there is ultimately only one outcome. But only the variables can be known."

"I don't understand." Malidora began to move around the banks of the spring toward the other side. "Are you Hableides, the great mind that the Vogus spoke of?"

"No," said the voice. "I am called Neristara. I was once like you, material, dimensionally limited. Before my ascension, I could only see the outcome."

"Where are you?" Malidora continued to the other side of the spring.

"My consciousness is in Averess, one of infinite realms of the Everance," Neristara said.

"How do I get out of here?" Malidora asked. "I need to help free this world of the Shadows."

"It is too late for Kandom," said Neristara. "The Nulvarians have gained too much life energy, their tendrils run too deep. But there are other worlds that can be saved."

"It's not too late. We have nearly defeated them," Malidora said.

"I'm afraid the darkness has swelled beyond your means to defeat them here."

"Help us then! Help us stop them."

"There are no variables that would lead to the outcome you seek. Return to the wellspring. Leave this world. Follow the blue light."

"The spring here? Inside this dream?"

"You entered Kandom by water and stone. Return there."

"But it was only a small pool," said Malidora. "It doesn't go anywhere."

"You've been through Nulvare and retain neutralized aethrum. Combined with your organic essence, you have all you need for the waters to take you. Dive into the pool and follow the blue light."

"Then what? Was I not brought to this world for a reason? To redeem myself and help save it from the monsters in The Hollow?"

"You do have potential, great potential. Your actions have opened new variables," said Neristara. "I will help you as much as I can. Listen closely. The nyalith before you, rarely do you find one so engorged with the tempestuous energy of a world in its death throes. This gives you a rare opportunity. Take a shard of this nyalith and bring it with you through the spring."

"What do I do with it?"

"You must find The Awakener," Neristara said.

"How do I find them?" Malidora was startled as a roaring ripped through the skies of this reality.

"I have faith that you will find a way. I'm afraid our interaction has attracted a dangerous presence," Neristara warned. "I must go. Find The Awakener and bring them to my slumbering body."

"No!" Malidora shouted. "I need to know more! Neristara!"

A buzzing roar drilled into Malidora's mind as a rush of a thousand voices surrounded her. Brushing by her like a fierce wind, the various expressions coalesced into one, a storm in the wilderness of an eternal dream.

There is no gulf of time nor space that we cannot reach. No realm, dimension, or universe that we cannot find you.

Even hearing the voice of Razinoth extracted memories from her mind. The images of all the faces of those she either killed or failed to save, her brother and sister, Legotian, and many others haunted her thoughts.

Once we have devoured this world and picked your soul from its ruin, we will take great pleasure in controlling you once again. Your consciousness will serve the Gaith for eternity as we peel back the layers of The Everance.

The power of the voice ripped through her as the world stretched away. She fell backwards into the black sludge that covered the ice. Either from the cold or the encounter with Razinoth, perhaps both, Malidora's body shook uncontrollably as she tried to sit upright.

"Are you okay?" said a familiar voice behind her. It was Dabradan, who came to her aid along with Evala and Ravetaria.

Steadying herself, she stared at the nyalith. She loosened her dagger from her belt and attempted to cut into the crystalized stone. It did little more than scratch the smooth surface. Malidora searched her clothing for other tools that could work but could find nothing better than the dagger she had already tried. Her eyes turned to Dabradan, "Can I borrow that claw?"

"What?" Dabradan said as Malidora grabbed the weapon. Using the sharp edge of the Whidge claw, she tried to carve a piece of the nyalith stone. Digging the claw into a corner of one of the facets, she managed to cut a line into the rock.

"What are you doing? It's freezing out here," Dabradan said.

"If we are going to destroy the remaining Shadows, we must do it now," Ravetaria said.

"Give me a moment." Malidora repeated the process until she had a triangular shape. She dug in from the other side until it loosened.

"A moment?" Ravetaria scowled. "You had us keep going to finish them off and now we're waiting for you?"

"Got it! Let's destroy them and get out of here." Malidora finished breaking the piece off. She held it between her fingers, examining the piece of crystal. Nothing unusual appeared or sounded from it. She placed it in one of the pouches of her battledress.

"What is that for?" Evala wondered.

"I feel like it could be useful," Malidora said. "Maybe we can study it later."

"Well, let's go then." Dabradan started forward. "Kill what we can while we are here."

As they moved on across the ice, they halted as the buzzing became loud. The source was near, pulsing with an odd dissonance. Hanovus launched a spark into the black ahead of them. Clusters of Shadows appeared in the light. More Nulthereals than Malidora had ever seen.

"Are you serious!" Evala muttered, closing her eyes in despair.

The sight of hundreds of Nulthereals soured the faces of everyone in the group. Dabradan threw a spark further left of the other with the same result. Nothing but rows and rows of Nulthereals in the darkness ahead. Several of the Shadows began slowly creeping toward them.

"We can't contend with this," admitted Ravetaria as she traced her black fingernails around the outline of the white stone around her neck. "Back to the defenses of the Shimatress!"

"You're right, let's get out of here!" Malidora turned and dashed across the blackened ground. The others quickly followed. The Nulthereals began moving toward them as Malidora looked back. She hit the ice and slid off her feet, backflipping onto the black muck behind her.

As the others caught up, she carefully walked over the ice as fast as she could without falling again. The buzzing increased. Malidora risked a faster pace as her heart pounded in her chest. The Vogus were more adept at handling the ice. Racing ahead, they ran and slid across the frozen surface.

Fluffy snowbanks lay ahead, illuminated by the glowing forest nearby. Malidora didn't want to risk attempting the speed the Vogus used across the slippery ground but knew the Shadows gained on them. Apparently, Nulthereals had no problem moving over water when it was frozen.

Hanovus lost his balance and overcompensated, dropping his rifle and causing him to tumble to the hard ground. Dabradan carefully turned around to help as Hanovus struggled to return to his feet. Malidora nearly fell as she turned around. Nulthereals closed on them. Hanovus rolled over to pull out the claw. He hacked into the first few to reach him. As they closed in around him, Hanovus slid across the ice, caught in the Nulthereal's grip. Dabradan slashed at another group of Shadows, the lunge causing him to slip. Malidora dashed for the sure footing of the snowbanks as Evala moved to give Dabradan a hand.

As she made it to ground, Malidora turned and fired a volley of shadow tipped arrows at the approaching shadows. One Nulthereal shattered, while two more were slowed as their forms cracked open. She continued loading her crossbow until, out of the darkness, came Evala and Dabradan, their hot breath filling the cold air around them.

The buzzing rose as more Nulthereals poured across the ice.

"They got Hanovus . . . ." Dabradan managed to get out between heavy breaths.

Running through the snow, they headed toward the glowing forest. Dabradan gained a second wind as another wave of Nulthereals drew near. The Shadows ate a path through the trees chasing them but seeming to lose speed as they did so. The Vogus had reached the syverns just as they all began to light up.

Malidora leapt onto one of the syverns, gliding away as Dabradan and Evala climbed onto theirs. Weaving through the trees, Malidora caught up to the green streaks of the Vogus as Evala and Dabradan trailed behind. The Shadows could not match the speed of the syverns allowing Malidora to relax and ease through the next group of trees.

As they approached the lights of the Shimatress, Ravetaria led them around to the main gate. They shut down the syverns, causing them to descend to the ground. There were no guards at the gate as they approached.

Ravetaria raised her arbow to her mouth. "Larkyn, why is no one watching the gate?"

They huddled in, waiting anxiously for a voice to come through the communication patch of Ravetaria's arbow. They were met with silence.

"Larkyn!" Ravetaria repeated.

More silence as Grathael sat down on the open ramp leading inside. Ravetaria's expression never wavered, even as any shred of hope rapidly dwindled. Dabradan and Evala exchanged glances as they reached for their flash weapons.

CHAPTER 18

"IS THAT YOU, Ravetaria?" said a voice through an output device in her arbow.

"Yes, Larkyn, is everything okay in there?" Ravetaria's nose wrinkled as if bracing for the worst.

"Everything is fine," Larkyn said.

Dameriel and Livoxian cheered while Grathael jumped to his feet. They rushed inside as Ravetaria followed. Breathing deeply, Dabradan trailed Evala up the ramp.

Neristara was right. This world was lost. Perhaps it was time to leave, but what would she say to Dabradan, Evala, Ravetaria and the others. How could she just leave them behind to die? Could she take them with her? Would they even go if she could?

Why did she even care about them personally? She was an agent of Sinavus; she didn't view people as individuals. She was supposed to help the masses. For the sake of the many you had to be willing to sacrifice a few along the way. Even the brightest light casts shadows.

Taking a step toward the ramp, she grimaced at the conflict inside her head. Had she lost her edge? Her emotion was winning against the cold logic that was supposed to be unbreakable. She may be the last Sinavus agent left to hunt down the Shadows, but at least that meant there were none here to see her weakness exposed.

The soft crunchy steps turned to metallic clanks as she made her way up the ramp through the main gate. Evala turned as she approached, and the rest of them walked slowly into the deserted entrance bay.

"Larkyn!" shouted Ravetaria impatiently as she stormed toward the hall ahead. Footsteps echoed from the path on their right as someone drew near. Larkyn stepped into the bay, joined by Kiriol and Tynex.

"What has been going on outside?" Larkyn inquired.

"In a moment," Ravetaria said. "We need guards in here, immediately! This is an egregious failure! Why would you have them leave their station?"

Larkyn moved further into the room, stopping in front of Ravetaria. "They were needed elsewhere. They haven't been absent for long."

"She's lying," announced Evala.

Larkyn turned to Evala, her green eyes turning to narrow slits. Kiriol and Tynex stepped in beside Larkyn as her eyes moved back to Ravetaria.

"We've been doing the best we could in your absence." Tynex glanced at Larkyn.

Kiriol rubbed the arbow on her wrist. "Everything has been fine, perhaps better than it was."

"We've been more productive, there is unity among us now." Larkyn placed her hands on her hips as if she were still in charge.

"Things are as they should be," Kiriol said, "without the brightlanders."

Ravetaria shifted her stance, spreading her feet slightly apart. "What are you trying to say?"

More footsteps approached from the hall, coupled with a low, vibrating buzz. Mitian walked out into the room behind the others, her hands out of sight underneath her robe.

"What is she doing here?" Ravetaria pointed her arbow at Mitian.

Mitian sauntered toward them. "They recognize that I am not the enemy."

Grathael and Dameriel trained their arbows on Mitian as well.

"I don't know what Mitian told you," Ravetaria said, "but I suspect him of assisting with the murders among us. He could be the killer himself, or he could have removed the barricade, letting that creature in!"

"That was us." Akranyx entered the room with Zaravell and Yelthai. The vibrating grew louder.

Mitian moved closer. "We hope you will soon see things from our perspective." He stopped and stretched his arms. "As you look down on us as stars in the sky." Mitian brought her arbow to bear on Ravetaria, launching celettes wildly into the group. Larkyn and the rest joined him, lighting the bay in flashes of blue.

Igniting her shield, Ravetaria deflected the celettes that whizzed toward her. Livoxian and Dameriel drew their shields as well, but too late to stop all the celettes as they slumped to the floor. Evala and Dabradan extracted their weapons, blasting into the crowd as the rogue Vogus were forced to switch to their shields as well.

Taking cover behind Ravetaria's shield, Dabradan fired, finding an unguarded zone on Kiriol's leg. As he lowered his shield to grip the wound, Dabradan fired again into his torso.

Malidora raised her pistol, but had to hold her fire with Dabradan, Evala, Ravetaria, and Grathael in front of her. As Evala rolled left into a crouch, Malidora ran into her vacant position, shooting at Larkyn as she deflected with her shield. Evala fired on Mitian, forcing him to switch from his weapon to a shield.

Malidora changed targets to focus on Mitian, combining with Evala to pummel his blue shield with a hail of fire. Leaping from her position, Evala continued shooting at Mitian. Unable to block both angles, Mitian was burned by the volley of flashes.

"Malidora, cover me!" Evala shouted as she charged at Yelthai.

Malidora turned and blasted a line of fire at their new enemies, trying to make sure they had to maintain their shields as Evala stormed ahead. "Evala, wait!"

Evala kicked Yelthai, knocking the shield away long enough for Malidora to put a bolt into her chest. She continued firing as Evala raced toward Larkyn.

"Evala, get to cover!" Dabradan shouted.

As celettes flew at her, Evala dove back toward the group. As she came toward them, she landed awkwardly and barreled into Malidora, sending both of them to floor. As Malidora tried to stand, a spatter of red painted the metal beside her. Grathael fell not too far from them, landing hard onto the metal floor, but the blood wasn't his.

"Fall back!" Ravetaria yelled as Dabradan grabbed Evala and dragged her off Malidora. With a kick up to her feet, Malidora dashed down the ramp behind them.

Launching celettes into the support stems of the ramp, Ravetaria severed them, making it swing closed behind them.

Following the trail of blood, Malidora found Dabradan holding Evala as they lay in the snow. She kneeled in front of them, the last few moments flashing through her head.

"You're going to be all right." Dabradan's hand pressed tightly on her side. "We're going to get you back home and get you fixed up."

Evala eyed him with a sheepish grin. "You're lying." Clouds rose from Evala's mouth as she breathed heavily into the cold air.

Letting out a shivered exhale, Dabradan mustered a smile. "Well, what do I know? I'm wrong most of the time. Which means you will be fine."

Clanging rose from the Shimatress as the Vogus inside beat on the ramp door.

"They'll be coming around through the processing bay soon," Ravetaria warned.

Evala began coughing as she tried to sit up. "At least I made it to Underveil."

"Yes, you did, you even got me out here," Dabradan quipped as dark thick liquid began to ooze between his fingers as he clutched her side.

"Malidora," Evala said, her voice growing weak, "you were right about everything. You're the only one I've known who never lied to me."

Ironic for someone to say that about her, with as many as she had manipulated and deceived when it was the most efficient course of action. She had not felt the need to lie here. It almost felt good to be recognized for something honest for a change.

"I did lie to you, though." Evala lifted one of her feet for a moment before it fell back on the snow. "I can't jump as high as you think."

"What do you mean?" Malidora leaned closer.

With a grin, Evala turned to Malidora. "I have repulsor boots. Take them off and use them. They'll adjust to your feet."

"But I don't—" Malidora's eyes darted back and forth, unsure what to say. "You should keep them."

"Wear them," Evala insisted. "Maybe you'll be as good as me someday."

Forcing a chuckle, Malidora nodded.

"Take them off me." Evala lifted one of her feet as well as she could. "I want to see you put them on."

Crawling gingerly to where her feet lay, Malidora lifted each one, following Evala's instructions to remove them. After taking her own boots off, she slipped her feet into them. Pressing on both sides, they snapped into place around her feet and ankles.

"Tell me you won't let the Shadows win." Evala glanced between Malidora and Dabradan. "You and Dab. Protect everything that is left. Don't let them take it."

Dabradan took her hand in his, holding on as if she were about to fall.

Malidora looked over at her. "They won't win." The words spilled out of her mouth before she realized what she was saying.

Evala smiled and closed her eyes as if to sleep, then quickly opened them again. "I've never seen so many stars." For the first time, the confident gleam in her eyes was replaced with a childlike innocence.

Malidora lifted her head to the clear black sky. "One of the Vogus told me they believe that when you leave this world you are reborn as a star among the heavens, like a candle burning in the dark."

"It is true," said Ravetaria, standing nearby. "The bravest warriors become the brightest stars. When you leave this world, you will stand out among many. It will be up to you to watch over us, protect us and guide us on our path. All the worlds of the universe will be at your feet."

"That sounds peaceful." Evala glanced at her. "To watch over everyone from above."

"I should have told you when it mattered," Dabradan said. "You are one of the bravest and most skilled Barandiers I've ever seen. I was harder on you than I should have been. I thought it was for your own good."

Evala's eyes began to close, but she fought to keep them open as she glanced at him. "It still matters, because I know you mean it. I know you're telling the truth . . . ." Evala's voice fell silent as her face went still. Clouds of breath no longer rose from her mouth.

Malidora's face felt as if it were breaking, a dam barely restraining a torrent of emotion. Not only for Evala but for the many that were cursed by knowing Malidora's name. The images came rushing back, but she had to black them out again. She had to put her mind in another place, to ward off the emotions the way Sinavus had taught her. The only way to save this world and avenge them all was to pull herself together and be strong.

Dabradan clenched his teeth as he swept his hand over Evala's face to close her eyes. Malidora couldn't bear to look at him. The hurt on his face only made it harder for her to quiet her own pain. She had to bring her focus to the mission, not on individuals. Sinavus taught her never to make decisions based on emotion, but they had already infected her. She had already made the choice.

Ravetaria stepped toward them. "I hate to be cold, but we don't have much time."

Dabradan began covering Evala's body with snow. Ravetaria and Malidora assisted until she was buried in a mound of white, illuminated by the green glows of the Shimatress. He placed her two pistols on top of her. Malidora laid her old boots at Evala's feet, keeping the repulsor boots as Evala wished.

Ravetaria started the syverns as Malidora and Dabradan ran toward them. Hopping on, they soared away from the Shimatress. Zooming over blankets of white, Malidora's head ached. So much loss. Too much to process. Maybe the best thing to do was exactly what Neristara told her. To get to the pool and leave this world to the Shadows. She could make a stand elsewhere. Perhaps that was the reasonable thing to do, but right now she didn't care about potential. She didn't care about variables and outcomes. Whatever logic-defying task it takes to preserve what was left of this planet, she would find it. She couldn't let Evala down.

"If you are heading back," Ravetaria sped ahead of them as she spoke, "I will lead you to the terminator."

Dabradan's long hair whipped with the wind. "You are welcome to come to Udamal with us, Ravetaria."

Streams of blue light rushed by them. Something hit Malidora's syvern as she shifted left. The rogue Vogus were behind them. Ravetaria accelerated, swerving as celettes whistled past her. The rear of Malidora's syvern exploded. She banked hard to her right, dodging a barrage of celettes.

The syvern shuttered and slowed. Smoke erupted from the damaged tail. As the three other syverns closed in, Malidora quickly turned into their path, ramming into the side of Larkyn's syvern. Malidora leapt from her crippled vehicle, leaving it to spin out of control. She grabbed onto Larkyn as they both struggled to stay on the syvern. Larkyn threw an elbow at Malidora's head, maintaining control of the vehicle with her other hand. Seizing her arm, Malidora turned Larkyn toward her, punching her in the bridge of the nose. She shoved Larkyn off the syvern, taking the steering controls as Larkyn tumbled through the thick snow.

Now behind the attacking riders, Malidora drew her weapon and fired. One of the riders was hit, slumping forward at the controls as the nose of the syvern pitched forward. Pieces of black metal from the shredded syvern rushed by as Malidora evaded them.

Ravetaria took care of the last rider as Malidora sailed toward their streaks to catch up to them. With the riders gone, Malidora took a deep breath. She moved closer to Ravetaria as she continued to lead them toward the terminator.

As they rocketed across the tundra for a while, the air began to warm. Approaching the twilight zone, between day and night, Ravetaria slowed. Silhouetted in the ghostly light, a flock of birds with incredibly long wings hovered nearby, oblivious to the troubles of the world.

The wind licked at Ravetaria's black strands as she cradled the stone around her neck in her palm. "This is as far as I can go."

"What?" Malidora glanced at Dabradan and back to Ravetaria. "Aren't you coming with us?"

"The brightlands are no place for Vogus," said Ravetaria. "The sunlight makes us ill. Boils our skin. I wouldn't last there."

Dabradan took his hands off the steering column. "You could stay in the buildings."

"My place is in Nestopa." Ravetaria glanced back at the open darkness. "I won't abandon it."

Malidora got down off the syvern. "What will you do? What is left here?"

The buzzing of the encroaching Nulthereals rose around them. "I'll find others." Ravetaria turned her syvern toward their left. "Others not under the shadow's sway. There must be more somewhere."

"Thank you for everything." Malidora put a hand on her shoulder. Ravetaria eyed her as if unsure of her intent. "I'll never forget you."

"I never thought I would have a friend in Underveil," said Dabradan "You're a great warrior, Ravetaria; it was an honor to fight beside you."

Ravetaria revved up the engine. "Likewise, perhaps we'll see each other again," she glanced from Dabradan to Malidora, "among the stars."

Her syvern streaked into the distance along the penumbra, around the coming Nulthereals. Malidora mounted her syvern as the buzzing came near. The Shadows swarmed in behind them.

Kill him. He is nothing to you. Draw your weapon. Even if you can resist our thoughts, do you think he can? Even now he hears our commands. He is thinking about pulling his weapon and ending your life. The only way to survive is to kill him before he kills you.

Malidora and Dabradan glanced at each other as if wondering what the voices told the other. It only fed her vanishing trust. While knowing this feeling came from the Nulthereals' deception, it was difficult to put the doubt aside. She gave Dabradan a nod and he returned it. They launched into the twilight speeding toward the glow at the horizon.

The first glint of light appeared. Shielding their eyes, they rode toward the sun. Malidora slowed as she began to grow uncomfortable with the speed. Suddenly it seemed too dangerous to be moving this fast. She lost confidence in her ability to control the syvern.

The Shadows began to catch up to them again. Malidora gripped the steering tightly as her breaths became quick and shallow. The buzzing of the Nulthereals vibrated in her chest. Ignoring everything her body told her, she accelerated. Dabradan matched her speed as they reached the flooding light of the sun.

Intense light flashed to her left. As her eyes adjusted, Malidora realized it was reflecting off the surface of moving waters. Malidora broke away, heading toward the river. Dabradan moved after her as she glided the syvern across the path of incoming Nulthereals. They flew over the rushing waters as the front of the syverns began to pitch forward.

She pulled back on the controls as they neared the riverbank. Dabradan hit the surface, his syvern skimming across until it splashed into the water. As Malidora raised the front of her syvern, the tail dropped into the river. The impact knocked her off the vehicle sending her into the wet spray.

The current rushed around Dabradan's shoulders as he moved through the river. Though shallow enough for him to stand, Malidora struggled. She strained to keep from being pushed down the river, unable to find any footing. She swam toward him but could not win against the power of the current. As Dabradan closed in toward her, she lunged at him, wrapping her arms around his neck.

As they made it to shallow water, Malidora found the riverbed underneath her. With her arms still around him, they turned across the river as a legion of Nulthereals gathered at the water's edge.

Dabradan watched the writhing mass of Nulthereals. "What made them stop?"

"The water," Malidora said. "They can't move over water."

She pulled him toward her. Tainted thoughts filled her head, some of her own and some from the Shadows. She ignored them both. Acting on her own impulse, she leaned forward and kissed him. He nearly stumbled with the shift in weight and probably a bit of shock.

His warmth infected her again, igniting every nerve. Ignoring the mandates of Sinavus, she let this desire overcome her. For a moment, the Shadows, the river, and everything else faded away, leaving nothing but two souls connecting.

Malidora's mind raced as she withdrew, her emotions still spiraling out of control. As much as she tried to keep a distance between them, it had become too much to resist. Even though she had crossed this line, she couldn't let it determine her actions.

She opened her eyes. The Nulthereals hovered away toward the night as they stood in the water staring at each other.

"Looks like they are leaving." She let go of his shirt.

Dabradan leaned back. "That's all you're going to say?"

"Perhaps we shouldn't indulge in these desires," she said, turning away. "Not while so much is at stake."

"If this is the end, let's enjoy what little time is left." Dabradan walked deeper into the river, grabbing one of the syverns.

She grabbed her syvern, dragging it out of the water. "I don't do well with this kind of thing. Someone always gets hurt or dies."

Dabradan lay on the sand staring at the sky. "We're both going to die someday; you may as well live while you have to chance."

His words echoed in her mind. They lay next to each other waiting for the engines to dry out. Perhaps he was right, but she couldn't take that chance. There was too much work to be done, too many wrongs that she had to right. She wasn't in a place in her life where she could allow someone into it.

Dabradan took out his communicator as they rode toward Udamal. "Cian, it's Dabradan. Can you hear me?"

She eased her syvern toward him to listen, but there was no response. Over glassy formations in the sand, through forests of yellow, green, and blue trees, Dabradan found landmarks he recognized. They adjusted direction, riding toward the sun until they approached the still broken walls of the Udamal.

CHAPTER 19

THE SHATTERED GATES of Udamal stood silent in the still air. Dabradan came to a stop, dismounting the syvern as he ran through the large cracks in the stone. More armored lizard creatures littered the area inside the walls. Some of their skulls caved in at the base of the wall. They had made it in further this time, destroying many buildings inside.

Bodies of Udamal residents were among them. Some appeared trampled underneath the giant creatures, while others were partly buried beneath toppled stones of the walls and buildings. These corpses did not look like the shriveled ones they had seen of late, and the odor of decaying flesh hung over the city.

"Anyone here!" Dabradan called out. He walked around the collapsed buildings near the center of town. "Cian!"

A loud snort nearby captured their attention. Rustling behind one of the jagged walls of a building, something lumbered. Loud, thunderous quakes shook beneath their feet as one of the giant lizard creatures rumbled around the corner. Dabradan grabbed his rifle, furiously firing at the creature. His blasts ricocheted off the thick armor of the monster, but he continued firing.

The giant lizard raised one of its front legs off the ground then stomped hard into the streets, sending cracks through the stone from the center of its impact. It stared at them for a moment. Then it charged. Malidora grabbed Dabradan pulling him with her as he continued to shoot. The creature plowed into the far wall that still stood, knocking out a small hole and pressing several blocks out of place.

"We need to get out of here!" Malidora shouted.

He turned to her, yelling back, "I've got to stop this thing!"

"We don't have the firepower." Malidora tugged on his arm.

Dabradan shrugged her away. "I'll get through that armor eventually!"

Her mind cycled through anything to divert his attention from the creature. The destruction of his city was another loss in a long string of losses.

"Evala wouldn't want you to die here," she said, gently stroking his hand.

Dabradan turned around, narrowing his eyes as he glared at her. He grabbed her hand, running toward the gate. The creature snorted as it recovered from the blow of the wall. The lizard charged again. Lunging headfirst at them, the creature plowed into one of the large buildings that remained in the center of town. The beast collapsed under the rubble, one of its hind legs quivering. It snorted a final deep breath as the pile of debris crushed further into its body.

As they moved out between the cracks in the walls, Dabradan paused and sat down. A plume of dust scattered as he let out a heavy breath. "We failed. I failed. I never should have left."

"You did the only thing you could do." Malidora kneeled next to him. "The only thing that would have saved Udamal was stopping the Shadows."

Dabradan threw his communicator into the air, watching as it landed in the sand ahead of them. "There's nothing left now. I would have been better off dying here."

"Kandom is still here," said Malidora. "Maybe there are others. There are always setbacks, but you can start again. You can build something better with the knowledge you have now."

"Setbacks?" He rolled over, laying in the dirt against the stone base of the wall. Perhaps giving him some time alone was the best approach right now. She wasn't very good at comforting anyone, especially through something like this. Stepping through the rocks and debris, she moved far enough away from him to feel alone, while keeping him in sight. She moved to the outer wall that remained, picking up a new scent.

Following the smell, she came across a group of footprints embedded in the dried mud. They all pointed in the same direction, angled slightly to the left of the sun.

"Dabradan!" she cheered. "There were survivors!"

After a few moments, he slowly came around the curve. "What are you talking about?"

"Some of them escaped." She pointed out the footprints. "See!"

Dabradan glanced down, tilting his head up as his eyes followed the tracks until they disappeared into the sand. Focusing on the horizon in the direction of the prints, he stood with his arms at his side. "They went to Vesta."

"Perhaps they are still there," Malidora said. "Let's go and see."

Hanging his head, Dabradan backed against the wall. "I'd sooner die."

"What's wrong with Vesta?" Malidora eyed him.

Dabradan shook his head. "Everything."

"It can't be that bad." Malidora's shadow fell over him.

"It's the worst place on this planet. Everything about it is corrupt. We left to build an independent city, and I swore I would never return."

"Every city is corrupt. If your people are there, you have to go. Let them know you are still alive too."

He slapped the dust from his trousers. "It's the principle. There's no justice in a world that allows that city to stand while Udamal lies in ruin. I would just as soon the Shadows destroy that place. Why would I want to live there?"

Malidora rested her hands on her knees. "We promised Evala we would save what is left of this world."

Dabradan closed his eyes as she spoke her name. "Evala thought Vesta was beautiful." Dabradan huffed. "She only saw it from a distance. She never knew what it was like inside the walls."

"We have to warn them," Malidora said. "If you grew up there, it can't be all that bad. If it still stands, we should help keep it that way."

Dabradan stood up straight, walking a few feet away. He traced the rough stone of the wall with his hand as he moved.

Malidora stepped into the sand in the other direction. Searching the soft lumps of dirt, she found the communicator that he threw away. She picked it up, heading toward Dabradan. "You know, corrupt cities are my specialty. I know exactly how to use their greed to my advantage."

He turned around, cocking his head as he stared at her. "You? That place will eat you alive."

Malidora grinned. "How little you know me."

Dabradan stroked his dark beard. "All right. We'll warn them. But don't count on me staying for long."

They returned to the syverns, soaring over the hilly landscape. Zooming alongside a thick forest, Malidora recognized the area. The water pool lay on the other side. She could veer off and enter it. She would follow the blue light and accomplish her new mission. She glanced at the black boots given to her by Evala. It did not seem right to leave yet. When the time was right, she would know.

Malidora broke toward Dabradan's vehicle. "So, tell me more about this place."

"Vesta . . . the City of Wonder," Dabradan added a sarcastic tone as he spoke the last phrase. "Imagine a city filled with one group doing all the work and getting little in return, while the rest get all the benefits while doing little work. The rules that are meant to help everyone are constantly bent to whims of the powerful."

"Sounds like your average city to me." Malidora swerved to avoid a large glass spike protruding from the sand.

"Udamal had its share of problems," Dabradan covered his eyes as they passed through a cloud of dust, "but nothing like Vesta."

"So, we can't lose." Malidora smiled. "Either we succeed in saving it, or—we get the pleasure of watching it burn to the ground."

Dabradan chuckled. It was the first time he had laughed in a while.

The sun hung low to their left as they sped over the smooth glass-covered terrain. A massive tower began to take shape ahead. Bathed in the orange light of the sun, Malidora had never seen its equal. The width and height of the structure seemed impossible. Light reflected off a large blue jewel at the top, shining so bright, it was like a second sun.

It was surrounded by massive stone walls rising to sharp points, like wings on each side of the tower. In the sky surrounding the tower were two sets of massive rings. Even at this distance, the architecture of structures and buildings rose above the edge of the surfaces of the rings.

City of Wonder, indeed.

"Beautiful . . ." she breathed out as her jaw slackened.

Dabradan scoffed. "Nothing more than a gaudy monument to greed and corruption."

"I'm having trouble finding fault in anyone capable of this," Malidora admitted.

"You sound like Evala, seduced by the alluring façade." Dabradan slowed as they approached the gate. "But its heart is rotten to the core."

The gate appeared to be made of orange light, somewhat like the shields the Vogus made with their arbows.

Dabradan brought his syvern to a stop. "To be fair, I'm told it was once an amazing place, the capital of Gesauren society." Dismounting the syvern, he stepped up to the translucent gate. A yellow light turned on from both sides of the frame. "Anyone could make goods and trade them. If you were industrious enough and worked hard, it was possible to make it from the ground level all the way to the second ring."

He turned his back to the gate as if knowing there would be a wait. "As the city grew, the thercon of each generation became increasingly more concerned with pleasing the high elites, those with the most money. As the wealthiest elites in Vesta, the high elites on the second ring are the biggest threat to buy them out."

"Buy them out?" Malidora cocked her head.

Dabradan glanced back to the gate for a moment before he returned his attention to Malidora. "Buy out the naldus of Vesta. Whoever owns the naldus is the thercon of Vesta."

"Interesting," Malidora said. "So, it all comes down to who has the most money. I guess in the end that's what matters most in these places."

Dabradan straightened his back. "The thercon ignores the ground level citizens' concerns because they are not a threat to his power."

A group of guards on the other side of the gate came toward them. "What is your business with Vesta?"

Dabradan leaned forward. "A shadow reaches toward the walls of Vesta. We wish to have an audience with Thercon Merrigan."

"Thercon Merrigan will grant no audience to independents."

"Many cities have been razed," Dabradan said. "I'm sure he is aware that Vesta could be next."

"He is aware, but unconcerned. There is no threat to us here."

Malidora walked toward the gate. "Legions from Underveil have crossed the terminator into the light. Preparations must be made."

"Who are you?" The guard poked Malidora in the shoulder. "You don't look Gesauren."

Dabradan brushed Malidora away from the guard. "Birth defects are common in the independent territories."

Malidora glared at him.

A look of disgust crossed the guard's face, but he couldn't seem to take his eyes off her. "Any force would be foolish to attack Vesta," said the guard as the other turned to leave. "Will that be all?"

Dabradan's lips twitched before he finally spoke, "Asylum. Our city has been razed. We have nowhere to go."

"We're no longer accepting refugees." The guard took another look at Malidora and began walking away.

Dabradan reached out his hand as if he could pull the guard back. "I happen to know that you took in refugees from Udamal."

The guards continued walking. "They were not refugees. They bought their way in."

Dabradan raised his shoulders, rubbing a hand through his hair. "We'll trade one of these vehicles for entrance and shelter."

The guards turned around. "Both vehicles and we have a deal."

"Can't do it," said Dabradan. "I need one for parts. If I can start a shop here manufacturing these, maybe I'll cut you in."

The guards glanced at each other, mumbling something back and forth. "We accept, but we'll be expecting the first one you build." He pressed some buttons on a device in his hand. "You're assigned to the Ruvak district. Block G-16. First thing you need to do is report to your district governor."

"Don't forget the other vehicle you owe us," said the other guard. "We'll be watching you."

The light shield faded, allowing Dabradan and Malidora to pass through. "We'll need a genetic sample to track your clearance." He shined a laser over Dabradan's hand and did the same to Malidora. "Your genetic code is not even right."

Malidora stuffed her hands underneath her belt. "You may not think so, but I am proud of my abnormalities."

"It's close enough," said the other guard. "You'll need to leave your flash weapons here. Grounders aren't allowed to have them."

The guards searched them both, removing Dabradan's rifle and Malidora's pistol. They left her crossbow alone and allowed Dabradan to keep the Whidge claw that he had tucked under his belt. Dabradan climbed onto Malidora's syvern sitting in front of her. He scooted back in the seat, sliding her toward the end.

"I take it you want to drive." Malidora wrapped her arms around his waist.

"I know my way around the city." Dabradan eased through the gate as the guards waved them ahead.

He drove slowly through the dusty streets as Malidora held onto him. The walkways in front of the buildings were crowded with Gesaurens passing by. Their clothes dirty and tattered, many of their bodies thin and malnourished. A mother carrying two children walked in from of them, oblivious to the syvern. An older child crossed the street, holding the hand of another. The children turned their dust covered faces toward them as Dabradan came to a stop

Nudging them across the street, a woman nodded her thanks as she herded the children into a cloth flap in one of the small buildings. Dabradan turned onto a side street, moving away from the crowd. This area looked largely deserted. The stone buildings were cracked, and vegetation grew over the road.

Making another turn, they made it back to the main street that seemed to circle the inside of the walls around Vesta. Loud pops and vibrations sounded through the area. Three men attended to a balton under a small awning. Metal pieces of all different shapes and sizes were strewn about on both sides of the road. Black stains decorated the walkways and parts of the street.

Dabradan slowed, gazing at the buildings as they passed by. A man ran out of one of the structures, gripping his arm. He sucked in air as he spun around in pain from some type of injury.

They continued on until Dabradan found what he searched for: Sector G. He stopped and let Malidora dismount before powering down the vehicle.

"Still think it's beautiful?" Dabradan moved around a stone structure, stained by rain and dark moss growing in the cracks.

Malidora turned around to take another look. High above were the two sets of ringed platforms with the tower in the center. The streets around her were dirty and covered with rocks, the grimy buildings poorly maintained. "There's room for improvement."

"At least no one here knows how to power up the syvern." Dabradan stopped at the doorway. "After you."

"Must be expecting a trap," she quipped as she grabbed the handle and pulled it toward her. Malidora entered the thin, musty hall. The sand on her boots ground on the rough floor with each step. Several rusted metal doors lined the corridor. Filled with voices and the cries of children, the building smelled of mold and body odor.

"You passed it," said Dabradan.

She turned around as he pointed to a rusty, faded sign with the number sixteen. Dabradan yanked on the sliding door, opening a little more with each tug. A few roaring scrapes ending with a final whine revealed a tiny space, barely enough for one person to lie down. Sunlight spilled into the room through holes in the roof. An old, tattered cloth lay on the floor, covered in loose pebbles and silt.

"I feel like I could sleep anywhere right now." Malidora brushed some of the tiny rocks toward the middle of the room. Settling to the floor, she curled around one of the darker corners of the room. Dabradan leaned back against the far wall, taking off some of his clothing to get comfortable.

Malidora removed Evala's boots, being careful not to hit the glowing blue lights on the bottom. "Aren't these going to lose power eventually?"

"They shouldn't. Those gain charge from your movements." Dabradan rested his head on a piece of board. "If they do, just move them around for a bit."

After drifting off to sleep, the cries of an infant and an argument outside woke her a few times. Ironically, she missed sleeping in the dark.

CHAPTER 20

MALIDORA WOKE TO a buzzing sound outside. Gently moving her feet from under Dabradan's head, she stood and walked into the street.

A group of young men in torn clothing stood around the syvern while two others worked the levers and buttons, trying to power it on. She strode toward them, standing in the group beside the vehicle.

"If you'll excuse me," she said, giving them a death stare, "that's mine."

The group left the vehicle and moved away down the road. Malidora sat down on the syvern. The thought of powering it up and heading out of the city entered her mind. She could take it to the water pool and search for the oasis she had seen in the nyalith. It would be much easier than staying here, but something compelled her to stay. She wasn't sure if it was Evala or Dabradan, or if the idea of saving another world would bring her redemption.

"You must be one of the new residents," said a nearby voice. Malidora glanced up to find a Gesauren man walking toward her. "There's supposed to be two of you."

He stared down at a square metal object in his hand as Malidora got down from the syvern. She watched him silently as he fidgeted with his clothes. He seemed uncomfortable with her lack of response.

"I'm Klevet." He bowed slightly. The smooth clean clothing and shiny jewelry he wore was a sharp contrast to the dusty street he stood in. "Governor of the Ruvak district. I need to get your name and the name of the other to match it to your genetic signature."

"Governor?" Malidora swung her neck back, shaking her hair into place. "I guess you have a lot of power around here."

"Only to be used for the good of the district." Klevet clasped his hands together over his gold belt. He had a mark on his arm, a triangle dividing a circle. It appeared to be a scar but for its symmetry. As two men carried a large rusty metal object across the street, Klevet remained in the middle of the road, forcing the men to go around him. "Meeting each new citizen of Ruvak is one of the positives, of course. They're more like friends, family even."

Malidora ground her boot into the gritty road. "Are you aware of the attacks on the independent cities?"

Klevet lifted an eyebrow as he stared her in the eyes. "Of course, I'm aware. There are rumors of creatures razing cities, driving the survivors here for protection."

Arching her back, she returned his gaze. "The attack will be coming here eventually. Vesta needs to prepare."

Klevet snickered. "The walls of Vesta are far stronger than those of the independents. Our technology, our weaponry, is vastly superior. We are quite safe here. You say we need to prepare. We already have."

The tall solid walls rose above the weathered buildings beyond them.

"You haven't prepared for this." Malidora turned as a group of kids ran past carrying bundles of dirty cloth.

"I can assure you, nothing will befall us here." Klevet played with the strands of jewels around his wrist as the kids moved by. "Now what is your name?"

Malidora swept her hands down the sides of her hair as she glanced at the great tower that rose above the city. "What do you need that for?"

"So, you can earn and buy." He bent toward her. "You want to find work, don't you? No one can pay you without it."

She looked down at her hands as she rubbed them together. "Does anyone ever refuse?"

Klevet straightened his back. "Who would refuse? There's no reason to be here if this isn't taken care of. You might as well be an independent."

"I should warn you that everyone I give my name to dies." She smirked. "Are you sure you still want it?"

"What are you talking about?"

Wiping the hair from her forehead, Malidora moved her attention further down the street. "It's a curse, or a blessing, depending on who the person in question is."

Putting the square device into his pocket, he moved toward her. "If you could just give me your name or whatever you wish to be called. The sooner we get this done, the sooner you can start earning."

Malidora stepped toward him. "There doesn't appear to be much earning around here."

"There are varied levels of initiative around here." He waved toward the street. "Workers earn, the lazy do not. It all depends on you."

Putting her hands on her hips, she raised an eyebrow as she glanced at him. "You're saying that most of these people are lazy?"

"Look, it makes no difference to me," he said. "I'll put a name down either way."

"Malidora." She held out her hand as a greeting.

Klevet took her hand, lifting it in an acknowledging gesture. "Welcome, Malidora. I look forward to your contributions to Ruvak." Before letting go, he rubbed her skin with his thumb. "How were you able to color your skin like this?"

"Something of an accident I guess," she said.

"Accident?" Klevet shook his head. "There's money in it if you would be willing to share the technique. We could start a company together. It would be a hit with the advanes."

He let go of her hand, staring at her orange, red, and black hair. "What is the other name? The other new resident."

It was a perfect opportunity to give some ridiculous name that Dabradan would hate, but there were more important things on her mind right now. She couldn't think of anything amusing enough. "Dabradan."

Klevet reached into his pocked, grimacing. "Where did I put that—" He tried the other pocket, digging his hand in as if he would surely feel it eventually.

"Looking for this?" Malidora held out the square device.

Rubbing the side of his head, Klevet stared at the device and then Malidora. "How did you get that?"

"Do you believe in magic?" Malidora winked.

Klevet snatched the device from her outstretched hand. "We don't take kindly to thieves around here."

"It's only a game," she said. "It is now in your possession."

He clenched the bridge of his nose before walking away. Malidora watched as he moved to the end of the street before exploring her new surroundings. After passing shops trading what appeared to be junk, Malidora came across a woman selling small colorful boxes. The boxes had pictures of fruit, animals, or plants on them.

Malidora realized how empty her stomach was after having not eaten in at least a day. "Is this food?"

The woman's eyes became slits as she watched Malidora cautiously. "Yes. Food."

"How much?"

"Two perculin for a box," said the Gesauren woman. "Or make an offer."

Taking inventory of her pouch, Malidora found the nyalith shard she had cut from the stone. Digging further, she felt some pebbles in the corner. She pulled out some tiny pieces of the shadowstone from the Whidge. She handed it to the woman.

"What is this?" the shopkeeper stared at the pieces of black rocks in her hand. "This is no good to me."

"Take a good look," Malidora said. "They're rare and valuable."

The woman brought the pebbles close to her eyes as she inspected them. Malidora slid a few of the boxes from the stack into her coat as the shopkeeper squinted at the small stones.

"No, sorry, this won't do me any good." The woman handed the rocks back to Malidora. "They are pretty, but no one is interested in rocks."

Malidora placed the little stones back into her pocket. "I'm sure I can find someone that will realize their worth."

Perhaps she was irredeemable, but the woman would thank her a thousand times over if she knew what Malidora was trying to save them from. Malidora was merely taking what the universe should have given her. What chance but she did this world have left. If the woman had accepted the stones, it wouldn't have been necessary.

Malidora was reminded of Evala telling her that she was the one person who had never lied to her. Though she had become nearly immune to the guilt of such things, the thought of Evala and Dabradan's disdain cut deep. Gritting her teeth, Malidora fought to replace these thoughts in her head with something, anything, else.

After walking around a corner out of view of the woman, Malidora opened one of the boxes. It was filled with seeds, nuts, and dried pieces of fruit. At first it tasted like dirt, but the more she ate the more she became accustomed to it. As long as she made sure she had a piece of the dried fruit in each handful, it gave the harsh saltiness a touch of sweet flavor.

As she was about to enter the building, Dabradan came out laughing with another Gesauren.

"Look who I ran into!" Dabradan patted the man on the back. "They put us in the same block house as Cian and the others from Udamal."

Malidora recognized him as the man talking to Dabradan when she first stepped into Udamal. "Great."

Cian tilted his head. "Isn't she the prisoner?" He turned to Dabradan, his mouth open as if prepared to say something as soon as he found the words.

Dabradan rested a hand on Cian's shoulder. "I forgot to mention that part. We were desperate. We set her free and she has helped us ever since. I probably wouldn't be here if it weren't for her."

Cian's eyes drooped. "If only you could have saved the rest of them."

"We're starting the business again," said Dabradan. "The one we had before we left Vesta.

We're going to buy scraps and make them into balton parts."

Malidora feigned an enthusiastic nod.

"Where is this vehicle you spoke of?" Cian looked around.

"Right over there," Dabradan pointed toward a corner of the building and turned to Malidora. "We're going to reverse engineer the syvern and sell them."

Malidora folded her arms. "For someone that hates this city, you sure seem happy to be here."

"Might as well make the best of it," Dabradan said. "May be the only city left."

"Isn't that what someone said earlier?" She tapped her chin with her index finger. "I got some food if you are hungry." Malidora took one of the dried chunks of fruit from the box she had opened. She leaned toward him, placing the fruit toward his mouth. Reluctantly, he opened his lips and let her guide the fruit into his mouth. She placed it onto his tongue, sliding her finger from his lips as he closed around the chunk of fruit.

"What else you got?" He grinned as he chewed the dried fruit.

Malidora handed him the box. "Here you go."

Cian had turned away by the time Dabradan took the box and walked him over to the syvern. Malidora turned and watched them as they excitedly pressed buttons and turned controls. "I suppose I'm not part of the business."

"We'll find something for you to do." Dabradan powered the syvern up as it emitted its distinctive whine.

Malidora stepped over the rusted junk laying on the walkway toward the syvern. "This world is nearing its end, remember?"

Dabradan glanced up. "That's why we are doing this, we have to sustain ourselves, and selling these vehicles may attract those with influence." His focus returned to the syvern as he pried up a panel with a sharp tool.

"How long is that going to take?" she wondered.

Dabradan's focus remained on the syvern as Cian leaned over to watch. "Hard to say."

Starting an honest business and working your way up from nothing would take too long in this place. Why bother? Malidora walked away from them, heading down the street. She took out another box, pouring a handful of its contents. This one was sweeter, with a tinge of bitterness. Continuing to eat as she walked, she came across a group of children playing a type of game on the walkway.

As she watched them from a distance, they took turns trying to kick a small stone into a piece of old pipe that lay on the ground. Many of the kids turned as she approached, while others focused on the game.

Malidora walked up into their group, bending down to be at eye level with them. "Do any of you know how one gets to the rings?"

One girl glanced at the others before turning to Malidora. "Maybe."

Malidora faced her. "So, tell me."

"How much are you paying?" The girl looked at her and then back to the boy about to kick the rock.

With a grin, Malidora moved toward her. "Smart kid." She reached into the pocket of her battle dress finding another one of the boxes. "What about this box of food?"

"Only money," said the girl.

Malidora bent slightly toward the girl. "What if I grew another box out of my hands?"

The girl put her hands to her hips while some of the other kids stared at Malidora. Malidora extended her hand, palm up, while covering it with her other hand. Removing the hand that covered her palm, Malidora gave the illusion that a box had appeared in her hand out of nowhere.

"Whoa!" A few of the boys ran over.

The girl lifted her hands. "What did you do?"

"Grew a box from my hand like I told you," said Malidora.

"No, you didn't," the girl stated, her hands returning to her hips.

One of the boys moved in closer. "Do it again!"

Malidora handed him the box and performed the trick again, handing the second box to the girl.

"So how would I get to the rings?" Malidora asked.

"Make some for me!" said another kid.

Another stepped forward. "Me too!"

Malidora stood up, crossing her arms. "If you don't give me the answer, I'll summon a monster that feeds on naughty children."

"Yeah, I wanna see that!" said one of the boys.

Malidora lifted her eyebrows. "There won't be much to see when it eats you."

"You have to buy your way up," another kid stepped toward her.

"Or you have to be a guest of one of the advanes," said another.

"Neither of those will ever happen," said the girl.

Malidora wandered the streets, watching some people collect junk and others make new things out of old ones. Some sold items from benches, and the cycle seemed to go back around. After going back to the community shelter they were assigned to, Malidora watched Dabradan and Cian take apart the syvern. She spent the rest of the day holding parts and handing them tools until a buzzing sounded through the street.

"What's that?" she asked as she set a cube with glowing wires on the clay beside her.

Cian stood, holding his back as he stretched. "Our shift is over and those on the other shift begin."

Dabradan and Cian were tired from their work and went to lay down inside the block house. Before long Malidora joined him. The constant daylight felt so wrong. Her body's weariness disagreed with what her other senses were telling her.

CHAPTER 21

THE BUZZING SOUND signaled the beginning of a new day as Malidora tried to stretch out the stiffness in her neck. Dabradan got up soon after as Cian stopped by the room. He led them to the district fountain where everyone came to bathe. The dark water in the pools looked anything but clean. Malidora stayed under the falling water hoping the flow would be the most sanitary.

She returned to the streets, walking around the shadow of the tower to get enough sunlight to dry her clothes. As she found a patch of sunlight, a man, wrapped in what appeared to be blankets, came running toward her. He tapped her on the shoulder even though she was looking right at him. It made her want to punch him, but she resisted the urge.

"Klevet wants to see you," the man said, and he gestured toward one of the side streets before running away.

Despite the uncertainty of Klevet's intentions, Malidora decided to see what he wanted. She had her crossbow if she needed it, and a small, concealed blade. Turning onto the other street, she noticed a tall house that stood out among the others. It was well constructed with appealing materials. Some of the wall sections were framed in the glassy haspere that she had seen on the way to Mortagon. It had to be Klevet's house.

With no handle to open the door, Malidora began to pound on it. Footsteps inside came lightly toward her, with no hint of urgency. After a brief pause, the steps started up again. The door slid open.

A Gesauren woman stood in the doorway. Dressed in a clean black suit with a frilly teal waistcoat, the woman glared at Malidora. "You don't have to cause a racket to announce yourself." The door closed behind her.

"I'm here to see Klevet." Malidora quickly bowed her head.

The woman smirked with a certain satisfaction, as if she relished this moment. "As would many, but he has no one scheduled today."

"Schedule?" Malidora traced her fingers along the doorframe. "I was told that he wanted to see me."

The woman closed her eyes for a moment, inhaling deep. "He will work you into to his schedule eventually, but today his time is filled with other matters that need his attention."

"Why don't you simply mention that I am here?" Malidora slid her hands down her sides, resting them on her hips. "If he doesn't wish to see me, I will quietly leave. Otherwise, you and I can continue chatting."

She looked away as if playing scenarios in her head. "Who shall I tell him is here?"

"Malidora."

The woman exhaled. "Wait here."

As the door opened, Malidora squeezed behind the woman into the house.

The woman quickly turned around. "I will call security! You are to wait outside!"

"I'm making sure you hold up your end of the bargain." Malidora eased past her into the dimly lit room. "If he doesn't want to see me, I will leave as I said."

The Gesauren woman tightened her lips, then turned and left the room. As she waited for the woman to return, Malidora wandered over to a display case in the corner of the room. Several white stones were pinned to a black material inside. Upon further inspection, the white stones were teeth, animal teeth. They appeared to all be teeth of predators of all sizes and shapes.

The same scent that surrounded the woman became more noticeable as her footsteps approached. "He will see you in the conservatory." The woman dramatically gestured toward a hallway to her left.

The hall opened to a room filled with windows displaying beautiful fountains, red leaved trees that curved in unnatural spirals, and docile creatures feeding on perfectly trimmed green grass.

"I noticed you admiring my collection," said Klevet as he sat in a large black chair made of thick animal hide, tanned, and polished.

Malidora took a few steps into the room. "You mean the teeth?"

"There is no weapon more primal." He grinned as he took a sip from a decorative glass.

Malidora gazed at the lovely scenery in the windows around them. "I don't recall the city around here looking like this."

Klevet laughed as he set his drink onto a sculpted haspere table beside his chair. "The view is artificial. The district unfortunately does not lend to the kind of ambience one could appreciate." He extended his hand toward a seat across from him.

Malidora sat in the soft seat, adjusting her position in the chair until she found a comfortable balance. "A shame. Perhaps if you did a better job helping your people, there would be no need for illusions."

"Yes, if only I could dedicate more time to finding a way to motivate everyone to work," Klevet crossed one leg over the other, leaning back in the seat, "but someone has to manage the funds distributed by Thercon Merrigan, assist promising businesses, help those who lack the ability to work, and maintain . . ."

Leaning back into the cushion, Malidora propped her elbow on the side of the chair. "Maintain what? Where is that money going?"

Klevet brushed some invisible lint from his pants leg. "It goes back to motivation. If the people won't work, the buildings can't be repaired."

"So, you're telling me that these people barely making it aren't willing to work to bring food to their children?"

"You realize that I could have you apprehended." Klevet picked up his drink from the table. "As I said before there is no place for thieves here."

"I found an item that you misplaced, I thought you would be grateful," Malidora readjusted her position in the seat. Nearly everyone she had met in a position of power had some dubious business connections, ways to make even more money on the side. With those types of connections came problems.

"As your district governor, it is my responsibility to ensure that you become a productive part of our society." Klevet took a sip of his drink, returning it to the table.

"That's good to hear." Malidora leaned forward. She didn't have time to feel him out, not with the Nulthereals coming. She would have to be bold. As anxious as she was, she couldn't afford to let it show. "I was hoping you could help me find work. You've seen one of my many talents. I have a knack for finding misplaced items. Surely, that would be of benefit to someone as yourself."

"That is why I called you here." Klevet rested his chin in his hand, tapping his cheek with a finger. "There is one task, particularly vexing, that may provide an opportunity for you to . . . shall we say, redeem yourself."

"I'm up for a challenge." Malidora watched as a bird landed on a perch outside the window. Her eyes were drawn to a metal decoration of a triangle obscuring a circle.

"That's what I like to hear." Klevet leaned toward the table again to pick up his drink. "There's a cleaning company in the Nirus district. Strictly interior cleaning." He took a big sip of the drink this time and set it back on the table. "They've had some recent difficultly cleaning a certain establishment. It has become quite a stain on our community, you see." Crossing his legs again, he placed his hands on his lap. "Someone with your bravado may be more willing to take the necessary risks."

Malidora rubbed her knuckles together. "The risk to clean this establishment?"

"Yes, you see, we can't risk these stains getting on our hands."

"And what do I get in return?" Malidora slid back in her seat.

Klevet's attention was drawn to the hallway, as the female assistant came into the room. "You will be well compensated." He moved his eyes back to Malidora. "Find Laudra when you get to the Nirus district. She resides in a place called the Black Sun and will give you the details."

Malidora took that as a hint that it was time for her to leave and stood up. Klevet grabbed his glass and took another drink. "You have nice teeth," he said. "Has anyone ever told you that?"

"That's not usually what people notice about me."

"I would love to add them to my collection." Klevet motioned toward the display cases. "If you were to cross me."

"How far is this Nirus district?"

Klevet got up from his seat. "Nearly the other side of Vesta. If you need transport, Pyrina here will give you the necessary funds to get there."

Walking past Pyrina, Klevet left Malidora to sit and stare at the artificial view through the windows. Pyrina came over and stood beside where she sat. "I transferred some credits to your account."

Malidora peered up at her. "What account?"

Pyrina ran her hands over her suit, smoothing it out. "It's tied to your genetic signature. Everyone has one."

Malidora moved out into the sunlight as Pyrina ushered her out the door. As anxious as she was to get started on this task, she decided it best to explain her impending absence to Dabradan. With all that he had been through lately, she couldn't leave without telling him.

When she arrived at the block house, Dabradan, Cian, and a few others were dismantling the syvern. She explained to him about the job she had acquired and that she could be away for a bit.

Dabradan frowned. "I thought we were working together on this."

Malidora leaned toward him. "We are. I'm doing my thing. You are doing yours."

"I haven't been trying to ignore you or anything," Dabradan assured.

Malidora chuckled. "Don't worry about it. I'll be back before long."

She turned away, about to head toward the main road. Clenching her teeth together, she turned back and opened her arms to give Dabradan a hug. She was not much of a hugger, but perhaps the gesture would feel more reassuring. As he enveloped her in his thick arms, the exchange of body warmth soothed her. Perhaps she needed it more than she thought.

Once she made it to the busy main road, the random noises of the city made it difficult for her mind to wander. After a few blocks, she came to a building lined with baltons like the one Dabradan drove from Udamal. These platforms were much larger and carried more people. A crowd stood outside the building, perhaps waiting for a ride.

Malidora moved into the crowd, waiting for the next transport. Some of the Gesaurens stared at her as she stood outside the building. Though most of her skin and hair was covered, her clean tailored black clothing stood out compared to their dusty, ragged attire.

The next transport moved alongside the walkway, and people began boarding. An attendant scanned her hand with a handheld device and allowed her a seat. Apparently, credits were transferred from her account, but she had no idea how many were taken or what she had left.

"Move all the way to the end and take the last available seat," announced the man driving the platform.

She walked down the row of seats, stopping near the end next to a man and woman. Before long, the platform rose from the ground and began to slowly move down the road.

An alert sounded from the platform, and children scattered off the road as the platform went through. The man shifted closer to the Gesauren woman in the seat. "You know what I heard last shift? The companies that bought the governorships, they are supposed to be next in line to move up to the rings."

"Yeah, everyone knows that," said the woman as she dug through a small bag in her lap.

The platform moved into a more open area. Trees and vegetation grew in rows alongside the street. "I wasn't finished," the man said. "I heard that the reason they haven't moved up is so they can keep the power they have here."

Pipes running up from the ground showered water onto rows of trenched soil. Workers holding containers picked berries from lines of bushes. Others bent to gather from plants growing just above the soil.

"So what?" the woman pulled out a blue glowing screen, much like the one Toberin used to write on.

The man turned his body toward her. "So, they are holding everyone else back. We can't move up to the rings if they stay in that position."

She looked up from her screen as they went by a sparse group of buildings where Gesaurens herded groups of animals. "What does it matter? We'll never be able to buy into a governorship anyway."

"They're supposed to be helping us," said the man. "Not using their power against us."

The great walls around the city slanted upward as they moved further around the circumference. From a distance, the walls were higher at two sides, like wings that rose half the height of the tower in the center.

The platform slowed and soon stopped alongside a raised walkway with people gathered around. A sign read, "District of Alfor". The couple got up from their seats with the rest of the passengers and left the platform. More passengers boarded the platform, searching for empty seats.

As they began moving again, the spacious area turned back to the crowded buildings that defined the Ruvak district. These buildings, however, were much more appealing and well maintained. The ambience darkened as they passed under the shadow of the tall wing section of the wall. Rhythmic beats and melodies soared through the streets ahead. Colorful lights decorated the buildings and streets, providing some illumination in the darkness.

They came to a stop, and several passengers rose from their seats. A sign on the raised walkway read "Nirus". Malidora hurried past the other seats toward the front of the platform. Fully in the shadow of the wing of the wall, Malidora had to wait for her eyes to adjust to the darkness before moving down the ramp onto the lower walkway beside the street.

It was like nighttime under the huge shadow. She walked down the main road until she came to a crowd of Gesaurens in the street. Gesaurens swayed and danced to music coming from a stage where several musicians stood performing. Making her way through the mass, Malidora noticed a side road that was less packed. She eased onto the less dense street, passing places that resembled taverns.

Entering one of the dimly lit taverns, Malidora moved to the bar. Taverns were hubs of information; she only wished she had the time to play it cool and relax a bit while gathering data. With an impending attack, she couldn't relax anyway.

Inside the tavern, people appeared to be playing a game, swinging glowing light sticks at each other. Some sat in chairs formed into a circle. Music with a quick tempo played at a fairly high volume and mingled with the voices of the attendees. The keeper leaned on the bar talking to two women. He walked toward her.

"Welcome, what would you like?" He set his arms onto the bar.

Malidora leaned on the bar's cold, sticky surface, raising her voice to cut through the noise. "What do you recommend?"

"I like barch." The man reached under the bar and set a flask down on the surface. "The advanes even order it sometimes."

"Advanes?" Malidora ran her fingernails across the slick top of the bar.

"You know, the people that live on the first ring." The man pointed upward.

Malidora set both hands on the bar, tapping her fingernails on the wood. "They come down here?"

The keeper smiled. "All the time. They pay extra for special treatment too. We earn most of our credits serving them."

"I'll try one," she said.

He scanned her hand, fortunately she had enough credits left to buy it. The keeper mixed three different liquids together, sprinkling some kind of dust into it, and set it on the bar. Malidora examined the dark green beverage as she lifted the metal flask. The keeper watched as she took her first sip. It had a smooth creaminess to it but tasted a bit bitter. She puckered her lips a bit as she swallowed it.

"It's an acquired taste." The keeper smiled.

Malidora swirled her tongue around the inside of her lips. This world may not be around long enough to acquire a taste for this. "It's not bad."

"Yell if you would like another." The keeper started toward the other side of the bar.

"Let me ask you something." She set the flask down, and he returned as she placed her hands back onto the bar. "Where can I find the Black Sun?"

The keeper winked. "New to the Nirus district? When you go outside, you'll see it; it's the tallest building in the district."

"Thank you." She picked up the flask and took another drink.

The keeper leaned closer. "It's pretty exclusive though. You probably won't be able to get in."

Just a few moments later, the streets outside were as loud as inside the tavern, but the resonance was much greater. Malidora spun around until she found the tall building silhouetted against the ambient light of the street. It was shiny and black, reflecting the lights all around it. It had to be the Black Sun.

Wandering through the maze of side streets to avoid the chaos on the causeway, Malidora came to the triangular door of the Black Sun. When she drew near, the door seemed to rotate within its triangle frame. One section of its rotation showed a translucent blue shield that passed by at regular intervals. As the shield came around again, she stared through it into a long hallway inside. It disappeared and reappeared again. When the clear shield came back around, a tall figure stood close to her on the other side.

Instinctively, Malidora stepped back. The shield appeared again and this time it came to a stop.

"Do you have an appointment?" asked a bald Gesauren man who was behind the screen. He wore a strange suit with fringes around the sleeves and shoulders.

Malidora stepped forward. "I was told to meet with Laudra."

"And what is your business?"

Malidora paused for a moment before recalling her conversation with Klevet. "Klevet sent me. For cleaning."

The translucent shield dissipated, allowing her to step through.

"Ah yes, Laudra has been expecting you." The man in the purple suit stepped aside as Malidora entered the hall.

The shield reappeared behind her as the man led her past the hallway through a room with soft chairs. "This way." He opened a door to a flight of metal steps.

She followed him up to the top floor of the building. The man walked through a doorway toward an open room with a huge window overlooking the lights of the city below. On the balcony behind the glass, a feminine form stood, silhouetted against the glowing ambience.

The glass window parted as Malidora approached. Immediately the din of the crowded streets cut through the quiet of the interior.

"Quite the view, isn't it?" She wore an elegant black dress revealing much of her blue skin. Glowing orange gems adorned her neck and wrists. "Have you ever seen so many gathered together, undivided, for a common purpose?" The woman inhaled deeply as though breathing in the sights and sounds around them. "No promises, no rousing speeches, not even the thercon can assemble an audience like this."

Malidora stepped toward the railing to peer out at the crowds of

Gesaurens below. Some were dancing in the streets, others cheered near stages, as music or theater was being performed.

"The pleasures of the senses . . ." The woman held a shiny glass of a clear pink liquid over the railing. "Entertainment is the most influential power."

Malidora surveyed the scene, watching as many stood outside taverns and other venues. Some sat in grouped chairs watching projected images on screens.

"We bring together grounders, advanes, and even high elites looking for an experience they can find nowhere else. Through the power of entertainment, we can change minds, influence communities."

"I often find that as one's power grows, the less responsible they become." Malidora watched a group of Gesaurens coming down the street wearing odd green and red costumes. They wore hats with winged pieces that stood straight out. Their collars were similar.

"Power cannot properly thrive within the constraints of responsibility." The woman swayed with the music that played through the street. "All of Vesta benefits from what we do here. And the better it is for everyone else, the better it is for us. There's a harmony to it, a balance. It's part of the city's ecosystem. What we provide is what holds this city together, what keeps it all from spinning out of control."

"I suppose that works," said Malidora, "if you can adapt. Ecosystems never stay the same for long. The hunter eventually becomes the hunted."

"You must be Malidora." The woman took a sip from the glass as she leaned against the railing. "As you may have guessed," she turned to face Malidora, her hands raised away from her sides, "I am Laudra, Governor of Nirus." She had black shiny hair, short at the front and slanted longer in the back. It was cut with perfect edges, swinging and bouncing with the slightest movement. There was a certain glamorous alure about her, and she obnoxiously knew it. "Would you like a drink?"

Malidora forced a smile. "I never turn down a drink."

"Please, sit, get comfortable." She held a glass toward Malidora, sparkling as if made of light. It was thick and smooth to the touch. She took the glass and settled into a chair beside Laudra.

"Why do you wear a hood?" Laudra poured a pale green liquid into Malidora's glass.

Malidora rotated the glass in her hand, examining its shine. "I try to stay unnoticed."

"Take it off, there's no need to hide here." Laudra leaned back into her seat as she tilted the glass to her lips.

As Malidora slipped off the hood. Laudra sat up, staring at Malidora's hair and likely her bronze-colored skin.

Laudra's eyes grew. "Where did you get that done?"

Malidora wanted to tell her it was natural, but that would lead to many questions and possibly some disbelief if she told her she was from another world. "In Udamal."

"Really?" Laudra craned her neck. "I had no idea independents had any sense of fashion."

"Most do not." Malidora took a sip from the glass. The drink was effervescent with a taste of fruit and spice.

Leaning onto her side, Laudra curled her legs up into the chair. "If you are wondering why you are here, Klevet believes you may have some talents that could be of use." Laudra kicked off her shoes and stretched out her feet. "With you as a refugee . . . a new citizen, our meetings with you are entirely legitimate. The thercon encourages us to help new citizens. It's a unique opportunity for all of us."

"And what does the job entail?" Malidora brushed through her hair with her hand.

Laudra crossed her legs, propping her feet on the crystal table nearby. "Nirus has attracted a lot of attention over the cycles. Especially from the advanes. Some of them do not see it for the pleasures of sight and sound it offers but for the money that can advance them up to the second ring." Laudra downed the rest of her drink. "They are beginning to open businesses here, encroaching on what we have built." Laudra sat up and leaned toward Malidora. "This is grounder territory. We cannot let the advanes take business away from us."

"Is there a reward for whatever it is you want me to do?" Malidora set her drink down on the table beside them.

Laudra placed a finger in her glass, playing with the single drop of liquid left. "Payments will come from a variety of sources, totaling three hundred arculine credits"

"I have a counter proposal." Malidora said as Laudra's left eyebrow twitched. "There is a great threat coming to this city. Rather than money, I need to use your influence to convince whoever is in charge of defense and tell them that their weapons maybe be useless against the coming threat." Malidora tried to relax, setting her hands on the arms of the chair.

Trapping the remaining liquid between her finger and the glass, Laudra slid it toward the edge. "Not the counter I expected. I must tell you, the majority of defense is on the first ring, under the control of Therin Veridius, but you needn't worry. They will have no problem handling the beasts that attacked your cities. The defenses here are impenetrable."

"The beasts are meant to weaken your walls." Malidora moved her thick skirt so that she could cross her legs. "The real threat is the Shadows controlling them. Shadows that cannot be destroyed with flash weapons."

Laudra sucked the last drop from her fingertip. "We have more than flash rifles."

"I've only seen one thing that can destroy this enemy." Malidora reached into her quiver, extracting an arrow.

Leaning forward to set the glass on the table, Laudra wrapped her hands together, resting them on her knees. "And what is that?"

Malidora worked the dark stone out of the bolt and handed it to Laudra. Eyeing the black crystalline object, Laudra turned it in her hand. "What is this?"

"I call it shadowstone," Malidora said. "It is a piece of the Shadows after their ethereal forms have been neutralized and broken into stone."

Laudra scratched the black stone with her nail. "So their stone can turn the others to stone?"

"We have enough to kill a few, and then we can arm others to use their stone as weapons to fight them," said Malidora. "The more we destroy, the more we *can* destroy."

Laudra set the stone onto the table. "It's a very interesting rock, but I'm not sure anyone will believe your story without real evidence. I'll see what I can do."

"When the attack comes, you'll be up to your neck in evidence."

Malidora's eyebrow twitched as she stared at Laudra. "You will need the stone."

"If that is true, then I thank you for the gift." Laudra placed the shadowstone in a small bag sitting on the table. "Let's get you a place to rest. My assistants will take care of anything you need. We have several guest rooms. It gives the Black Sun a bit more legitimacy if it is used to house our citizens. In the next cycle, meet with my friend Brogin. He will give you further instruction."

CHAPTER 22

HOW PLEASANT IT was to sleep in the dark again. The windows turned to opaque black, blocking out the glowing lights from the street. A few dim lights illuminated the room with a blue color. Malidora stared at them from the bed. She imagined them as candles burning in the dark, binding nightmares to the darker places of the world outside. It brought a glimmer of comfort to a dire situation. Knowing the Nulthereals were out there and could attack the city at any moment—It was difficult to let herself relax and go to sleep. She glanced back at the light. How she was going to prepare the Gesaurens for this, she had no idea. Still, these events stirred something in her, it felt like being in Sinavus again. Perhaps if she was able to convince one person with enough influence, they would believe her.

When Malidora woke, she was given directions to a place called Fearmark, the location where Brogin would be. Laudra did not seem concerned with Malidora's warnings. It was doubtful that she would risk her standing on something she didn't believe. Malidora knew she had to find someone else. There had to be someone that suspected something strange about the attacks on the independent cities and was at least slightly concerned. Until then, she would have to play this game for a while longer.

The crowd outside had subsided only slightly. She worked her way around a group of onlookers as five dancers dressed in reflective white costumes performed. Malidora stopped to watch the strange dancing. Their dance, set to music, was a series of quick movements between dramatic still poses they would assume for a moment before moving again.

Soon she found the illuminated Fearmark sign with several Gesaurens in line waiting to enter. Malidora walked past the crowd and entered the building. The inside was illuminated in dim violet. Those inside relaxed in soft chairs, drinking silver-colored drinks. The clientele here mostly dressed in complicated clothing and smelled better than the crowds on the causeway.

Malidora walked toward the counter where two women and a man seemed to be setting up orders. Leaning against the white counter, Malidora turned to the man. "I'm looking for Brogin."

The man slowly turned in her direction, staring down his nose at her. "Name?"

The genetic signatures they used in this city made anonymity impossible. It was another aspect of Isodonia that she missed, the ability to craft a false persona.

"I go by Malidora," she stated.

The man's expression softened. "Oh yes, you're a bit earlier than he expected, but it's fine. Go ahead and take the lift."

He nodded toward a round platform behind the counter. As she stepped onto the platform, it rose, taking her to the next floor.

Striding onto the oddly soft flooring ahead, she moved toward an open room where a man stood over a girl who sat reclined in a raised chair. The man held a bladed object to her skin below her neck. Malidora paused, uncertain what she was witnessing. He began cutting into her skin as the girl winced in pain.

Malidora moved toward the man. "Whoa—What are you doing?"

He raised up to acknowledge Malidora. "What do you think I'm doing?" He went back to cutting the girl. "I'm creating art."

The girl opened her eyes. "Wait your turn! Don't interrupt while he's doing my scar!"

Malidora took a seat in one of the chairs on the other side of the room as the man finished the cut. He picked up a bottle and scooped out some gray gel inside. Removing a red stained cloth, he put some of the gel in the girl's wound. She yelped as he tapped his fingers on the wound, rubbing the gel into the cut.

After wrapping the area with a sticky fabric, he helped the girl out of the chair.

"This is going to look so good!" She smiled as she walked to the lift, pressing her hand over the taped wound.

Malidora stood and moved toward the chair as the man put his hands under a cylinder, cleaning them in the rushing water that poured out.

"You must be the refugee." He blotted his red stained hands onto a cloth.

"Brogin?" Malidora set her elbow down on the back of the large chair.

"Yes." He turned around and moved toward a table with many small cutting tools. "Would you like a scar designed specifically for you?"

"No thank you, I have enough already." Malidora pulled up her sleeve to reveal remnants of an old wound on her forearm. She recalled the face of the man who got the better of her, a swordsman with a mustache. She let him get too close before jackknifing to safety, dispatching him with two bolts to the chest. Her scars served as reminders of her mistakes.

Brogin crossed his arms. "Where did you have yours done?"

"They were a gift from my foes," Malidora said. "I gifted back, but unfortunately for them they were never able to see my work."

"Battle scars? Interesting. You never see those anymore." Brogin squinted as if examining the scar. "Perhaps Laudra sent the right person this time and your refugee status makes it so much easier to deny involvement."

"Are you going to tell me what the job is?" Malidora studied his face, attempting to read his expressions. "I'm a bit weary of the runaround."

"Straight to business," Brogin said. "I like it." He turned away from Malidora, pacing around the room. "There's a new shop in Nirus, called Embliss, doing body modifications." He spun around. "Things like that hair you have and your discolored skin, but they also do designer scars like we do here."

"Ah, this is about competition," said Malidora.

"It's more than that." Brogin began pacing again. "This business is funded by an advane named Yevallo. This business will funnel money to the rings, money that should go to grounders."

"Or to you specifically." Malidora ran her hand over the soft cushion of the back of the chair. "So, you want me to put them out of business."

"Not exactly," said Brogin. "He has a competitive advantage. With access to information available to the first ring, he and the other advanes could pose a serious threat to our businesses. Give us that information, and we will be unstoppable. Yevallo holds a device that can access the entire network of genetic signatures. We need you to steal it and bring it to us. We have people that can break the security on it where we can use it as we wish. Laudra controls security forces in Nirus. She will see to it that no one is in your way. Just remember, if you decide to talk, no one is going to believe a refugee over a district governor."

"Of course." Malidora moved over to a surface extending from the far wall. "I know how this works."

"The payment will be transferred to your account signature," Brogin said. "Don't expect it to be all at once."

"How will I find the target?" Malidora picked up a clear book with words and pictures made of light, showing various designs of scars to choose from.

Brogin wiped his hand over his mouth, "The target is the business. He comes down about every three cycles. Sometimes he stays over a cycle. That should put him here two cycles from now."

Thumbing through the book, she said, "I need somewhere to stay in the meantime."

"A room has been arranged for you at Teravane," said Brogin. "It's one of the many places Laudra owns."

❧

Malidora spent the rest of the cycle watching the musicians and other entertainers in the street. Some of the large buildings offered supposedly premium shows, but there was a cost to enter. Her room at Teravane was comfortable, allowing her a place to bathe, food to eat, and a soft bed to sleep on.

Even with so much to distract her as she waited for the day of the advane's arrival, Malidora grew increasingly antsy. The image of the horde of Nult-hereals they saw in Blackfrost weighed on her mind. Flashes of the recent dead plagued her. Toberin, Hanovus, and Olien slumped over the control panel. She saw the defeated look on Dabradan's face when they returned to a deserted Udamal. The child-like innocence in the eyes of Evala as she drew her last breaths peering up at the clear, starry skies of Underveil. Ravetaria's weary expression as she left Malidora and Dabradan at the terminator.

To steal this device, she would have to study the target carefully. Following him for day or weeks would be necessary to learn his movements. She would need to see him use it and observe where he keeps it on him. Time was an expense she could not afford. What was coming for them would not wait.

Her mind went to Plagat teaching her how to siphon elu from their crystal constraints. *You can't wait for something to happen, you have to make it happen.*

It was unlike Malidora to dwell on those she crossed paths with, but it was the only reason she was still on this planet. She checked her pouch to ensure that she still had the nyalith shard. If things went bad, she may not be able to get back to the pool and leave this place.

On the cycle before the advane was to arrive, Malidora could no longer wait. Time was not on her side. The Nulthereals were surely closing in. Even though the Whidge was destroyed, they had the numbers to turn all of Vesta against itself. She had to find someone who would listen.

She loaded her crossbow and marched toward Embliss. Shining in blue lights, Embliss was wider than Fearmark but only one floor. As she pushed her way through the crowd outside, someone grabbed her shoulder.

"Hey! Get back in the line!" shouted a man, grabbing her from behind. Malidora clutched his arm and forcefully shoved him back. As he lunged at her, she shifted her leverage, using his imbalance against him as she flipped him to his back onto the ground. She had planned to go the subtle route, but now she had intimidated those who stood in line. The more direct approach was in play.

The crowd stepped back as she strode past them into the building. Malidora pushed aside a customer talking to a man at the main desk. "I need to see Yevallo."

The man pursed his lips as his eyes moved from his screen to Malidora. "He's not here today."

Malidora leaned toward him. "Who's in charge?"

The man took a deep breath before he began. "If you have a complaint—"

"Who's in charge?" she roared.

The man at the counter said nothing but swayed his head toward a hallway behind him. Storming down the hall as it turned right and then left, she passed several white rooms, some with doors closed, others open. Through the glass of one of the shut doors a team of people wearing masks stood over a woman lying on slanted bed. Her eyes were closed as if she were asleep. One of the masked people standing over the woman glanced toward Malidora as she walked by.

At the end of the hall was a door made of grained wood, it stood out from the sterile white rooms in the rest of the building. As she reached for the door console, clomping footsteps moved quickly toward her. The sound was accompanied by the scent of adrenalin.

Malidora removed the crossbow from her side, and its arms snapped into place as its tension cord was pulled taut. Shifting her weight on the tips of her toes, she charged quietly toward the sound. As she approached the corner of the hall, a man wearing a black utility suit stepped out sooner than expected.

He aimed his flash weapon as she fired two arrows whistling into his arm and shoulder. As he gasped in shock, Malidora charged in, swiping the heel of her hand into his nose. The man lunged back, absorbing most of the blow. With momentum leaning her toward the wall, she spun and brought her left foot under his chin. The blow sent him off his feet, bouncing against the ceiling, and into a limp pile on the floor.

Confused by the strength of her kick, she realized that she was wearing Evala's repulsor boots. Apparently, they had applications other than high jumping. Malidora retrieved her shadowstone arrows from the man's unconscious body and dragged him into one of the open rooms. She picked up his rifle from the floor.

When she got back to the wooden door, she attempted to open it with the control box, but it would not budge. Blasting the controls with the rifle, the door popped loose from the hold. As Malidora slid open the door, a girl came running toward her.

"What is going on out there—" the girl asked as Malidora grabbed her, holding her body in front of her. The girl tensed up and began to struggle against her grip. A man with short red hair stood from his desk, turning toward her. "What is the meaning of this?"

"I need to see Yevallo." Malidora pulled the girl toward her and slid the door closed.

The man took a step toward her. "Who are you?"

"My name is a mark of death." She pointed the rifle at him before moving it back to the girl. "Anyone who hears it will die. But I'm hoping it won't come to that."

Laying his arms at his sides, the man stared at her. "Why would I allow Yevallo to meet with a killer?"

"Killer?" Malidora said. "I haven't killed anyone, yet. This is strictly business."

The girl stopped fighting and began to relax, perhaps resigned that she couldn't break Malidora's hold. As she circled the room, the door slid open suddenly. Two men and a woman in black uniforms moved into the room. Malidora took the girl she was holding and slung her by the arm into the first man. As he stumbled back, Malidora fired a flash bolt into his chest. Before she could turn, the second man kicked her between the shoulder and neck, knocking the rifle from her grip. Springing backward, Malidora reached for an arrow. As the man charged toward her, she fired a bolt into him as she rolled to her feet. The female guard fired as Malidora grabbed hold of her weapon. The girl ran out of the room as the guard and Malidora fought to get the upper hand.

The guard was stronger and able to control Malidora's movement. As the guard swung her arms to the side trying to break her hold, Malidora ended her resistance. She allowed the guard to snatch the weapon from her and throw her to the ground as Malidora used the momentum to catch the floor and spring up with her hands while shoving her foot into the guard's chest. The force of her boots launched the woman backward into the wall and crumbling to the floor. So much for making this clean.

"Not a killer?" The man waited in front of the desk.

Malidora stood, adjusting her clothes. "A girl should be allowed to defend herself, don't you think? If you're not the hammer, you'll end up the nail."

"More will be coming," the man warned, "if you leave now, you may be able to escape."

Irredeemable, said a voice in her head. Though it sounded like Razinoth, it was her own conscience. Malidora tried to shake the thought from her mind as she quickly went over her options. She had already decided to flip the job Brogin gave her into something else. Something that had more chance of getting what she needed. Working for the governors wouldn't get her anywhere, not in the short amount of time she had to save this world."

Malidora brushed her fingers through her hair. "I'm trying to help you. I came to warn Yevallo that they want him dead."

"Who wants him dead?"

"Brogin." Malidora folded the crossbow together, placing it in the holster at her side. "And some of the district governors."

The man's eyes wandered around the room. "That's quite a charge. How would you know this?"

"Because they hired me to do it." Malidora bent down, pulling the female guard by the arm toward the wall where the other two lay. *You're the only one I've known who never lied to me,* Evala's words made her want to live up to that sentiment. To think of them now as she was doing this made her feel sick, but she was doing this for her. To make sure that her death was not in vain.

The man took a deep breath. "What do you want?"

"First, I'll need protection." Malidora pulled an arrow out of one of the guards on the floor and placed it into her quiver. "I need to get on the first ring."

"I can't get you on the rings!" The man sat in the chair in front of the desk. "What about credits? Credits I can do."

"If all I wanted was credits, you wouldn't be alive right now," Malidora moved toward him. "If you can't get me on the rings, I have no use for you. The governors want this place shut down. If I can't get to Yevallo, I'll have to give you to them."

The man rubbed his forehead. "Let me speak to him. Privately."

"No, it has to be in front of me." Malidora pulled both of her gloves down tight.

"All right." The man stood up and walked to a table on the other side of the room. Picking up a small device, he returned to his seat.

"Don't try anything stupid. This kill order won't end with me," Malidora tapped her fingers above her elbow as she folded her arms. "Yevallo's only chance is with me. If something happens to me, they will simply hire someone else to finish the job."

The man pressed a button on the device. His breaths came short and quick as he waited. After a few moments, a voice came over the device. "Esid? I trust this is important."

"I believe it is," the man said. "I'm here with someone that is stating your life is in danger."

"What makes you think this is credible?" the voice said over the device.

Esid inhaled deeply again. "She says she was hired to kill you and needs protection. She wants to be moved to the first ring."

Yevallo laughed. "And who is she saying hired her?"

"Brogin and some of the district governors," said Esid.

There was no response for a moment as Esid glanced at Malidora.

"What is this person's name?" Yevallo inquired.

Esid cleared his throat. "She doesn't wish to give her name."

"I need to find her signature code," Yevallo said. "I can't verify without a name."

Esid's eyes cut to Malidora. "He needs your name."

"I heard," she said.

"You're not going to kill me if I hear it, are you?" Esid said.

"That depends." Malidora smirked. "Can you keep it secret?"

Esid nodded.

"Malidora."

"Did you get that?" Esid spoke into the device.

"I'm looking it up now," said Yevallo. "Here it is. Only one Malidora in Vesta. Registered a few shifts ago as a refugee. From one of the independent territories, interesting."

Esid glanced at Malidora as he spoke into the device. "What do you make of it?"

"Analytics check out. What is going on with your signature?" said Yevallo. "Your genetics are outside the parameters."

Malidora leaned toward Esid's device. "They keep telling me they are going to fix that."

"Ah well, if they don't care, I don't care. Let's see, met with the Ruvak governor, standard procedure. The only thing slightly odd is that she met him the second time at his home. The governor of Ruvak doesn't typically invite new residents to his home. That's only happened—twenty-two times."

Malidora paced in front of Esid as he stared at the device. After a brief pause, Yevallo continued. "Seems he sent her to Nirus for work, pretty normal. The Nirus governor then sent her to Fearmark, presumably for assigned work. Fearmark does have openings for sterile environment clean up."

Esid eyed Malidora. "You don't believe her story?"

"The analysis doesn't bear it out," Yevallo said. "No arculine transfers except for some metal tools she sold and transportation."

Malidora moved closer. "I didn't sell any tools, but they did put some credits on my account."

"Even though the analysis doesn't show anything suspicious, her story adds up," Yevallo said. "They did a good job of keeping everything looking normal. And she's a refugee from the independent territories. She has no credibility if something goes wrong. We knew Brogin would try to interfere, but we didn't know he would go this far."

Turning away from Malidora, Esid raised the device to his mouth. "What do you want to do?"

"I'll meet with her. Only her. No weapons. With my security unit present. I have some questions I would like her to answer," said Yevallo. "Send her to the tower elevator. I'll be at the fifty-five-mark platform. I'll see to it that her status is changed to first ring access."

CHAPTER 23

MALIDORA RODE WITH Esid through the shadow of the high wing of the wall. The dirt street became patterns of brick as they entered the light near the huge base of the tower. She could not keep doing this. If she was ever going to join real society again, she had to stop harming others, even for a noble cause. She could hear Legotian and Trace arguing in her head. Trace would be proud, but even though Legotian was the biggest motivation for this, he would be scolding her for it. Malidora promised Evala she would not let the Shadows win, but was not sure either Evala or Dabradan would approve either. The balton slowed to a stop, and Esid pointed his eyes toward the tower as if a gesture of what she needed to do next.

Despite no scents of adrenaline or other chemicals associated with fear or malicious intent, Malidora kept her guard up. Stepping out onto the hard brick street, Malidora put on her hood. An arched pathway tunneled through the base of the tower to where it stood on four huge legs at the surface. Monuments and statues adorned with bright blue flowers and flowing fountains underneath the tower made it the most beautiful place she had seen of Vesta so far. It was a shame she didn't have more time; she would have liked to have taken a better look.

Trying to avoid appearing lost or new, Malidora headed straight to one of the lifts. She passed two security patrol guards armed with flash rifles standing near the lift. A group entered the lift as she walked toward, but there was enough room to accommodate her. She slipped inside as another small group of Gesaurens boarded.

Before it started, an alarm sounded, causing the two guards to run toward them. Malidora shuffled behind two people that looked to be a mother and daughter. The guards continued rushing toward the lifted. She hoped it would take off into the air before they reached her, but it didn't move.

A red light began flashing from the floor as the alarm continued to screech. The guards entered the lift, stopping at the red flashing octagon shaped section of the floor. The other passengers moved away from the red floor section occupied by a young man.

"You don't have clearance to the rings!" one of the guards shouted as they led the man out of the lift compartment. Malidora exhaled, relived they weren't after her. After a few moments all the octagons lit up blue and the lift started. The city shrank beneath her through the thick glass until their view became obscured by metal pipes and cables. Once they passed the through the inner workings of the ring, the light returned as the lift came to rest on a new surface.

She stepped onto a firm mesh ground as the others disembarked the lift. A circular runway filled with buildings of varied sizes and shapes stretching ahead against a backdrop of clouds and pale sunlight. Arms of streets extended from the tower like the spokes of a wheel, reaching to the circular platform of the ring.

The ground level, mostly chaotic and dilapidated at the bottom, displayed order and significance from up here. Searching for a glimpse of Ruvak, she couldn't make out anything familiar. For a moment, her focus waned. She hoped that Dabradan was well. All the loss she had witnessed in the past few cycles came back to press on her mind. She hated to imagine what it did to him. Though it made her feel a little better knowing that he had made the same mistakes as she in her first encounters with the Shadows.

Malidora pulled her hood tight against the breeze. She walked with the crowd toward one of the large arms that extended from the tower platform to the exterior ring. The streets were almost clear with a tint of yellow and white markings that covered it. Some streets seemed made for baltons only while others were for walking. Between the streets were unusual trees and plants that curled and spiraled around themselves. Perfectly smooth buildings and clean shops were grouped together along the roads.

Etched into a stone monument was the number ninety. Unsure what the numbers signified, Malidora continued down the street toward the ring. After what proved to be a long walk, she came to the circular ring that surrounded the tower. Much wider than the arms joining them to the tower, the ring was like a city unto itself. Beautiful parks of lush green grass and trees were surrounded by pristine structures of haspere and stone. More of the spiraling trees on multi-tiered walkways bordered by flowing water that cascaded over terraced stone. Peaceful music mimicked the running waters, played from everywhere around her.

The street around the arm led to a round platform bulging out from the rest of the width of the ring. The number ninety was etched on a few of the monuments standing in the area. Around the outside of the circle was a path leading into a small structure overlooking the horizon below. She was supposed to be on platform fifty-five. Another monument read, one hundred thirty-five and pointed toward the other direction. Nearby she found one that said fifty-five and pointed the direction she faced. Hoping that meant she was heading the right way, she continued further on.

Fifty-five marked the arch over the next round platform. A wall of shrubbery separated the pathways, making it confusing like a maze. As she moved down the sloped path, separations in the hedgerow revealed a fountain in the middle of the platform. It was surrounded by sculpted haspere in the form of four-legged animals she had not yet seen in Kandom. Slender and muscular with fierce teeth and eyes, a symbol of both beauty and strength.

Two children placed the bulbs of a pink flowers into the reservoir of the fountain as an older woman stood behind them. The water splashed, tossing the flowers around the pool as they watched.

"You're not from around here." The statement from somewhere to the right seemed directed at her. Malidora turned to find a medium-aged man with white hair. He wore a coat, nearly black, with two bands of material that tucked under his belt and hanging down the sides of his lighter colored pants.

Malidora turned back to the fountain as a cold wind wrestled with her cloak. "What tipped you off?"

"You're too young to be as out of style as I am," he remarked, grinning as though it was a clever joke.

A man in a black suit, like the uniforms of those she had fought in Embliss, approached from the row of bushes surrounding the fountain. Another black-suited security person drew her attention from a different direction. Five in total, walked toward them. They stood around her silent and still.

"If you would follow us," the man said, "this will be less conspicuous."

As the man and the security detail moved from the walkway on the platform to the clear street of the ring, Malidora trailed behind. From the large street, they took a path around a small park, through rows of trees twisted into various shapes.

They came to a multi-level apartment with many windows, the outside made of light brown stone with deep textured lines. The roof was smallest in the middle and swept up at both ends of the building. One of the uniformed guards moved up a row of steps to the second level, standing beside one of the doors.

"As you have probably gathered, I am Yevallo," the white-haired man said. "You are invited to the feast at the 6.7 cycle mark."

Malidora's nose wrinkled. "What does that mean?"

"The 6.7 mark?" Yevallo checked a device on his wrist. "Don't worry about it, you will be summoned. For now, purify yourself, I'll arrange for some appropriate clothing to be delivered."

Up the stairs she ran, excited at the thought of a bath. She walked past the guard, and the door opened automatically as she drew close. After sliding the door shut behind her, she barely noticed anything about the room as she searched for a means of cleaning herself off. Around the corner at the back, there was large pool with a fountain in the middle.

As she inspected the fountain, water began jetting from slits all around it. The water was warm and inviting. She quickly began removing her layers of clothing, excited to get in. After taking off the vest coat, she reached into one of the pouches on her belt. Malidora pulled out the nyalith shard, staring at its faint green haze shining from the inside. She had no idea what she was supposed to do with it, but she couldn't afford to lose it. Evala, Olien, Hanovus, and Toberin, if they died for anything at all, that shard was the only hope left. She placed the shard carefully back into the pouch. Piling her clothes on the floor, Malidora stepped into the pool.

"Your dress is here," said a voice outside the door.

After feeling clean and a bit more relaxed, Malidora climbed out of the pool as the water drained and warm air dried her off. She found a dark robe hanging on the wall nearby and put it on. As she slid the door open, the guard handed her an oblong container. She opened it to find a silvery blueish dress made of shiny reflective material. It had a hard, shoulder piece that held a sash across the front. The sash was the same color as the dress but sparkled with tiny glittering objects. She tried it on. The dress split above her waist, exposing her stomach, and flowing into two ribbon pieces that hung over her legs as part of the skirt. Three more ribbons made up the rest of the skirt over her hips and in the back. Sparkling translucent leggings ending at her thighs were included to wear underneath.

It wasn't something she would have chosen on her own, but it was fun to play the part of someone else. Perhaps someone she could have been in another life. At least on this occasion, she would be Malidora, advane on the first ring in the city of Vesta. The more she thought about it, she could hardly believe she made it here. Thousands of people on the ground seemed to have lived their whole lives never seen the first ring and she had made it in a few days. Maybe there had been some luck involved, but it was mostly her ability to adapt to unexpected or changing situations.

The guard patted her down as she exited the room, then escorted her to a platform vehicle that took her to platform 180. As she exited the vehicle, she stood in front of a structure mostly made haspere, cut like gemstones. The building was comprised of round buildings fused together each with domed roofs. Clear glass squares fanned out around the circumferences of each structure, while vertical pieces stood between them.

For a moment her stomach tingled. What was she doing here? She was completely out of place in this world. She must look like a fool trying to fit in. Malidora took in a slow deep breath, holding it until she could get into the right mindset. Reminding herself she had done this many times in Sinavus. The only difference was this was on a foreign planet. All it took was the appearance of strong confidence. Once she played that part, the confidence became real. She exhaled.

Surveying the room, she found a large room filled with red cushioned booths. Most of them filled with Gesaurens, old and young, with oddly styled hair and unusual colors. One woman had dark pink hair swept into different levels. Another showed off her lengthy unnatural fingers. Scars shaped into various symbols adorned the skin of others. Some had striped skin patterns. In this place, her hair and skin would not stand out.

Yevallo stood from his seat and waved her over. He wore a red and white suit with a raised, serrated collar that stuck out like blades. A man and a woman sat on each side of him. The man wore orange and blue and twirled a glass cylinder that placed in his mouth. The woman had golden horns on her forehead that parted her green hair.

Malidora sat in front of Yevallo, waiting for him to speak first. He took a tube from a dish on the table and squeezed the contents into his mouth. After chewing for a moment, he fixed his eyes on Malidora. "From an independent town to the first ring of Vesta. You look as though you've lived on the rings forever."

"Must be the dress," she said as she adjusted herself in the seat.

Yevallo continued chewing. "No, you have the look. Your hair, your skin . . . you're novel . . . individual . . . divergent. A true first ring advane, not compliant to what the high ring think you should be. What do you think, Gima?"

The woman with horns eyed her smugly. "She's on her way, I suppose."

Yevallo waved at someone behind Malidora. "We've given you protection. Now I hope you will indulge some of our questions."

The man beside Yevallo took the cylinder from his mouth. "There are rumors that some, maybe all, of the district governors have conspired together to find ways to keep themselves on the ground, never moving to the rings."

"Apparently the thercon never expected the governors to want to stay on the ground and never move to the rings," Yevallo said.

Gima rested her arms on the table. "When you control where the money goes, you hold all the power."

"The concordance needs to be changed," said Yevallo. "It was believed that when the owner of a company bought the governor position that they would be the best to manage funding to their districts. Part of moving up to the rings is showing how you can make your district flourish."

Two men in white rolled a cart over with small slices of meat, mixed with red and yellow plants. The combination of meat and plants were held together with a stringy material weaved through each piece. They placed three of the mixed strands of food onto all four of their plates. The food resembled a necklace with different jewels strung on it.

The man in orange and blue put down the glass cylinder and picked up the item of food. Holding both ends of the limp string, he nibbled on the pieces it held together. "I've only been to Nirus. What does the rest of the ground look like?"

Malidora watched as they held the strange food up to their mouths taking small bites of it. "Ruvak is horrible. The people there are miserable. It's dirty. The buildings are—"

"We get the idea," said Yevallo as he finished half of the oblong food. "Do you believe that Ruvak and Nirus are conspiring together for their own ends, ignoring those they serve in their own districts?"

Malidora picked up the stringy ends of the food and held it close to her lips. "The governors? They are definitely working together. To what purpose I couldn't say." She took a bite but got too much. She broke the stringy plant tying it all together and the contents spilled out onto the table and into her lap.

Yevallo raised an eyebrow, searching the room like he was uncertain what to do.

"I spotted some colleagues of mine." Gima stood up from the table. "I am going to sit with them."

Malidora tried to put herself somewhere else in her mind and avoid the embarrassment that began to flood into her.

One of the attendants came over and helped clean the table and Malidora's dress. After they finished eating, they moved outside. Yevallo called someone to drive Malidora back to the apartment.

"We'll discuss this further in the next cycle," he said as baltons floated in a circular area on one side of the restaurant. "We may need you to keep up your employ with the governors and have you go back to the ground. There's some planning we need to do first."

Malidora pivoted toward him. "I don't want to go back. I need to speak to those in charge of defense."

Yevallo glanced toward the street. "That may take some time, but we'll handle it. In the meantime, you will be well taken care of."

The vehicle arrived, slowly making its way around the circle. Malidora climbed onto the platform, riding around the ring the way she came. As they came to platform fifty-five, the thought of staying in a boring room under guard watched did not appeal to her.

"Drop me off here," she told the driver.

He slowed down but continued toward the apartment. "I'm instructed to take you directly to the apartment."

"The apartment is right there. I just want to get some fresh air before going back to my room. Then I'll walk over."

The vehicle came to a stop on the part of the street that went through the platform area. "Very well, it's easier turn around here anyway."

She walked past the fountain and around the hedgerow maze toward the edge of the ring overlooking the sky. Her long shadow cut through the orange reflection on the stone path as she headed toward an observation deck. Moving from the path into a climate-controlled structure with large windows, Malidora sat down in one of the seats nearby.

Violet-gray clouds floated near the sun as the ground area was bathed in orange light. The low sun hung permanently in the dust of the atmosphere. It must have been dustier on this cycle making the sun appear larger than normal.

After all the fighting, the fear and mind-bending madness, what a contrast it was up here. Peaceful, blissful silence, only the sounds of the flowing fountain and the occasional breeze as she stared at the painted sky. It was odd how the farther away you get from other life forms, the more peaceful the world seemed. It was perfect and calm, unstained by the drama of living creatures. If only this moment could be frozen in time.

Perhaps stasis was the state of true perfection. A singular moment captured and unchanging. Afterall, it was action and change that gives way to chaos. One event leading to another, a chain reaction that turns serenity into bliss and sorrow. A candle lit with a motionless, eternal flame.

A huge bird soared through the sky just past the observation deck. The graceful creature seemed to notice her before it flew off toward the light of the sun and out of sight into the great beyond. On the other hand, perhaps perfection could not encapsulate beauty. Maybe it was the unpredictable, the roll of the dice, the lovely calamity that change brought.

Could it be the flicker of the candle that was truly beautiful? The risk of wind that either feeds the flame to its brightest or extinguishes it completely. Perhaps this is why the universe had to allow the bad along with the good. As much as she had seen of the bad, she couldn't let the Shadows put out the universe.

She wasn't sure what her next play would be, but whatever it was she had to find it quickly. At least at this moment there were no Shadows coming toward them on the dusty horizon. Reclining in the chair, she took in the view allowing her thoughts to drift unwarily. Before she realized, her eyelids began to drop. Like a feather falling side to side slowly easing its way to the ground, Malidora passed into the numbness of sleep.

An alarm sounded nearby, startling her awake. "Attention. Please move away from balconies and observation points."

Malidora stood up, searching the area to determine what was happening. Soldiers in helmets that covered half of their faces wearing gray and black armor moved toward the observation deck. Ushering people away from the immediate area, the soldiers spread out into two columns as a young man, possibly around her age, came dashing toward the observation point.

"What is the latest report?" The young man had perfectly coifed, short white hair that was slightly spiked upward on each side. He was dressed in a regal black suit with blue ridges on its sides. The suit top lay below his waist like a skirt but remained tight against his hips. Gold threading highlighted details on the jacket. Over his shoulders was a black cape with red lining, flowing behind him with the breeze.

One of the soldiers lifted a bright screen from his vest to where he could see it in front of his face. "Still closing."

The man rushed ahead toward the structure where Malidora stood watching.

"My therin, we have not cleared that area yet," informed a soldier that did not wear a covering over his face. His vest bore red marks on the shoulders.

The man in the cloak ignored the soldier and continued on the observation deck until he entered the room with Malidora.

"Advanes are not supposed to be in this area." The man walked up to the glass, staring out into the open.

Malidora moved toward the window beside him. "Then why are you here?"

He pointed excitedly. "There they are!"

Malidora gazed out the window toward the clouds of dust near the horizon. Rows of armored beasts were running full speed toward Vesta. The same beasts that wrecked the independent cities.

CHAPTER 24

THE REGAL WHITE-HAIRED young man eagerly leaned on the glass. "This is going to be fantastic!"

"They'll be in range in point one seven." The voice of the unmasked soldier was closer.

With a whirring and the sound of metal sliding on metal, huge cylinders extended from below the rim of the ring.

Malidora eyed him as he stared at the approaching beasts. "You know those things have thick armor, right?"

The man in the cloak kept his eyes on the view of the charging animals. "It doesn't matter, our flash cannons will take care of them."

"I've seen these creatures take down the walls of Udamal and Mortagon, flash rifles didn't do much against them," said Malidora.

"Rifles?" the young man scoffed. "These are ploxor flash cannons, quite a difference from rifles."

The unmasked solider entered the terrace. "What are you doing here? Take her away at once!"

"Let her stay, Trinavus." The man smirked. "I want to see her reaction when our cannons shred these creatures."

"Very well, my therin." The soldier held up his hand to the encroaching troopers. The other soldiers stopped in their tracks.

The dust subsided temporarily, revealing multiple rows of beasts.

"Where did these things come from?" The therin briefly eyed the solider.

Trinavus stepped closer to the window. "Unknown."

"They came from Underveil," advised Malidora.

"Underveil? I thought Underveilians couldn't see in the light," said the therin.

Trinavus glared at Malidora. "You are correct, my therin. She must be joking."

Malidora turned around to face them. "They are being controlled, running blind."

"What? Who could be controlling them?" questioned the therin.

"Shadows . . . Whisperers . . . Nulthereals." Malidora watched their reflections on the glass. "Whatever you want to call them. They have the ability to persuade, control minds. They are the true threat to your city."

Trinavus moved around the therin to grab the shoulder of Malidora's dress. "You realize who you are speaking to, advane! This is Therin Veridius, son of Thercon Merrigan and heir to the Naldus of Vesta. You are graced to be in his presence!" Malidora stared back at Trinavus with a smirk on her face. Only great actions impressed her, not titles or fancy clothing.

"Almost in range!" shouted a voice from below them. "Prepare to fire!"

Veridius turned back to the window, pressing his face to his hands that he had shaped around the glass. Trinavus let go of her dress, focusing on the scene before them.

"Fire!"

A low boom ending with a high-pitched squeal rang out as red sizzling bolts launched from the cannons below. The energy blasts came from underneath the rings, flying toward the line of armored creatures. The booming of the cannons filled the air, breaking the serenity and shaking the deck they stood on.

The terrain exploded with fiery energy as the blasts hit, scattering debris and dust. Lines of creatures moved around piles of dirt and craters caused by the blasts. The cannons continued firing at the rows of beasts as they seemed to come to a stop at the wall of clouds of dust and debris.

"This is amazing!" Veridius clasped his hands together, nearly cheering.

As the smoke and dust abated, it became clear that piles behind them weren't piles of dirt. It was the remains of the armored beasts annihilated by the powerful cannons. Trails of dust stretched out from the craters, mixed with dark red. Malidora stared, surprised at the damage the large guns had wrought on these armored monsters that had been a complete menace to the smaller cities.

The guns fell silent as the last animal was destroyed.

Veridius turned to Malidora, smiling gleefully. "What was that you were saying about their armor?"

"Impressive," she replied. "Though I'm not sure we'll be so fortunate when the Nulthereals arrive."

"Vesta is untouchable." Veridius extended his hand toward the smoking corpses on the ground. "There is nothing capable of reaching our walls."

"Nulthereals are not solid like those beasts." Malidora crossed her arms. "Unless your cannons can connect with them, we are still in grave danger."

"Lies! You have insulted our therin enough!" Trinavus snarled.

Veridius held up a finger in front of Trinavus. "At least lies can be intriguing. Much more so than these tiresome meetings you keep dragging me to."

Trinavus gave a quick nod. "Speaking of meetings, therin, we're going to be late for the lorus ball."

"Dreadful . . ." Veridius turned, leaving the covered terrace as Trinavus followed after him. Malidora peered out at the carnage in front of the walls of the city.

Veridius walked back into the terrace, standing in the entryway. "I didn't get your name."

Why did everyone around here ask for her name? She used to walk through the streets unnoticed on Isodonia.

"Malidora."

"Malidora, seeing as you are already dressed for it," Veridius extended his hand, "would you accompany me to the ball?"

She almost forgot she was still wearing the sparkling gown. Malidora glanced at his hand then looked away. The beckoning hand of governance, promising everything and delivering nothing. This young man represented everything she despised about those who had been given unearned power over others. "I'm afraid I don't have access to the second ring."

"Nonsense." Veridius waved his hand. "Trinavus, see to it."

Trinavus pulled a small device from a pouch on his belt. It projected a larger blue square, and Trinavus moved his fingers to different locations inside the square. She couldn't tell what he was doing inside the projection but supposed it was something only seen from his side of the screen.

"A moment ago, you said it would be dreadful," Malidora said. "That's not exactly selling me on the idea."

"You would refuse Therin—?" Trinavus huffed as he peered at her above the screen.

Veridius placed his hand on Trinavus' chest. "That will be all, Trinavus." Veridius grinned as he turned back to Malidora. "It would be dreadful without your company. Your novel beauty will be the talk of the ball. What's that word, Trin? The one the advane use. Derelict?"

"Divergent, I believe," Trinavus continued moving his fingers inside the projected light.

Veridius nodded. "The elder elites hate the unconventional appearances that you advanes seem to love. I want to see their faces when you walk in with me. Isn't that what the divergent live for?"

"I suppose it would pass the time until my other obligations." Malidora took his hand, and he led her past the soldiers around the hedges to a shiny silver vehicle surrounded by guards waiting for him. This vehicle was sleeker than the baltons. It was smaller and covered on all sides with windows shaped around it. Veridius assisted her as she climbed into the seat and then walked around to the other side of the vehicle to sit in place beside her.

The vehicle lifted from the surface, and Malidora was caught off guard when the vehicle continued to rise high toward the second ring above. They climbed past the pipes and cables that ran along the underside of the second ring until the surface lay beneath them. The platform came to a gentle rest on the ring near the street.

The streets on this ring were silvery like highly reflective chrome. The buildings gleamed like polished jewels. Many residents, both men and women, stood about wearing flowy loose gowns. Veridius offered his hand again as she exited the vehicle.

He directed her to the front of a large, sparkling structure of red stone; its strange architecture was imbalanced and unsteady in appearance, leaning to one side. They walked into the huge vestibule. Small, shiny objects dangled from the ceiling while faceted smooth stones, cut in various shapes and angles along the walls, made the whole room difficult to comprehend. The whole interior distorted and reflected everything like a room full of mirrors. At the far end, a double staircase went up to a giant window between them and then continued up to the higher floor.

Veridius lead her up the stairs, passing by a lovely view over the edge of the ring in the clear crystal window. They entered a large dining hall where some Gesaurens sat at a long table, while others stood further away, having private conversations.

Attendants wore high shoulder pieces on their gowns with an elliptical disc behind their heads. One of them came over to aid Malidora into a seat.

"Seat her next to me," Veridius ordered, as he began greeting others seated nearby.

Malidora felt the icy stares of the guests as she and Veridius moved near the end of the table, and he helped her into the chair. Circular patterns of blue and white ran across the smooth surface of the long table. The attendant emphatically motioned for Malidora to stand back up. She leaned up in the seat, uncertain what the problem could be.

"That's where I'm sitting," said a man in an orange cloak.

Veridius came over. "Not this time, my friend."

The noise began to drop as everyone moved out of their clustered groups to their seats at the table. An ornate black chair at the end of the table stood empty as they all turned toward it. After a moment, Veridius raised both arms to the room, and everyone not already seated sat down.

"I take it Thercon Merrigan won't be coming . . ." The woman across from Veridius wore a light pink gown.

Veridius folded his hands on the table. "He rarely comes to these events anymore."

"I hope he is in good health." The woman pressed on the hair knotted up on top of her head.

"He is." Veridius glanced at his hands as he patted on the table with his fingertips. "He just never has time for some of us anymore." He lifted his eyes back to the woman. "You know how he is, always working."

The woman studied her own reflection in the table, then eyed Malidora. "What's this advane doing here?"

Veridius raised his eyebrows. "Why don't you ask her?"

Scoffing, the woman turned to speak to the man beside her. The attendants brought in bowls of creamy brown liquid, placing one in front of each person. It smelled like a hearty concoction of meat and plant, along with some other spices and scents unknown to Malidora.

As a bowl was placed in front of her, she inspected further: perfectly cut pieces of a light-colored meat with squares of green, yellow, and something that was nearly pink in color. It was all mixed into a light brown sauce.

Wishing for a taste, she searched for a utensil, but there was nothing else on the table. She eyed Veridius, beginning to feel out of place. Several attendants moved in behind the people sitting at the table across from her, as someone moved in behind her.

The attendants carried a long-handled spoon, one of them dipping it into the entrée in front of her. They began to hold the spoon to the mouths of those who sat at the table. The attendees opened their mouths as the attendants placed the small utensil inside their mouths. Eating from the spoon, the attendees sat back in their chair as the attendants wiped the excess from their mouths.

"Signal when you are ready, please." The attendant waited behind Malidora.

Malidora wrinkled her lips. "That's quite all right. I'll do it myself."

"You are a guest of the Naldus of Vesta, Malidora," said Veridius between chews. "Allow yourself to be served."

Malidora squeezed her eyes closed and opened her mouth, allowing the shallow spoon to be placed on her tongue. Closing her lips over the utensil, she took the exchange of the saucy food as the spoon was pulled from her mouth.

The meat was tender and succulent with a tasty blend of spices and seasoning. The vegetable bits featured a variety of textures, some crunchy, others soft. Together it made for a pleasant combination. As the meal went on, she began to ignore the weirdness of the attendants feeding her. It was nice to be able to relax and have someone do most of the work for you. The attendants were even attentive enough to stop whenever anyone was about to speak.

She nearly laughed out loud at the thought of Dabradan seeing this while he worked on the dusty streets of Ruvak, eating dried fruit and sleeping on wet dirt and rocks. At the same time, she felt a tinge of guilt; after all he had been through, he probably deserved this more than she.

After everyone had finished the meal, many of the guests began chatting, and the room was filled with chaotic, unintelligible vocalizations.

Veridius leaned toward her. "Was that to your liking? The deca louch?"

"The what?" Malidora glanced toward the man beside her then back to Veridius. "Oh, the food?" Malidora replied.

"Yes, did you enjoy it?"

She rubbed a smear of sauce that had spilled on the table. "It was very good, very tasty."

Veridius smiled. "I bet you never had anything on the first ring that compares."

One of the attendants rushed over to clean the table in front of her. Malidora leaned back as they wiped it down. "I must admit I have not. It was undoubtedly one of the best things I have ever tasted."

Veridius leaned on the back of his chair, stifling a laugh with his hand covering his mouth. "I nearly made a scene laughing at your expression when the attendants fed you."

Malidora's lips stiffened. She loosened them deliberately before asking, "So why exactly did you invite me here? To laugh at my discomfort in a situation I'm not accustomed to? So you could impress someone beneath you with your wealth?"

"Quite the contrary." Veridius chuckled. "I invited you because you are not impressed. You talk to me as if I am more than a title. Not like the sycophants or the elites of rival companies that agree with anything I say. They would just as easily stab me in the back if it would help their standing."

"What do you mean?"

Veridius looked around at the other guests as they were engaged in conversations of their own. "My family and the rest of these so-called elites are no more than empty shells. All they care about is their appearance, their social standing, their power. Advanes are usually too intimidated by my title to speak to me."

Malidora turned to the woman across the table as her attendants primped her hair. "I guess that comes with the territory."

As soft but lively music began to play, several of the guests rose from the table. They came together in pairs, dancing on the large, open part of floor behind the table. With elegant motions, they swung their arms high then suddenly stopped in a frozen pose. They leaned back and spun their feet slowly on the floor, ending in another pose before resuming again.

"I just wish I could show them I am not like my father," he said. "I find the advanes far more interesting than the high elites."

"What about below the rings?" Malidora propped her arms on the table.

Veridius curled his lips. "Grounders are dirty. They are lazy, unintelligent, spending all their earnings on instant gratification. Even their governors fail to be industrious enough to move up to the first ring."

"The governors want to keep the power and control they have on the ground." She tugged at a loose strand of hair as she waited for his next reaction.

"But what good is power on the ground?" Veridius leaned against the back of the chair. "Who would want to live there?"

Malidora placed her palms onto the table. "Some have no choice. Isn't it your responsibility to make the whole city a better place for everyone?"

"I suppose." He shuffled in the seat. "Each one of us has a responsibility to improve our own lives. The system is designed to reward the hard-working, the innovators, the bold. None of the grounders meet that description anymore."

Leaning over the table, she took a deep breath before she began. "Have you ever been on the ground? There *are* hardworking people. You should get to know them. Their struggles, their needs."

"It's best for me not to get directly involved with anything on the ground," Veridius said. "I can lead better from up here. Difficult decisions are best made from afar. I serve the needs of all of Vesta not just a few hardworking people."

This is what she despised about the governments of cities. They became machines that served to keep themselves running rather than help the people.

"How can you lead them if you don't know them?" said Malidora. "If you don't care about them as people?"

Her face began to warm as she realized her hypocrisy. His was the same philosophy held by Sinavus. Even though their goals were to shift the balance in the people's favor; to put leaders in place that were weak and corrupt, easy to bribe and manipulate; they kept the machine intact and used it to their advantage for the outcome of making things better for the commoners. They valued no individual over the whole, but hearing it spoken back to her from a city leader made it feel all wrong.

Veridius chewed on his bottom lip. "What would you have me do? I can't change the system."

Malidora sank into the back of the chair. "Then what power do you really have?"

"Perhaps you are right." Veridius rubbed both sides of his face as the attendants placed another spoonful into Veridius' mouth and he stopped talking. He took a bite and raised a finger to Malidora, as if he had more to say. "This is why I need your company. I've spent too much time among these hypocrites. I'm afraid that I'm becoming more and more like them. My father once told me to surround myself with people who disagree with me. You learn nothing from those that side with you all the time. Of course, my father never followed his own advice."

Malidora waved her attendants away as they began to bring food toward her mouth. As easy as it was to get caught up in the splendor of this place and in the argument with a city leader, she didn't have the luxury of time. The Nulthereals were coming. She had to take the chance and move the conversation to the looming threat.

"The biggest problem facing you right now is the incoming attack by the Nulthereals," Malidora said. "Show everyone that power you have and send an army to meet the Shadows before they get here."

"If you don't think our cannons would suffice, what makes you think an army would do any good?" Veridius bought up his hand to prop his chin on.

"You need a stone that bridges the gap between matter and aethrum," Malidora said. "I happen to have some in my apartment. Destroy one Shadow with it, and you have the means to destroy ten more."

"I would ask you to dance, but I'm afraid my interest in this ball is waning." Veridius slid his chair back. "I thought having your company may spice things up enough to endure it. Please take no offense, it would have taken a miracle." Veridius stood from his seat as the attendants slid it back under the table. "I would like to see the stone you speak of. Your high ring clearance will remain active as long as you return next cycle." He signaled toward the corner of the room, and Trinavus came to him. "Be a good assistant and take Malidora home."

Trinavus reached for Malidora's hand, but she didn't let him take it. "I'll follow you," she said, and they began walking out of the hall.

"Actually, Trinavus." Veridius waved. "Why don't you fetch her belongings from the apartment and have one of the palace guest rooms prepared. She can stay here over the cycle."

"How are you going to get into my apartment?" Malidora wondered.

"Leave that to me." Trinavus stood tall, straightening his posture. "Won't be a problem."

Veridius' attendants surrounded Malidora, walking her out of the great hall and into a corridor tall enough for a giant. Twisting curls of carved designs embellished the columns that met arches in the ceiling. Their footsteps were silent in the soft spongy surface along black and rose-colored patterns on the floor.

The attendants opened the door of the guest room, freeing the fresh aromas inside. The enormous interior included a rippled ceiling opening to a crystal window at the top with a view of the sky outside. A few faint stars dotted their dark blue medium through the octagonal opening. A sprawling, white covered bed with fluffy pockets of material like clouds sat directly below the window. Malidora collapsed onto the bed. She sunk in deep for a moment but rebounded into a comfortable softness.

Malidora couldn't wait to tell Dabradan about this, making it all the way to the highest ring. She lay in blissful peace, gazing up at the twinkling stars. The dome was surrounded by orange and pink clouds lined in silver. It was so still and quiet that the threat of the Shadows seemed so far away. If only it would stay that way. As much as she wanted to get back to Isodonia and rebuild Arkanthis, she could see herself content here for a long time.

CHAPTER 25

TRANQUIL MELODIES ENTERED her ears, increasing in tempo as Malidora became aware of herself and her surroundings once again. Malidora opened her eyes as new formations of clouds floated by through the window in the roof. It was odd to wake to the same degree of light that she fell asleep to. She wasn't sure she would ever get used to this lack of day and night cycles.

Exploring the large room, she found a doorway to a huge multileveled bath with cascading waterfalls flowing gently into a misty pool. As she entered the room, a projection of a serene forest covered the walls and surrounded the water, making it appear to be outdoors.

She entered the water, breathing in the woodsy fragrances that normally accompanied a forest. Even animals appeared around her, calmy eating grass, adding to the peacefulness of the scene. Malidora couldn't help but feel like a goddess, even though it was an illusion.

Once she finished the bath, she found her clothes and crossbow laying on a table. The clothes were clean and folded perfectly. She put on her tunic and battledress, panicking for a moment as she checked the inside pouch. Relieved as she pulled out the energized shard of nyalith, affirming visually that everything was still intact, she collapsed the crossbow, placing it inside her coat. She strapped on the quiver filled with shadowstone arrows underneath her battledress.

Sliding open the door slightly, Malidora peeked into the

hall. Only a few Gesaurens roamed the quiet corridor at the moment. Closing the door, she made her way down the hall into a large circular room. Moving images lined the walls, as some gathered to stare at them. As she passed the banquet hall, three attendants ran up to her.

"Your presence is requested in the garden," one of them said.

Malidora paused, though she knew the answer, she felt she needed to vocalize the question. "Who is requesting?"

"Therin Veridius." The attendant lifted her robed hand.

They escorted her through another hallway to a set of doors. As the doors opened, the outside sun filled her eyes with glittering light. The garden abounded with life. Tall, leaning trees surrounded the broad waters of a shimmering pond. Shrubbery with flowery blossoms lined a stone path crossing the water by an arched wooden bridge. White blooms floated on the water, urged by an occasional breeze. It was difficult to convince herself that this place was on the second ring suspended far above the ground.

Veridius placed his glass next to another on the table beside him and stood from his chair as she approached.

"It's good to see that some get to enjoy nature's beauty," Malidora glided toward the chair on the other side of the table. "while others see nothing but dust and stone."

Veridius curled the corner of his lips. "There is a farming district on the ground. You can't get more nature than that."

"Have you ever been there? There is no beauty there. It's industrial," Malidora tucked the thick skirt under her as she sat. "Nothing like this place."

Veridius waited for her to settle into her chair before returning to his. "The governors get to decide what to do with their district. I could have a garden made, but they would want it removed in the interest of maximizing space for practicality."

"I suppose its best that you get to the root of the problem then." Malidora's eyes followed a dark blue and gold bird gliding merrily from tree to tree.

Veridius crossed his legs. "And what is your diagnosis?"

A new breeze played with the leaves that hung over the pond from a nearby branch. Malidora turned toward the sound, watching the limbs curl and dip into the water. "I would say the amount of control the district governors have, if it were not for the imminent attack on this city."

Veridius bounced his propped foot up and down. "No one seems to share your concern, I'm afraid."

Malidora sat up straight in her chair as a strong gust stirred the tops of the tallest trees. "No matter how many times this happens, no one ever believes it until it's too late."

"Perhaps if you could provide some evidence . . ." He uncrossed his legs and leaned forward.

"Evidence?" Malidora fumbled for the glass next to his to quench the sudden dryness in her throat. "The evidence is all around you. How many cities need to be leveled to the ground before there's enough evidence?"

Veridius carefully lifted his glass from the table and brought it to his lips. "Surely you are not referring to the creature we obliterated before they even got close to the walls."

"You wanted to see the shadowstone." She repositioned herself in the chair to confront him, grasping one of the black stone pieces in her pouch.

He examined the iridescent black stone as he turned it between his fingers. "Where did this come from?"

"From a Nulthereal that was destroyed," Malidora slid to the edge of her seat, as the wind made textured patterns in the pond. "Only this can connect with them. Anything else goes straight through."

"Assuming what you say is true," Veridius held the stone to one eye, "this is but one. How would we destroy an invasion with one stone?"

"Shadowstone begets shadowstone. Break one shadow and you have the means to destroy ten more." She could see the doubt in his face. This was pointless. It didn't matter how many ways she tried to explain it, no one ever believed her until they saw it for themselves. By then, it was too late. Malidora rose from her seat and started down the incline toward the path around the pond. Hearing Veridius' footsteps behind her delivered a spark of hope.

"Their most dangerous weapon is us." She turned around to face him. "They can take your memories, your feelings, and your thoughts and use them against yourself or others. The only way to resist is to recognize the difference between thoughts you would act on and those you normally would not."

“What you say defies all understanding,” Veridius continued behind her as she walked along the walkway. “For your sake, I hope you are not delusional. For our sake, I hope you are.”

Malidora came to the wooden bridge that crossed the pond. “If they get close enough to the city walls, it’s over. This city will devour itself.”

“I’ll have all reports of any unusual activity sent directly to me,” Veridius said. “That’s the best I can do for now.”

Malidora made her way across the bridge, stopping in the middle where the arch was highest. The trees opened up here, providing a lovely view down the length of the pond. Veridius reached into a small container under the railing, pulling out a handful of what appeared to be pebbles. He tossed them into the water beneath them. Malidora bent over the rail as a small fish came to the surface, splashing as it ate the food floating on the water.

“That’s a feisty one!” Veridius watched the fish dart between each morsel.

The fish was long and thin, turquoise in color. Malidora took a handful of the food, throwing it into another spot as a few more fish quickly gathered in the area.

“Do you think they wonder how it happens?” Malidora sat on the railing. “Nourishment raining from the heavens, or do they simply accept their good fortune without questioning it?”

“Probably the same as us. Questioning, seeking, learning new things along the way but never finding that ultimate answer. In the end, we accept it as a part of nature until our curiosity begins again. The cycle never ends. I wonder if it all would have been more satisfying if we simply enjoyed the majesty of the nature of the universe around us.”

Malidora allowed a smile to bend her lips. “But how then would we know that high elites and advanes are better than grounders and that therins and thercons are better than everyone else?”

Veridius’ eyes tightened until he noticed the smirk on her face. “Ah, when you bite, you bite hard.”

“Perhaps it is inescapable. If it is in our nature to be curious, then questioning everything is our way of enjoying everything around us.”

Veridius nodded as he tossed the dry food into the water. More fish gathered around the bridge. Malidora lost track of the one especially feisty fish they had spotted before.

"What is it about a multitude that diminishes the value of one?" Malidora said as she watched the frenzy of fish eating as much as they could.

"What do you mean?"

"One can be interesting, unique," said Malidora, moving her arms from the rail, "but it quickly gets lost in a crowd, and suddenly it's not so special."

"It's still the same." Veridius brushed the residue of fish food from his hands. "It's your perception that has changed."

"Exactly." She turned her body to face him. "Somehow, I failed to see this before."

Veridius tilted his head toward his shoulder. "I suppose you're referring to the comments I made about the grounders."

"In another life, I was in a group called Sinavus because I hated the ruling system. I would've liked to see them ended, but unfortunately, we need systems to function. Sinavus operated in that system, using its corruption to our advantage. We stole for funding, lied to stir controversy, even killed if it was deemed necessary to benefit the right people. We thought ourselves heroes, fighting for those who could not fight for themselves. We made gains as some were hurt, a few suffered. For the good of the many, we said. For the good of the commoners. Now I wonder if I lost sight of what really matters."

Veridius leaned against the railing, staring out across the water. "What made you hate the system so much?"

Malidora stared across the pond as the treetops settled. "An old man I used to know had a small farm, but he made the most of it, and it was quite successful. Though he wasn't my real father, I often pretended that he was, and I think he liked it that way." Malidora rubbed the skin near her eyes, she rarely told this to anyone and was not sure how she was going to react. "He let me stay in the barn, took me in when no one else would. I used to hate all the chores he made me do to help keep things running, but I became attached to this farm. Took pride in it like it was my own." She rubbed the sides of her face as they grew warm. "The magnos came and took his land, all because they didn't protect the farmland they had. For the good of the many they said. But not for us."

"Perception can make hypocrites of us all," Veridius said.

"Indeed," said Malidora. "Perhaps serving the masses is useless if you lose sight of the individuals making it up."

"When I was growing up, I wanted to be like what I thought my father was," said Veridius. "I wanted to make a difference in this city, not just this city but the whole world. But everyone wants something different. The most I've accomplished is making things for the elites a little bit better. There's so much wrong on the ground, I wouldn't even know where to begin."

"Perhaps you start with a single person, one who needs it the most and go from there," Malidora pondered.

Veridius traced his finger along the grains in the wooden railing. "Yes, there will be some changes around here."

Veridius spent the rest of the cycle giving Malidora a tour of the palace. As time wore on, he took her to the council chamber. They moved outside onto the balcony overlooking the world of Kandom. He handed her a pair of frames to wear over her eyes that magnified the view when you touched the right side.

A river wound its way from a large forest toward the city walls. A channel split off from where the river curled away from the city. The channel appeared to run directly into the wall itself, not far from where the main gate would be. Pockets of forests and grassy fields were scattered among the sandy plains and glass formations.

"The corpses of those armored creatures are still out there." Veridius scanned the land around them. "That sullies the view a bit."

Malidora turned in the direction he was staring until she found the group of craters and scattered carcasses. Zooming in with the frames, she took a glimpse of the decimated creatures. The blast holes in their armored coverings were enormous. The cannons had shredded them.

Movement from behind one of the creatures caught her eye. Someone was out there among them. Malidora observed as they used something to cut what was left of a leg from the body of the beast. As she continued watching, she noticed more figures moving around the bodies and pieces of the creatures. "There's someone there."

"Where?"

"Among the dead animals." Malidora widened the view.

Veridius touched his frames turning his head toward the row of corpses. "Rovers," he said. "I've never seen them this close to Vesta."

"I guess they couldn't resist a free meal," Malidora quipped.

Veridius twisted his mouth in disgust. "That meat can't be good. Surely, not good enough to risk getting in range of our cannons."

"Are you going to kill them?"

"No." Veridius watched as some of them carried parts of the creatures into the distance while others stayed, cutting them into smaller bits. "Not while they're clearing the area. As long as they come no closer, there is no reason to fire on them."

The rovers marched back and forth between the forest and the plains. Malidora and Veridius watched until weariness or boredom got the better of them.

❧

The next cycle when Malidora left her quarters, the great hall was filled with a chaotic clamoring of voices. Upon entering the hall, she found no one as the voices trailed from the vestibule further on. A crowd gathered at the midpoint of the stairs outside the balcony, while the balcony itself was full.

As she was about to descend the steps, an attendant ran toward her. "The therin has been asking for you."

Malidora stopped for a moment then took another step. "He knows where I am, he can come himself."

"Please," said the attendant. "There is something he wants you to see."

Malidora turned back to the crowd. It would take some time to get to the balcony to see what they were looking at. "Very well."

She followed the attendant through the great hall to the council chamber where Veridius stood staring over the rails of the veranda. He flinched as he heard her approach but did not turn in her direction. Malidora grabbed a pair of frames from a table as she stepped out into the natural air.

Veridius stood aside, inviting her to stand beside him. She gripped the railing, leaning onto it as she gazed over the landscape. Nothing out of the ordinary until her eyes wandered to one of the forests.

The trees were blackened, bent toward the ground, as if no longer able to support their own weight. The vegetation was dead, but rather than dried up plants, it appeared more like rotting flesh. Dark residue oozed from the forest into a basin.

She felt Veridius' eyes on her as she stared at the blight. He took a long breath before he spoke. "There are only two forests left. If reports are true."

Playing scenarios in her head, Malidora fixed her eyes on the dead forest. They had to leave the city. Take the fight to the Shadows before they could get close. The only problem with that is they couldn't take on the thousand Shadows they saw in Blackfrost.

"Have you seen anything like this before?" Veridius inquired.

The only way it could work was to isolate a small group of Shadows first. Slowly, they could arm the masses with shadowstone that way.

"Malidora?"

"It's the Nulthereals." She faced him. "We have to find one alone and destroy it for anything we can use as weapons."

"I'll send a team to scout the area," Veridius said. "We need to know exactly where they all are and how many. We can't afford to go in blind."

Malidora stepped into the council chamber. "We can't afford to wait!"

"They'll get data back quickly." A gust of wind caught Veridius' cloak. "If anyone spots them approaching Vesta, we'll fire the cannons once they are in range."

"The cannons—" Malidora started.

"If the cannons don't work, we'll meet them head on with whatever we have."

Malidora grabbed his shoulder. "We need to find Dabradan!"

"Who?"

"He came to Vesta with me. He knows how to fight Nulthereals," she said. "He has a shadowstone weapon!"

Trinavus guided the platform past the first ring toward the Ruvak district on the ground. Searching the rooftops for something familiar, Malidora pointed toward one of the streets off the main road. With a swirling cloud of dust, the vehicle closed toward the street.

The syvern had been mostly dismantled. Parts lay against the block house where she had stayed for a cycle. Malidora surveyed the street, searching for a sign of Dabradan.

"Stay away from that!" someone shouted.

Malidora turned to find the dust- and grease-covered face of Cian as he came running from the shade of a hut nearby.

"Cian, where is Dabradan?" she continued to turn, searching in all directions.

"Oh, it's you," Cian said. "He's in the room getting some rest."

Malidora entered the block house, turning through the halls toward the small room they had been assigned. As she opened the door, Dabradan rolled over and got to his feet, particles of dirt and other debris matted in his hair. "Dabradan! The Nulthereals are getting close. Do you still have the blade?"

Nearly stumbling against the wall, Dabradan began to recognize her. "Where have you been? I was worried about you."

"I'm fine," Malidora propped him up with her shoulder. "Come with me to the rings. Help us figure out how to stop the Shadows."

Rubbing his eyes with his knuckle, he propped the other hand against the wall. "Where are we going?"

"I'll show you," she said. "Come on!"

Shielding his eyes from the sunlight beaming through the holes in the roof, Dabradan gripped the Whidge claw.

"Cian, I'll be back soon. Don't let anyone near the parts." Dabradan followed her toward the shay."

Cian waved. "We'll be here."

Trinavus opened the doors as they approached.

"Cian." Dabradan turned and walked back toward the syvern parts. "Better get the syvern reassembled while I'm gone, we may need it soon."

The shay lifted off and soared over the city. Flying them toward the first ring. They passed into the shadow of the tower as it obscured the sun.

"How are repulsors getting this much lift?" Dabradan inquired.

Trinavus turned toward Malidora and Dabradan sitting in the back. "These aren't repulsor engines. There are only six vehicles in Vesta like this."

"You could sell these to grounders and have enough to buy Vesta." Dabradan stared out the window.

Trinavus flew past the first ring, moving between the crossing arms to the second. "If anyone on the ground had these, they'd be able to get to the rings without clearance."

"Yeah," said Dabradan. "Can't have that. You know I don't have clearance, right?"

"You do now." Trinavus brought the shay to a stop by the red crystal palace. Veridius stood outside waiting as they got out of the vehicle.

Veridius walked toward him. "You must be Dabradan."

Malidora stopped when she noticed Dabradan frozen in his tracks. "Yes, it is." She patted Dabradan on the shoulder.

He leaned toward her ear and whispered, "Is that who I think it is?"

"Veridius? Yes."

"Therin Veridius?" he whispered.

"He doesn't entirely believe me," Malidora said, "but he's willing to listen."

Dabradan shook his head. "How did you get an audience?"

Malidora smiled. "Persistence."

"I mean no offense," Veridius said, "but we should get you to a bath. You'll stick out here in a bad way covered in dust and . . . everything else."

Malidora pulled him close, looking Dabradan in the eyes. "You really should."

CHAPTER 26

AS MALIDORA AND Veridius sat at the table in the dining hall, Dabradan hesitantly entered the room dressed in a sleek black suit with red ribbons spilling down below the collar. He found Malidora and lowered himself into in the seat reserved beside her.

"Look at *you*," Malidora quipped.

An attendant came over and set a plate in front of him, placing two pieces of meat, some fruit, and a stalky cooked vegetable.

Veridius, who had been talkative earlier, ate quietly once Dabradan arrived. Dabradan said nothing either, focused on eating as the attendants fed him. She couldn't blame him. He had likely been eating the small fruits and whatever else he could find on the ground.

"You know Dabradan doesn't like the City of Wonder motto of Vesta." Malidora hoped to start something to get Dabradan talking. She also wanted to see his reaction. Veridius glanced up from his plate while Dabradan glared at her. "He aways says it sarcastically. He said that this city is nothing more than a monument to greed and selfishness.

Dabradan's eyes grew big as he swallowed the mouthful of food. "I never said that. Not in that exact wording anyway."

"You're not completely wrong." Veridius eyed Malidora. "I've been attempting to see things from a different point of view lately. I've been told that I need to empathize more."

"There's no opportunity here." Dabradan took the glass

handed to him by the attendant. "It's either suffer on the ground or leave Vesta altogether, yet you all seem surprised that anyone would want to be independent."

Veridius tapped his fingers together as his hands rested on the shiny table. "That is something I intend to correct. I've been going over the concordance, but I can't remove the governors unless they have committed a crime."

Malidora scoffed, "Crime is their whole operation."

"One step at a time." Veridius cleared his throat. "It would be easier to strip their power, giving the management of funds for the ground districts over to the first ring."

Dabradan tested the drink, making a sour face before tilting his head as if having a change of heart. "I'm not sure what that would solve. Taking away more power from the ground."

"But it may give the governors enough incentive to move on to the first ring," Veridius said, "providing an opening for others."

Dabradan rubbed his chin. "I don't care what you do if it works." He took another drink, making the same sour face he did before.

"It's an acquired taste, Dabradan." Malidora took a drink from her glass. "Kind of like you."

Dabradan smirked as he took another sip, making her chuckle quietly to herself.

"Malidora tells me you led a security team in Udamal." Veridius took a cloth from his lap, wiping his palms with it.

As the attendants placed a leafy vegetable in his mouth, Dabradan paused his chewing to respond. "Mostly escorting shipments between cities. Rovers like to ambush the shipping routes."

Taking time to chew the piece of meat that the attendant placed in his mouth, Veridius paused before speaking again. "If Malidora's perceptions regarding these events are accurate, perhaps you can advise one of my squads. You have experience in combat with these so-called Shadows."

A rapid succession of booms sounded in the distance, causing a commotion outside the banquet hall. Veridius set his utensil on the table and put on an earpiece. "Trinavus, status."

The thunderous noises stopped. Malidora stood, anxiously waiting to hear what happened. As tempted as she was to walk out to the vestibule terrace, she decided to stay and hear it from Veridius.

"What did he see?" Veridius began to pace around the table. "Who gave the order?" Malidora glanced at Dabradan, who sat calmy chewing away as the attendants fed him.

Veridius returned to the table, standing in front of his chair. "Someone fired the cannons." A repeating tone came from his earpiece. "My apologies, I must finish this conversation privately. It's my father." He walked into a quiet corner of the banquet hall.

Taking another bite of meat, Dabradan seemed indifferent to the situation. Malidora sipped her drink, her hand shaking as she held the glass. After a few moments, Veridius returned to the table. "One of the gunners thought they saw something heading toward the city. Came out of nowhere, there was no time to report it. After the dust cleared nothing was found. The gunner has been relieved of his position."

"I don't like the sound of that." Malidora handed the glass back to the attendant to hold.

Veridius got back into his chair and placed the cloth on his lap to finish eating. "I also checked in with the scout team. They haven't seen anything yet."

After they had finished eating, Veridius left to attend a string of meetings, some related to the cannon issue and some already scheduled. Malidora showed Dabradan around the palace, at least the areas she could access. As the cycle wore on, one of the attendants informed them that Veridius regrettably would not be able to meet with them again until the next cycle.

Malidora opened the door to her room. "Where are you going to stay? I don't think they want you lounging around in the hall."

"That's my problem," Dabradan quipped. "I'll figure something out. There's probably a rule against letting someone else in there."

Malidora pushed the door open further, inviting him in. "I'm sure no one would say anything if I broke the rules."

"There's only one bed . . ." Dabradan hesitated. "I suppose I could sleep on the floor."

"Only one bed? Don't be ridiculous. Look at the size of that thing.

That's ten beds put together." Malidora removed her battle coat, leaving only her thin cloth top and leggings. "As long as you leave me enough space, we'll be fine."

Dabradan stepped inside and removed his armor shell. Malidora pounced on the bed, and he sat down on the edge at the other side.

❧

Malidora woke to the sound of tapping on the door from outside. Moving Dabradan's arm from around her waist, she got up to answer the door. She was surprised to see Veridius standing there. "We have a problem." His eyes moved past her to Dabradan asleep on the bed. Veridius tightened his lips together as he tilted his head toward the floor, as if a bit disappointed.

"He didn't have another place to stay." Malidora hoped to diffuse the situation.

"Get ready as soon as you can and meet me outside the palace." Veridius turned with a bit of a stomp and moved down the hall.

Malidora took a quick bath and dressed, taking her quiver full of bolts with her. She hurried past the bed as Dabradan still slept.

When she made it outside the palace, faint shouting from somewhere echoed in the air. Standing in a garden on the other side of the street, Veridius waved her over. The shouting became louder as she walked toward him. Rhythmic chants from a crowd below combined with random metal tapping. She followed him to the edge of the ring that overlooked the city itself.

Through the first ring, at the base of the tower, a crowd gathered. Several of them had mallets and picks beating against the stone legs of the tower where the arches allowed visitors to walk beneath and view monuments and the history of Vesta. Another group of grounders pushed on the other side of the pillar. More grounders were marching through the streets toward the tower in the middle, seemingly intent on joining.

Malidora glanced at Veridius. "What are they saying?"

He gazed over the crowd. "Tear it down."

"Has this ever happened before?"

"There have been small riots here and there, but the security forces keep things under control." Veridius turned as Trinavus approached, crossing the street with a group of soldiers, heading toward them. "This time they were overrun."

"You're going to have to take action, my therin." Trinavus suited up, carrying a helmet at his side. "They pose a serious threat."

Veridius straightened his shoulders. "Do you think they could actually damage the tower?"

"With enough bodies dedicated to one purpose, you can do just about anything," said Trinavus. "We have to shoot and end the threat."

Veridius leaned toward Trinavus. "Absolutely not. They are Vestian citizens!"

"They have injured and killed members of security, they are criminals," Trinavus said. "Once we begin firing, they will disperse."

Malidora stepped beside Veridius. "It's the Nulthereals. The Shadows are controlling them. They are probably using the disdain the grounders already have for the advanes and high elites."

"Shadows," Trinavus sneered. "We've yet to see any evidence of this."

"What more evidence do you need?" Malidora gestured toward the swarm of Gesaurens below them.

Veridius glanced at the massing crowd. "Trinavus, take her on the shay, see if you can find any sign of these Shadows."

Covering his right ear, Trinavus appeared to be listening to something in his earpiece. "I'm afraid Thercon Merrigan has countermanded your order. He's sending us to engage the crowd directly."

The lines in Veridius' face deepened as he grabbed his own earpiece, putting it to his ear, "What? I am in charge of our security forces! Why is he doing this?"

Trinavus looked back at the chanting crowd. "You failed to act."

"Get him on the line!" Veridius fumed.

Malidora's heart pounded with each moment that passed. The amplitude of the chants increased.

"Tell my father I must speak to him immediately," Veridius said into the device Trinavus handed him. "I don't care who he is meeting with. This is urgent!"

"He's already given the order, accept it." Trinavus stood by with his arms crossed.

Veridius snapped his eyes toward him. "No. I will not accept this."

"Tough decisions are not for everyone. Be grateful he made this one for you," said Trinavus.

"Either I'm in charge or I am not," Veridius said. "This is the one thing that I'm allowed to control. I'm not giving that up, too."

Trinavus eyed Malidora. "You wouldn't even care if she weren't here."

The arguing, the sounds of the crowd, it was all happening again. Her hand began to tremble. Her pulse raced and her breaths came quick and shallow. Like a nightmare she couldn't wake up from, the world was caving in on her.

She could no longer take this.

"That has nothing to do with it!" Veridius said as she moved down the silvery street on the way to the tower. There had to be a way to get down there without being swallowed up in the mob. The chants grew louder as she came to the elevator. As she circled the platforms around the tower, she spotted a service ladder that went down the shadow side of the tower to the first ring. It wasn't ideal but perhaps it would work.

Ahead was another elevator. Grounders ran by the pillar the elevator led as they headed toward the swarming crowd. They were spread out enough that it shouldn't be dangerous there.

Malidora boarded the elevator, descending past the first ring to the ground. She dashed by the archway, evading the Gesaurens running and shouting toward the pillar that the crowd was shoving and beating on.

Scattered fights raged in the streets, though most seemed drawn toward the tower. The main gate, still shielded with its translucent blue barrier stood, between the Alfor farming district and Ruvak. The walls of the city appeared to be perfectly intact as she scanned as far as her eyes could see.

Sprinting through the alleyways, she headed toward Nirus. At the edge of the huge shadow cast by the high winged wall, she stopped to catch her breath. From the darkness ahead, a woman staggered through the cluttered street between rows of small buildings. Malidora's fingers found the crossbow inside her vest, just in case.

A balton sped through one of the crossing streets behind her as she stepped into the dark. The strange woman stumbled over a metal box laying along the side of the street, steadying herself against the wall of a building. As Malidora passed her, the woman stood tall, staring at her.

She began shaking, reaching toward Malidora. "Do you hear them?" The woman moaned. "Whispering behind the stars . . ."

Malidora walked on without responding.

The woman turned as she moved by. "They're calling us!" she screeched. "Calling us to the serpent's dream."

Though winded from running earlier, Malidora sped up.

The woman matched her pace. "They have milked this world of its blood."

She didn't have time to deal with this woman. Not wanting to have to hurt her, Malidora bolted ahead, dodging pieces of refuse scattered in the road. The woman began running after her. "Our lives are the key to the gate!"

As the silhouette of the Black Sun rose above the structures ahead, she heard loud crashes of the woman falling over come from behind her. The guard at the back door lay silent on the steps as Malidora walked toward the three-tiered building. Grabbing him by the arm, she dragged him up the stairs near the door.

Before she could get any part of the guard close enough, the rotating door clicked as she backed toward it. Could it be the clearance Veridius gave her worked here too? The inside was clear as she entered the building. She crept into the stairwell, hurrying up the steps toward the third floor.

As she made her way toward the balcony, a voice echoed into the hall. "Foolish girl, you return to the very lair of those you betrayed?"

"There's been no betrayal." Malidora drew her crossbow. "I've come to fight the Nulthereals with you or anyone who would stand against them."

She was met with silence until she approached the open doorway leading to the large glass window in front of the balcony. "I see you have somehow gained clearance to enter the Black Sun." The door began sliding shut. "Fortunately, the doors in my penthouse were disconnected from the thercon's security grid."

Malidora loaded and fired, hitting the dark figure sliding the door closed. Before the door could shut all the way, it jammed on the arrow protruding from the guard as he fell against the door.

She reached the door, pushing it open as the guard crumbled to the floor. After extracting the arrow from the guard, Malidora turned to the huge window. The two doors on each side were already closed.

Ripping the flash pistol out of the guard's side holster, she fired it toward the glass. Burning holes began to melt through the glass at the bottom of the window, until a section collapsed under its own weight. Malidora crunched on the crystalline pieces, slipping through the break in the window to the outside balcony.

A quiet breeze met her as she aimed the pistol at the group sitting at the table. Laudra, Klevet, and two others she had not met. She could only assume they were governors of other districts. The view below was quite different from the last time she was up here. Many of the lights were off. No longer filled with music or theatrical presentation, the streets were now riddled with small pockets of fighting and inebriated thrill seekers staggering over the passed-out bodies that lay in the street.

Laudra sat back in her chair holding a glass of sparkling liquid. "Some people just can't take a hint."

Malidora lowered the pistol and walked up to the table. "Do you still have the arrow I gave you, with the shadowstone?"

Laudra glanced at Klevet and back to Malidora. "It was added to my collection." She stroked the black shadowstone threaded into a gold chain around her neck.

"This is happening just as I told you it would." Malidora looked at Laudra. "Are you not going to help save Vesta?"

Laudra took a sip of her drink, savoring it on her tongue. "Vesta doesn't need saving. Chaos will come to order eventually. In the meantime, we have fights in the streets to entertain us."

"This is more than disorder," said Malidora. "It won't stop until nothing is left alive. It's up to us to end it. Order your guards to help."

Setting her drink on the table, Laudra displayed a light flashing on the band around her wrist. "I've already alerted the guards, but not to help you."

The blunt impact of footsteps sounded from downstairs as a group of figures illuminated by the dim lights outside ran through the streets toward the Black Sun. Klevet reached for a pistol in his coat. Before he could take a shot, Malidora kicked the table, the repulsors on her boots sending it flying into Klevet and Laudra as the other two leapt to the floor. The impact knocked Klevet into the window behind him and Laudra into the metal railing on the corner of the balcony.

Malidora lunged at Laudra, ripping the chain from her neck as the guards made it to the third level. Leaping over the rails, she hurled toward the streets below. Everything went into slow motion as she fell. Flipping her body over, she managed to get her feet pointed at the ground. The repulsor boots absorbed some of the shock as her legs gave out on impact. Rolling onto her back, Malidora carefully made it to her feet. The ligaments in her knees popped as she stretched her legs, rushing past the people in the streets.

"Take her down!" Laudra yelled as Malidora sprinted around the curve of the main street near the outer walls. Heading toward the light where the high wing of the wall tapered down, she came to a ladder that scaled to the top of the barrier.

CHAPTER 27

HAND OVER HAND, Malidora climbed the ladder to the ledge leading to an alure. Looking out over the city, she could see many Gesaurens leaving the Alfor district, heading toward the tower. Moving through the alure, she glanced outside the city toward the curling river. One of the last living forests stretched out in the distance.

Leaning over the terraced edge, her eyes traced the base of the wall, and she spotted it. Writhing against the orange hues in the sand, a Nulthereal hovered nearly out of sight. Even while staring directly at it, Malidora questioned whether it was truly there.

She hurried along the pathway for a better shot. A cold stillness sprung within her as she neared the Nulthereal. As she peered over the edge, her stomach churned, anticipating the sight of the mind-twisting Shadow. Malidora exhaled as she spotted it, almost directly beneath her along the wall.

Trying to remind herself that this abnormal anxiety was influenced by the Nulthereal, she loaded a black tipped bolt into her crossbow. Her heart quickened as she aimed, trying to hold the crossbow steady as her hands shook. As she tried to correct her aim, a bolt of red light whizzed by her, disrupting the air. More blasts skid against the stone nearby as a group of guards fired on her from below. Malidora dropped to her knees behind the terraced siderails around her. Cold sweat formed on her forehead as she froze in place. Bits of broken rock rained onto her as the guards continued to fire.

She took the arrow out of the crossbow and drew her flash pistol. Taking a peek behind the stone, she realized there was now only one guard. As she scanned for the other two, the sound of hollow metal caught her attention.

The other two guards were climbing the same ladder she had used earlier and were trying to get to the top of the wall. Malidora stood and bolted down the alure as the guard below continued firing. The other guards made it up on the wall, shooting bolts at her from behind.

Another guard joined in from the ground as she continued to dash across the wall. With no cover from the two gunmen firing down the pathway toward her, she had no other choice. She leapt off the wall outside of the city, using the repulsor boots again to absorb some of the impact. She ran as fast as she could, away from the gunmen and the Nulthereal. The two gunmen above lost their line of sight as she hugged the base of the wall.

Somehow, the buzzing of the Nulthereal grew closer. Increasing her pace seemed to only make the sound louder. Then she realized why. Another Nulthereal floated along the wall ahead. Could they not go through the stone as they could through the trees of the forests? Perhaps they preferred to hide outside the city, making the residents do their bidding.

Reloading the black arrow into her crossbow, she kneeled and aimed at the Nulthereal in front of her. She turned back, the shadow behind flew toward her, but there was enough time. Firing the arrow, she hit the Nulthereal. The arrow stuck, sending ripples of cracks into the Nulthereal's now hardened shell. It continued to move toward her, no longer dancing like flame.

Malidora dropped the crossbow into the sand, pulling out the flash pistol. No need to waste shadow arrows. Some of the flash bolts ricocheted off the Nulthereal while others burned into it. It continued flying toward her until one of the blasts hit the shattered spot where the arrow stood. The Nulthereal burst into bits. Dust and debris landed all around her as the buzzing from the shadow behind her came near. Grabbing her crossbow off the sand, she pulled a handful of bolts from her quiver. She had no time to switch weapons now.

Twisting awkwardly, she fired, loaded another bolt, and fired again. The Nulthereal dropped to the ground, crumbling into three large pieces. Taking a moment to catch her breath, she was interrupted by bursts of dirt nearby. Flashes of light from the guard's weapons motivated her to use every bit of energy she had left.

She ran along the circumference of the wall, headed for the main gate. As the guards began to close in, Malidora drew her pistol, stopped, and turned around. Pressing the trigger as fast as she could, she launched a hail of fire at the guards. They dropped, taking cover behind the ramparts along the wall.

Quickly, she sprinted toward the gate, regaining some ground from her pursuers. The translucent blue shield now visible, Malidora began to slow, taking a breather the rest of the way. As she made her way up to the shield, no one stood behind the gate. No one to let anyone in or out.

She tried to call for help but her voice did not project. Her body pulsed, growing numb, as a loud buzzing approached. Whispers began to fill her mind. Refusing to hear the words, Malidora fed on chaotic thoughts. Playing a cycle of images, emotions, and dreams, she drowned out the formation of the Nulthereal's words.

Two of the whispering Shadows appeared from nowhere, closing in on her. She fired her pistol, forgetting for a moment that the laser blast would do nothing. Throwing the flash pistol to the ground, Malidora reached for her crossbow. She grabbed a bolt, trying to place it into the groove as fast as she could before the Nulthereals were close enough to pull her in.

In her haste, the arrow slipped out of her hand before she could get it into place. With the Nulthereals bearing down on her, she turned and ran. The arrow flew from the ground into one of the Shadows as they followed her. She hoped the arrow would at least damage the Nulthereal on the way through, but it did not. Heading for the river, she bolted through the sharp formations of glass across the sand.

Voices invaded her mind as she struggled to resist.

Do not go near the water.

Malidora ran toward the channel that led from the riverbend through the wall of the city. Ignoring the need for oxygen that her lungs couldn't provide fast enough, she dashed for the water. She splashed into the shallow water, wading further into the deeper part of the channel. The Shadows stopped as they approached the white sandy banks. The water surged around her waist as she moved to face them.

Step out from the water. Come to us.

Hands shaking, she reached into the water seeking her quiver. As she aimed her crossbow at one of the Shadows, Malidora found an arrow, pulling it above the water. As she pivoted to load the crossbow, her plant foot slipped on loose rocks along the bed of the channel. Correcting her fall, she stepped into deeper water. Before she realized what happened, she was caught in a stronger current. Her body was thrown down the channel, tumbling out of her control. Her arms and legs plowed into hard objects as she came to a stop. The outside air touched her face as she broke the surface. Tangled in the gnarled roots of an old tree, Malidora gasped to fill her lungs with air.

She pulled herself up onto the shallow waters of the ford. Her stock of arrows remained in her quiver, but her crossbow was gone. Not far ahead was a large pipe that went through the walls of the city. Carefully running along the gravel in the ankle-deep water, she headed toward it. The shallows became deep again before she made it to the pipe, but the current was not as strong.

Swimming toward the wall, she found the pipe covered in a metal grate that prevented access into the city. Grabbing the steel bars, Malidora pressed her feet against the stone wall below the surface. She tried to pull the grate out enough where she could enter the tunnel, but it wouldn't even budge.

A buzzing sounded further up the channel. She stopped pulling on the grate, hanging on the metal bars to keep herself above water. Any sense of hope drained out of her. She should have stayed on the second ring. If she had been more patient, perhaps Veridius and Trinavus would have finished arguing. Patience had never been her strength. The anxiety of bad things happening around her was never something she could ignore. She couldn't simply wait and do nothing.

She should have learned by now. She couldn't save the world by herself.

Even though she had tried to plant seeds in the right people, no one ever believe or helped until it was too late. She should have listened to the voice in the nyalith and left when she'd had the chance. It was all over now. Nothing left but the dying. Perhaps it was best to let go of the bars and drown in the waters below. At least that way she wouldn't have to face The Hollow again.

The buzzing grew louder as her right hand released the grate. She swung around with her back to the wall. The Nulthereals moved along the banks to the tunnel. They eased over the shallow water, reaching out. The soaked tips of her hair stretched toward the Shadows as they moved close enough to nearly suck her in.

A low whine joined the buzzing as a cloud of dust swept the landscape behind the Nulthereals. Emerging from the dust, a silver shay moved low to the ground. Someone jumped from the vehicle, charging behind the Nulthereals. Her hair fell flat against her face as the Shadows focused on a new target.

One of the Shadows was sliced in two pieces that tumbled past the old tree, splashing into the channel. The dust began to clear as Dabradan brought the Whidge claw down on the other Nulthereal before it could consume him. Malidora exhaled, uncertain how long she had been holding her breath.

She turned loose of the bars and swam to the bank. Barely feeling her legs, she crawled up the sand toward him.

"What were you doing out here alone?" Dabradan offered his hand to pull her up.

She grabbed on and made it to her feet. "Veridius and Trinavus kept arguing. I tried to find someone that would help, but I should have known better," she replied, still catching her breath. She propped herself on the old tree. The muscles in her thighs felt heavy and sore.

"You didn't wake me up." Dabradan stood nearby allowing her a moment to gather her strength. "You're as reckless as Evala," he spoke with a joking tone, mixed with an inflection of concern.

Dabradan guided her toward the shay as it touched down. "Don't forget this." He placed something into her hand.

She closed her fingers around the object and gazed down at her crossbow. "How did you find it?"

"It was right there." Dabradan pointed at the roots of the tree. "You stepped on it."

Malidora kneeled by the remains of one of the Nulthereals, taking a handful of its splintered remains. Dropping the fragments into the pouch inside her vest, she stood up and headed toward the shay.

"Malidora, I'm pleased you're unharmed," Veridius said as she slid across the seat making room for Dabradan.

"Did you see the Shadows?" she asked.

"I saw you hanging on that pipe," Veridius said. "Good thing there're sensors around to show your location."

Malidora tried to catch her breath. "Dabradan destroyed two of them. You didn't see that?"

"Must have been when he was underneath the trees," said Veridius.

She glared at him between the wet strands of hair hanging over her face. "Willful ignorance won't make them go away."

Trinavus took the shay upwards, flying over the wall. As they moved over the city, she leaned over Dabradan to get a glimpse of the base of the tower. The crowd, even more massive now, shoved on all the pillars of the tower. Some put their weight on them, while others worked on loosening one stone at a time. Another group chipped into the rock, swinging hammers. Some even had flash weapons they were firing into the legs of the tower.

"A unit was sent to break up the crowd by any means necessary," Trinavus said. "They were overwhelmed by the grounders."

Malidora settled back into her seat. "Now they have flash weapons."

"I told you it was a bad idea." Veridius shook his head.

Malidora grabbed Veridius' shoulder between the seats. "Don't start this again."

"You're right," Veridius said. "I don't know why I keep getting so agitated."

"Nulthereals," Malidora let go of his metal shoulder guard, "they're making us do the work for them."

Examining her crossbow, she noticed the bowstring was pulled loose from its limbs. Malidora breathed out her frustration.

"What's wrong?" Dabradan inquired.

"It's broken again." She wiped wet strands of hair away from her eyes.

Dabradan reached out. "I used to be a mechanic, let me see it."

She handed him the crossbow. He studied it for a moment, pulling on the bowstring and the limbs. "When was this made? It looks ancient." He continued to play with the string.

"I thought you were a mechanic," Malidora said.

Dabradan turned it back over squinting inside the slot where the trigger was. "With normal equipment. I don't understand how this works."

"Give it back before you make it worse." Malidora grabbed the crossbow from his hands.

Dabradan glanced at her as she folded it back up. "If it was built with newer tech, I could do it with no problem."

Veridius leaned between the seats. "Maybe you should improve it with new tech. I bet a repulsor on that would give those arrows more range."

"Yeah, if I could just slap one on there," Malidora said.

"Let one of my engineers look at it." Veridius looked at the window as they neared the second ring.

"As long as they don't break it," she said.

Veridius moved back into the seat as the shay moved over the red palace. "Isn't it already broken?"

CHAPTER 28

THE SOFT CUSHIONS cradled her as she settled back into her room, lying on the bed. Aside from the soreness in her legs, she was quite relaxed. Though weary from her encounters with Laudra and the Nulthereals, sleep would not find her. Events played through her mind in a loop.

Don't enter a fight you cannot win. It was part of the Sinavus Code. She hadn't obeyed that particular rule so far, why start now? It was what she should do, but she always had a hard time letting things go. Most of her life had been chasing down the Blight Whidge on Isodonia and destroying it. She never imagined this was a much larger problem across multiple worlds.

Contrary to what the voice in the nyalith said, this was her punishment, and the only hope to redeem herself was to save this world and eventually end the threat of the Gaith and the Shadows forever. Evala had reminded her of that.

Once she relaxed, she slept longer than she had in a while. When she finally awoke, she walked into the hall searching for Dabradan. A soldier sitting in the great hall, set his device on the seat beside him and stood. He began marching toward her, removing his helmet. "Ah, finally, I thought I was going to have to watch your door for the next period." Trinavus rested his helmet under an arm.

"Where is Dabradan?" she asked as a unit of soldiers moved through the hall past her. "And Veridius?"

"Have a seat in the dining hall." Trinavus placed a device on his ear. "I will inform them to meet you there."

The attendants ushered her to a chair at the long table. She sat and waited as the attendants brought her food and drink. This time they didn't stay and feed her. After she had finished nearly half the meal, Trinavus and Veridius walked in with Dabradan trailing behind them.

Veridius placed her crossbow in front of her and sat down. Malidora picked the weapon up and gripped the handle. They'd kept the bowstring, but it was now mainly decoration. The new addition was an oblong black box at the back of the guide where the arrow rested.

Veridius pointed to a switch on the back of the grip. "Press this first."

Malidora pressed it, and the box glowed blue, making the crossbow hum in her hand. The trigger had been replaced by a new design. It had more of a curvature to fit a finger. When she pulled it, the initial response required more pressure than she was used to, but after the first bit of effort it slid back easily the rest of the way. The blue glow pulsed with her test of the trigger.

"Seems nice." She bounced the crossbow in her hand. "We'll see how it works in a fight."

Dabradan pointed to some layers in the grip material. "It was my idea to use corvex chargers. Every motion you make will feed the cells. It should never run out of power, but if it does, shake the weapon rapidly."

"Like the boots," Malidora said. "Excellent."

"There was a second wave to contain the grounders." Veridius leaned toward her as she picked up a piece of meat from her plate and began eating again. "It too, failed."

Dabradan set his hands on the table. "Many of the soldiers just stood there while the grounders killed them."

"They are getting ready for another wave." Veridius tightened his shoulders together. "This time they are sending nearly every soldier and guard we have, but at least they are heeding my warning."

Malidora swallowed. "What warning is that?"

"Killing some of the grounders is not dispersing them," Veridius said. "And even my father knows we can't kill a significant number. Aside from the immorality of such an act, the grounders do all the stonework, the farming, the engine repair, all the work the advane and the high elite don't want to dirty their hands with."

"You need them more than they need you." Biting off another piece, Malidora raised her finger to let them know she was about to speak. "How are you going to accomplish this?"

A flash pistol was tucked between the middle console between Trinavus and Veridius.

"Many of them will be armed with farum weapons," said Veridius. "If you aren't familiar, they paralyze the target, allowing them to be captured."

Just in case, she quietly slid the pistol loose and tucked it under her belt.

Rubbing the back of his hand, Dabradan faced her. "Farum bolts are still dangerous. There's a small chance the paralysis doesn't abate. Other times the target is even killed."

"If you have a better idea," Veridius said condescendingly, "we'd love to hear it."

"I didn't spend my whole life being raised to be in charge. I'm only a simple independent," Dabradan mocked.

Malidora was quick to interrupt before an argument started. "We need to get back down there and find the rest of the Shadows before any more of them come."

Barely able to keep still, she waited for them to finish their meal.

Trinavus guided the shay toward the wall, as four other vehicles moved to land in a clear area just outside of the central district where the grounders beat tirelessly against the tower. Dabradan gripped the Whidge claw tight as they glided along the outside.

Staring at her crossbow, Malidora's hands began to shake. Despite all the danger she had faced over the years, something about Nulthereals made her more anxious than normal.

"Slow down." Dabradan stared out the window. "I think we just passed one."

Trinavus turned the vehicle around. The Nulthereal hovered near the wall like black smoke. Opening the vehicle door, Malidora grabbed an arrow. She loaded the crossbow, aimed, and fired.

The recoil surprised her as the repulsor launched the arrow faster than any bow she had seen. The bolt landed in the stone wall behind the shadow; she'd missed. Loading a second arrow, she tried to make sure she remained still this time, but the movement of the shay and her shaking hands made it difficult.

Her shot missed again.

The Nulthereal flowed toward the shay. As it stretched its inky blackness toward the vehicle, Trinavus tried to lift off, but they were caught in the shadow's force. He managed to turn the vehicle, bringing Veridius face to absent face with the otherworldly entity.

Veridius scurried from the window as the door began to bend. He ended up in Trinavus' lap as he continued to lean away from the shadow. "Get it away! Get it away from me!"

Malidora leapt from the vehicle, lining up another shot as the shadow moved closer.

"Malidora, wait!" Dabradan yelled as he climbed across the seat toward her door. She fired again. There was a sound of an impact, but the arrow disappeared as it went into the Nulthereal. The shadow went after her, but it was too late to run. As it stretched toward her, its pulsing body froze. Breaking in half, the Nulthereal fell into the dirt in front of her.

One of the jagged pieces of shadowstone that remained revealed a small tunnel from one end to the other. Her arrow had gone completely through. She retrieved her arrow from the wall and another sticking up from the sand but could not locate the third.

Malidora climbed back into the shay. "So, believe me now?" She smiled, as a nervous Veridius moved back into his seat.

"You meant shadows," Veridius said between breaths, "quite literally."

They rose above the wall, flying toward the tower.

"We need to check on the raid," Trinavus reminded them.

Covering the whole circular area around the tower, grounders pushed through the massive crowd. A brigade of armored soldiers fired their weapons into the outside edges, but barely made a dent in the multitude. Another transport landed at the edge of the Nirus district, making a push toward the tower.

Veridius' face turned sullen as he stared out the window.

"They are only getting started." Trinavus continued to circle the tower. "Once they begin to divide the crowd, they will flow through the mob with ease."

"If annihilating these Shadows will stop it, let's continue the search," Veridius said.

Zooming low over the wall, Veridius pointed at another Nulthereal hovering along the edge. They moved outside the wall, descending toward the ground.

Veridius turned to Trinavus. "Don't get so close this time."

Gripping her crossbow, Malidora put her hand on the door. "I can't hit it with all your moving around."

She opened the door and climbed out. The Nulthereal immediately sped toward her as she lined it up in the sights. Her hands began to shake as soon as she heard the buzzing. She pulled the trigger, launching the arrow into it.

The impact sent a shockwave of cracking damage from the puncture, but it continued to move toward her. Malidora began to move away from the vehicle as the Nulthereal advanced. Pulling Trinavus' rifle from between the seat, Dabradan fired through the open window. His marksmanship came in handy, as he fired a shot straight into the fractured point of the shadow, splintering the Nulthereal into small fragments.

A flurry of flash fire bashed into the metal doors of the shay, cracking Veridius' window. Trinavus took the vehicle into the sky, flying away from the threat. Malidora stood, alone on the ground as more vibrations and buzzing cut through the air. Two soldiers atop the wall continued firing at the shay as it flew off. Loading a new arrow, Malidora aimed and fired. The bolt went through the soldier's armor plate, pinning him against the stone ramparts.

Bursts of dirt and sand moved toward her as the second gunman turned his fire to her. Bolting toward a group of trees away from the wall, Malidora pulled another arrow from her quiver. The shay turned and flew back. Redirecting his fire toward the vehicle, the soldier fired several bursts. As the shay approached, some of the bursts began peppering the vehicle.

Being less proficient at long range shots, Malidora rushed toward the wall. Noticing her approach, the solider turned back to Malidora, aimed his rifle toward her as her arrow pierced his neck.

The shay turned around again, flying erratically as the buzzing around her grew, filling her ears. A shadow moved in from her left. Taking the arrow from the shattered remains of the Nulthereal she killed, Malidora ran the arrow into the guide. A rumbling from behind drew her attention as she waited for the Nulthereal to come closer. A second Nulthereal moved in from the rear, while several more Shadows slithered around the curvature of the distant wall.

Her delay gave the encroaching Nulthereal time to get closer than she intended. She fired the shot moments before it vacuumed her in. As the Nulthereal burst into bits, Malidora dove out of the path of the one behind her. She tumbled over the sand as the shards were sucked into the other Nulthereal as it moved in.

She hoped the broken stones of the shadow would damage the other as they entered, but they did not. Confused, she staggered back, losing ground to the Nulthereal and having to accelerate to find a safe distance. Now was not the time to debate the physics of the Nulthereals and shadowstone. Malidora stopped suddenly and pivoted on the heel of her boot, launching an arrow as she spun in the direction of the chasing shadow. The arrow glanced off the Nulthereal as sparkling dust spilled from the cavity.

Malidora took another arrow as she leapt into the air, somersaulting over the shadow with the assistance of the repulsor boots. Landing behind it, she turned and fired another arrow as it wafted toward her new direction. The Nulthereal exploded.

She felt invincible as she kicked at the debris left behind by the Shadows, recovering three of her arrows. A swarm of dust clouded her view ahead as the group of oncoming Nulthereals disturbed lose dirt and debris. Malidora moved further from the city. Climbing natural steps of hardened clay, she worked her way up a small hill.

Thorny red plant growth protruded through breaks in the rock as she reached the top. A four-legged creature stood at the edge of a pool of collected water, eyeing her as it lapped it up with its tongue. From the higher vantage she was able to see seven Shadows among the scattered dust, heading to the hill. She would pick off as many as she could and escape down the backside of the hill when they came near.

As the Shadows came to the base of the mound, they split up. They surrounded the hill as if waiting for her to make the first move. Malidora expected them to move as a group, using their numbers in a single clustered attack. Her one advantage to this strategy was, with them separated, it allowed her to deal with fewer at a time. That only worked if she could keep enough space between her and them. If any got too close, they could easily converge, leaving her no escape.

A low growl reverberated behind her as a primal scent filled the air. The brown furred creature crept around the water hole, its hairs standing on end. Baring its fangs, the animal walked to her left side, maintaining a certain distance. Malidora turned, moving her crossbow in line with the creature.

It charged, leaping at her. The weight of the creature knocked her backwards onto the hard dirt. She slid toward one of the Nulthereals on the ground as the animal's weight knocked her back. A small avalanche of pebbles and dirt covered her face as she came to a stop halfway down. Three of the Shadows floated up the incline toward her as the creature clawed her neck below her right ear.

Holding the animal at bay as much as possible, she had no way to get to the blade inside her vest. The creature bit into her shoulder as she struggled to push against its weight.

As she fought to get the beast away, her hands found its neck. Squeezing with all her strength, the animal released its bite. It gasped for air in rasping breaths as Malidora continued to crush its neck. It swiped furiously as she turned it away from her, trying to keep its strikes from her face.

She quickly drew one hand into her vest, slashing the creature across the middle with her blade. It curled up around the bloody wound. Malidora climbed to her feet, kicking the beast down the hill toward the Nulthereals. The three Shadows rushed over to the animal, draining a wispy essence from its body.

Another cloud of dust stirred near the wall ahead as Malidora made it back the top of the hill. She picked up the crossbow, aimed, and fired, destroying the shadow in the middle. The other Nulthereals followed as she retreated toward the pool of shallow water. Loading another bolt, she launched into the shadow on her left. The bolt made streaking fractures across the form of the shadow, but it remained intact. Fumbling in her quiver, she found another arrow as the Shadows moved in. The other Nulthereals surrounding the hill had advanced, tightening around her.

Malidora refused to let them take her back to The Hollow, but there was no escape from this encroaching darkness as the Shadows collapsed on her position. The Sinavus Code repeated in her mind: never be taken alive. She grabbed the blood covered knife, moving it toward her chest. She thought of Evala's face as she took what could be her last breath. Is this the way she wanted to go out? This was no heroic sacrifice; it was a coward's death. She may be a lot of things, but she was no coward. Why make it easy on Razinoth and his Shadows? *Candle burning in the dark.* If she had to go down, she would not go quietly.

The sound of thunder rumbled as the ground began to shake. The vibrations beneath her steadily grew stronger as the Shadows stopped. A fissure formed in hardened clay, widening as the world around her crumbled.

The hill tossed her about, collapsing her into the ruptured stone. She came to a stop as sediment spilled over her. Nearly upside down in the shaft, Malidora tried to bring herself upright. Using mostly her legs, she pulled her upper body forward but could not get higher than where her feet rested in the stone.

As she twisted her body, one foot broke out of the tight crease into a larger space. Light beamed through a crack between the rocks. Kicking at the sides of the crevasse, the rocks began to give way. Sand rained on her as she broke through. Rolling her body out of the hole, the rumbling began to subside. Making it to her feet, she bent over while the fuzziness in her head cleared. The sky seemed to darken.

The Nulthereals buzzed down the hill as she turned toward the city walls. Clouds of dust swirled in the wind as it blew, a dark shape moving within. Malidora checked her crossbow, sliding another arrow into the guide. Someone limped out of dust and debris, making their way toward her as the six Shadows stormed down the hill.

She shot the Nulthereal on the far left of the row, giving her more room to maneuver that way when she needed. Covered in dust, the limping figure moved toward the Shadows. Whipping through the air, their blade lashed at the Nulthereal on the right end. Dabradan quickly slashed another coming toward him as their force began to tug at him.

Malidora changed targets, firing at the one closest to him. Fragments of shadow floated in the air between the pull of Nulthereals as Malidora and Dabradan broke them. Picking them off as they surged toward Dabradan, she grabbed one of the last few bolts in her quiver. The arrow streaked as it fired, whipping through the air as it shattered the last Nulthereal.

CHAPTER 29

THE BLUE SKY darkened as the sun slowly dropped toward the horizon. Dabradan's shadow grew long as he marveled at the strange event. "The sun is moving . . ."

"No, Kandom is." Malidora stared as the sun touched the tops of the trees of the withered forest.

Dabradan closed his eyes as he brushed away the soot. "Kandom always moves, but the same side always faces to the sun. It must be rotating faster now."

Malidora brushed the dust from his forehead. "That quake. Did it have something to do with it?"

"I wouldn't know," Dabradan said, as he wiped grains of sand and dirt from his hair. "It's never happened before."

Malidora turned to him as the sun settled behind the trees. She reached her fingers to his hair, stroking it to help brush out the remaining debris. "What happened back there? Where's everyone else?"

"Trin went crazy," Dabradan closed his eyes as her fingers got close. "Veridius got a little singed from flash fire, and he kept yelling about getting him to safety. Even with Veridius ordering him to go back, he kept saying the thercon would kill him if he let anything happen to Veridius."

Malidora rubbed the smears of dust from the bridge of his nose. "You came back for me."

"You're surprised?" he asked, as she traced her finger from his nose to his lips.

Dabradan leaned in close, cradling her neck as their foreheads bumped together. Their lips found each other as his grabbed hold. Malidora closed her eyes as electric fire spread over her face and down her neck.

Malidora hesitated, afraid of what could happen if she gave in to these feelings. She never should have stayed with any of them for so long. Dabradan pressed his body against her, and she stopped resisting, riding the storm of emotions to wherever it may lead her. It was too late to turn back now. This feeling, this connection, she had forgotten what it was like.

She had been fighting for the wrong reason: Vengeance. Though she convinced herself that it was more about saving the world, saving people, that was another lie. How can you want to save everyone without caring for anyone? The only people she loved had been taken from her.

The walls around her heart were more impenetrable than the walls of Vesta. Yet something had gotten through, infecting her from the inside. She could no longer deny it.

Her mind slowly came back into focus as they separated. "How did you get here?"

Dabradan moved his hand from the back of her head, tracing her neck to rest on her shoulder. "There was fire coming from the tower area. Trin flew low outside the wall for cover. He stopped at one point, and I jumped out. The shay kicked up a load of dust." He slapped more dirt from his clothing.

Twilight was upon them as the sun vanished behind the land. Malidora collected as many arrows as she could find while Dabradan cleaned the dust from the exhaust ports of his rifle. From someplace unseen, the buzz of Nulthereals pulsed in the rising darkness.

"We'd better get inside the gate," Dabradan warned.

"We can't." The nerves in Malidora's hands began to twitch with the vibrations of the Shadows. "There's no one at their post to let us in."

Dabradan moved toward the wall as twilight faded to night. "There has to be someone to let us in."

"How are they even going to see us in the dark?" Malidora walked over to him as he lifted his head toward the ramparts.

In the pitch black, she could hear his footsteps as Dabradan stepped along the stone base. "I'm getting in there one way or another."

He pulled out a spark, shining it along the top of the wall as she followed.

"There's a grate." Malidora's heart began to quicken. "Where the channel comes through from the river. Where you found me before. If you have a way to cut through the steel, perhaps we could get in that way."

"Flash bolts may do it," said Dabradan, as they moved around the edge of the city. No sign of the channel or the front gate. Dabradan sped up. They had to be getting close.

Suddenly the sand and dirt crumbled, the light of the spark partly eclipsed by something ahead. Malidora stopped as the sound of sliding sand rained into a cavity in the ground beneath her.

"Dab? Are you all right?"

He responded with a low moan before speaking, "For the most part."

Malidora clapped her hand over her mouth to prevent herself from the giggle that was about to come. He had fallen into a hole, possibly caused by the quake.

"Do you need help getting out?"

"Possibly."

Malidora lowered herself to the ground, crawling toward the edges obscuring the light. She extended her hand but could not see him.

"Can you see my hand?" she asked, stretching out as far as she could.

Pebbles slid further as he moved around. "I can't find you."

Malidora waved her arms hoping he would see the movement. "Can you stand? Is there anywhere to pull yourself up?"

"I'll try." Sand and rock ground against the dirt for a moment as he moved, but then stopped.

"Everything okay?" She leaned further over the edge.

"I think I see something."

"What?"

"Lights . . ."

"Lights?" Malidora teased. "Did you hit your head?"

"No," Dabradan stated. "Well yeah, but that has nothing to do with it. I think it's lights from the city. I think this pit goes underneath the wall."

"Are you sure?"

"Yes, get down here."

Malidora moved from the edge, sitting in the dirt. "Are you able to get out? No point in both of us getting stuck."

"Yes, there's a slope on this side that's easy to climb."

"Why don't you climb out first and make sure."

Dabradan sighed. "I just need a little boost to get out. Then I can pull you up."

"You said it was easy to climb!" she yelled into the dark crater.

"It *is* easy. It's not a big deal."

"I don't like stepping into something I can't see."

"At least you know the pit is here," Dabradan said. "That's more than I got."

"We need a different plan," Malidora was done crawling through these dark enclosures. The images of the canals and cavities she unknowingly inhabited during her time inside the body of Razinoth made her queasy.

"Are you serious? After we've been nearly sucked into Shadows, run over by armored beasts, and shot at, you're afraid to climb into a little pit?"

"All right fine, I'm coming down there, but only to shut you up." She lowered her right leg over the edge, letting her body sag as she stretched for ground. Finding nothing, she slid her hip across the lip of the pit, stopping at her waist. Still, she could feel nothing below her but empty space. "How deep is this?" she demanded, pushing aside the thoughts of the last time she'd been in caves, draining the elu out of the life forms there.

"I can't be sure," Dabradan grumbled. "I didn't daintily climb in the way you are."

"I do have a pistol. I can shut you up from here," she said playfully.

Malidora let herself slide further while gripping a handful of sturdy roots of grass, stretching to find the bottom, and yet there was nothing but the side of the pit she could kick with the toe of her boot. Stretching a little more, she lost her grip on the roots and slid down the side of the pit into the hole.

Her foot hit a loose stone, causing her to tumble unbalanced into the hole. She landed on her side on a pile of gravel and dirt.

"That wasn't so bad." Dabradan snickered.

She almost regretted ever kissing him as she propped herself up on a rock. Dim lights inside shined against the dark, hazy sky.

"Cup your hands together so I can step up," Dabradan said. "I just need a little boost."

Malidora ducked into the stone foundations of the wall toward him. "Why don't you boost me up?"

"Do you have the strength to pull my weight up there?"

"I guess we'll find out." She stared up at the tower. Lights from the rings reflected on it as it seemed to sway.

"I'll have to get up first so I can pull you," said Dabradan.

She clasped her hands together, making a step for him near the side of the pit. Lifting his foot into her hands, he nearly made her drop as he put his weight on her. She pushed his boot up as much as she could until he lifted himself out.

Dabradan kneeled at the edge of the pit reaching toward her. She could not quite get to his hand as she tried to maneuver her way between some rocks to get higher. Their fingertips touched as she hoisted herself up.

Dabradan leaned further, grabbing her hand, but no longer had the leverage needed to pull her. Still holding on to her, he got to his knee and lifted himself up, towing her with him.

They came up behind some of the square living structures, similar to the ones in Ruvak. Dabradan moved onto the main street. Scattered fires on some of the wooden buildings lit the roadway in their flickering light. The streets were deserted but for a little girl who sat on the steps outside one of the shops.

Malidora walked toward her. "Do you need help? Do you know where your parents are?"

The girl stood up. "Get away from me!" she yelled and ran off into the dark.

"We're not far from Ruvak." Dabradan moved quickly down the road as Malidora followed.

As they made it to the blockhouse, they spotted the syvern leaning against the old building, fully assembled. Dabradan ran toward the entrance. "Cian! Where are you at?"

Dabradan continued calling him after he went inside the building.

After a moment she no longer heard his voice or anyone else's. Another moment passed and still silence. Concerned, she opened the door. She stepped into the dark tight hallway, feeling her way along the wall. "Dab!"

"I'll be right there," he responded quietly.

Malidora rounder the corner, heading toward the glowing reflection of the spark on the walls ahead. She found him kneeled on the floor, placing a thin piece of wood over the head of a body lying there.

"He deserves better than this." Dabradan covered Cian's body with whatever he could find.

Malidora kneeled behind Dabradan. "When this is over, we can make it right."

"Will it be over?" he asked. "I don't know even know what we can do."

Malidora rubbed the back of his shoulders. "I have some of the shadowstone with me," she said, putting her hand into her vest to make sure. "Are there any weapons we can use to launch these at the Nulthereals?"

Dabradan exhaled. "We'd need to build weapons like yours."

Malidora sat down, pressing her feet against the wall. "Aside from aesthetics, the functionality of my repaired crossbow is nothing more than a repulsor with a trigger on it. Could we get some repulsor things from somewhere?"

"Yes . . ." Dabradan stood. "Every balton has them. If they are as abandoned as these streets, there's nothing to stop us from taking them."

Malidora rose to her feet. "If any soldiers out there are in their right mind, they could fire these shards at the Nulthereals, while we gather more of their pieces."

Dabradan rushed past her, heading outside the building. As Malidora ran outside, he was starting the syvern.

"We'll look in Nirus," said Dabradan as the syvern began to hum. "Plenty of lights there."

"Not so plentiful now, but more than there are here," Something zoomed overhead as Malidora climbed onto the back of syvern. A shay circled the outside of the city as Dabradan turned the syvern around. They rode through the quiet back streets, mostly deserted except for a few soldiers plundering through housing units. Flames poured from the windows of Klevet's villa. The road in front of the house, normally clean, was now as littered as the rest of Ruvak.

As they moved into the outskirts of Naldus Circle, the mob still hacked at the pillars of the tower. They had removed a portion of stone blocks on one of the pillars, exposing the metal skeleton inside. Using some of the soldier's flash weapons they blasted into the metal. Some of the soldiers battled with groups that had spread away from the mass cluster at the tower. Bodies lay scattered on the ground as carrion insects flew over them.

A loud thunder erupted around them as they entered the edge of the Nirus District. Buildings began to shake as they entered a tight alleyway. The whole landscape seemed to vibrate. Even with the syvern hovering over the street, it knocked against the vehicle as it rose with the quake.

Parts of the road bowed up, rippling toward them from behind, breaking the stone and loosening it from the street. One of the buildings ahead had its roof cave in before the whole structure collapsed. Dabradan turned down a sideroad as the building crashed to the ground spreading dust and bits of rock all around it.

The circling shay flew by again, likely unable to see much on the dark landscape. The quake continued to worsen as a deafening squeal rang out behind them. Shouting rose from the crowd in the circle accompanied by grinding and squeaking.

Dabradan stopped the syvern and turned around. The tower swayed dangerously, and the rings around it bowed and rippled. One of the arms holding the second ring to the massive tower broke away from the ring. The sudden jolt caused the whole tower to pitch forward.

The tower continued to slowly tip as metal ground against metal, making a dissonant melody like an instrument out of tune. Dabradan turned the syvern around, flying between the crumbled debris. He drove back past the circle, turning on a side road toward the main street. They headed through a small alleyway as Dabradan dodged a large, pointed stone protruding through the dirt road. Malidora turned back for another glance at the large stone: A nyalith.

A horrible crash rocked the city as they neared the main gate. A strong gust of wind blew around them as Malidora turned back. The tower had fallen. It lay near the farming district, propped up by the first ring for a moment before momentum sent it further, snapping off the arms of the enormous ring and breaking the tower in half.

"Hit the switch on the gate!" Dabradan yelled as he drove up to the guard station.

Malidora reached for the control box, punching the button to open the gate. The first ring broke free of the tower, falling over with another boom. The second ring and top half of the tower flipped over and crashed into the ground.

Dabradan drove through the gate as clouds of thick dust and debris flooded the city. The crashing continued as they crossed the river. The sun had risen, mostly hidden by dust and smoke in the air.

"I don't know where I'm going." Dabradan drove toward the remaining green forest. "There're no towns left. I suppose we could live off the land. Build a house. Start a new civilization together."

The world started to quake again. The sandy landscape to their right began to separate, collapsing into a large sinkhole. "I don't think that will be an option for long," Malidora held tight as the syvern shifted violently with the rapid changes in the terrain. "There's only one thing left to do."

"What's that?" he said as they moved into the forest. They passed through crisscrossing trees, uprooted from the craters and fissures scattered across the devastated terrain.

"Head that way," Malidora pointed as they came out into the open plains. Dabradan turned toward a wooded area along the horizon, the forest where she had first seen Gesaurens hauling logs to repair the walls of Udamal. "We have to leave this world."

"Are you sure this is where you want to go?" Dabradan steered around a patch of blighted foliage. Gummy liquid decay dripped from the trees like melting candle wax.

Malidora rested against his back. "Yes, it's not too far ahead."

Between the fleshy trees, a dark figure emerged from the black growth, feeding energy to it from its hands. Its red eyes turned toward them as it stopped what it was doing, firing black celettes at them as Dabradan guided the syvern away. The Gaith had sent another Whidge. Like the one before, it appeared to be possessing the body of a Vogan. Dabradan accelerated, speeding them through the brush and out into the rocky plains.

Several patches of dark growth littered the landscape as they crossed the purple and pink stripes of sand she remembered on her path toward the forest. As Dabradan winded around large crevasses in the surface, Malidora pointed to the stacked rocks with the small, twisted tree growing between them. She motioned for Dabradan to stop as they approached.

She climbed off the syvern as it settled to the ground. Running over to the peculiar tree, Malidora searched for the pool that brough her into this world. The rock and hard mud where the pool should have been was now a giant crater. The water of the pool was gone. Dabradan caught up to her, staring at the wide hole in the clay surface.

"It was right here!" Malidora huffed as a warm rush enveloped her.

CHAPTER 30

DABRADAN TURNED AS they heard a shay flying somewhere behind them. Even with the sun higher than it had ever been in this part of Kandom, the dust in the sky made it difficult to see far, but they were apparently not the only ones to survive. Malidora swept her hair back as her fingers began to tingle.

She should have done what the voice in the stone had instructed. Now all hope was lost. Dust brushed by her face as the wind picked up, forcing her to shield her eyes.

The dark form of the Whidge rose from a pool of black growth nearby. Emanating vibrations caused a tremor in her elbows moving up to her wrists. It began to walk toward them through the ashen haze. Malidora reached for her remaining arrows as Dabradan raised his weapon. Celettes whizzed by as Malidora crouched and fired. The celettes stopped as the Whidge switched to its shield, covering its head in time to deflect Dabradan's shot.

Circling the Whidge, Malidora put herself on the other side of Dabradan with the Whidge at the point of the V between them. Forced to choose between blocking her shots or Dabradan's, the Whidge brought its shield to stop her arrow. The blast from Dabradan's rifle burned into its back. The Whidge fed white energy into the wound from its hands.

Malidora continued to pump arrows into the crossbow as fast as she could as the Whidge parried with its shield. Another blast from Dabradan hit it in the chest as it reeled from the blow. The Whidge charged at Malidora, blocking her arrows again as its invisible force took hold.

Malidora somersaulted backward, the repulsor boots allowing her the force to escape the Whidge's grip. The Whidge deflected Dabradan's bursts as it healed a freshly received wound. Malidora rushed to get back into position.

She had a horrible idea. A thought that she would likely regret. It was the last thing she wanted to do, but circumstances had left her little choice. Malidora folded her crossbow and tucked it into her belt. Taking out the flash pistol, she rapidly tapped the trigger sending a flurry of bolts at the Whidge. The barrel began to glow bright red with her sustained rapid firing.

She hit its chest and shoulder before the dark Vogan could protect itself. A necklace broke free from the shadowy Vogan and fell onto the sand, its white jewel gleaming in the light. As the Whidge healed the damage to its Vogan body, Dabradan wounded it again with a hit to the side of its face.

The end of Malidora's pistol burned with orange heat as she tapped the trigger as fast as she could. The shadow Vogan projected its shield sideways in the air, stepping on top of it. The shield vanished as a new one was projected in front of it. The Whidge leapt from shield to shield, projecting them as platforms as it climbed into the sky above them. It was the same technique that Ravetaria had used.

The ground vibrated again, as a pocket of reddish-brown sand nearby began to cascade toward a widening hole in the center. The crater continued to divide, sending rocks and haspere sliding in. They blasted at the Whidge as it crouched on a shield overhead. Their shots hissed off the blue energy as they fired from below.

Malidora and Dabradan both backed up to get an angle as the shay that had been circling the area flew low toward them. Malidora continued firing, hoping to get a bolt around its defense. The shay hit the hard dusty stone, bouncing off a few times before skidding past them. Releasing the shield long enough to launch a salvo of whistling celettes, the Whidge forced Malidora to dive for rocky cover.

The tremors became more intense as sections of rock broke away and mounds of stone shifted. The cracks around them separated as the world convulsed. Dabradan aimed and fired, getting some shots dangerously close to the shadow Vogan.

"Malidora!" a voice called out over the sand. Veridius dashed toward them from the shay.

Malidora ignored him as she launched a continuous barrage at the Whidge, burning the barrel white hot. Energy crackled as the shield deflected and absorbed the flash bolts. The Whidge shieldwalked in the air toward her. It stopped directly above Malidora preventing her from gaining any line-of-sight advantage. Dabradan took aim, firing methodically, and forcing the Whidge to tighten its body within the safety of the shield. It had to ensure nothing was left exposed.

Turning off the shield, the Whidge dropped, falling toward Malidora. As the Whidge was about to land on her, it re-ignited the shield, knocking Malidora off her feet. Before she could recover from the blow, the Whidge formed the shield into a blade of light. The blade flashed, scalding her sight for a moment as something forced her down. Red sand scattered from her breath as she exhaled. Malidora pushed herself up, readying her pistol as her vision began to clear.

"Dab!" Malidora heard her voice cry out before she felt her mouth move. Time seemed to slow to a crawl as she blasted at the Whidge that was using Ravetaria's body. The dark Vogan removed its light blade from Dabradan's chest. Snatching the rifle from his hands, the Whidge slung it onto the sand behind them. Reconfiguring the light into a shield it deflected Malidora's bolts before receiving more than minimal damage. It strode toward her as the shield continued to flicker, absorbing the energy bolts as fast as she fired them. It knew it now held the advantage.

She tried to back away but the Whidge had Malidora inside the range of its control field, pulling her with invisible force. She struggled in vain to escape as it began to drain the life force from of her body. Her senses started to fade.

Suddenly, her focus returned as she heard flash rifle fire from another source. It's blasts burning into the Whidge. Malidora gathered herself as the essence flowed back into her. The Whidge shielded itself against the new attack, leaving its back open to Malidora. Taking aim, Malidora pulled the trigger. Nothing happened. Quickly examining her pistol, she realized the barrel had melted from the heat.

Malidora threw down the weapon and leapt toward Ravetaria, kicking her in the back. The force of her repulsor boots sent the Whidge tumbling across the sand. The Whidge ignited its shield as Malidora stepped on its arm, preventing it from using its arbow to protect itself.

"Shoot it!" Malidora shouted as Veridius rushed over, training his flash rifle on the Whidge. Snatching the rifle from his grip, Malidora fired into its chest until the shadowy body went limp. Malidora removed her gloves as ran to Dabradan. Crouching beside him, she took his hand in hers. His pulse was weak. "Why?" she whispered. "It should have been me!"

"I couldn't let anything happen to you," he spoke with a voice barely audible. "Besides . . . You're our best chance . . . to complete the mission . . ."

Leaning over him, she pressed her lips to his cheek as his body went limp. Memories she had tried to repress rushed into her head. The images of the night she had returned to the forest where she and Legotian camped near the capitol of Gildanel. Though she hadn't liked his strict rules and discipline, something made her want to stay. He had believed in her. He'd seen her as more than just a thief, turning her into someone with self-respect and regard for others.

The images of that night were so clear. Legotian had sent her off in the rain to fetch water from a nearby stream. It didn't make sense at the time. They'd already had water. She hadn't questioned him, but Legotian must have known that the red-eyed Blight Whidge was hunting them. Now she realized that Legotian had sent her away hoping she might live.

As she'd waded into the flowing waters with her bucket, the Blight Whidge had come near. Her hands had shaken as she'd closed her eyes, but the Whidge did not enter the water. Once it had moved on, she'd mustered the courage and ran back to the camp site. When she saw Legotian's hollow stare, she'd known the Blight Whidge had been there. She knew then that she was cursed.

The images faded as shadow spilled from the wounds of Ravetaria, returning her form to its normal state. Ravetaria lay dead in the dust, her fierce and beautiful face now at peace. The nightmare, at least for her, was over.

And Dabradan . . .

The quaking continued as the entire surface of the world seemed to collapse around them. Rising from the sand, the sludging ooze began to take shape as the true form of the Whidge. Malidora rested Dabradan's cold hand gently beside him. Something could drain the life energy from his body to be used for the Gaith's ends. And she? She could do nothing.

Veridius steadied himself, helping Malidora to her feet. Reaching into her quiver, she pulled out a shadow-tipped arrow.

"Take this!" She thrust the arrow toward Veridius. "Hold onto the stone. No matter what happens, don't let go."

The gurgling mass of the monstrous Whidge stretched ten feet above them, forming long arms and three snakelike legs. Malidora grabbed Veridius.

"What are you—!" Veridius muttered as she shoved him as hard as she could toward the monstrosity. Veridius' horrid scream ended abruptly as he vanished into the devouring void of the Whidge.

Reaching into her quiver, she found nothing to grab. She stretched deeper, but no arrows remained. She had either miscounted, or they had spilled out during the fight. She searched the nearby sands as her hand touched something at the bottom pocket of the quiver. Malidora pulled out the shadowstone attached to a gold chain that she had ripped from Laudra's neck. A smile spread across her lips as she gripped the stone tightly into her hands. As the monster's tendrils began to generate, Malidora charged at the Whidge, closing her eyes as she was enveloped in darkness.

CHAPTER 31

C*ANDLE BURNING IN the dark. When nightmares come to take its spark, I need not hide in fear or fright. For even shadows need the light.*

Malidora's eyelids wrestled against the blinding bright as she sat on a rounded stone at the edge of the water. Ripples upset the reflections in the crystal-clear spring as an airy breeze disturbed the long, hanging fronds of crimson. Peering above the trees, a large red sun tried to console her with its warmth on her skin. Flares of light silhouetted the trees as its raw energy burned from the horizon she had traveled from.

Her visage, battered and bruised in the mirrored surface, did not fully resonate the pain surging within her. Burying her face into her hands, she could no longer restrain the deluge as the emotion poured out of her. Her name truly was a mark of death. Whether by her hand or the misfortune of being in her company, everyone close to her ended up dead.

"I found some berries!"

The voice startled her as she wiped the smudges under her golden eyes. Veridius came to the edge of the water, offering red and black berries from his hand, blackened from shadowstone.

Malidora hid her face. "If there is food and water here, I will leave if you wish to stay."

"No, if you're leaving, I'm coming with you." Veridius lifted his cloak as he sat in the sand beside the stone.

Malidora peeked between her fingers as the wind eased the

orange ends of her hair across her cheek. "I'm cursed. You're better off being as far away as possible."

Veridius rose to a knee beside the stone, facing her. "Cursed? You saved my life."

"My brother, my sister, my father Legotian," Malidora began, "half of my planet, Dabradan, Evala, your entire planet. Everything and everyone I get close to dies."

Veridius sat on the rounded stone next to her. "You're fighting a war. There are always going to be casualties. Some would say you are fortunate to still be alive."

"I've been fighting against myself as much as the Shadows, justifying my actions, taking the quickest path, no matter the cost. Until I atone for that, I will always be cursed."

"We've all done things that we need to overcome. You've given me another chance. I had power and did little good with it. Maybe without it, I can be what I should have been all along. I can only hope it's not too late to make a difference somewhere." Veridius leaned toward her. "Were you crying?" he asked as she turned away.

"No!" She unwittingly raised her voice. "I had to wash some mud off my face."

Her tears began to burst anew. She quickly covered them, rubbing her eyes as if that would seal up the sorrow within her.

"There's no shame in emotions," Veridius said. "I'm sorry about Dabradan. I'm sorry I didn't get there sooner. I should have believed you at the very beginning."

Malidora brought her hands away from her eyes. "It was *my* burden. *My* chance at redemption, but I failed once again. I'd hoped that this was my purpose. My reason for existence."

Veridius moved in front of her, looking into her eyes. "We're still here, we have a chance to get it right the next time."

"How did we get here?" Malidora stared at the red leaves swaying in the wind. "I can't even remember what happened."

"You were incredible! You guided us through the void, away from those terrible voices. When you found a thousand pathways in the blue tempest, you seemed to know the way. You led us out of a dark cavern to a dry spring. Fortunately, after walking for a while, we found this oasis."

"The oasis!" Malidora reached into her coat and pulled out the nyalith shard. "Now I remember! The Awakener! I need to find The Awakener."

Then came the smell of pheromones wandered on the wind, signaling the approach of living creatures. Malidora held her finger to her lips, warning Veridius to keep quiet. Voices unseen approached.

Two figures brushed through the trees toward the spring.

"Look, here's one we haven't explored yet," said the girl to the boy.

The boy pointed toward white flashes of light in the sky near the horizon. "They've taken another world."

The girl walked ahead, her magenta hair glowing like embers. The boy paused for a moment staring at the sky before following her toward the water.

"Oh—we didn't realize anyone would be over here in this region." The girl started but quickly regained her composure as she stared at Malidora and Veridius standing motionless by the spring. "Are you friends of Ambrielle?"

"I don't know anyone named Ambrielle." Malidora studied the face of the girl. "But you look very familiar."

"I'm Sidaire." She moved closer to the water. "And this—"

"Sidaire! Kazial!" Malidora stood. "You made it out of The Hollow!"

"You know us?" Sidaire squinted as she studied Malidora.

"You were in the mindstream," said Malidora. "Ilganok's dream."

Sidaire suddenly opened her eyes wide. "It was *you!* You got us out! If it weren't for you, we would still be in that nightmare. When we made it back to this world, neither of us could remember how we'd escaped."

"I'm glad you are both safe." Malidora smiled. "Do you know where we are?"

"We're on Solsellion." Sidaire moved her hand along the horizon. "What's left of our home. We've been working to hold off the Nulthereals."

Malidora put her hands over her face. "They are everywhere."

"Yes," said Sidaire. "We've been trying to find all the springs so that we can regrow the life they took away."

"We're looking for The Awakener." Malidora's eyes switched between both of them. "You don't happen to know anything about that do you?"

"The Awakener?" Sidaire glanced at Kazial as he shrugged. "Never heard of anything like that, but we will help find them."

Malidora dried her eyes with her glove, and Veridius gave her a wink as he introduced himself to Sidaire and Kazial. After a couple of moments, they all walked together out of the oasis, across the dunes on the horizon. Perhaps even in her mad quest for vengeance, she had done something right.

It was clear now that the Shadows were too vast to take on by herself. To win this war it had to be more than revenge. It was about saving the universe and all those living in it. Her thoughts went to Legotian, Dabradan, and Evala.

Maybe she wasn't as cursed as she thought. She had been surrounded by those who believed in her despite the things she had done. They had sacrificed themselves because they believed she was the best chance to complete the mission. She would not allow their deaths to be in vain. What if she did have great potential as Neristara said? It was time she found a way to realize it.

Malidora was familiar with darkness, yet the candle had been lit. She was no longer alone, whether she liked it or not.

Perhaps it was time to open the door again and step out of the dark, for even shadows need the light.

END

Bewilderness will be a five book series and Book 4 will be coming soon!

THANKS FOR READING!

I would love to know what you thought of Neverscape.
Please don't forgot to leave a comment on Amazon!

JOIN MY NEWSLETTER AND GET A FREE BOOK!

Get my short story, Elyravess, free when you sign up to my newsletter at *https://bewildernessseries.com/*
The newsletter will give you monthly updates on upcoming books in the series, behind the scenes, and artwork!

In ancient Elyravess, a young boy's chance encounter with the daughter of a galactic archaeologist leads to a discovery that will alter the course of their future and the fate of their worlds.

ACKNOWLEDGEMENTS

I would like to begin by expressing my gratitude to God for providing me with the strength, guidance, and inspiration to complete this book. Without His blessings, this accomplishment would not have been possible.

To my family, who have always been my pillars of support and encouragement throughout my life, thank you for standing by me every step of the way. Your belief in me has been a constant source of motivation and inspiration.

To my friends, thank you for your unwavering support, your kind words, and your valuable feedback. Your presence in my life has enriched me in ways I cannot express.

A special thank you to Emily Katzenberger, who believed in my writing since my first published book and has been a constant supporter throughout this project. Your feedback and advice have been invaluable, and I am grateful for your encouragement and guidance.

Once again, thank you to all those who have contributed to the creation of this book. Your support and encouragement have meant the world to me.

ABOUT THE AUTHOR

Author Kevin Cox has always been fascinated by the splendor of the universe and the mysteries it holds, using his imagination to fill in the vast unknown. Though he never planned to be a writer, he often had ideas for stories playing in his head. After deciding to write a single chapter to see if he could do it, he discovered a love for writing he never knew was there.

Much of his inspiration comes from growing up during the 80's, reading and watching all the fantasy and science fiction stories he could find. Ideas come to him during long drives or while listening to music. He often listens to music while writing, especially songs that match the mood he is trying to capture.

He believes that a good story needs great characters that each have struggles and desire to find ways to overcome them. Kevin hopes that his readers will see their own struggles in these characters and are inspired to find their own strengths and always be learning and improving to be the best version of themselves. Connection with friends and willingness to help others are central themes in his writing.

Kevin lives in southwest Georgia in a small town called Leesburg. When he isn't writing, he enjoys playing guitar and video games.

Please contact or follow on social media. for the latest news and info on the next book in the series.

Email: authorkevincox@gmail.com

Instagram: @kevincoxauthor

Twitter: @authorkevincox

OTHER WORKS

Bewilderness: Book One and Shadowsphere

Available on Amazon.com *https://www.amazon.com/dp/B09J3Z9J2F*

Named one of the Best Books of 2022 by Kirkus
"This meticulously crafted YA journey will challenge readers' expectations until the last page."

— Kirkus Reviews (starred review)

When a young girl wakes up in an unknown world and encounters dark forces that threaten the universe, only she can change its destiny.

Accessing portals to other realms, Ambrielle journeys across multiple worlds as she searches for answers to find her way home.

Sixteen-year-old Ambrielle has no memory of her life. In fact, she doesn't even know if her name is Ambrielle, the name her new alien friend gave her when she woke up mysteriously stranded in a desolate world with no humans. As she slowly cobbles together bits and pieces of her life, Ambrielle tries to fit in with the many alien species she encounters and settle their divisive conflicts, all while eluding shadowy entities from a realm beyond the universe as she seeks a way to return to Earth.

www.ingramcontent.com/pod-product-compliance
Lightning Source LLC
Chambersburg PA
CBHW020258030826
48979CB00026B/1388/J

* 9 7 9 8 9 8 6 6 3 6 8 5 6 *